LIDYA

The DCI Tom Tallis stories

SEAS THREATEN
UNHOLY WAR
LIDYA

LIDYA

JOHN MALYON

First published 2022 by John Waldram
Copyright © John Ryder Waldram 2022
Cover photo © John Waldram
The author's moral rights have been asserted
All rights reserved
ISBN 978-1-7399165-4-1
Computer typeset in Palatino
Printed and distributed by KDP

FOR
SARAH, DANIEL,
BETH AND ANNA

The cover photo shows McLean's cross
which stands beside the ancient
Street of the Dead
on the Isle of Iona

PART I

Suspect

For five days at the end of November, frost gripped South Devon; but by the beginning of December, the biting wind had died and snow began to fall, gently, dusting the moor and headlands. From Plymouth Hoe, the Sound showed placid pewter beneath lead, the breakwater a hard line against the open sea beyond; at Queen Anne Battery the tarpaulined yacht park was packed, the frosty pontoons deserted.

A few miles to the south-east, one Wednesday afternoon, Detective Chief Inspector Tom Tallis had left Yealmpton behind and was finding the snow thicker along the country road. To avoid the snarls of Newton Ferrers he chose to ease his old Corolla down Widey Hill, and the car slithered a little as he reached the shelter of trees at the steep valley bottom. At Bridgend, he found the tide out in the creek, a solitary fiercely-pied oystercatcher stabbing at the mud; but further along there was water, and a few boats stood patiently over their moored reflections. As he took the upper road through Noss Mayo, Tom saw how thickly the snow rested already on the roofs. He turned the Corolla sharply left, crunching towards Brookings Down Wood.

At the footpath corner, he parked in the lay-by to his right, recalling springtime bluebells in the wood beyond the stream, their bulbs hidden now under the swelling white duvet. Plenty of time in hand: the layby would give him somewhere to think. The air was very still. He opened his briefcase and extracted a file, so thin he didn't bother to open it.

*

A very odd business. Fortunately (from Tom's point of view), the Super had allocated the main task to Iain Gemmill. Unfortunately, however, it had been decided that Tom was the man for the bit requiring maximum tact.

On Tuesday the Super had called Iain in, relieved him of his other work, and sent him to Exeter to be briefed by Special Branch. When he returned at five, Iain had walked straight in and settled himself on the end of Tom's desk, his tweed jacket still buttoned against the cold.

Tom looked up.

'David Manfield got me up to speed.' Iain switched perch to the radiator and sat on his hands.

'And?'

'You're in on this one, too, man.' This in Iain's usual quiet Kilmarnock.

Tom tipped his chair back. 'Whose authority?'

Iain grinned.

'Not "John Smith" again?'

'You've guessed it. He rang the Super to clear it.'

Tom groaned. 'What's it all about?'

'Another terrorist… But this one's British.'

'A British Muslim?'

'Forty, export–import.'

'What sort of British?'

'Newton Abbott. Public School, Blundells. Business studies at Exeter… Drinks a bit.'

'A Muslim who drinks?'

10

'Patronises that unofficial mosque in George Street, the one Aliza investigated. When he's not away on business.'

'Name?'

'Ralph Slade.'

'You and I need a rest from this stuff, Iain! How did this guy get to be a Muslim?'

Iain raised his eyebrows and smirked. 'Making some deal, I gather. With a cotton exporter, old-fashioned Cairo gentleman. Ralph caught a glimpse of his luscious daughter. Shouldn't have been able to see the women of the family, but he managed it, somehow. The lassie made eyes at him, he wanted to marry her—so he had to convert.'

Tom laughed. 'As simple as that?'

'Then, after two years, the marriage failed—but the Islam didn't rub off so easily. Ralph was hooked.'

'Interesting! … And the terrorism?'

'They're not sure. The guy trades all over the Middle East, but the link that interests MI6 is in Peshawar. He imports ethnic cottons. They're brought down from the hills by pack horse, put into containers. Train to Karachi, home by sea. The ISI reckon his business partner's al Qaida.'

'ISI? Pakistani intelligence?'

'According to them Ralph is bringing explosives into England.' Iain shivered a little.

'Want some coffee? … And MI6 agree?'

'They're not sure either. He's shown no obvious signs. It may be no more than religious tomes for Bradford bookshops.'

Tom had got the kettle going. 'Sounds like a can of worms… What are we supposed to do?'

'The ISI guys reckon there was something big on a container that came into Bristol on November 10th.

MI5 is arranging with Customs to go through it. I'm to interview Ralph.'

'What do you tell him?'

'They want to scare him off, or maybe bounce him into an admission. So I'm to say it's a terrorism investigation, no bones about it. I'm off to his Exeter office tomorrow.'

'OK.' Tom filled the mugs and spooned in coffee-mate. 'And where do I come in?'

'Dates… The container left Peshawar on September 16th. Ralph *said* he wasn't there until the 20th, but the Pakistanis say he arrived on the 10th.' Iain slurped gratefully, and set his mug down leaving a wet coffee ring on a briefing paper. He frowned and wiped it with his handkerchief. 'They have bugged transcripts of a conversation between Ralph and the al-Qaida guy about the forthcoming shipment. While I'm interviewing Ralph, they want you to talk to his wife, find out what she knows about his movements.'

'His *wife*? He married again?'

'Sorry, yes. Two years ago.'

'Name?'

Iain looked in his file. 'Lidya Slade. Lidya, L–I–D–Y–A. Not L–Y–D–I–A.'

'Do I tell her what I'm investigating?'

'Yes.'

'But not let her ring Ralph?'

'Exactly.'

Tom sighed. 'Address?'

'I've set up a file for you. Victory House, Stoke Road, Noss Mayo. Big house, up above the village… John Smith told me she was young and rather good-looking.'

'Right.'

'And one thing David said you ought to know,

though it's nothing to do with the case. They had a cot death. Upset them a lot. A year ago.'

*

He'd thought: better be tidy for this one—there was a tie under his scarf and blue issue raincoat. He closed his brief case, checked his Filofax, rummaged in the boot to find an old black umbrella. He pulled on a pair of rubber boots and locked the car; then crossed the road, skidded on the steep steps up to the kissing-gate and found the narrow footpath up to Stoke Road. As he clumped cautiously along it, the snow began to fall more thickly. He was rising steadily, but Newton Ferrers, over the narrow creek, remained invisible behind the gently swirling white curtain.

Once in Stoke Road, he turned left. The snow there was already six inches deep, with a few car tracks, but no traffic. After a hundred yards of trudging, he found on his right a white-barred gate labelled 'Victory House' set into a neatly trimmed yew hedge. The snow behind the hedge was untouched, the house itself out of sight. Tom closed the gate quietly behind him and set off up a winding path marked by low patio lights. He passed white-burdened roses on either side and left them behind.

The snow paused for a moment and suddenly the house stood revealed: large, modern, but low and more tasteful than Tom had for some reason expected. Its front façade was in smoothly dressed masonry, a severe creamy limestone, and there were several picture windows. The curtains to the right of the front door were drawn across, but glowed with warm light. Tom squared his shoulders, walked up to the door and rang the bell.

13

A distant light voice called from behind the lighted curtain: 'Door, Elspeth! Can you? Please?' A clatter along the hallway, an indistinct figure behind the glass, the door opened. Gawky, fair, and might have been a sixth-former.

'I'm sorry to bother you,' said Tom. 'I'm looking for Mrs Slade.'

'Oh,' said Elspeth. 'Right.' She looked over her shoulder.

Tom waited.

'Who shall I say it is?'

'She doesn't know me,' said Tom. 'If you fetch her, perhaps I can introduce myself.'

Elspeth hesitated. Then she turned and entered the brightly lit room leaving Tom on the doorstep. 'A man, for you.'

'A *man!*' The voice was light, slightly husky, conspiratorial. Firm steps on carpet, a little slow; the door to the room swung open.

Tom's first impression was of a shift dress in orange and scarlet gracing a tall and elegant shape, but then he blinked. Lidya's face was deep brown, dark enough to make him feel unsure, in the light from above, where her amused eyes were anchored.

'Mrs Lidya Slade?' asked Tom. Her high cheekbones recalled for him, disconcertingly, something in naval architecture, the curves of some delicate hull perhaps.

And she was decidedly pregnant.

The eyes searching his had become more serious, but she laughed, and put her head a little on one side. 'Yes,' she said. 'I'm Lidya.'

Lidya

'Mrs Slade,' said Tom formally. 'I must explain that I'm a police officer.'

'*Police?*' she said, and one hand strayed protectively to her belly.

'Yes,' he said. 'I need to ask you a few questions.'

She remained stock still, upright, apprehensive.

Tom produced his warrant card, and paused. She peered closely at it. 'Perhaps there's somewhere we could talk?' he suggested at last.

She looked around distractedly. Her sitting room carpet was fluffy, white and new.

'Should I take these off?'

She looked down at his snowy footgear and smiled. Tom hauled his boots off, parked them dribbling on the front door mat, removed his raincoat, and hung it on a brushed steel hook. He padded into the sitting room in his socks, and settled onto the cream leather sofa she gestured towards. He opened his briefcase.

She sank into the corner of a matching armchair, four yards from him, head erect.

'I don't quite know where to begin,' said Tom, as disarmingly as he could. 'It only concerns you very indirectly... You'll understand that the security services are very concerned about terrorism just now?'

She nodded, and cleared her throat. In the brighter light Tom could see that her skin was not black but a deep chocolate, her lips red. He wasn't sure whether

15

she was using lipstick.

'It concerns your husband's contacts in Peshawar,' he said. 'The authorities are interested in various people there, and it turns out he may have met some of them.'

'During his trip last September?

Tom nodded.

'I see,' she said. She seemed a little relieved. 'But you'll have to ask Ralph about that.' Her accent was educated English, with a hint of more musical vowels. 'Shall I ring him at work for you?' She made as if to stand.

'No,' said Tom. 'We have his number. In fact my colleague Inspector Gemmill is interviewing him as we speak. What I need is simply what you know of his movements. If you happen to have the names of anyone he was meeting, that would be a bonus.'

She took a deep breath, rose silently, and fetched a desk diary from an elaborate walnut bureau that gleamed under the wall lights, and remained standing as she turned the leaves. She looked up. 'You mean, you want *me* to give you the dates? Independently?'

Tom nodded again.

'But why?'

'That's what Special Branch has asked for.'

'*Special Branch?*'

'Yes.'

For a moment Tom thought she might refuse to cooperate. Her lips parted. But then with one finger she traced very slowly down the page. 'Well,' she said at last, doubtfully. 'He left home on 14th September… Then he called me from Islamabad two days later…'

Tom wrote discreetly in his Filofax.

'And I think he called again to say he'd reached Peshawar.'

16

'Can you remember when that was?'

'I'm not sure… Yes I am: Elspeth was here, it must have been a Monday. That makes it the 19th.'

'Not the 26th?'

'No, it was only a day or two after he rang from Islamabad. And he was back here by the 29th.' She was running one hand through her hair: it was black and curving, framing her dark face and almond-shaped eyes, but ended in wispy curls.

'Thank you. Did he say who he'd be seeing?'

'No, I don't think so. I assumed he'd be seeing Mostar.'

'Mostar?'

'His partner. Mostar al Hamri.'

Tom wrote some more.

'When he came back, he was cross because Mostar had loaded the shipping container without letting my husband inspect the goods. Ralph made them unpack it again… And he'd seen Jim McVeigh.'

'Who's that?'

'Ralph's investment banker. Ralph wasn't sure why Jim had chosen to come out to Pakistan, but he was pleased with how the money talk went.'

'Anyone else?'

'Not that he told me. But he's sure to have seen lots of people. Ralph schmoozes. He loves it.'

'His business is import–export?'

'Yes.'

'Do you know what stuff?'

'Cotton cloth, mostly. Made-up garments too, if he can get the quality.'

'And Ralph's a Muslim, I think? He converted?'

Lidya looked anxious again, but then laughed, a liquid, musical ripple. 'Yes,' she said. 'When he was in Cairo.' She didn't elaborate.

'And you attend the mosque in George Street?'

'Oh, no! That's Ralph's business.'

'You're not a practising Muslim, then?'

'I'm not a Muslim at all!' She looked disconcerted.

'Sorry!' said Tom. 'I got the wrong end of the stick.'

'That's all right.'

'Perhaps I should ask where you come from?'

'Addis.'

'Ethiopia? Addis Ababa?'

'Of course. And that's where I met Ralph... He was trading with my father, you see.'

'Perhaps that makes you Christian?' said Tom cautiously.

She smiled. 'So you *do* know something about us. Yes, I'm a Copt.'

'An ancient Church, isn't it?'

She laughed. '*Very* ancient... Saint Phillip converted the treasurer to the Queen of Ethiopia.'

'As described in the Acts of the Apostles?'

She smiled with pleasure. 'Exactly.'

'Does your husband visit the George Street mosque regularly? Does he know the people there?'

Now she looked really concerned. 'Look,' she said, and paused. 'I don't know much about that mosque, but it's not a hotbed of extremism, if that's what you're thinking. You'll have to ask Ralph about it... He's not a very conventional Muslim, you know.' She laughed, uneasily. 'Plenty of alcohol in the house. He drinks with his business contacts. We serve wine when we have guests. None for me just now, of course, but Ralph doesn't hold back.'

Tom smiled. 'D'you know England well?' he asked.

'Quite well. My father sent me to boarding school here, in Cheltenham.'

'The Ladies' College?'

She laughed again. 'Yes, the sixth form. And then I've been here with Ralph.'

'How long have you been married?'

'Two years.'

Tom wrote that down, then paused and riffled through his notes; he could think of nothing else he needed to know. 'I think that's about it,' he said at last. 'Thank you.' He pushed the papers back into his briefcase and stood up.

She rose too and led the way towards the front door.

Tom hesitated. 'I'm very sorry to be a nuisance,' he said. '… But can I use your toilet?'

She nodded gravely. 'Of course. But the downstairs one is broken, I'm afraid.' She came with him to point the way up the stairs. 'Turn right along the landing, and then on the left.'

As Tom climbed, she retreated to the sitting room, and he caught a glimpse through the door of her orange and scarlet dress subsiding again into the easy chair. Her eyes were closed.

Padding over the pastel carpet of the landing, he passed the open door of a bedroom, and saw that it had been decked out as a nursery. The curtains were a colourful print of zoo animals peering through a green jungle. A basket cradle, a plastic baby bath on a delicate wooden frame, and a neat pile of baby clothes, all blue, stood awaiting the new arrival.

When he came down again it was Elspeth, anxiously smiling, who came to show him out. The sitting room door was now closed, and he could just hear Lidya's anxious voice on the phone. 'That's to be expected,' he thought to himself.

He dragged on his rubber boots, thanked Elspeth, and set out once more into the still-falling snow.

*

As he cautiously negotiated the white-filled lanes around the head of the creek, images of Lidya and her well-appointed house flitted through Tom's head, and he wondered what Jane would have made of her. How old? Late twenties? Younger than Jane, anyway. In most respects Jane's age no longer troubled Tom, but he did sometimes notice that her thirty-five years weighed up new acquaintances differently from his fifty-one.

The car skidded a little, and Tom corrected the slide smoothly, without thought... 'All those blue clothes,' he muttered. 'They must have had a test.' Hardly surprising. That longed-for infant would surely have been subjected to every test available.

He caught himself imagining... That particular question had never found its way onto his and Jane's radar. But things had been settling down: the unsatis-factory short-term locums with local GPs were over, her part-time appointment as registrar at the Derriford was going well. She'd sailed her *Ariel* solo to Rosslare and back... He found himself smiling, then frowned with an obscure determination to bring himself down to earth.

Thrumming to itself, his car climbed softly to the Yealmpton road, and came to a squeaky halt. Sounds were muffled. Careering white flakes splotched onto his windscreen, and survived melting for a moment before being whisked away on intermittent wipe. Through the ghostly kaleidoscope he saw that a snow plough had passed that way since he'd come. With a small nod of satisfaction, he turned right and acceler-ated gently towards home.

Developments

Next morning, Tom's office was chilly again, and Iain, carrying a folder, came to settle on Tom's radiator, which was groaning to itself.

'How was Victory House?' he asked.

Tom looked up. 'I reckon John Smith was right,' he said.

'Swept you away, did she Tom?'

'You never told me she was Ethiopian.'

Iain's eyes opened wide. '*She hangs upon the cheek of night, like a rich jewel in an Ethiop's ear...* And I'd taken her for an English rose. Tall and coal black, then?'

'More dark milky coffee... And she was pregnant.'

'Yes, he told me.'

'What was he like?'

'Sharp suit, public school accent. But it was strange, Tom...'

'Go on.'

'Not brash, drives a discreet Lexus.' Iain was rubbing his hands together beneath his chin. 'But his secretary told me he drives it like a maniac round the Devon lanes...'

'Ah.'

'Not as secure in himself as you might expect... On the other hand, quite a physique. Thickset. Shoulders too broad for his jacket... Sure enough, serious long-distance swimmer. Does the length of the Exe estuary each summer.'

'Adventurous type, then?'

'Not sure, Tom. Felt more like it was to compensate for something.'

'What?'

'How should I know? Perhaps his dad despised him and his mother drank.' Iain gave Tom a slow, speculative look.

'This isn't like you, Iain!'

'Drinks a bit himself anyway. I could see the glassware behind the curtain.'

'They had that cot death, I suppose.'

'Yes… Didn't want his wife upset. Made damn sure I knew about the new baby. Fair enough… Excited at the prospect. Touching.'

'Might he have been expecting your visit? Fortifying himself?'

'No. Too taken aback.'

'So how did the interview go?'

Iain shrugged. 'Dead straight.' He opened his file. Tom slid his own notes out of his desk drawer.

'Dates.' Iain ran his finger down a list. 'Flew to Islamabad 14th September.'

'She agrees.'

'So do the flight records, and immigration.'

'Reached Peshawar on the 19th. Hotel confirms.'

'He rang her from there the same day.'

'Right…   Left Peshawar on the 24th, back in London late on 28th.'

'And back in Noss Mayo on 29th. That all fits… But hold on, you told me yesterday he said he reached Peshawar on the 20th, not the 19th. Where did that come from? Did MI5 quiz him?'

'No, they just got Heathrow Immigration to ask him a few innocent-sounding questions. He may not have been that precise in his answers.'

'Perhaps he meant the 20th was his first working day... But anyway, the ISI reckon the container with explosives left Peshawar on the 10th, long before he left the UK?'

'That's right. I pressured him a bit. He only got really upset when I told him you were questioning his wife.'

'What did he say about al Hamri?'

'Confirmed they'd met, said they'd been partners for years. Staggered that MI5 knew about their conversations—and then worried, of course.'

'Admit anything?' Tom was in probing mood, chair tipped back, hands behind his head.

'Agreed with the substance of the bugged calls. But that was only dates and arrangements. When I suggested Mostar might be a Taliban sympathiser, he just laughed.'

'They all are, north of Peshawar?'

'That's what he meant. Admitted Mostar often did the final sealing of the containers and dealt with Pakistani customs and thought it quite possible he had al Quaida links. But at the UK end the containers are unsealed by Customs in his own bonded warehouse— said nothing could be extracted there without his knowing.'

'Lazy, not to have worried more about arms smuggling?'

'He's a merchant-adventurer, not a civil servant.'

Tom frowned. 'His wife said something about meeting someone... an investment banker.' He hunted through his notes. 'Jim McVeigh.'

Iain consulted a notebook. 'I asked him for his Peshawar contacts, and he named three... Here we are... No McVeigh.'

'Perhaps they met in Islamabad. He spent several

days there.'

'Have to check.'

'Did you quiz him about his religion?'

'I did. Made no bones about his marriage, laughed about it. But interesting about Islam.' Iain got off the radiator and settled onto the papers on Tom's desk. 'Asked whether I was religious, quoted the Holy Book—translating the Arabic. Read me off stuff about Jesus and Mary.'

'They appear in the Qu'ran?'

'Seems so… His secretary told me he makes donations. Orphans in Palestine and Iraq, a medical charity in the UK, another promoting women's education in Egypt… Didn't sound very Islamist.'

'Did you ask about the George Street mosque?'

'Said he went there mainly for Friday prayers, and didn't know the people very well. He'd met Dr Said, though, said he admired him.'

'We know Said's OK… Sounds like you agree with MI5, Iain? Nothing suspicious?'

'He was alarmed, of course, to have attracted their interest, but his story hung together.' Iain paused, head a little to one side, still seated on Tom's papers. 'I rather liked him. He's got curly reddish hair, a tad greasy.'

*

The next day Tom had a doctor's appointment. He managed to leave Charles Street at the official knocking-off time of 5 pm. After stop-starting to Crownhill through rain-spattered evening traffic, he drove up into the housing estate and parked in broad Sumach Avenue, its large houses far enough apart to leave plenty of spaces. The rain was easing, and the moon, glinting between ragged clouds, made obscure silver shapes on the polished wet tarmac.

The steamy waiting room was packed, and he carefully folded his damp raincoat before reporting. 'Dr Mikailan this evening, Tom,' said Clarence, whose previous employment had been as a clerk in the County Court. 'Forty minutes, I'm afraid.'

'No problem,' said Tom, tapping his brief case. 'Plenty to do.'

A man with a white streak in his glossy black hair made space on the leatherette bench, and Tom settled down to review his notes on Dane Street Motors and the ringed Aston Martins. It wasn't a high priority, but it would absorb his attention peacefully.

Fifty minutes later a firm hand settled onto his shoulder. Igor, head of the practice, his jutting beard modelled on Lenin's, liked to summon his patients in person. 'Ready Tom?'

Tom followed him into the consulting room and sat down. 'Afraid it's my ear again, Igor.'

Igor raised his eyebrows and consulted his computer.

'The left one?'

'Yes.'

Igor clicked his tongue, found an auriscope, checked that its light came on, and applied it to Tom's ear. 'Um,' he said. 'Better rinse it out.' He fiddled over the sink, ran the water heater. 'Keeping well otherwise?' He rummaged in a drawer.

'No problems.'

'Jane enjoying herself at the hospital?'

'Yes, she is.'

There was a long pause while the water warmed.

'Changing the subject, Igor,' Tom ventured suddenly.

Cradling his syringe, Igor looked up.

'D'you have any experience of cot deaths?'

'You're not investigating one?'

'No. But I came across a case recently, and it made me think.'

'Ah, Tom... Lacerating. And more common than young mothers seem to think... Ready now? Tilt your head.'

The Victoria Falls roared in Tom's ear, and coursed down his neck onto a scratchy towel.

'And worse still when the police get involved...' Igor took another look. 'That's cleared it... That case you mentioned... It wasn't Lidya Slade, by any chance?'

Tom said nothing.

'I remembered seeing your old car parked by Brookings Down Wood, a couple of mornings ago... Discharge from the inner ear. Drum inflamed. Been scratching at it, have you?'

'I expect so,' said Tom guiltily, took the offered towel and dried his neck. '... Were you involved in Mrs Slade's case?'

'Only through Elizabeth Mayhew. She came round for a chat...'

'She's the GP?'

'Yes.'

'Was she worried?'

Igor pondered. 'You're not investigating it, you said?'

'No.'

'Not seriously worried... But this is in confidence, Tom.'

'Of course'

'The Child Death Review was due... Her own judgement was, nothing to worry about—or that's what she said. But, let's say, for a GP of thirty-four, she's surprisingly unsure of herself. Likes to talk her issues through. All of them. *Ad nauseam.* And I'm the poor sod she wants to do it with.'

'And you agreed with her?'

'Oh yes... Classic case. Male infant, four months. Mother breast feeding, last feed two in the morning. Put the child in the nursery, on its back, all proper, in a basket cradle... Come the morning, mum exhausted, still asleep, but dad hears no noises on the baby alarm. Investigates, child not breathing, wakes mum, panic. Mother calls the ambulance... Paramedics confirm dead at the scene. Horror all round... Pathology inconclusive, as usual, slight excess of fluid on the left lung. Dedicated parents, no hint of ill-treatment...'

'But at 2 am, Lidya was alone with the baby. How fast did they call the ambulance?'

'Very fast.'

'So why was Elizabeth Mayhew concerned?'

'Battle-axe of a practice nurse told her the mother was too calm, not natural to have called the ambulance so collectedly... You'll need an antibiotic, Tom.' Igor dotted incomprehensible hieroglyphs onto his prescription pad. '...That nurse had once encountered a real case of infanticide. Probably over-suspicious.'

'How did the nurse know the mother was calm and collected? Was she there?'

'Don't see how she could have been... Here you are, Tom. Know the routine? Be sure you finish the course. See me fast if it flares up again... Now, off with you, I'm behindhand today... '

'Thanks Igor.' Tom snatched up his briefcase and retreated backwards through the door. He pocketed his new prescription thoughtfully and collected his raincoat from the now almost empty waiting room.

*

The following Thursday there was a yellow post-it note on Tom's desk, asking him to drop by. Iain's office was larger than Tom's, but had no outside window. Iain graciously offered him a chair, and Tom took it with a grin.

'MI5 aren't happy,' said Iain. 'They want to talk. This afternoon.'

'Damn.'

'At Dawlish Warren. Can't think why. Are you free?'

'If I work late.'

*

Iain had a habit of using his family Passat for police business and claiming expenses. After lunch, as they wound their way towards the sea along the Teign estuary, Tom felt renewed irritation at being dragged out on this chilly and tedious drive for no obvious reason. But gradually, he relaxed, and found himself thinking about children again.

'How's your Al doing?' he asked.

'Fine,' said Iain. 'Margaret still says the house is too quiet.

'Too *quiet?* I thought you'd bought him a synthesiser.' The air was keen, and Tom was shivering a little beneath his issue raincoat, though the Passat heater was toasting his feet.

'We did. But he was very good about it. And it's an attic bedroom.'

'Media Studies at Stirling, isn't it?'

'Bit different from chilly old Strathclyde.'

'I thought you enjoyed university, Iain?'

'Well I did, but now I just don't get it. Al's into gritty Scots culture and his Glaswegian's so thick we have trouble following. But not into careers and job interviews. Not girls. At least, we think not girls. He's composing for a Polish pop group… Who all have a much sharper eye for the main chance than Al has.'

'Margaret's worried?'

'I'm worried. He's in his last year.'

Tom nodded. He'd been lucky with Miranda and Jack.

The estuary on their right was leaden and flat, the water nudging gently at the kelp mounds beside the road, the sky featureless, matching the water. There were no gulls airborne. The mounds of weed were topped with dirty half-melted snow, but the tarmac ahead was dark and clear.

*

The rendezvous was a single-storey wooden café in the Dawlish Warren confusion of caravan parks and holiday chalets, its northern roof still snow-streaked and dripping. Inside they found John Smith seated at a wicker table with a glass top, settling into an unseasonal cream tea, his professional ability to melt into any surroundings challenged, Tom thought, by resentment at the grottiness of Inspector Manfield's choice of venue. Unable to order beer, the Special Branch man had settled for Darjeeling with a double helping of toasted teacake, and his moustache showed signs of melted butter. Tom and Iain draped their regulation raincoats over a black bentwood hat stand, and ordered Earl Grey and cheese scones for two. There were no other customers and the proprietress

29

pulled up a mobile heater belching paraffin-scented hot air. She clattered cheerfully from the kitchen with the new orders, and set a CD playing on the audio system—birdsong, a continuously burbling rookery. She asked whether they liked it.

'Thank you,' said John Smith, 'very nice.'

'Those ruddy birds loud enough?' asked Mansfield when she'd retreated. He wiped his moustache with his paper napkin.

'For Chrissake, David—she's miles away.'

Tom relaxed.

John Smith cleared his throat. 'So,' he said to Iain, 'Thank you for coming. My impression was, you reckoned the target was in the clear?' He ladled sceptical strawberry jam onto clotted cream and tipped his head back.

'Not exactly,' said Iain cautiously. 'His story hung together.'

'No suspicious contacts in Plymouth?'

'No.' Iain examined his cheese scone and looked up. 'But we wanted to know: have you confirmed his agent Mostar as definite al Qaida?'

'Can't comment.'

'If he is, Ralph's known him a long time, long enough to have picked up a shrewd suspicion.'

'True.' John Smith's lips were compressed in his tanned face.

'And likewise,' persisted Iain, 'he's been attending that unofficial mosque in George Street a long time. We don't know of anything wrong there—but it seems a likely place for making Islamic contacts.'

John Smith said nothing.

'Have you discovered yet what was in the container?' Tom asked David Manfield.

David glanced for confirmation at John Smith, who

nodded. 'We have,' he said. 'Heaps of cotton cloth. And a lot of religious books—but they were all on the manifest. Just one bit of weaponry, that wasn't: a magazine for an AK 47.'

'A *magazine*? No ammunition? No explosives?'

'No.'

'Is importing the magazine illegal?'

'Illegal to leave it off the manifest. Otherwise, not.'

'Dummy run, then?'

John Smith nodded. 'Very likely. If they think it's gone smoothly, we can expect the hand grenades next time, or the time after.'

'I presume Customs repacked it all, and you'll be looking to see who collects the magazine from Ralph's warehouse?'

'Of course... And we'll be bugging the house.'

'The Noss Mayo house?'

'Yup.'

'So, take it all together, you're still reckoning Ralph's suspicious?'

'We've another line of enquiry that says so.'

'And what line is that?' persisted Iain.

'Can't tell you.' Over a third scone loaded with cream and jam, John Smith was beginning to look a little irritated.

'They say Pakistani intelligence is riddled with Islamic sympathisers.'

'So it is. But our chaps on the ground know who to trust.'

Iain turned to Tom and shrugged.

Tom turned to John Smith. 'I damn well hope you do your bugging discreetly,' he said. 'Those people need a bit of peace.'

Peggy

The following day Tom's desk phone rang at 8 am.

'Mrs Peggy Harford, Sir.'

'Never heard of her. What's she want?'

'Says it's confidential, Sir.'

Tom sighed. 'Put her on, Sam.'

There was a pause, and the line clicked. 'Chief Inspector Tallis?' A light Devon voice, cautious.

'Speaking.'

'Oh good! I have some information for you, Chief Inspector.'

'Yes?'

'About a family I work with.'

'What family?'

'You interviewed her last week—Mrs Slade.'

He felt his eyebrows shoot up. He had been disciplining himself to disengage from worrying about the Slades.

'Can we talk face-to-face?'

'Phone not good enough?'

'No.'

Tom made a face at the receiver. 'Can you be here by nine?'

'I can manage that.'

'Ask at the front desk.'

At five to nine the desk sergeant rang through again, and Tom made his way down to the main entrance. Sam nodded towards the row of battered stacking chairs set out by the window. A grey-haired figure was plumped broadly upright on one of them, a black bag and a pink cycle helmet parked beside her. A nurse's uniform showed under her raincoat. Sam jerked his head at her. She rose and walked briskly over to the desk.

'Mrs Harford?' Tom asked.

'Yes,' she said, looking determinedly up at him.

'Tom Tallis. Better go to my office.'

She followed him along the corridor and bustled beside him up the stairs, taking one riser at a time alongside Tom's loping two.

Tom unlocked his door, found her a seat. She placed the bag and cycle helmet tidily on the floor and settled herself.

'The Slades, you said?'

'They're expecting a baby,' said Peggy.

'I know.'

'And she's *terrified* you're going to arrest her husband.'

'Is she?'

'*Yes.*'

'And how do you come into the picture?'

'I'm the midwife... And she's very, very *fragile* Chief Inspector. They lost their first baby, eighteen months ago.'

Tom nodded.

'You know already?'

'Yes.'

Peggy seemed stopped in her tracks. 'Well,' she insisted, a little lamely, 'this time round, we've got to take every precaution, haven't we?'

'Meaning what?'

'CONI. Care of Next Infant.'

Tom had to be careful: collaboration between police

33

and social services is nowadays encouraged. 'Does one cot death make another more likely?' he asked cautiously.

'Not necessarily. It's the *parents* I'm concerned about, Chief Inspector.' Renewed determination was spreading over Peggy's face. 'She may seem confident to *you*. But more than a year it took her, just getting off the anti-depressants. And *he* started drinking… It's a miracle they're as positive as they are today, a living miracle.'

Tom nodded again, slowly. Peggy leant towards him, and for a moment he was afraid she was going to take his hand. She saw him draw it back a fraction, smiled confidingly. 'And now, you see, you've sent her spiralling down again,' she said.

Tom considered.

'So *are* you?' she persisted.

'Am I what?'

'Going to arrest him?'

'I hope not.'

She opened her mouth to speak. Her concerned eyes seemed to be saying: is that *really* the best you can do?

Tom raised his eyebrows. 'I can't say any more than that, Mrs Harford,' he said.

'But if you take Ralph away, Lidya'll surely go to pieces,' she urged, leaning forward again. 'And even if you don't, he'll be drinking again. Baby'll suffer…' She looked sternly at him. 'Black women need protection, too, you know, Chief Inspector.'

Tom's annoyance boiled over. 'Sometimes,' he said, 'people, black or white, just have to cope with us… How tough d'you reckon Mrs Slade is?'

'Whatever sort of a question is *that*?' she asked indignantly.

Tom set his jaw.

Peggy looked at him. 'She's strong,' she said, 'a sensible, warm-hearted woman…'

Which had been Tom's impression also.

'…Religious, too. But Chief Inspector, baby-stress like this is as hard as it gets for a woman, really!'

Tom took a deep breath. 'Not in my hands.' he said at last.

'Supposed to be *terrorism*, isn't it?' said Peggy cannily. 'That's what she told me. What nonsense! That wouldn't be the ordinary police, would it?'

Again Tom said nothing.

Peggy looked at him and said fiercely, '*Someone's* got it terribly wrong, haven't they?' Then switching instantaneously to winning innocence: 'Could you, just possibly, speak to the person whose decision it is?

Tom imagined her thirty years earlier, a rosy-cheeked country girl wheedling in the school play-ground. He laughed.

'Or maybe *I* should?'

'No,' he said. 'I can't even give you his name. But I hear what you're saying…   I'll certainly do what little I can.'

Peggy looked at him, and hesitated for several seconds. Then she smiled. 'Right,' she said. 'OK. Thank you…   I'd better leave you my number.'

'You realise I'll probably be in no position to tell you anything that's happening?' said Tom sternly. But he found her a sheet of paper.

'I understand.' She tore the paper in two, wrote the number on one half and returned it. 'Now, have I got your name right?' She wrote busily on the other half, and showed him.

'Correct.'

'Thank you.' She slid the paper into a side pocket of

the black bag.

'When's this baby due?' asked Tom, thinking ahead.

Peggy found and consulted a diary. '20th January,' she said. 'Just over a month.'

Tom escorted her back to the main entrance, and after a moment's hesitation, shook her hand and watched her disappear through the glass doors.

*

Christmas arrived. In Tom's house Miranda made up a bed for Jack in his old room, and he was barely over the doorstep before he'd volunteered to put up holly and find a tree. On Christmas Eve Miranda's Hamish dashed in for a two-day visit, enthusiastic as ever, and Tom cooked supper. Jane joined them for the meal (which happened to be her first meeting with Jack) and afterwards, Miranda and Hamish reminisced about sailing to Brittany with her the previous summer.

'Any chance of getting *Ariel* up to Scottish waters this year?' asked Hamish, who worked near Oban. Jack, having missed out last time, looked up hopefully.

'Far too early to say,' said Jane firmly.

On Christmas Day Jane was with them again for Miranda's turkey and mince pies. Jack said he would tackle the washing up, and Jane offered to help. Jack looked down at the other three slumped in their chairs, nodded, and he and Jane disappeared together.

Tom settled again to crystallised ginger and his bookish present from Miranda, but after a while became aware of distant talk in the kitchen. He could tell, slightly to his surprise, that the usually silent Jack was monopolising the conversation, and Jane was laughing at him.

*

On 30th December, Tom heard that Victory house had been bugged. The usual method was to disconnect the phone, and, when the target reported the fault, to send around what appeared to be a BT engineer to fix it. It made him dissatisfied: pregnant Lidya shouldn't have been left phoneless. He had taken a policy decision not to discuss the Slades with Jane, but was finding the constraint irksome.

On 5th January he found another post-it note from Iain on his blotter. He made his way to Iain's office and stuck his head round the door. Iain was shuffling paper work, his lips tight.

'Morning!' said Tom. 'Good weekend?'

'Fine,' said Iain, scratching his head. He had a scarf wound around his neck, its long ends trailing down his back. 'It's Monday morning brings the trouble.'

'What's hit you?' Tom found himself a chair.

'MI5 again. They want Ralph questioned.'

'Oh no... When?'

'The twelfth.'

'That's not great timing.'

'Why?'

'Their baby's due on the twentieth.'

'Don't think I knew that.'

'Any danger they'll arrest him?'

'No. It's to be me, not them. We bring him in here, me to reel off the questions while John Smith sits and listens, or so he says. The bug's shown up nothing, so far. And no other new evidence... They're just trying to bounce him.' Iain was flexing his plastic ruler incautiously.

'Not justified, then?'

'Not by my reckoning. Just bloody persecution.'

37

Jane

It was a glorious winter's Saturday, shiny and windy—and Tom was coming to put up shelves. Jane's maisonette was flaunting itself even more airily than it had on the agent's web site in May. She walked to her bedroom, where the orange and scarlet check of the duvet cover smiled up at her, and eased out from the back of the tall cupboard an artist's portfolio. She carried it to the kitchenette, laid it on the sheets of newspaper arranged ready on the whitewood table, untied the ribbons and slowly opened the heavy cardboard. A chalky whiff of unfixed pastel tickled her nose.

She looked down and felt a momentary surge of doubt. Confident Miranda would surely have brought more *rebellion* to the chrysanthemums and vase.

'How old is she?' she wondered aloud. 'First year of teaching… Twenty-two? And ready to marry… Jesus.'

But Miranda, after all, was her mother's daughter. Beth too, from all that Jane had heard, had been so spontaneously, so overflowingly artistic, earthy—so beloved. Warm-hearted women, it seemed, had just tumbled into Tom's earlier life.

But self-doubt could not survive for long on such a sparkling day. Only two days ago, she reminded herself stoutly, that glowing duvet had been swept aside in unaccustomed disorder… And Tom wanted to make frames for her pictures.

She located a plastic store bag and dug out a bottle of fixative and spray. She assembled the device and tried it out on newspaper. She sprayed her work evenly, set it to dry on the worktop, and carried the empty portfolio back to the wardrobe, with a passing conspiratorial grin at the orange and scarlet check.

*

The bell rang. It was his voice on the door-phone: a whole hour early.

'It's you!' she said. 'I'll be down.'

On the doorstep, the sun made a halo of his hair. She laughed. Leaning down, she kissed him on the forehead, drew him inside.

Tom raised his eyebrows cheerfully and stepped into the stairway. He dumped one of the bags he was carrying and closed the door behind him. She felt herself gathered towards him by his free arm, sensed her heart thumping against his chest.

'Come on up!'

Tom hauled his bags up the staircase and deposited them in her sitting room. He settled onto her sofa. She went into the kitchenette to make coffee, thought for a moment, and found a jug of cream to set on the tray with the cups and biscuits. She filled the cafetière and placed the tray before him.

'What's this?'

'Don't you like it?'

'Course I do.' He sipped. 'Got those pastels fixed?'

'I've made a start.'

He grinned encouragement and selected a short-bread without asking. 'What a gorgeous day.'

'Yes.'

'I brought a measuring tape.'

'You don't have to rush, Tom.'

'About fourteen feet of books, you said?'

'Yes… But I can buy shelves, you know.'

'No,' said Tom. 'You need something tailor-made, to make best use of that space. But before I start messing around, can I ask you something?'

'Of course!'

Tom made a face. 'Cot deaths.'

She glanced at him. 'Sudden infant death syndrome—SIDS.'

'Ever had to deal with a case?'

'Oh yes. They're not that unusual.'

'How common?'

'I'm not sure. Most GPs will have seen several.'

'What happens, exactly?'

'Nothing much. That's the whole point. The baby dies in its sleep: just stops breathing.'

'Do they know why?'

'Occasionally it's a bug. But usually for no detectable reason… That's why it hits the parents so hard.'

'Because there's nothing to blame?'

'I don't think the mothers ever recover, not really. "I let him get too hot." "Should have realised he was breathing irregularly." "Should have looked at him more often." "Should never have let myself go to sleep." "I should… I shouldn't… I should!" You see it in their eyes… Tough business, parenthood.'

Tom looked at her. 'Has its rewards too,' he said.

The sun encouraged Jane to smile.

He stirred his coffee.

'When there's no recognisable cause, there has to be an autopsy, and the poor parents have to face the prospect of their little one being sliced up.'

Tom nodded.

'And then, if the autopsy finds nothing, there's the

40

awful possibility of infanticide to be investigated, because there's no obvious way of distinguishing SIDS from smothering with a pillow… And then the police have to come in, and, God help her, the poor woman has to face being a murder suspect, on top of everything else… I heard about a case like that last year.'

Tom looked up.

'When I was doing that locum with Elizabeth Mayhew.'

'You weren't personally involved?'

'No. But the mother turned up in my open surgery twelve months after losing her baby, for something quite different, and I took the opportunity to read up her case notes.'

*

After the coffee, Tom made his measurements. At first she thought of quizzing him about the construction he had in mind, but then thought better of it. The work in his own house was good, she said to herself, I liked it, didn't I? And now he wants to make something for me with his nice competent hands. She sprayed a second coat of fixative.

When Tom had finished his measurements, they wrapped up and went out for a walk, arm in arm in the wind, around the local streets. They found Mai Doo house open, and Jane bought chow mien and egg-fried rice for an easy lunch.

'Remember Brookings Down Wood?' asked Tom, as they set off again.

'Last Easter? Another windy day.'

'It looks mysterious under snow. I was there just before Christmas. Walked up the footpath opposite.'

'Did you?' said Jane, thoughtfully.

41

Tom said nothing, and she looked up at him. But he still said nothing, and they walked on.

At last Jane said, 'That footpath takes you up to Victory House, doesn't it?' She looked at him doubtfully.

Tom sighed. He thought for a while. 'I'd better come clean,' he said, and looked at her quizzically.

Jane looked up at him and nodded. 'I remembered the address, you see, and worked out where the house was later, one day when I was in Noss Mayo to see another patient.'

Tom thought for a moment. 'Classy bit of architecture,' he said.

'Her bloke must be in the money... But we don't have to talk about them if you don't want to, Tom.'

'He's a trader.' Tom hesitated, and took a deep breath. 'Look... This is the bit you *must* keep to yourself, strictly. Promise?'

'OK.'

'He's a convert to Islam... And the security services think he may be a terrorist.'

'Jesus!'

'Iain and I think he almost certainly isn't, but we're afraid the poor bloke is about to get arrested. And the thing is, they've tried again—she's heavily pregnant.'

Jane looked up sharply. 'Oh,' she said.

'Not my business, of course. But if he does get detained, what sort of support can she count on?'

Jane considered. 'That's up to Elizabeth and Social Services.'

'Will Dr Mayhew have got in counselling support?'

'Not necessarily.' Jane considered. 'There's something called CONI for a second pregnancy after a cot death.'

'I gather that's going ahead.'

'Well, that's good. There'll be the usual post-natal, I suppose… Don't know what Elizabeth would do if the husband got arrested. She's not a very decisive woman.'

'That's what Igor said.'

'You spoke to Igor too? This *is* on your mind, Tom.'

'I was seeing him anyway, about my ear.'

'So you interviewed her?'

'Yes… I saw their nursery.'

Jane felt herself frowning a little, and rather deliberately pulled Tom's elbow closer.

Tom was looking down at her. 'All in blue,' he said.

'Hard for them, the risk is higher for boys.'

'Oh. Why?'

'I don't know… What's her husband like?'

'English. Iain liked him. But a streak of uncertainty, he thought. Drinks too much.'

'Poor chap.'

'He may need to pull himself together.'

'Well, yes,' said Jane. On a sudden impulse she added: 'Look, Tom! When's this baby's due?'

'The twentieth.'

'Only a week! How would it be if I rang Elizabeth, just to be certain she's got things in hand?'

Tom hesitated. 'I suppose you could.'

'No time like the present.'

'Hell, Jane, it's the week-end!'

'Won't hurt her, she likes talking her cases over. It'll put your mind at rest. Let's do it.'

Tom said nothing. Jane pulled her mobile from an anorak pocket. She stopped under a kerbside plane tree, whose leafless branches were thrashing overhead, then moved away to find a quieter spot in the sun beside a wall. He watched, arms folded.

She sheltered the phone from the wind with her free

hand. 'Elizabeth?' she said. 'It's Jane Allison,' and waited. An unstoppable stream of news seemed to be flowing from the other end. At last she said: 'Well, I was really calling about a patient... Lidya Slade.' Another long pause. 'Peggy told you, then?' ... 'That suits me very well...' An even longer pause. 'Super, Elizabeth. Thank you. See you then. Bye for now! Bye!'

'What was all that about?' asked Tom.

'Chit-chat, mostly!' said Jane, and laughed. 'But she wants to talk to someone about Lidya, anyway.'

'Really?'

'I can see her tomorrow morning. The midwife seems to have told her already there was some threat of arrest. She knows already it's about terrorism.'

Tom looked down at the pavement and up again. 'All right,' he said at last. 'But don't harp on the security aspect. And keep my name out of it. Just try to make sure she gets some decent support.'

Elizabeth

Jane's interest in the Slades had been provoked by rather more than merely wishing to do helpful things for Tom: her encounter with Lidya the previous year had sparked a reaction of its own. The spare beauty of Lidya's face, the quiet way she'd risen and walked off with her prescription, had somehow provoked in Jane a longing—for what? For *discourse*, maybe. Perhaps she'd seen in Lidya a possible sharer of wounded feelings.

*

She arrived promptly next morning at Elizabeth's surgery. It was next to the pleasant old stone house in which she lived, set back behind an untidy hedge in Yealm Road. It being a Sunday, there was no receptionist there, but a nurse answered the door, crisply uniformed. Jane assumed she must be the practice assistant who'd been on leave during her locum—Elizabeth had run on frequently about Marsha Stone's habits and opinions.

'Dr Allison?'

'Yes,' said Jane, smiling against the odds. She won a wintry smirk in return, but no further conversation, and was shown into the untidy office behind the consulting room, where Elizabeth was seated in an executive chair drinking coffee, and rotating herself idly, left then right, using her bare feet to push off against an ancient footstool.

She looked up and grinned cheerfully. 'Glad you could come in. Sherry?'

Jane smiled quickly. 'Coffee would be great, if you've enough.'

'I'll make another pot.' Elizabeth ran both hands distractedly up through her short blond curls, stood up, and wandered off to fill an electric jug at the sink in the consulting room.

'Peggy told you what was happening with the Slades?' shouted Jane through the open door.

'Yes… But the thing is, I don't quite know what I should do.'

'Well,' Jane said, 'if her husband does get arrested, she's going to need support. Probably needs it anyway.'

Elizabeth returned for the empty cafetière. 'But, Jane, she's *got* support.'

'CONI, d'you mean?'

'They asked for it two months ago.'

'Which bits are they getting?'

Elizabeth swung the chair round, rolled it to her desk and consulted a computer file. 'The midwife twice a week, and the apnoea alarm. Plus symptom and weight diaries.'

'And the usual briefing?'

'Peggy does that.'

'OK. But what I meant was *emotional* support. She's had one cot death. And now she's afraid her husband's going to be whisked away—she's surely terrified something'll go wrong with her new baby. Proper counselling.'

'D'you really think so?'

For a sane well-trained practitioner of thirty, you *are*

thick, thought Jane tartly—or perhaps, just harassed. With no children of your own, you don't want to think about the terrors of motherhood. 'What about other things? Does she have help in the house?'

'No idea. Perhaps Marsha... Marsha!' Elizabeth yelled, and disappeared again to make the coffee.

Steps sounded in the corridor. The nurse slid quietly into the room and settled her weight into the remaining easy chair, knees slightly apart. The ageless type, thought Jane. Fifty? Thirty-five?

Elizabeth returned with the steaming pot, and looked up. 'Jane here's wondering how much help Mrs Slade has in the house, Marsha.' She poured out for herself and Jane.

'That black woman? Over in Noss Mayo?'

'Her husband's been questioned by the police.'

'*Has* he though?' Marsha's look suggested she wasn't surprised. 'What for?'

Elizabeth looked at Jane. 'I don't know,' said Jane diplomatically, and Elizabeth said nothing.

'And a new baby coming... Help in the house? I don't know. She used to have a sixth-former two days a week. The midwife will be going in.'

'Do you know them?' asked Jane.

'I saw a lot of her before their cot death... She probably will need help.'

'Why?' asked Elizabeth.

'You remember, Lizzie... Ignorant. Wanting to swaddle that baby tight in a scarlet cloth. Silly woman. Might look like a fashion plate, but never had enough milk.'

'It was her first,' said Jane. 'I saw her in surgery last summer, and she didn't seem stupid to me.'

'British girls have more common sense.'

'Well,' said Jane, deciding not to argue. 'How

47

would you feel Elizabeth, if I called in myself to check the situation?'

'You?'

'I don't want to do anything unprofessional. But I heard what was happening, and I remembered her.'

'D'you really have time, Jane? Feel free. I'd be grateful. Want to see her notes again?'

'I'll have a re-read, and tell her I'm there on your behalf. I guess I could call in with Peggy, sometime?'

'If you think Lidya needs psycho support, were you thinking of organising it, Jane?' Elizabeth sounded relieved.

'You'd have to make the formal request.'

'I can do that, sure.'

'But would it be a good idea if Marsha looked in fairly regularly, too, once the baby's arrived?'

'D'you really think that's necessary? We've got practice priorities to consider, haven't we Marsha?'

'We do indeed.' Marsha made a face, but didn't seem surprised to be consulted. 'But I could find half an hour twice a week, Lizzie. Tuesdays and Thursdays at four, maybe, when I'm over to Bridgend for Mr Stokes' diabetes.'

Elizabeth seemed to be considering.

'Good,' said Jane. Marsha had responded more positively than she'd expected, and probably knew how to conceal her critical spirit when face-to-face with a patient. Jane sipped her coffee and changed the subject before any objections were raised.

'I should *hate* running a one-woman practice, Elizabeth,' she said. 'How do you find it?'

Marsha pulled a face and got up to leave.

'Sorry, I didn't mean to drive you away!'

'That's all right, Dr Allison. Catching up on reports.' Marsha's feet were quiet on the carpet as she stepped firmly to the door, but then echoed into the distance on the parquet of the corridor.

'The practice? Can be a strain,' admitted Elizabeth. 'But I talk things through a lot with Marsha. She's very down-to-earth. Reminds me of all the admin I've forgotten.'

'She was off on leave when I was with you. How long's she been in the practice?'

'Since I started down here. Seven years.'

At that moment the phone on Elizabeth's desk rang loudly, startling Jane. For a stupid moment she thought it might be for herself: Tom, perhaps, with some urgent new information.

Elizabeth leaned forward, grabbed the receiver and cradled it under one ear.

'*Speaking!*' she said. Jane could hear a male voice, raised and peremptory as though used to giving orders, but couldn't pick out the words.

'Of *course*,' said Elizabeth, 'I'll be with you *directly*.'

The voice continued.

'Oh please calm down,' said Elizabeth, 'there's nothing whatever to worry about!'

The voice quacked even more urgently, and at some length.

Elizabeth cast her eyes up to the top of the bookcase facing her and allowed her gaze to rest there. 'Yes indeed,' she said at last. 'Of course. As *soon* as ever I can.' The phone clicked, and she returned the receiver to its cradle.

She turned to Jane, with a frown. '*Well!*' she said. 'That changes our perspective a little,'

'What d'you mean?'

'*Why* do the men always panic?' She looked anxiously around her office. 'Baby's on its way!'

'That was the husband?'

'It was indeed.' Elizabeth jumped to her feet and peered into a cupboard. She distractedly stuffed her stethoscope and a packet of surgical gloves into a scuffed leather bag.

'Gosh! Early, isn't it?'

'Eight days, he said.'

'How far have they got?'

'Waters broken. Contractions strong and frequent...' Elizabeth ran off to bellow instructions to Marsha.

Jane paused, listening to Marsha's mumbled replies from a distant room, and then, sure that Elizabeth would leave her to her own devices, found her coat and let herself out of the surgery. She pulled the street door closed behind her with a vigorous click—a click, in fact, of something oddly like elation.

Arrival

Next day, alerted by Jane, Tom tried to get Ralph's interview deferred, but was told this was impossible, so he called her at the Derriford.

'ENT ward.'

'Can I speak to Dr Allison?'

'She's seeing patients. Is this urgent?'

'It's a police matter. Chief Inspector Tallis.'

A long pause. He allowed his pencil to tap periodically on the desk.

'Tom?' came Jane's voice.

'No go, I'm afraid. Ralph will be hearing he's wanted in three days' time.'

'Oh dear... I'd better visit them—I cleared it with Elizabeth yesterday before we knew the baby had arrived.'

'Are you sure that's a good idea?'

'It's the practical thing.'

'Well, don't get too involved. Concentrate on getting the help she needs.' Tom scowled at his handset.

'I'll drop by with Peggy when she visits tomorrow morning... She's the midwife. Splendid, concerned, apple-cheeked body.'

Tom smiled.

'Oh—and it was a girl, not a boy.'

'Really?'

'Someone muddled the tests... Can't talk now,' went on Jane. 'I'll ring tomorrow evening. Will you

51

have time?'

'I'd better.'

*

It was still very cold at 9.50 the next morning as Jane turned her Clio towards Widey bottom and changed down for the hill.

The morning's business, she knew uneasily, was at least partly something of her own that, far from setting Tom's mind at rest, was making him uneasy. But then, as she reached the hill bottom patches of snowdrops on the dun verge by the trees, exclamation marks trumpeting new life, stabbed at her consciousness, and her mood quickened.

The Clio purred quietly on beside the still water of the creek, through Noss Mayo, and climbed the hill. Peggy was waiting, parked in the lane, and they walked up the path to Victory House together, its limestone shining in the wintry sun. Jane rang the bell, and heard after a moment a thumping of male steps on the stairs. The door was unlocked and opened slowly.

She saw a not very tall man in a double-breasted suit that contoured around broad shoulders. His face was tanned, but a little red too. 'Morning, Peggy,' he said very cheerfully.

'A lovely morning it is, Mr Slade. This is Dr Allison.'

'Ah, yes.' Ralph shook hands, bent to pick up the milk basket, and ushered them in. 'I'll just put this away in the kitchen. Go on up.'

His hand had felt warm in hers. Jane followed Peggy over the fluffy carpet, up pastel stairs and into a sunny nursery. Lidya was seated in a low chair, gently rocking a basket cradle with one hand, a shiny new novel open but face-down on the floor beside her.

Lidya smiled enquiringly up at her, as Ralph reappeared and came delicately into the room.

'This is Dr Allison,' said Peggy.

'I remember,' said Lidya.

'A septic cut, wasn't it?' said Jane, smiling. She shook hands and peeped into the basket. The baby was just awake.

'Grey-green eyes in milk chocolate!' enthused Peggy.

'*Gorgeous*!' said Jane, meaning it.

Ralph looked delighted. Lidya smiled a little, her oval face tilted to one side.

I was right, thought Jane: they *are* a lovely couple. 'I'd better explain why I'm here,' she said.

'Please find chairs,' said Lidya, without taking her hand off the basket. Peggy brought two bedroom chairs over, and the women settled themselves in a ring of three. Ralph quietly stationed himself behind the cradle and took charge of the rocking.

'I was talking to Dr Mayhew yesterday,' explained Jane. 'I'm here to make sure you get all the support you need.'

Ralph smiled and nodded. Lidya remained impassive, but seemed to accept Jane's contrived explanation. 'Thank you,' she said simply.

'I often work with Peggy,' Jane went on, 'and she was getting me up to date.' Peggy nodded vigorously. 'How are things going with baby?'

'We've hardly had time to get used to her,' said Ralph.

'Peggy tells me she's feeding well... Oh, I ought to have asked—does she have a name yet?'

Ralph frowned briefly and glanced down at Lidya.

'We were *thinking* of Ayana,' Lidya said quietly.

'That's nice! Is it Ethiopian?'

'Amharic, yes.' She nodded. 'It means beautiful blossom.'

'But not settled yet?'

Lidya pulled a face, and looked up at Ralph, who seemed a little shamefaced. 'We were expecting a boy, you see,' she said. 'Poor Ralph hasn't had time to think.'

Jane leant forward. 'What about practical help? Have you got what you need?'

'We're well off for that,' said Lidya, her slender hands quiet in her lap.

Peggy said briskly: 'Maybe I should bath baby to-day, Lidya? If you three want to talk?'

Lidya seemed to hesitate.

'You go downstairs,' said Peggy firmly.

'Yes,' said Lidya. 'Thank you, Peggy.'

Peggy leant over the cradle, looked in, smiled, and ran her little finger delicately over one tiny brown cheek. Then she set off for the bathroom, leaving the baby in the basket.

Lidya and Jane rose. Ralph cleared his throat and said: 'I'll be in my office.' He smiled again at Jane and turned to Lidya. He left the bedroom door open behind him, and marched to another room along the landing, closing its door behind him with a firm click.

Lidya paused for a moment, then silently led the way down to her pristine sitting room. Jane followed, stepping cautiously out onto the fluffy carpet in her sensible walking shoes. Lidya indicated one of the soft leather chairs and settled herself into another, curling her feet gracefully beneath it. Jane sat down, her back straight, and smiled hopefully.

But the smile was not returned.

'You were asking about assistance, Doctor. We're doing very well, thank you. Peggy's coming in every day.'

'But she'll have to taper off soon.'

'And Elspeth is here with me as mother's help on Mondays and Fridays, which fits with her lectures. And Ralph is taking time off work, plus we have Mrs Biggs, who cleans for me on Wednesday afternoons.'

'But later, when Peggy has to cut down, d'you think more professional back-up might be a good idea?'

'Professional?"

'Nursing help. Would it be good if Marsha called in sometimes?'

'Marsha?'

'Dr Mayhew's practice nurse. I think you know her.'

Lidya's eyebrows lowered a fraction. She turned her head to stare abstractedly at the white carpet.

'Would that be helpful?' persisted Jane.

Lidya looked up. 'Doctor... I'm sorry, I forget your name.'

'Jane Allison.'

'Yes, Doctor Allison. Why do you feel we need another medical person, please? Is Dr Mayhew worried?'

'About your baby, you mean?'

'Of course.'

'No.' Jane smiled again, as gently as she could. 'Not at all. One cot death doesn't make another more probable, you know... Dr Mayhew explained that, didn't she?'

'She told us, yes.'

'We were thinking of *you*.'

'Me?'

'You and Ralph.'

Lidya looked up.

'Peggy told me something, you see,' said Jane.

'About the police coming.'

Lidya's face became stony.

Jane pressed on. 'You must be worried.'

Lidya was silent for a long time. At last she said: 'Of course I'm worried… You have children?'

'No.'

Lidya raised her eyebrows eloquently, sighed, and turned to look out of the window. 'Where I come from…' she said at last.

Jane's encouraging smile withered somewhat.

Lidya looked coolly back. 'Where I come from,' she repeated, '*mothers* advise mothers. But then, most families can't afford doctors.'

Jane swallowed. 'D'you have friends with babies?'

'Back home, of course.'

'Anyone nearby?'

'Not near. One in Birmingham.'

'Birmingham?'

'An old school friend… I call her every day.'

'That must be a help. Do you call Ethiopia too?'

'Yes. Two of my sisters have children, now. And cousins have babies too—but no telephones.'

'No phones?'

'In the mountains, you know, in the Amhara.… Do you know Ethiopia?'

'No, not at all.'

'My mother was a shepherdess there, when my father first met her. Or that's what he likes to say—she was a goatherd, really.'

Jane looked up, but there was still no smile.

'She was seventeen, very beautiful. My father was wealthy, an educated man from Addis Ababa.' Lidya straightened her back. 'He is related to Haile Selassie.'

'The Emperor? Really?'

'Yes… Now, I want to ask you, doctor. You say

that one cot death doesn't make another more likely. But in the mountain villages, there are some families with many deaths. My own mother's eldest sister lost three.'

'Your aunt lost three babies?'

'Yes.'

'How awful! Were they ill, before they died?'

'No, they were all healthy.'

'And they died in their sleep?'

'Yes.'

'Before the age of one?'

'Yes.'

'Well,' said Jane. 'I'm sure the cot death research says that's surprising, very unlikely to happen in one family. But I'm not an expert, I'll check it out for you. You need to be sure, don't you? I can see that it's worrying.'

'Yes.' Lidya's face was almost rigid now.

'And on top of that you've had the police here?' said Jane gently.

Lidya stared at her. At last she said quietly: 'A Chief Inspector came... He was polite, but he asked horrible questions. And a different man questioned Ralph. We're afraid Ralph may be arrested, very much afraid.'

'All at a time when you desperately need him by you?' Jane meant this to be sympathetic.

Lidya glanced quickly upwards towards Ralph's study. 'I also need him sober,' she said, and blinked. Her eyes glistened, suddenly.

Jane, taken aback, raised her eyebrows, and Lidya tightened her lips, as though she regretted having said so much.

'When did that start?' asked Jane, cautiously.

'Drinking? Not when Gabriel died, if that's what

you were thinking.'

'Gabriel? Your first baby?'

Lidya sighed and nodded. 'Not then. Ralph started as a teenager—too much gin in the family home... He tried to cut it out when he converted.'

'Converted?'

'You didn't know? He became a Muslim in Cairo, before I knew him... But he was drinking again by the time we met. My father told him he must stop.'

'And did he?'

'Yes.' Lidya paused. After a moment, she settled herself deeper into the soft white leather of her chair, peered cautiously into Jane's eyes.

'Yes,' she said, 'we called him Gabriel... Can you imagine losing a baby?'

'I can *try*,' said Jane. 'But I doubt if I can imagine right.'

'Well,' said Lidya, 'I had him for two precious months. After he was born, I mean.'

'And you wanted to be the perfect mum?'

'Like my mother... And then we let him die. *I* let him die.'

'Don't say that!'

Lidya broke eye-contact and looked down.

'Did your mother get to see him?'

'Oh no, no. My mother died, you see, when I was thirteen. I had to look after my brothers and sisters.'

'You were the oldest?'

'Yes. And Gabriel was the first grandchild. When he arrived, I was *being* my mother, can you understand that?'

'Yes, I think so.'

Lidya nodded. 'When we found him dead, I screamed like a mad woman for two hours... After that, a day and a half in an exhausted dream. But then

Ralph and I talked, we told each other we'd get over it, I thought we could be strong... But on the second day I found Ralph drunk.'

'How awful.'

'I collapsed. I was in bed, unable to act, gibbering. Ralph was scared out of his wits. But he stopped drinking, pressured the GP, found someone for me.'

'A therapist?'

'A hospital psychiatrist. She talked to me for a while, but then she started ladling out those pills.'

'SSRIs?'

'Yes.'

'Oh! And?'

'I hated them.'

'Like having your soul sucked out?' asked Jane.

Lidya looked curiously at her. 'You have experience?'

'Yes.' It was Jane's turn to break eye-contact.

Lidya paused. 'They let me slide away from reality... But then I couldn't get off them. Stuck in bed, with lost Gabriel floating in front of me, every hour of every day.'

'Lost Gabriel... Did you name him for the Archangel?'

'Perhaps. Ralph liked it. Gabriel is in the Qu'ran, too.'

Jane thought for a while. 'Look,' she said at last. 'You've an awful lot on your plate just now, a lot of stress...'

Lidya looked up sharply, then shrank again into her chair and looked suspiciously at Jane. At last she said: 'What are you trying to tell me, doctor?'

'I thought—we thought—you might need some emotional support...'

'But I might not want it from *you*.'

'Have I overstepped the mark?' Jane asked hurriedly. 'I didn't mean…'

'Perhaps I've been telling you more than I intended.'

'I'm sorry…'

Lidya again looked carefully into Jane's face, and gave a little smile. 'You don't know what resources I have,' she said.

'That's perfectly true,' said Jane. 'I suppose I just naturally felt you were a long way from home, your husband's been drinking, you've no mum to chat with… No church to turn to either,' she added.

Lidya looked at her coolly. 'And perhaps I just naturally preferred to manage my problems in my own way!' she said, and paused. 'No, I'm sorry… I'm grateful for your concern… I will mention one thing.'

Jane looked up.

'It's true I have no Coptic priest near here. But there's an Anglican priest in Plymouth, Father Barnabas.'

'Barnabas Gresley? St James?'

'You know him?'

'He's on the Primary Care Trust.'

'Ah yes. I talk to him.'

Jane nodded.

Lidya's face suddenly lost its strain. '… And my father is coming soon, to see his granddaughter,' she added.

'When?' asked Jane.

'It's not settled.' Lidya sat up straight and stretched her arms towards the floor.

Faintly from upstairs, Peggy's voice sounded, and Lidya went to the door. 'What was that, Peggy?'

Again Jane couldn't catch the message.

'She says she's finished the bath,' said Lidya. 'Shall

we go up again?'

'I ought to be going,' said Jane, 'but can I have one more peep?'

Lidya made space, and Jane hastened up the stairs ahead of her. In the nursery, Peggy was smiling down at the cradle.

'Ah,' said Jane. She looked up from the tiny face, and was a little surprised to discover that Lidya was examining her intently, neither smiling nor frowning. She recovered herself. 'I really must be going.'

Lidya seated herself by the cradle and didn't follow Jane downstairs, but Ralph must have heard the goodbyes, for he emerged from his office to show her out. At the front door, she eased into her winter coat and pulled on her driving gloves.

'Very nice to have met you, Doctor,' said Ralph. His farewell smile was encouragingly warm.

'I'm not sure I've helped very much,' said Jane. 'But good luck with everything,'

Thin clouds had covered the sun, and as she paced down the winding path between leafless bush roses, a light mizzle dusted the wool of her coat. She felt suddenly disconcerted. Had she been far too pushy? Tom would almost certainly think so. And what, oh what, had Lidya made of *her*?

As she opened the door of the Clio, Jane remembered the Toni Morrison lying face-down beside Lidya's chair. And why not? she thought. *I* read novels and so does she. She recalled also the Southern community brought so vividly to life in its pages. Those black characters, she thought, they're just as alien to her as they are to me—they've nothing in common with black Ethiopians, nothing whatever. But *Britain* she knows: *I* probably don't seem very weird to her at all.

Ariel

On the Thursday morning Iain and John Smith questioned Ralph, and late on Friday Iain brought Tom up to speed.

Ralph had complained bitterly about the effect on his wife. He'd been straightforward about Jim McVeigh. Jim wasn't one of his Peshawar contacts—he had an office in Islamabad, but they'd met, by arrangement, at the railway station. Jim, he said, was a US citizen he'd first encountered in Cairo ten years earlier. Ralph's enterprise was small beer for McVeigh's investment bank, but as a favour for an old friend Jim had recently put up some capital, which conveniently arrived at a moment when Ralph had cash flow problems.

'How much?' Tom asked.

'Two hundred thousand dollars.'

'Plausible'.

'And he gave us Jim's contact details in Pasadena.'

That was about it. John Smith had asked no questions and they'd allowed Ralph to drive home, angry and rattled. By Friday morning the CIA had checked McVeigh out. They'd found nothing suspicious. Ralph wasn't even over-extended in business.

But it was obvious that John Smith was still taking the security case very seriously.

*

On Saturday Tom was booked for supper with Jane. She had a morning ward round but was able to dash out at lunchtime for ingredients. By 7.45 fish pie odours were enlivening the flat and liquid was bubbling up through the mash. 'Sauce too runny,' she muttered. 'But he won't be able to resist the smell.' She walked into her sitting space to check her still-life, now on the wall, and returned with satisfaction to the cooker, blobbed oil over the sliced courgettes and was wondering whether to start heating them when the bell rang and his voice was on the door phone.

'Coming,' she shouted, hurried downstairs, and opened the door.

'Sorry,' said Tom, shaking rain off his waterproof. He settled it on a hanger in the entrance, followed her up to the bright flat, and noticed the still-life.

Jane watched him.

'Just right,' he said. 'Are you pleased?'

'I think so.'

'That pie smells good.' He dropped onto the sofa and picked up her Saturday magazine supplement. Promptly at eight, she had her first course on the table.

'When did you rustle that up?' he asked. 'Weren't you on duty?'

'That was this morning. I had time to shop.'

'Lucky me.'

She served, and they ate in satisfied silence for a while. Then he looked up and said:

'You said you'd seen her?'

'Yes.'

'How did it go?'

'I'm not sure. She doesn't want counselling.'

'Did you like them?'

'Very much. And the baby was lovely. But I'm not

sure Lidya likes me.'

'Ah.'

'What d'you mean, ah?'

'Well,' said Tom. He ate on methodically for a while, then leant back, looked at her, and wiped his mouth slowly with his napkin.

'Go on.'

He pushed out his lower lip. 'More stuff has come in from Special Branch.'

'About Ralph?'

'Yes... Look.' He seemed to be appealing. 'I've been thinking it over... I really must stop discussing the Slades with you. This is national security stuff.'

'Oh!' said Jane.

'And I want you to stop seeing her, too.'

'*Me*? Why? What d'you mean?'

'How much did you let out on Tuesday?'

'I didn't say I knew you.'

'But what happens when she finds out?'

'How can she?'

'All sorts of ways,' said Tom, a little crossly. 'Peggy knows, doesn't she?'

Jane said nothing.

'I'm sorry—you're worrying about them, aren't you?'

'You're right,' said Jane. 'I *am* worrying. I like her. She's a lovely person.' She cleared away the plates and fetched her sweet.

'What's this?' asked Tom.

'Zabaglione. Egg yolks... I should have used Marsala in it, but you're getting sherry.'

He took a spoonful. 'Mm! Good stuff... Better if you don't. Even if I take care not to tell you things... This help for Lidya: have you got it sewn up now?'

'I suppose we have, between us. I'm not sure she

needs very much.'

'Well, then.'

She considered. 'I'll buy what you're saying up to a point, Tom... It might be tactful, anyway, not to push too hard. But if anything goes wrong with the baby.'

'No. You stay away from them altogether!'

Jane's eyebrows shot up. 'But I've promised Elizabeth.'

'You *offered*. She's Elizabeth's patient, not yours.'

'You're accusing me of being unprofessional?'

'Aren't you, rather?'

'Hey!' Jane swallowed. 'Look,' she said at last. '*I'm* the one to take responsibility for that.'

Tom said nothing.

She considered. 'All right,' she said. 'But under strong 'protest... I won't visit her again, not without discussing it first. But I may ask Elizabeth from time to time how things are going. Will you accept that?' You'd better, she added to herself.

Tom hesitated. 'OK,' he said at last. 'But could you have a word with Peggy, too? Not to let on to Lidya that you know me.'

*

The following Friday. Jane called Tom at breakfast time.

'They're putting *Ariel* in the water tomorrow,' she said. 'Would you be free to help? I should have asked earlier.'

'Sounds fun... Early in the season, isn't it?' Flakes of snow were drifting down past his kitchen window.

'Not really. I'm just keen to be sailing again.'

By the time he reached the marina next morning, the desultory snow had more or less stopped and a weak

65

sun was making the water glint occasionally. A team of men in baggy yellow oilskins had removed *Ariel*'s tarpaulin, and a huge crane already had her poised in slings over a monstrous hydraulic launcher. Jane, in green sweater and seaboots, was watching the men at work.

Tenderly, and with a great creaking, *Ariel* was eased down onto the straps of the launcher, her deep keel sliding smoothly between them. There were grunts of satisfaction, and the crane withdrew. Perched high in the air and wearing earmuffs, the foreman started the growling engine of the launcher, and manoeuvred the whole contraption across the yacht park and down the launching ramp. He squeaked to a halt at the water's edge, and two men climbed aboard to attach fenders to *Ariel*'s port side. They returned to the ramp, a pair of mooring lines snaking after them. A muffled shout, and the foreman drove the launcher firmly into swirling icy water. As she sank into it, *Ariel* stirred on the straps, and was left swaying gently, afloat. The foreman climbed down to release and roll up the straps, then perched himself again in the driving seat and withdrew the launcher up the ramp, taking his noise with him.

The men with the lines worked *Ariel* gently forward to her berth, pushing occasionally with a foot to keep her away from the pontoon. They made fast, dusted their hands, and grinned. A puff of cold wind from the harbour rattled halyards against the masts around.

'Hi, Tom,' said Jane. 'Now for the mast.'

*

Forty minutes later, the sleet had held off and the mast was safely wedged in its housing. The foreman

66

shook hands with Jane and retreated up the ramp with his two assistants. Tom and Jane set up the bottle-screws to get forestay, shrouds and backstay as tight and balanced as they should be. The stainless wire ropes gleamed in the cold air.

'Now we can go anywhere,' said Jane. 'At Christmas Hamish was talking about a cruise.'

'Feeling positive?'

'How about up the Irish Sea to the Hebrides?'

'Sounds tremendous.'

'Ready for some coffee?'

They went down into the cabin and settled on opposite sides of the saloon table. Jane filled their mugs from a thermos. Tom slurped and wiped his lips. Jane passed him a packet of Devon toffees; he selected a piece and unwrapped it very slowly.

'I've been thinking,' he said at last, and lowered his eyes uncertainly.

Jane raised her eyebrows.

'Off and on for a while now…'

'About what?'

'About… We've never talked about it… Your biological clock.'

'*Oh*!' She frowned.

'It's ticking.'

'We're not settled enough.'

'Aren't we?' He took another gulp of coffee.

'What set you off about that?'

'Thinking about you, I suppose.'

'Was it Lidya's pregnancy?'

'No. Earlier than that.'

She thought for a while. 'I suppose she's made *me* think a bit.'

'Yes,' said Tom. He raised his eyebrows a little. 'We *could*, if we wanted.'

67

'But you've got Jack and Miranda.'

'So what? We might want some kids that were yours.'

She stared at him, and after a while, blinked a few times. 'I've been trying not to think about it.'

A corner of Tom's mouth lifted a fraction. 'Why not?'

'Can't you see?'

'See what?'

She paused. 'Kids need *love,* don't they?'

Tom smiled gently again, but ran one hand anxiously over his chin at the same time. 'Who says you can't give love?' he said at last. 'I think you'd make a super mum, Jane.'

Her mouth suddenly tightened. 'Not now, Tom,' she said. 'You've caught me unawares... Please.'

'Well,' said Tom, 'All right. But under protest. I couldn't help noticing how little Ayana's got under your skin.'

Jane flinched momentarily, and turned away. Tom felt a pang of doubt.

But she was still considering. 'You thought it was the baby?'

'Yes.'

Jane looked deep into her mug. 'No,' she said. 'It wasn't. It was Lidya.' She selected a toffee for herself, and raised her eyes to Tom's. She sucked, looked down into the mug again, and slowly finished her coffee. Wrinkling her nose, she turned herself around and grasped her anorak, still sucking.

Tom washed up the mugs, collected together the tools and tidied away the toolbox.

Crisis

The next four days passed quietly: they were a little warmer, but with intermittent rain, and the air felt exceptionally heavy. On the Thursday Tom was lunching in the canteen, at a table on his own, when he felt a tap on his shoulder. It was Iain, an empty tray swinging from one hand. 'Don't go away,' he said sharply, and marched off to the servery.

From there he looked back towards Tom. The queue inched forward, Iain's fingers were drumming on the stainless steel of the counter. He was arguing at the checkout. At last he returned, bearing his usual roll, smoked mackerel and green salad.

'Says he'll be here at three,' he remarked, and disappeared again to fetch a portion of butter and glass of water. He returned, crumbled and buttered his roll and bit into a mouthful of the fish.

'*Who* says he'll be here at three?'

'The coroner.'

'What coroner?'

Iain stared at him. 'Didn't anyone tell you?'

'What?'

'The baby, Tom! The Slade baby!'

Lidya's delicate nursery swam suddenly before Tom. '*What*? What's happened?'

'Yesterday evening. Someone called the ambulance. Paramedics took the baby to the Derriford. Dead on arrival about 8.20. The parents arrived earlier.'

'Before the ambulance? Why?'

'No idea. *She's* still under sedation.'

'And him?'

'Don't know…   No obvious cause of death…   I think you should be involved.'

'Which coroner? Phil Thompson?'

'Yes.'

*

A grizzled head appeared around the door of Iain's office.

'Phil! Come in, sit down. Coffee?'

'Thanks. Hullo Tom! You in this too?'

'May be.'

Iain's spoon tinkled in jar. He fired up the kettle, filled and distributed the mugs.

'Sugar?

'Please.'

Iain obliged. 'You want a full investigation, Phil?'

'I think so.' Dr Thompson eased his tall frame back in the metal chair, and stroked his chin with his left hand, eyeing them both. 'I'll make up my mind after we've talked.'

Iain had found himself a new exercise book. He bent its cover back, pencil poised. 'What've you got so far?'

Phil opened his brief case and consulted a file. '999 call at 7.32 pm, ambulance arrived at the Derriford 8.21. The paramedics attempted resuscitation *en route*, but the infant was dead on arrival.'

'And the parents arrived earlier?'

'At the hospital by eight.'

'How was that?'

'They weren't at home when it happened.'

'Not at home?'

'I spoke to the father this morning. Apparently it was the first time they'd left the baby with a baby sitter... Father's elderly aunt, name of Bridget Phillips, big house in Salcombe. But there was a teenager there too, name of Elspeth Cukay.'

Iain was writing busily. 'The mother's help.'

Dr Thompson looked up. 'What's this? You know the family already?'

'That's why Tom's here.'

'I interviewed the mother before Christmas,' said Tom levelly. 'About a national security matter. There's a risk the husband, Ralph, may be arrested.'

'Hm. Complicates my job.'

'Where had the parents gone, Phil?' asked Iain

'Supper party with a local GP.' Dr Thompson consulted his file. 'Dr Said.'

Tom glanced at Iain. 'We know Said,' he said. 'Serious Muslim.'

'That'll be the connection,' said Iain.

Dr Thompson looked puzzled.

'Ralph is a convert,' explained Iain. 'I suppose the baby-sitters called them at Said's?'

'Yes. About 7.35. The parents drove straight to the hospital.'

'And who was last to see the baby?'

Dr Thompson turned over a page. 'Mother fed it in the nursery. The two sitters arrived at 6.30 and went up to talk to her. Then they both went downstairs. She finished the feed and put the baby down, drawing the curtains, turning off the light, and shutting the door as she left. That was immediately before she and Ralph went out at 6.45. Nobody else saw the baby at that point, so she was the last.'

Iain's eyes met Tom's again. 'So,' he said, 'the baby

sitters left the baby to sleep and didn't go up to check until about 7.20, when they found it dead?'

'Presumably. I haven't spoken to them.'

'And the medical evidence?' asked Tom.

'Autopsy proper tomorrow. No bruising. Very slight laceration on the chin. Much like last time.'

'You were involved then as well?'

'I was.'

Tom shifted in his chair. 'Assuming the autopsy shows nothing, are you sure we need to take this up officially?'

'Two unexplained infant deaths in the same family? Dereliction of duty not to... Yes, they're a nice couple. But the stark fact is, she had unobserved opportunity, on both occasions... Stresses of motherhood can do funny things.'

Tom stretched out his legs and examined his shoes. He looked up. 'Will you complete the autopsy before we pull out all the stops? You may find some other cause of death.'

'I may. I didn't last time, however.'

'But surely we ought to start immediately,' said Iain. 'Check round the house, at least? Talk to the baby-sitters?'

Dr Thompson looked at Iain and Tom in turn, and slowly rubbed one ear.

'You're right,' said Tom. 'But we could aim to keep it unobtrusive... How about using Aliza, Iain?'

Iain sat back in his chair and considered.

Dr Thompson closed his folder thoughtfully, but kept it on his knee. 'Who's Aliza?'

'My sergeant,' said Tom. 'Aliza Akinci, Turkish, knows the Muslim community.'

'I think that would work,' said Iain. 'Low key, till you've got the autopsy results... What about the mother?'

'Heavily sedated this morning... He's not in good shape, either. Always horrible, cot deaths.'

'Have you had a double one before?' asked Tom.

'No. But they do happen.'

'Timing,' said Iain suddenly. 'It's four now. Can we examine the house today? Where's Ralph?'

'Still at the Derriford,' said Dr Thompson. 'Mrs Phillips was keeping him company, planning on going home this evening.'

'So much the better; nothing will have been disturbed... But heavy-handed to be requesting a search warrant this early.'

'And too late to get one today,' said Tom.

'Don't worry, you're OK,' said Dr Thompson. 'I told Mr Slade we might need to look around, and he didn't object. Told me to get the key from the mother's help. I'm not sure he took in the implications.'

'Easy, then.' Iain closed his file.

*

Iain set off to the Derriford with the coroner, hoping for an initial interview with Ralph. Tom found a brief moment in which to give Jane the appalling news, but there was no time for talk: he and Aliza were to pick up Elspeth Cukay and examine Victory House.

It was dusk by the time Sgt Akinci ghosted the big police Volvo up the drive and squeaked to a halt in front of the garage. Elspeth, who had been sitting mesmerised in the back with Tom, came to life and snuffled into a small hankie.

The house was in darkness. Tom got out, carrying the evidence bag, walked firmly around the car, and opened the door for Elspeth. They crunched together over white marble gravel beside the smooth stone side of the house, to the back door. All sound ceased for a moment as they came to a halt. Sniffing, Elspeth searched in her purse and found a yale key. She handed it to Tom.

As Sergeant Akinci arrived, Tom unlocked the door and felt around for the light switch.

'S'on the right,' said Elspeth, and when Tom failed to find it, stepped inside ahead of him, and there was a click.

The kitchen was large. On a marble-topped table were the remains of a pizza supper.

'Oh shit,' said Elspeth, and moved forward.

'Don't touch,' said Tom, gently.

'How would you like to make us some coffee, Elspeth?' said Aliza, 'To keep us all going.'

It took Elspeth a long moment to take in the request. She looked puzzled. 'Filter coffee, you mean?'

Aliza smiled. 'That'll suit Tom very well,' she said. 'Thank you.' She removed the elastic band from her notebook and settled herself on a stool at the gleaming breakfast bar.

Elspeth slowly filled the kettle.

'Shout when it's ready,' said Tom. He picked up the evidence bag and disappeared. They heard his muffled footsteps on the stairs

'Now,' said Aliza. 'Would you mind just going over again what you told us in the car. You cycled?'

Elspeth looked up tearfully, her eyes red. 'Like I said, they told me to come at 6.30.'

'And that was when you did arrive?'

'Yeah. Mrs Phillips was just parking her car.'

'You know her?'

'Yeah. She's OK… I locked up my bike, and we went round the front. Ralph opened the door, all

74

dressed up.'

'To go out?'

'Orange tie. He said Lidya was upstairs.'

'And where did you go, exactly?'

'We hung up our stuff, then we went to the kitchen. Ralph showed Mrs Phillips the pizzas for supper... After that we heard Lidya calling, and we went up.'

'To the nursery?'

'Yeah. We said hullo to Ayana.' Elspeth smiled wanly.

'Lidya was breast-feeding?'

'Yes. She joked a bit. I asked where they were going, and she said, Dr Said's, hadn't she explained? I said no, and she told me who Dr Said was, he was very nice, but Ralph knew him better than she did.'

'You said she joked?'

'Yeah. Nothing special. She was looking down at the baby and smiling. We were all smiling.'

'What happened next?'

Tears were creeping again down Elspeth's cheek.

'Take your time.'

Elspeth found another tissue. 'She told us she would put Ayana down when she'd finished. She said she'd be setting the baby alarm, and it would be best for us not to go up till Ayana had settled. Give it half an hour, she said.'

'I see. Hold on a minute.' Aliza wrote carefully. 'Go on.'

'We went back downstairs. I started grilling the pizzas, and Bridget was looking up the telly programmes. After a while Lidya came down. She was just pulling on a white mac, stylish. She came into the kitchen and checked the baby alarm.'

'This is it?' On the dresser there was a blobby pink device with a stub aerial, stencilled with a leaping lamb.

'Yes. She put her ear to it, and said: "I think she's off already." I listened too. But I couldn't hear anything.'

'Nothing at all?'

'No. But I wasn't used to it. I didn't know how loud the baby's breathing would sound.'

Aliza wrote again, and paused.

'Want me to go on?'

'Please.'

'Then Bridget came back from the TV. She asked Lidya if she was sure they didn't want to take the baby with them.'

'As though she'd thought that might have been a better arrangement?'

'Yeah.'

'What did Lidya say?'

'She was quite certain.'

Aliza wrote carefully, and looked up.

'Then she and Ralph said goodbye.'

'And Lidya still seemed happy?'

'Oh, yes. It was their first night out, after Ayana was born. She was really excited. We heard them drive off. Then I microwaved some soup to go with the pizzas, and we watched the telly, in the sitting-room. I took the baby alarm with me, but I still couldn't hear anything. In the end, I asked Bridget what she thought, and she couldn't hear anything either. But she's a bit deaf, anyway. Then after a while we thought we ought to have a look...' Elspeth swallowed.

'You went up to the nursery together?'

'Yes.'

'Think carefully... What exactly did you see?'

'We just had the light from the door at first. Ayana

76

seemed, like, too *still*—and I couldn't hear her breathing. I couldn't see her face, it was in shadow. So I looked at Bridget, and so as not to wake the baby I turned up the light dimmer, just a bit. Then we were sure something must be wrong, and I turned it right up. Her little eyes were open, but not moving. Just glassy. Her skin wasn't blue or anything, but I knew at once she wasn't right. Then Bridget picked her up, and her head just flopped.'

'How long did it take you to be sure something was badly wrong?'

'No time at all. Bridget gave a sort of gasp, then pulled herself together. She put Ayana down in the crib and called 999 on her mobile. It was awful—the woman started telling us stuff. What to do. Bridget was on the phone, but I had to do it... Sod it, she wasn't my baby... Gentle shaking. Nothing... Shit! Opening her throat, trying to breathe into her... Pulse inside her arm... Nothing... Quick hard pushes with two fingers on her poor little chest... Then the ambulance came. Thank God. The men had a big machine. But they looked grim, it was all too late.'

'So then you called Ralph and Lidya at Dr Said's?'

'Bridget did. She had Ralph's mobile number. He screamed at her.'

'Why? What did he scream?'

'I couldn't hear. Then Lidya came on. She was very sharp, trying to shut Ralph up. She told us they'd go straight to the hospital, and rang off.'

Aliza realised she'd been holding her breath. She breathed out, and saw that Elspeth was watching her anxiously, tears running down her cheeks. She leant forward and took Elspeth's hand. After a while, she let go the hand and started writing again, steadily and neatly.

'When you went into the nursery, was everything as usual?' she asked at last.

'Yes.'

'And did you leave everything just as it was?'

'Yeah, I think so. When we were trying to get her heart going she was on the floor, and things probably got moved when the men came. We never tidied up, just locked up, and jumped into Bridget's car, and drove like crazy to the hospital. Bridget had her foot flat on the floor, but she couldn't keep up with the ambulance. Afterwards, she drove me home.'

'And Ralph and Lidya arrived ahead of you?'

'Yes. We saw their big car outside, all skew. They were in emergency. Ralph looked wild. Lidya had got a sight of Ayana as they bundled her through, and I think she knew...   It was soon after that she collapsed.'

'Collapsed?'

'Standing by the desk. She crumpled, and slid down onto the floor. Ralph started shouting again.'

*

Tom crouched and opened his evidence bag. He located in a sterile wrapping a thin pair of white cotton gloves, pulled them on, stood, and cautiously opened the nursery door. He felt for a switch, and found a dimmer knob. Pastel brightness swelled from walls and ceiling.

The room was arranged as he remembered, apart from a scarlet cloth tumbled untidily onto the floor. He moved forward. The cloth was much longer than it was wide. The basket cradle beside it was tidy and empty. No bedclothes or pillow.

He pulled a small camera from his pocket: its flash

made alien stabs at the gentle scene. He checked the images, opened his Filofax to record them. He extended his metal tape with a squeak, and jotted down a dimensioned sketch.

A pink baby alarm transmitter, cousin to the receiver he'd noticed in the kitchen, sat centrally on the cushion of the nursing chair beside the crib. It was still switched on. Tom switched it off and zipped it into a plastic exhibit bag.

Apart from the scarlet cloth, nothing seemed out of place. He found a small dried-out milky dribble on one side of the nursing chair, but no vomit or damp on the smooth plastic mattress of the cradle. The cloth itself would have to wait for the technicians; gingerly, he picked it up, folded it, and slid it into a second exhibit bag. It seemed clean and dry.

He turned to search for soft items. The cushion on the nursing chair was hard and thin. The only possibility in the open was a woolly lion, but it was very small. There was a clothes chest full of baby clothes, but all were neatly folded and apparently clean and unused. A fish mobile swung gently in a gentle flow of air from the half-open window.

*

On the landing he found a dirty-clothes basket, empty except for a man's shirt and a pair of socks. The master bedroom and two other bedrooms had pillows where one would expect to find pillows, but none seemed at all disturbed, indeed, the bedspreads were all arranged very precisely.

Tom noted it all down. Medicines? Nothing in the nursery. In the master bedroom, the left-hand bedside table drawer contained hay-fever remedies and a few prescription medicines in Ralph's name. A brandy glass stood on the same table, a trace of liquid at the bottom of its bowl. He sniffed: whiskey. The right-hand cabinet contained a lace handkerchief with a sachet of pot-pourri, but no medicines. The ensuite bathroom, on the other hand, contained a large assortment of medicines in Lidya's name: iron for anaemia; Edronax, a year out of date; StilNoct, current; plentiful supplies of Co-codamol and Ibuprofen. A diaphragm in a handsome black lacquer case. Lubricant. He examined the waste-paper baskets: twists of paper, a little hair, nothing to suggest recent use of drugs.

Tom hesitated. There was one other thing, but he knew it would be harder to find. Before settling down to search, he made a final general survey of the nursery and other upstairs rooms, but discovered nothing to excite his interest. Plenty of finger prints, but they would have to wait.

It took him half an hour of methodical work, but at last he had it: a tiny grey lozenge, a millimeter across by five millimetres long with an almost invisible two-centimetre wire projecting from it—so thin it could have been a human hair. A smear of superglue had been used to fix both parts to one of the vertical surfaces of the cradle's mattress frame, on the under-side, so that it wouldn't be seen unless the cradle was inverted or dismantled.

Suspicion

Friday was cold and bleak. Tom got himself to work in good time. After sorting his desk and diary he was about to find Aliza when his phone rang.

'Dr Mayhew, Sir.'

'Put her on, Sam.'

A brief pause. 'Chief Inspector Tallis?'

'Speaking.'

'My name's Elizabeth Mayhew, Inspector. I'm calling about my patient, Lidya Slade.'

'Ah yes,' said Tom. He thought for a moment. 'The coroner's been in touch.'

Elizabeth cleared her throat. 'There was an earlier case,' she said.

'We're aware of that... This is being handled by Sergeant Akinci, can I put you through to her?'

There was a pause. 'Perhaps I should talk to someone more senior.'

'My sergeant is very competent.'

'Can't I discuss it with *you*?'

Tom raised his eyebrows and pulled a pad towards himself. 'Perhaps you'd better.' He removed the cap from his biro with one hand.

'I've been talking it through with my practice nurse you see, Chief Inspector... Marsha always thought there was something wrong about the *first* death.'

Tom waited.

'But I didn't agree with her, at the time. I overruled

81

her.'

'So her suspicions never got reported... What were they?'

'She said the mother had been alone with the baby when the first death happened, and that she'd called the ambulance too calmly. Much too *cold*, she said.'

'How did she know? Was she there?'

There was a pause. 'No, I don't think she was. I'll have to ask her...'

Tom sighed, but not too loudly. 'We'll need to question both of you formally later,' he said. 'Is there something you want to tell me now about the *new* death?'

'Well, Marsha said the mother had opportunity this time too. She talked to the mother's help.'

'Ah!'

'Yes. And having two purely accidental deaths in the same family is very unlikely, Inspector... She was involved in a case of infanticide before, you see.'

'Ah.'

'In a hospital where she worked. A nurse was poisoning babies, but it was a long time before they realised. So she's alert to the danger.'

Tom sighed again. 'I'd better get some details,' he said. 'What's Marsha's surname?'

*

Tom went to find Aliza, who shared an office with Sgt Howe. Howe was preparing to go out, but looked round expectantly when Tom appeared.

'It's Aliza I want, Sergeant,' said Tom.

Howe buttoned up his raincoat and closed the door behind him.

'Want to talk it through?' Tom asked.

Aliza smiled. 'Wouldn't mind.'

He straddled a chair back to front and faced her, his hands crossed on its back. 'So, what did you make of Elspeth's account?'

'Nothing suspicious apart from the baby alarm.'

Tom nodded. 'Let's come to that in a minute... Everything else seemed to fit with a genuine cot death?'

'I thought so.'

Tom nodded slowly. 'Me too.'

'Did you find anything suspicious upstairs?'

'There's a cloth and cushion—have to see what the lab makes of them. But, if it really was a smothering, I'd have to say that Lidya tidied up unbelievably coolly and effectively afterwards.'

'And *timed* her attack remarkably stupidly.'

'Picking a time when she'd have to act very fast, and then immediately seem calm and collected in front of the baby-sitters?'

'And quite likely be caught in the act, too.' Aliza gave a little shrug.

Tom looked at her. 'And she's obviously not a stupid woman... However, you need to know. The GP's suspicious.'

'Really? Dr Mayhew?'

'She called me just now.'

'What does she know about it?'

'Almost nothing, so far as I could tell... It seems her practice nurse Marsha Stone had suspicions the first time round that we never heard about.'

'Mm.'

'You're going to have to interview her... But I can't see Nurse Stone would have known anything about that first death, either—wasn't in the house when it happened. Probably over-suspicious: I gather she came across a real case of infanticide once, earlier in her career.'

Aliza wrote fast.

Tom watched. 'OK,' he said. 'Now, the crunch point. The alarm.'

'Odd. On the face of it. *Why* couldn't the baby-sitters hear the baby breathing, if she wasn't already dead?'

Tom said nothing.

'The alarm might not have been working properly.'

'True.'

'On the other hand, the transmitter and the receiver were still switched on when we got to them, and both power lights were showing green.'

'Which means they were almost certainly OK. I switched them both off last night so the lab technicians could assess the states of the batteries.'

'But it would have been so... *blatant.*' Aliza smoothed down her page and looked up at Tom.

'Calmly telling Elspeth she could hear the baby breathing, if she'd really just smothered it?'

'Yes. But hold on.' Aliza turned back a page of her ring binder. 'She never said she could hear breathing, not exactly. What she actually said was: "I think she's off already." According to Elspeth.'

'You mean, she might have meant she *couldn't* hear the baby?'

'Yes. It might have been *normal* to hear nothing when the baby was asleep.'

'Yes. You'll have check what Elspeth thought she meant. And check how sensitive the alarm system is: another lab job.'

'But whatever Lidya may have said, the crucial fact is that neither Elspeth nor Bridget could hear any breathing.'

'That's true,' admitted Tom. 'And it's the sort of thing that could easily sway a jury.'

*

On the Saturday morning, rain was tippling down. But by three o'clock it had cleared, and Jane firmly suggested the Blackstone Point car park as start for their walk.

'If you think I'm going to drive you right past Victory House, no,' said Tom, and he took the lower road past Brooking's Down Wood, where the bare trees were still dripping. The cliff top car park was deserted. They locked up and set off westward along the National Trust cliff path.

'When did you first hear?' she asked.

'Lunchtime on Thursday.'

They marched on, Jane a little ahead of Tom.

'I guess this does change things a bit,' he added after a while. 'Seems only fair to tell you at least roughly what's happening.'

'Can you?'

'Aliza's in charge.'

'That sounds a good idea.'

'She's interviewed everyone now, except Lidya herself. Elspeth, Mrs Phillips, Ralph. Plus Elizabeth Mayhew and Marsha.'

Jane slid slightly on a muddy patch, and regained her balance. A weak sun had appeared, and there was a musty smell of gorse. Low mist clung to the sea on their left.

'Based on those interviews, and the evidence in the house, there's nothing to suggest it wasn't a second cot death.'

'That's a relief.'

'But there are other considerations.' He explained about the baby alarm, and Elizabeth's phone call.

'Whatever's she up to?' said Jane angrily. 'It's Marsha, isn't it? Igor was sure there was nothing suspicious about the first death.'

'And we've got the results of the preliminary post-mortem.'

'So?'

'Nothing serious. Slight abrasion on the chin, prob-ably caused in the resuscitation attempts, and some fluid in one lung, like last time. No bruising around the neck.'

'That sounds all right. Who did the PM?'

'Dr Ken Jones. One of our regulars. But he wants to call in a cot death expert before deciding.'

They were crossing a stile, Tom ahead. Jane looked up. 'Who?' she said sharply.

'Sir Ambrose Eaton.'

'Oh dear,' said Jane, the corners of her mouth turn-ing down.

'You know about him?'

'Very hot on child abuse… Why did this Ken Jones take that line?'

'Statistics. Says two cot deaths in the same family is very unlikely. He wants to be sure, and Ambrose is the expert.'

'I suppose he's right, technically,' said Jane. 'Once she's had one purely accidental death, it must then be very unlikely she'd suffer a second.'

Tom frowned. 'Are you sure?' he asked after a while.

'It's obvious, isn't it?'

'If you toss a penny and get heads, are you then less likely to get a head if you try again?'

'You *must* be,' said Jane. 'Suppose you got five

86

heads in a row. Surely you're then *extremely* unlikely to get another—the probabilities have got to even themselves out.'

'Well, I'm no expert...   But you *might* say, if you've just had five heads in a row, isn't that evidence of a biased penny? Perhaps the chance of another head now is *greater* than fifty-fifty?' Tom looked unsure. 'Look, how dramatic!' The Mewstone had come into view, poised craggily black in oily water against a background of wreathed mist luminous in the low sun ahead of them.

Decision

On Monday lunchtime, Tom was back at his desk and wondering slightly desperately how to organise his afternoon, when Jane rang.

'I called Peggy.'

'You did?' Tom tapped his pencil on the file in front of him.

'She was at the Slades' this morning.'

'Lidya's back home, then?'

'The hospital let her out on Saturday. It's not her in a state now, it's Ralph.'

'She's coping, you mean?'

'He'd been drinking. But Lidya knows how to stop him, and somehow she's found the strength to do it.'

'Extraordinary.'

'It's just never leaving him alone, Peggy said. And Lidya says he needs comforting.'

'*He* needs comforting?'

'Over something *so* tiny. He's distraught that he ever objected to Lidya's choice of name... Little Ayana.' Jane's sniff reached Tom's ear. 'That trusting tiny face... So hard to grasp she's gone... Lidya goes up to the nursery to weep, Peggy said, and rocks the empty cradle. But quietly, and not for very long.'

'Isn't she on tranquillisers?'

'She's set her mind against them, this time... She called Father Barnabas, and he came round. On Saturday afternoon... And on Sunday she telephoned her father.'

'How did that go?'

'The two of them are very close. He was quite phil-osophical, because a lot of babies die in Ethiopia… Will Aliza have to interview her?'

'That's still to come. But it should be a formality.'

'Let's hope it all calms down, and your nasty MI5 man leaves them alone. But, oh… I wonder what the two of them will do, now. It would take incredible courage to try again.'

Tom considered. 'Wanting kids is a strong instinct,' he said.

There followed such a long silence that Tom was tempted to ask whether she was still on the line, but thought better of it.

'Tom,' said Jane at last.

'Yes?'

There was another pause. 'No, forget it… Maybe we can talk this evening? You need to get on.'

'OK,' said Tom. 'I'll call if I hear any more.'

*

During the next two weeks Aliza interviewed Lidya and submitted her report to the CPS. The information reaching Jane through Peggy was encouraging: Ralph had stopped drinking, and was giving Lidya strong support, while Lidya herself seemed at least to be coping with her loss, and was dealing with practical matters. Jane was content that they had enough support, and pleased Tom by being ready to keep a low profile for the time being.

*

On the Friday of the second week, Tom was in a squad car on his way to pin down Dane Street Motors about the ringed Aston Martins, when he was radioed.

'Message from Sergeant Acinki, Sir. Request you telephone her.'

He pulled off the road and called up Aliza on his mobile.

'It's about Mrs Slade, Sir. They've decided to prosecute.'

'*What? Already?*'

'Yes.'

'No discussion of the evidence? No ifs and buts?'

'No Sir. Can we talk?'

'Give me ten minutes. In your office?'

*

Sgt Howe's desk was empty, and Tom commandeered his swivel chair. 'When did you hear?' he asked Aliza.

'Just before lunch.' She opened her tidy but by now thick file. 'Infanticide is murder, so not the local office. CPS in Exeter, Mr Sandy Clutterbuck.'

'Never heard of him.'

'He's a Higher Court Advocate, intends to handle the court appearance himself.'

'You spoke to him?'

'Yes.'

'Did he explain the basis for their decision?'

'No. He just thanked me for our reports. But he did say he'd consulted Sir Ambrose Eaton… I reckon he didn't have much option.'

'Sir Ambrose insisted?'

'Sounded like it.'

Tom pursed his lips. 'She'll be bailed?'

'Yes. We're to call her in, charge her, police bail to the magistrates for next week. They'll remand to Crown Court in Exeter, probably June.'

'This poor woman's innocent, isn't she Aliza?'

'That's my gut feeling, Sir.'

'What the hell will this do to her?'

Aliza made a doubtful face, and twisted in her chair.

'Charge straight away? You want me there?'

'If you wouldn't mind, Sir. That's why I wanted to put you in the picture. He's given me the charge wording, bar a few details. I'll call you when we're ready.'

'Anything else for now?'

'No. But I'd like to talk more later.'

*

For a while Tom thought of ringing Jane. But he knew she'd need time to blow her top once he'd told her, and deferred it to the evening. Just before five Aliza rang, and he took himself down to the front desk.

Lidya was already there, upright on one of the moulded plywood chairs by the window. She was wearing a grey wool suit, and gave Tom the impression of watching proceedings from a distance. A small man in a tweed suit with thinning hair and a tooth-brush moustache was leaning one elbow on the counter, facing Sgt Budd; Ralph was beside him, jigging up and down and muttering volubly. Tom walked towards them.

The small man looked up. '*Where* is the officer conducting my client's case, Sergeant?' he demanded, sharply insistent.

91

'On her way down, Sam,' said Tom. 'Has she booked an interview room?'

'Number three, Sir,' said Budd. Then he looked up and gestured towards the lift. Aliza was emerging from it, a bundle of files under one arm. She looked around, and hurried over to Lidya, who stood up to meet her. They spoke. Aliza turned to look briefly at the man in the tweed suit, nodded, and walked briskly to the group by the desk. Lidya rose and followed, more slowly.

'Mr Cormack?' Aliza asked.

'Indeed.'

'Of Grieves & Partners?'

The little man inclined his head. 'You are the investigating officer?' he said sharply.

'Yes.'

'Aliza Akinci? Rank of Sergeant?'

'That's correct.'

'And this is?'

'Chief Inspector Tallis,' volunteered Tom.

Mr Cormack looked Tom up and down. 'Your role in this case is?'

Tom smiled equably. 'Sgt Akinci asked me to be here,' he said. 'I took some part in the investigation.'

Mr Cormack raised his eyebrows, but said no more. Aliza looked around. 'I think everyone's here,' she said. 'Could you all please follow me?' She turned and led the way.

After a moment's hesitation, Lidya followed, and then Mr Cormack and Ralph, who exchanged glances. Tom took up the rear.

Interview Room 3 was windowless, but clean and tidy, with a plastic table and three light upright chairs. Aliza indicated that Lidya and her solicitor should sit down, and they did so. Aliza set her files on the table, and seated herself facing them. Ralph and Tom were left standing to her right.

Lidya looked down at the files.

'As I explained when I called Mr Slade,' Aliza said, her face impassive, but speaking quite gently, 'the Crown Prosecution Service have taken their decision, and they intend to prosecute. On their instructions I have now to formally charge Mrs Slade. I hope the position is clear?'

Ralph cleared his throat, but then found nothing to say.

Mr Cormack turned towards Tom. 'And you, Chief Inspector, have approved this preposterous charge?'

Aliza looked up. Ralph shifted his feet. Lidya's face remained lowered.

'Mr Cormack,' said Tom quietly, 'as I'm sure you know, the decision to prosecute lies with the CPS, not with us. It isn't my business either to approve or to disapprove, and the same applies to Sgt Akinci.'

Mr Cormack bowed his head in irritated acknowledgement, and Aliza turned to Lidya, who slowly raised her head. She showed no sign of emotion, and Tom was suddenly struck by how well-groomed she was: her glossy black hair was arranged in two smooth wings framing her face, and the grey suit she had chosen was beautifully cut.

'Mrs Slade, in order that the charge can be correctly worded, could you confirm that your infant daughter, who was born on 12th January and died on 29th January, had no birth certificate?'

Lidya frowned.

'That's correct,' interjected Ralph, his voice husky. 'We hadn't registered her.' He coughed.

'However,' said Aliza, 'am I also right that she was known by the family as Ayana?'

Lidya looked briefly at Ralph. 'Yes,' she said in a low but clear voice. A small tear was running down Ralph's cheek. He nodded and wiped it away.

'Thank you,' said Aliza. She checked the spelling of the name, and added a few words to the sheet lying on the table before her. 'I'll now read out the words of the charge,' she went on. Lidya, her head still raised, quietly placed both hands on the table before her, clasping one on top of the other. 'Mrs Lidya Slade, I charge you with the murder, by asphyxiation... ' There was a catch in Aliza's voice, and she cleared her throat. '... by asphyxiation, on the evening of the 29th January 2003, of the infant daughter born to you on 12th January 2003, known to you and your husband as Ayana.' She looked up. 'You do not have to say anything, but anything you do say will be recorded, and may be used in evidence.'

Lidya glanced at Mr Cormack; her dark face remained rigid. Aliza turned to Mr Cormack, who shook his head, and intoned: 'Nothing to say—my client has nothing whatever to say in response to this ridiculous charge.' In a delicate little gesture, he patted Lidya's clasped hands on the table beside him. Lidya swallowed and bowed her head.

There was a moment's pause in which no one else moved, then Ralph stepped around the seated figures and placed his hands firmly on her shoulders. His forearms were shaking; but Lidya's hands remained steady, one curved over the other on the plastic surface of the interview table.

*

'Lidya's been charged,' said Tom, standing damply just inside Jane's front door.

94

Her arms dropped and her eyes flickered. *'Charged?'*

'Yes.' He shrugged out of his raincoat, and hung it on a peg.

'With what?'

'Infanticide. Murder.'

'Bloody hell, Tom!' She stared at him for a good two seconds, then her mouth screwed. But that lasted only a moment, and then her face set. They climbed the stairs slowly and in silence.

Tom offered to make coffee.

'You can bring me a stiff gin if you want.'

After a moment's hesitation Tom obliged and found himself an orange juice.

'Don't you idiots have a *scrap* of common sense?' she burst out.

'Not our call,' said Tom. 'And the CPS didn't have much option,'

'For God's sake, Tom!' she shouted.

'What?'

'Do you *always* have to defend our impossible British legal system?'

'I don't defend it,' said Tom. 'You're absolutely right. It's a juggernaut. Nothing can now stop it feeding Lidya into the meat-grinder.'

'Jesus.'

'I hope to God she gets off, but it'll take for ever. And even if she does, the effect on her is sure to be appalling.'

'You think she's innocent, then?'

'Yes!'

'Who did the charging? You?'

'Aliza. Lidya had a lawyer, and Ralph was there.'

'Did she shout?'

'Aliza did what she had to do, as straightforwardly

as she could. Lidya didn't give us any dirty looks—I was surprised. She said almost nothing. Perhaps she guessed Aliza and I don't think she's guilty.'

'And no signs of collapsing?'

'Not yet.'

'What was her lawyer like?'

'Pompous. But he understood she needed support. He told me straight off the charge was preposterous. And he put his hand over hers while they were sorting out bail.'

'When does the case come up?'

'Next week at the Magistrates, but that's a formality. The judge and jury stuff comes up at the Crown Court in Exeter, probably in June.'

'God.'

'Ralph was in quite a state. But he's got himself in hand, pulling himself together. I guess they're not short of money for lawyers.'

'Nor short of courage, either.' Jane broke off, downed her remaining gin. She looked at Tom and opened her eyes wide. 'So much so, she's making me ashamed.'

'Of what?'

'Of being scared I couldn't be a caring mother.'

Tom looked up sharply. He said nothing.

'Mothers who've had cot deaths get scared about themselves, too. They blame themselves.'

'So it was courageous of Lidya to push that feeling away and try again?'

'Of course... And now she's being investigated for murder. Just like me last year. Only in her case, she didn't actually kill anyone. And she has to face a trial, which I never did. But she's not flinching.'

'We don't know that,' said Tom. And, he added to himself, if determination to have kids is the point, I'd be amazed if Lidya and Ralph tried a third time. He was assailed by an unwanted unease. Jane's voice had become buoyant, reminding him suddenly of her occasional readiness, when deeply involved or moved, to rush into misguided action. He tried to push the feeling away, but the horror of little Ayana's death somehow deepened his unease. 'What do you want to do?' he said at last, lamely.

Jane looked up, surprised. 'Fight!' she said. 'Fight for her! For both of them.'

Trial

Lidya's trial was scheduled for early June in Exeter, and since it was now a murder case, the Super placed Tom officially in charge. He and Aliza reviewed her investigation, but the medical and lab reports were now going direct to the CPS, with only occasional details seeping through to Tom's office. In February he and Iain arranged a meeting about accessing the MI5 surveillance tapes. At first John Smith seemed sympathetic. But after three weeks, he called back.

'Sorry, Tom. No can do.'

'You want an innocent woman convicted?' shouted Tom.

'They won't bend.'

'Even if it leads to a miscarriage of justice?'

'Yes.'

'What if the defence subpoena the tapes?'

John Smith sighed. 'The Home Office would get a declaration of nullity from the Minister,'

'Saying what?'

'That the subpoena was contrary to the interests of national security. And *you*'d have broken the Official Secrets Act by telling the defence of the existence of the bug. Probably finish up in jug.'

'But *why?*'

'You *know* why, Tom. Mustn't show the other side how we work.'

Tom swore.

He and Iain were even more disgusted when, in May, John Smith told them that the security services were no longer interested in Ralph.

'I hope we can *inform* the poor guy!' insisted Iain. 'He's got enough on his plate.'

'No way!' said John Smith. 'He could easily pop up again on the radar.'

*

The death and arrest had come to Jane like blows to the head. Because Tom was now officially involved, he'd been obliged to warn her once again to break off direct contact with the Slades, but she knew from Peggy that Ralph and Lidya were preparing to fight. Mr Cormack had engaged a QC. Ralph had stopped drinking. Lidya was seeing Father Barnabas regularly.

Towards the end of May, Lidya's father arrived, and stayed for three weeks. Jane saw him once, walking alone by the creek in Noss Mayo: tall, glossy-skinned and composed, in a light suit and straw hat.

She put much energy into consulting medical colleagues with experience of cot deaths, but discovered nothing that might help Lidya's defence. She checked out Sir Ambrose's views and history, which left her anxious and gloomy. She even sounded out Elizabeth on the possibility of organising a support group, but Elizabeth refused.

*

The days lengthened, and eventually spring ripened into hot summer. The trial was to open on Monday 16th June and scheduled to last ten days. Jane, determined to see something of the legal battle, rearranged hospital sessions so that she could attend. On the first day she drove up to Exeter. The Northerhay Gardens by the Castle were lavender-scented and bright with petunias. But the corridor outside the old courtroom in the Sessions Hall, once she had penetrated to it, smelled of ancient books.

There were seats free in the public gallery, which ran around three sides of the court room, and she found herself pushing along to the middle of its right-hand arm. The room, forbidding in its Georgian panelling, was hot and murmuring with talk. To her right, considerably raised, was a handsome high-backed walnut chair, presumably awaiting the judge. Close below her, in a boxed-in section, she recognised from Tom's description Sandy Clutterbuck the prosecutor, seated with his back to her, staring into space. The dock to his left was empty. After a few minutes a younger wigged and gowned man appeared from under the centre section of the gallery. This new figure made Jane uneasy: perhaps it was the fussy pince-nez, or the actorly set of head—a man too conscious of an audience agog for drama, she thought. He paused and looked back, and after a moment Ralph and Lidya came into view. He led them ceremoniously to adjacent chairs in the well of the court, facing the judge's chair and immediately in front of the dock.

There was a buzz of anticipation. Lidya, in a blue and grey silk suit, looked anxiously around before seating herself. Jane's stomach clenched: Lidya's predicament today mirrored too closely the nightmares she herself had been holding at bay eighteen months earlier. Ralph was dressed equally impeccably. He looked determined, and smiled at the defence barrister.

100

There was a new murmur as the jury were led in by the usher and clerk. Jane studied them as they settled into the jury box, which faced her on the opposite side of the court. Seven men and five women. One of the women black, young, alert and quite well-dressed, and two others professional-looking, one in glasses, chatting as though already acquainted. A much older man with a red, weather-beaten face. A young chap in a tank top, looking bored.

The clerk, in legal bands and gown, settled himself at a table facing the judge's chair, and the usher disappeared through a door to Jane's right. After a few more minutes of general anticipation, he re-appeared, stood waiting impressively for a moment, and then intoned 'All rise!' Great shuffling ensued. A door in the dark panelling behind the judge's chair was swung open dramatically by an unseen hand, and a small neat woman in short wig, bands and violet gown appeared. She marched to the judicial chair, whose elaborately carved back seemed almost to swallow her. The noise of people seating themselves subsided. She nodded to her clerk.

The clerk got the jury back on their feet and administered the oath. The jury members mumbled the required words and self-consciously settled back onto their benches.

The judge leaned forward and rapped twice with a pencil on the bench before her.

'Members of the jury,' she said briskly. Their faces turned towards her, and she paused and allowed them a smile of encouragement. 'Members of the jury, the case on which we are about to embark is a serious one. A mother, Mrs Lidya Slade, stands accused of the infanticide, which means the murder, of her own child. The defence have indicated that she intends to plead not guilty. That being so, the prosecution will wish to present a good deal of evidence to you. Your task will be to listen carefully to this evidence, and to give your verdict on the facts; that is to say, you will have to decide at the end of the trial whether, as a matter of fact, Mrs Slade did indeed murder her child, or not. You may, if you wish, make your own written notes as the trial proceeds.

'We expect the proceedings to take ten days or a little longer. I must remind you that your verdict is to be based solely on the evidence presented to you in this court, and not at all on anything you may have heard about the case elsewhere. If you happen to have previously read or heard anything related to Mrs Slade or to the death of her child, you must put it out of your mind entirely.

'During the course of the trial you should not discuss any aspect of the case with anyone other than your colleagues on the jury—not even with your partner at home, if you have one.'

The judge nodded severely and the jury looked suitably impressed. Jane felt reassured that things were to be handled crisply and decently, but had a sense too of massive machinery gathering momentum. In her own case she'd had to prepare herself mentally for the prospect of a court appearance and exposure in the media, but at some deep level she'd never doubted that British justice would eventually grind out a fair conclusion—Tom had been there, after all, and on her side. Now, for the first time, she was suddenly terrified that British justice might after all fail, that sensible, loving Lidya was about to be entangled and ensnared.

The judge nodded again to the clerk, who stood, approached Lidya, and led her to a boxed-in dock in front of the jury and facing Jane. He opened a little wooden gate for her, leaving her standing in the compartment, her hands resting on a polished brass rail. There was a deep hush, and Jane felt her stomach clench again. The clerk faced the compartment and said:

'You are Lidya Slade, of Victory House, Noss Mayo, in the County of Devon?'

'Yes.' Lidya's face was impassive. 'I am.'

'Lidya Slade, you stand accused of the murder by asphyxiation of your infant child, known as Ayana Slade, sometime on the evening of 29th January 2003. How do you plead, guilty or not guilty?'

Lidya glanced toward her lawyer, who pursed his lips and nodded.

'Not guilty,' said Lidya, loudly.

The judge looked towards her. 'Mrs Slade,' she said quietly, 'counsel has suggested, and the prosecution has agreed, that in this case there is nothing to be gained by your remaining in the dock. You may sit with your husband if you wish.'

Lidya seemed to have been expecting this, opened the little gate, and returned to her original seat, but Jane felt surprised.

The judge now glanced towards the prosecution bench and said quietly: 'Mr Clutterbuck, if you please.' The Higher Court Advocate selected a file from the stack in front of him, rose slowly, and faced the jury. Jane thought he looked a little tense, but his voice, when it came, was rich and firm.

'Members of the jury, I represent the prosecution in this sad case, and it is my task to present our evidence to you.

'The evidence concerned is in fact comparatively simple.' Mr Clutterbuck paused, and extracted a single sheet of paper from his file. He glanced at it and looked up again. 'It is not disputed that on the evening of 29th January last, Lidya Slade and her husband went out to dinner, leaving her baby Ayana, then two and a half weeks old, in the care of baby-sitters at her home in Noss Mayo. Some time after they left, the two baby-sitters discovered that Ayana was not breathing, and telephoned the emergency services. The baby was pronounced dead at the Derriford Hospital in Plymouth shortly after that.

'I shall present our evidence in the following order. First you will hear of the events of the fatal evening, most of which, as I have already indicated, are not disputed by the defence. This will make it clear that Lidya Slade and no one else had opportunity to smother her baby, Ayana.

'Then you will hear from two expert doctors, pathologists. One of them is the doctor who performed the autopsy on baby Ayana Slade, to determine the cause of death. The other is an expert on child abuse.'

There was a very slight rustle in court. Ralph looked up sharply at the defence lawyer to his right. Lidya was staring at the floor, and Jane could see that her lips had tightened.

'Their testimony will show you that Ayana's death was not an accident, but that she was in fact smothered.

'Next, we shall demonstrate that, when she left her home on the evening in question, Lidya Slade indicated to the baby sitters that her baby was alive and well, when in fact she knew it was already dead.'

At this Lidya's head jerked up; she stared at Mr Clutterbuck, who had paused for effect. Again there was a slight murmur in the courtroom. Lidya's head went down again.

'Then, we shall present evidence on the question of motive. As you will hear, infanticide is happily very rare, and when it does occur, it is not always easy to understand why a mother has chosen to attack her own child. And in this case in particular, where the mother was living with a devoted husband in easy circumstances you may find it especially puzzling.'

During this passage, Jane noticed that both judge and defence barrister had leant forward; now the pince-nez were turned questioningly towards the judge.

Mr Clutterbuck paid no attention. 'Finally,' he went on, 'I must point out to the members of the jury that this is not the first time in this family that a very young child has died. In October 2001 Mrs Slade's first child Gabriel died aged three weeks, and the event was recorded as a cot death, due to natural causes.'

Several of the jurors sat up straighter. But, Jane was thinking furiously, they're not *allowed* to bring that in. Surely not. Why doesn't her lawyer object?

'It is important for you to understand that Gabriel's death was investigated by the police at the time, but no prosecution was brought. And I must make it clear that Mrs Slade is not *now* being accused of responsibility for her son's death.

'Under such circumstances you, the jury, would not normally have been told of the earlier death: it would have been judged irrelevant to the present case, and likely to bias your judgement of Mrs Slade's later actions. However, the prosecution has argued, and the court has in pre-trial discussion agreed, that in this case the earlier death is relevant in assessing the *probability* that the second death, Ayana's death, was not due to natural causes. This is why I am informing you now of the first death.'

Mr Clutterbuck dipped his head in a tiny bow, and turned towards the judicial chair.

Sneaked in by the back door, thought Jane. Bugger them! *Bugger* them!

The judge frowned, and said: 'That completes your summary, Mr Clutterbuck?' She glanced up at a large clock on the wall facing Jane.

'Yes, your Honour.'

'Thank you. Very succinct… It's now only 11.20. A little early for lunch, but I suggest nevertheless we take a recess. There are one or two points that I might usefully take with counsel… Prosecution evidence at two?'

'Thank you, Your Honour.'

The judge looked towards the pince-nez, which flashed as their wearer nodded curtly. She smiled to herself and left the courtroom by her private door. The two lawyers looked cautiously at each other, bundled their files together and left in the same direction, through the door that the usher had used.

*

Tom was due to give evidence during the afternoon session, and he and Jane met for lunch in a slightly shabby self-service café downhill from the Castle. Jane was still fuming.

'Hum,' said Tom, examining the menu by the door. 'Beans on toast, I think.' There were, however, green salads available, more than half-decent, and Jane found some smoked trout and lemon to go with hers.

They found a table. As soon as they were settled, she sat back in her chair and pitched in: 'I'm *seething*, Tom! Absolutely furious!'

'Why?'

'Mr C. told the jury about the earlier death.'

Tom's eyebrows shot up. 'That would be excluded, usually.'

'That's what I thought. But he said the judge had agreed.'

'Did Clutterbuck explain the reason?'

'It's because they want to talk about probabilities.'

'Ah.'

'It's *so* fucking two-faced. Any talk about probabilities is bound to suggest to the jury the first death *was* murder. Even though in his opening speech dear pompous Mr Clutterbuck assured them he's arguing no such thing... The defence barrister's *hopeless*, no terrier instincts. Who is he?'

Tom looked up. 'Frank Irwin, QC. Exeter practice, quite successful. I've seen him in action before. Suave, isn't he?'

'I didn't like him.'

Tom smiled. 'Too self-satisfied?'

'Yes. And he should have stopped the jury hearing about the first death.'

'Wait and see how he does later.'

Jane sniffed and started on her trout. 'What time do you come on?' she asked at last.

'I saw the schedule,' said Tom. 'Elspeth, then Mrs Phillips, followed by me and Aliza.' He sliced and speared neatly a strip of bean-laden toast. 'Usual pattern, events first.' In went the beans and he started to chew.

'That's what Mr Clutterbuck said. I think the pathologists come later.'

'Tomorrow,' said Tom with his mouth full. 'Then the other technical chaps on Wednesday, followed by that practice nurse.'

'What does she know?'

'No idea. Surprised to see her on the list.'

'What about defence witnesses?'

'They've got their own pathologist, probably on Thursday.'

'Who?'

'Can't remember the name, a woman. Baby specialist.'

'Where from?'

'Sheffield, I think.'

'Don't know who that would be.'

'Five character witnesses. Then Ralph—and Lidya herself.'

'I thought husbands couldn't be forced to give evidence against their wives.'

'He's a defence witness, they've chosen to put him up. But he'll have to face cross-examination. They both will. It'll be tough.'

Jane thought for a while. 'In his statement,' she said eventually, 'Mr C. said there was evidence that Lidya knew Ayana was dead, before she left the house.'

Tom looked up. 'That baby alarm.'

'Must be… and Tom, there was something I didn't follow towards the end. He started talking about Lidya's *motive*. The judge and the defence lawyer both looked up pretty sharply when he did.'

'Um,' said Tom, wiping away tomato sauce from his mouth with a paper napkin. He leant back on his creaking bentwood chair and thought for a moment. 'The defence are supposed to be told in advance what evidence they'll be facing—the prosecution aren't allowed to refer to anything they don't have proper grounds for. Perhaps he's got something new on Lidya's supposed motives, and the judge wasn't sure what he was referring to.'

'What the hell could that be?'

'Hard to see, isn't it?' Tom paused, and put one hand gently over Jane's. 'How are you finding all this court stuff?'

'Quite stressful.'

*

Back in the courtroom after lunch, the judge indicated that the defence had waived its right to address the jury at that point, and the presentation of evidence began. The witness box, like the dock, faced Jane.

The evidence given by Elspeth and Mrs Phillips was gone through in great detail, but was much as Jane had expected, and nothing new emerged. Elspeth confirmed she'd not been able to hear Ayana's breathing on the baby alarm—and though she'd been expecting it, Jane's heart sank. Mrs Phillips hadn't been able to hear breathing either, but it was established that she was a little deaf.

When it came to cross-examination, the defence lawyer asked Elspeth:

'When Mrs Slade herself listened to the alarm in the kitchen, what did she say?'

'She said, "I think she's off".'

'What did you take her to mean by that?'

'Asleep.'

'And was she surprised that you couldn't hear any breathing?'

'I didn't tell her. She handed the receiver to me, and I couldn't hear anything. But I didn't say. I didn't know what to expect.'

'I see. And did she say that *she* could hear the baby?'

'Not as such, no.'

'So she *might* have meant that she *couldn't* hear any-

109

thing, that being normal when the baby was asleep?'

'I suppose so.'

*

As Tom walked to the stand and took the oath, Jane checked her watch: it was nearly three o'clock. She found herself keyed up: she'd never seen him in public action. But she needn't have worried. He described systematically the organisation of the police enquiry and the search of Victory House the day after Ayana's death. Mr Clutterbuck pressed him hard, putting it to him that Lidya had both opportunity and means to murder Ayana, but Tom quietly made clear the lack of evidence that any of the soft objects available to Lidya had been used in a smothering. He described in detail the lab tests that had been requested, and demonstrated the near impossibility, in the time available to her, of Lidya having used and effectively hidden some extraneous pillow or pad. This all took a long time, and Jane found it hard to concentrate on the detail.

When it came to the cross examination, Mr Irwin asked:

'Inspector, my client is accused of smothering her baby. How much time was there available during which she could have done so?'

'That,' said Tom, 'has been difficult to determine precisely. Our best estimate of the time available between Mrs Slade's going upstairs to feed Ayana and her coming down again prepared to leave the house is twenty minutes, certainly not more than twenty-five minutes.'

'And part of that time would have been taken up in changing for dinner?'

'Yes. The witnesses have confirmed that Mrs Slade changed her dress.'

110

'Is it not extraordinary, Inspector, to suggest that my client, if she intended to smother her baby, would have chosen an occasion on which there was so little time available, and when there were several other people in the house who might easily have disturbed her in the act?'

'That is a fair point—one that we did in fact include in our report.'

'I put it to you that such a choice of time would only make sense if my client had become so disturbed in her mind as to be reckless of all danger of being detected?'

'I think that is a reasonable conclusion.'

'Very well, Inspector. According to your investigation, *did* my client show any sign of being deranged, or at all upset, on the evening in question?'

'Not according to the witnesses we examined.'

'They considered her to have been happy, simply pleased at the prospect of going out?'

'Yes.'

Mr Irwin smiled. 'No more questions.' he said, and Jane breathed again. She looked again at her watch, and realised that Tom had been on the stand for more than an hour.

Aliza was equally professional. She added more detail of her interview with Elspeth, and confirmed Tom's estimate of the time available for a smothering.

It was now nearly five, and that ended the evidence for the day. Well, thought Jane as she drove home, Tom's evidence had been pretty helpful, without sounding biased in Lidya's favour. And Mr Irwin had managed to make some good points, too. She felt a little relieved, even mildly encouraged. But her lunchtime gloom and fury were submerged, not banished.

Experts

The following day Jane had planned to be at work. But she dreamed overnight of a series of disastrous court scenes, each worse than the last, and on waking found herself unable to stay away. After much arm-twisting of annoyed colleagues, she drove fast to Exeter, hurried through the gardens, and arrived only slightly late for the opening at 10 am. As she crept towards her seat, the first of the two doctors was being sworn, his right hand resting on the court bible held up to him by the clerk. He was perhaps forty, in pink shirt and green tie, but no jacket. A slim yellow ring binder lay before him on the ledge of the witness box.

Mr Clutterbuck rose. 'You are Dr Kenneth Jones, pathologist at the Royal Devon and Exeter Hospital?'

'I am.'

'You regularly perform postmortem examinations for the coroner, and other pathological examinations for the police?'

'That is correct.'

'And the court has evidence of your professional expertise and standing?'

'I believe so.' Dr Jones turned to the judge, who nodded very slightly.

'Did you perform a postmortem on the child known as Ayana Slade, on the 31st of January last, at the Derriford Hospital in Plymouth?'

'I examined the body of an infant identified as Female Baby Slade on the hospital records.'

'And what did you conclude as to the cause of death?'

Dr Jones found and slid on a pair of reading glasses, opened his ring binder and glanced at the first sheet in it. He looked up again, removing the glasses. 'I made my examination bearing in mind that the parents had reported the loss of their daughter as an unexplained cot death, but that the police had raised the question of infanticide. I should explain to the jury that when a family has suffered an earlier unexplained cot death, the police raise that question as a matter of routine.'

'Please go on.'

'I first examined the body externally. I found no bruising of the neck or face. There was a noticeable abrasion on the chin, but I understood that a paramedic team had attempted to revive the infant before removing it to the hospital, and I considered that this abrasion was likely to have been caused by their oxygen mask. I also found a few fibres of cellulose inside the left nostril.'

'How many fibres?'

'Seven, a very small amount. Probably originating from a cleaning tissue.'

'Did you draw any conclusion about how the fibres came to be inside the child's nostril?'

'They could have been breathed in as fluff or dust.' Dr Jones looked questioningly at Mr Clutterbuck, then consulted his file. 'When I examined the internal organs, I found no indications of disease or trauma, and the laboratory tests showed no signs of infection. The blood tests were normal, apart from severe depletion of oxygen, indicating a failure of respiration.' He glanced quickly at the jury. 'The hyoid bone of the neck, which is often broken in cases of manual strangulation, was intact.

'I did, however, find a good deal of fluid in the left lung. I also found some small hypoxic haemorrhages in the brain. These symptoms are associated with failure of respiration, and as such are found both in cases of unexplained cot death and in cases of smothering by a soft object such as a pillow. I found no petechial haemorrhages of the facial skin or in the eyes, which are often but not always found in cases of smothering.'

At this point Mr Clutterbuck led Dr Jones through a maze of medical questions about the symptoms of oxygen deprivation and different types of microscopic haemorrhage that Jane found confusing, in spite of her medical background. Dr Jones seemed to find some of them confusing too. Eventually the court adjourned for a coffee break. After the break, Mr Clutterbuck began again:

'So what, Dr Jones, did you conclude finally about the cause of death?'

'The cause cannot be determined from the medical evidence alone. The baby may have died from an unexplained failure of respiration due to natural causes. Equally, she may have been smothered with a soft object. She was not violently strangled.'

Sensible man, thought Jane. Thank God. Pity he couldn't rule out smothering, after all that fuss.

'Thank you. No more questions.'

The defence barrister rose slowly and rubbed his chin. 'Dr Jones,' he asked, 'are there *any* medical signs that can convincingly distinguish cot death from smothering?'

'There are some signs, such as facial bruising and scratching or bleeding around the nose and mouth which would not be expected in a cot death.'

'But these symptoms were not apparent in this case?'

'No, they weren't. On the other hand, they aren't present in all smotherings, especially if the perpetrator avoids unnecessary violence.'

'The fact is, therefore, that this could perfectly well have been a cot death?'

'It could. It could also have been a smothering.'

'I take it that the only foreign material found in the nasal passages was the very small quantity of cellulose fibre that you mentioned?'

'Correct.'

'No wool or cotton fibres?'

'No. Nor synthetics.'

'Thank you…   How long, in general, do you think it would take, Dr Jones, to smother an infant of this age?'

'How long? That is a difficult question. In most cases an infant will not normally resume breathing if effectively deprived of oxygen for five or six minutes. However, a sharp stimulus such as a blow to the chest within a further twenty minutes or more is sometimes capable of restarting the breathing reflex, or breathing may restart without any obvious stimulus.'

Mr Irwin hesitated, and glanced at the jury. 'So any intending smotherer would probably need at least ten minutes, to be sure, and maybe more?' he asked.

'I would say so.'

The judge coughed. 'That is your considered expert opinion, Dr Jones?' she said quietly.

Dr Jones looked worried, and paused. 'Yes,' he said at last. 'It's my opinion, but it's not possible to be exact.'

The judge frowned.

Mr Irwin continued: 'In your evidence you mentioned the previous cot death. A postmortem was performed in that case also?'

'Yes, and I had access to Dr S. P. Siddawi's report.'

'Could you describe to the court the conclusions drawn by Dr Siddawi in the previous case?'

'Certainly.' Dr Jones found another paper in his ring binder, and looked up. 'In the case of Gabriel Slade, who died aged two months, the symptoms were rather similar: no facial bruising, no signs of disease or trauma, and a quantity of fluid on the left lung. Dr Siddawi concluded there was no evidence of foul play, and the death was registered as a case of sudden infant death syndrome.'

'Thank you, no more questions,' said Mr Irwin.

Dr Jones picked up his reading glasses and ring binder, eased himself out of the witness box, and took his seat at the back of the court.

'Your next witness is likely to require some time, Mr Clutterbuck?' suggested the judge.

'Yes, your honour.'

'Once again, we're a little early, but I think we should take lunch at this point.'

'Certainly,' said Mr Clutterbuck.

Jane found her way to yesterday's restaurant; she felt anxious, and without the energy to do more than repeat her order for trout and salad.

*

After lunch, the prosecution lawyer resumed by selecting a new folder from the pile before him. He rose, and peered slowly around the court. 'Call Professor Sir Ambrose Eaton,' he intoned. The two professional-looking women jurors both craned forward for a first view of the new witness.

A slim figure seated three rows behind counsel stood and walked firmly to the witness box; he fished a black leather-bound notebook from his breast pocket and laid it on the bench in front of him. The professor was tall, his light grey suit well-cut, yet not quite clean at the cuffs, and his blue FRCP tie was a little weary. He looked alert, but relaxed. So he should be, thought Jane: he's done this so many times.

'You are Professor Sir Ambrose Eaton, of Guy's Hospital?' asked Mr Clutterbuck.

'I am.' Lidya looked up, and Jane could see her face in profile. Her dark eyes seemed to be appealing to the witness.

'You are an experienced pathologist, and have specialised for some years in cases of child abuse?'

'Twenty-three years.'

'A substantial period. And you might be described as the leading practitioner in that field?'

'I believe I might.' Sir Ambrose smiled, a little grimly.

'You examined the body of the infant Ayana Slade, professor?' At the name Lidya flinched and her head dropped.

'I did.'

'At what stage?'

'I was consulted two days after the death, at Dr Jones's suggestion. I made it my business first to read thoroughly his report, and I examined the body nine days after the death.'

'And what did you conclude about the cause of death?'

'I concluded that the child had been smothered.' He said it rather loudly. Lidya's face was now invisible to Jane, but her shoulders quivered. After a moment, Ralph's left hand moved tentatively towards Lidya.

He seemed to hesitate, then squeezed her upper arm gently and briefly.

'On what evidence did you base this conclusion?'

'As you have been told already, the smothering of an infant with a pillow or other soft object may well leave the body unbruised. That was so in this case.'

'From your personal observation?'

'Yes. But more particularly from Dr Jones's. He examined the body eight hours after the death. That is significant, because bruising caused by other types of violence, strangulation for instance, would certainly have been visible eight hours after death, though possibly not after nine days, even on a refrigerated cadaver.'

'So what makes you believe this child was smothered, and did not die naturally, in a so-called cot-death?'

'The direct evidence might be described as relatively inconclusive. It lies first in the substantial abrasion on the chin observed by Dr Jones. I cannot agree with him that this damage was most probably caused by the paramedic team. I have considerable experience of examining infants who have been asphyxiated. Smothering takes some determination, and in most cases the pillow or other pad is pressed down with great vigour, in order to be certain that the desired effect is achieved. I have frequently found scratches in such cases, even though there is no bruising. A paramedic team, on the other hand, may be expected to act rapidly but comparatively deftly and gently.

'Secondly, in my opinion the *degree* of hypoxic bleeding in the brain suggests smothering rather than cot death. This is a matter of judgement, but judgement based in my case on experience of a very large number of cases. However, although the abrasion on the chin and the hypoxic bleeding do suggest smothering, the indirect evidence is much stronger, in my professional opinion.'

'Please explain to the jury what you mean.'

'The indirect evidence has two aspects. One concerns the behaviour of the mother at the times of the deaths.

'I did not, of course, observe the mother personally on either occasion, but I have read reports of it. What I can tell the court, as an expert with very wide experience of investigating child abuse cases, is that coldness and absence of grieving in the mother is a leading indicator of guilt.'

Jane felt her jaw tighten. The judge looked very sharply at Mr Irwin, who did not respond. Her pencil tapped again. 'Mr Clutterbuck,' she said. 'No evidence of the mother's behaviour has yet been presented.'

'That is to come, your honour.'

'Yes. That being so, I must direct the jury to view Sir Ambrose's last comment with some caution. His expert opinion will only carry weight if it can subsequently be shown in this court that the mother was indeed cold and did not grieve.'

'Indeed, your honour, the prosecution is well aware of the point, and is grateful for your emphasis.' Mr Clutterbuck gave a little bow, and turned back to his witness. 'Professor, is it not very unusual for a mother to harm her own child? Especially, perhaps, one in comfortable circumstances?'

Sir Ambrose's chest expanded, and he turned more directly towards the jury.

'For any mother to attack her own child is, of course, not at all common. But it is, sadly, less uncommon than is often recognised, and I am sorry to say that until recently too many cases of child abuse and infanticide have passed undetected.' His voice had risen in pitch. 'Far too many. Fortunately we now have an expanding cadre of well-trained experts, and more cases are being brought to light. It is most important to understand that such crimes are by no means restricted to obviously dysfunctional families. On the contrary, appalling acts have been perpetrated secretly within the most comfortable homes, and by people who appear to be pillars of the community, for motives that are frequently deeply concealed. It is therefore important to be fearlessly guided by the physical evidence.'

'Thank you, Sir Ambrose. I believe you mentioned a second aspect of the indirect evidence?'

'Ah, yes. As the jury has been informed, a previous child in this same family died in infancy in very similar circumstances.' The professor said this with a sharp emphasis, and glanced at the jury. One of the two professional women looked uncertain and the young juror in a tank top had pursed his lips. 'In such a context it becomes important to consider the likelihood that a genuine cot death could occur twice in the same family.

'Cot deaths are rare. Of the live births that occur in this country only about one in two thousand is followed by a cot death—that is to say, an unexplained death from natural causes during the first year of life. In other words, if you choose a newborn at random the probability that it will subsequently suffer a cot death is low, one in two thousand. A real tragedy for the couple concerned.' Sir Ambrose directed an empathetic smile at the jury.

'But let us now consider families in which there have been *two* births. Of these families, only one in two thousand can expect their first baby to suffer a cot death. And of those very rare families, only one in two thousand *of them* would be expected to have the *second* baby die in the same way. This means that of all families with two births, only one-in-two-thousand of one-in-two-thousand would be expected to have *both* babies die. Now, one-in-two-thousand of one-in-two-thousand is *one in four million*.

'And one in four million, members of the jury, is really a very low probability. In fact, it's so extremely low that we are forced to consider other possible causes. And the obvious alternative is a mother who is smothering her babies, because it's hard to distinguish a smothering from a cot death.'

I *hate* this man, thought Jane. She felt her scalp crawling, struggled to remain calm, to listen carefully.

'I can illustrate the point further,' went on Sir Ambrose, 'by considering a hypothetical case in which *three* apparent cot deaths occur in the same family. The chance of that happening by bad luck is *one in eight billion*, far more than the total number of families in Great Britain. In such a case, my professional judgement would be that the probability of its happening by bad luck is so low that one could be virtually *certain* that foul play must have occurred. To summarise the point, I like to say that *one sudden infant death is a tragedy, two is suspicious and three is murder, until proved otherwise.*'

At this point Jane saw that Lidya was whispering to Ralph, silently banging her right fist onto her left palm as if to emphasise a point, her face drawn yet animated. Ralph nodded, and turned to speak to the defence lawyer. Mr Irwin listened, also nodding, but then seemed to be telling Ralph to wait.

Sir Ambrose had glanced down and paused. 'In the

present case,' he continued at last, 'the deep suspicion aroused by the extreme improbability of two cot deaths in the same family is compounded by the physical evidence that a smothering actually occurred, combined with the mother's recorded behaviour, and I have no hesitation in giving it as my professional opinion that a smothering occurred in this case.' Sir Ambrose turned away from the jury, and seemed to sag a little, as though tension had drained out of him.

Mr Clutterbuck nodded, as if totally convinced by all that he had heard. 'No more questions,' he said, and sat down, his face dour.

The judge turned towards the defence desk.

'A moment, your honour,' said Mr Irwin, and having received a nod of agreement, twisted round again to Ralph and Lidya. Whispered talk resumed, and Jane could see that the lawyer was making notes on a scrap of paper.

At last he stood up to face Sir Ambrose.

'Professor,' he said, and paused. 'As our learned judge has pointed out, you appear to be convinced that my client behaved coldly and showed no signs of grieving over the deaths of her two children, but no evidence of this has yet been presented in court. On what did you base this conclusion?'

'On the police report.'

'Which part of the report?'

'The information volunteered by the GP.'

'Which, if I remember correctly, the GP in turn obtained from her practice nurse. Did you yourself talk in detail to the nurse, to find out exactly what she meant?'

'No. I relied on the report, which was quite explicit.'

'But is it not difficult to assess any apparent coldness and lack of grieving of a parent in the immediate aftermath of a tragedy?'

'Yes. But I would expect an experienced practice nurse to be a perceptive judge.'

'I see... Now, you also mentioned that in cases in which mothers are known to have abused or killed their own children, their motives are sometimes hard to determine. Have you formed any opinion on what the accused's motive might have been in this case?'

'I have not: to do so with integrity would require a background in forensic psychiatry, which I do not have. However, it is not difficult to suggest possible motives which have proved relevant in similar cases in the past.'

'In the absence of evidence, that would be pure speculation, would it not?'

'The speculations of an experienced expert, might, I suggest, make a puzzling case a little less puzzling to the jury. The accused, for instance, might have been suffering from Munchausen's syndrome by proxy.'

'Sir Ambrose,' interrupted the judge, 'am I right in thinking that you have no direct evidence bearing on the mother's actual motives?'

The professor looked blank. 'Nothing direct, no.'

'Then perhaps Mr Irwin should move on.'

'Thank you, your honour,' said the defence lawyer, and glanced down at his file. 'Now professor, these abrasions on the chin, on which you and the previous witness appear to be at some degree of variance, can you please describe them to the jury?'

'I may consult my notes?'

'Of course.'

The professor picked up and leafed through the black notebook, and examined a particular page for a little while. 'I see that I have written down that they covered an area of 5 cm by 3 cm, but it now occurs to me that on the chin of a neonate that might be an overestimate. Let us say an inch by half an inch.'

'So you didn't actually measure the area?'

'No.'

'I see. And how *deep* were the abrasions? In your earlier evidence concerning cases in which an infant was known to have been suffocated, I believe you referred to finding not abrasions but scratches. Were these in fact deep scratches?'

The professor hesitated. 'No. But the skin had been scraped raw over a substantial area.'

'And you have no hesitation in identifying that as a sign of determined smothering?'

'No hesitation.'

'Really?'

The professor did not respond, but Mr Irwin merely raised his eyebrows.

'Finally, professor, may we return to your probability argument? It appears to be based on an assumption that the likelihood of a cot death is the same in all families. But might it not be the case that certain families are abnormally vulnerable, for genetic or other reasons—in which case your argument might prove to be very misleading?'

Yes! rejoiced Jane.

'You will not be surprised to hear, Mr Irwin, that this general point has been put to me many times before. My response to it is twofold. First, we have no evidence that any families in the UK population are exceptionally vulnerable. None whatever. And secondly… '

Mr Irwin held up one hand. 'A moment, professor. We must remember, must we not, that my client is Ethiopian by origin. I am informed that several infant relatives of hers have suffered cot deaths in Ethiopia, and that a close relative, her mother's sister, lost no fewer than three babies in this way.'

One of the professional-looking jury women glanced down at Lidya with some interest, but the professor was smiling.

'I'm afraid that anecdotal comments of that sort are of very little value, Mr Irwin. We have to consider the possibility of undiagnosed disease in Ethiopia. And infanticide, too—I fear that the lives of babies are often held of lower value in other parts of the world.'

Jane's eyes swung round to Lidya: her face was lifted towards Sir Ambrose, blank with astonishment, her mouth momentarily open. Then her head slowly fell, and she swallowed. Beside her, Ralph's fists had clenched, and Jane saw his jaw muscles tighten.

'My second point, however, is perhaps more important. We must notice that any tendency of some families to be particularly vulnerable, if it occurs, is *already included in the statistics*—the probability of one in two thousand is obtained from the measured rate of cot deaths, and therefore already includes the effects of any exceptionally vulnerable families. One musn't fall into the trap of allowing twice for the same effect. I'm afraid that this possibility, if it exists, is already included in the figures, and does not affect the statistical argument.'

That *must* be wrong, groaned Jane to herself, this is farcical. She could see that the judge and several of the jurors were frowning, and Ralph was whispering again to Mr Irwin. Mr Irwin eventually straightened up and asked:

'Can we be clear on this point, Sir Ambrose? Your professional opinion as a statistician is that the probability you quoted, of one in four million, would not be altered by the presence in the population of particularly vulnerable families?'

'That is correct. As I said, there is no evidence that vulnerable families exist, but, yes, if they do, their effects will have been already taken into account, and the statistical argument stands.'

Mr Irwin stood for some time, apparently checking the page in his folder. At last he announced 'no more questions'. Sir Ambrose smiled, inclined his head slightly to one side, and walked slowly back to his seat.

Fuck the man, thought Jane: he knows he's been given an easy ride. And God rot that useless defence lawyer!

Campaign

Alarmed at how Tuesday had gone, Jane wasn't able to be in court the following day. But Tom and Aliza would be there: they'd been recalled to give evidence about the baby alarm. At lunch time Tom called her. 'Case adjourned,' he said. 'We need to talk.' He sounded very gruff.

'Supper at mine this evening?'

By seven he was ringing the doorbell. He shrugged out of his anorak without a word. She led the way upstairs. He followed close, flung himself down on the sofa. 'All unravelling,' he said.

She dropped into an easy chair facing him.

'Our stuff went OK. We explained how we found the baby alarm system when we searched the house, how I'd switched off the units to preserve the battery states. But then came the forensic technician. He reckoned Ayana's breathing should have been perfectly audible on the alarm—if she was still alive... Extensive trials with real babies, right distance away from the microphone, blah, blah... Careful and thorough, has to be said.'

'No ifs and buts?'

'None at all. So they brought back Elspeth. She was upset, but still quite clear she *hadn't* heard anything. Stuck to it when they pressed her. Of course, Clutterbuck made hay; the jury were all nodding.'

'What d'you think?'

'If this evidence stands up, we may be forced to accept she's guilty.'

'What's your gut feeling?'

He hesitated. 'No.'

'Why?'

'She's not stupid. Why not a termination, if that was what she wanted?'

'Is there any way round this evidence?'

'I don't know, Jane... There was a possible explanation. The alarm had a volume control, a knob in the base, away from the on/off switch—I was a damn fool not to have noticed it. The guy explained they did their tests with the control set as they received it.'

'You think it might have been moved?'

'It might have been low when Elspeth tried it, and somehow got turned up later. I might have turned it up myself.'

'Could you have?'

'No idea. Don't think so. They had it exhibited in court, it was a small knob and recessed.'

'Did Irwin ask about that?'

'He never did, bugger him. I was itching to yell out, tell him he must.'

'Can't you do that? Send him a little note... '

'I'm supposed to be on the other side.'

'This *awful* system, Tom. She's so totally dependent on that one lawyer. If he's no good... It's terrible.'

'Seen it often enough. If the defence don't make the right case, nobody else is going to.'

'Tom... Elspeth tried that baby alarm first before Lidya and Ralph left, didn't she?'

'That's right.'

'Wouldn't you have expected Lidya to warn her not to turn the volume down, if she was concerned about Ayana?'

'That's one point Irwin *did* pursue. But he only made things worse—Elspeth said firmly Lidya never mentioned it.'

'Oh... And the whole case could turn on this evidence?'

'I'm afraid it could. If they manage to convince the jury Ayana wasn't breathing when Lidya came downstairs, I guess it's all over...' Tom had twisted himself at an odd angle on the sofa, his hands grasping his neck from behind.

She repeated her earlier question: 'You and Aliza *still* think she's innocent?'

'Yes,' he said, releasing his neck and running both hands forward through his hair. 'I asked her in the car coming back, and she agrees.'

'Me too,' said Jane quietly. She leaned forward and placed a hand gently on his knee.

He looked at her with some surprise, then placed his hand over hers. 'What did Eaton have to say about the probabilities yesterday?' he asked.

'Didn't you hear? Incredibly emotive. He said the chance of getting two SIDS in the same family is low, one in four million. And he had this mantra: *one's a tragedy, two's very suspicious and three must be murder.*'

'Did Irwin challenge that?'

'Not as such. But he did suggest some families might be specially vulnerable. He pointed out that Lidya's aunt lost three babies.'

'What was Eaton's response?'

'That they probably *killed* more babies in Ethiopia.'

'God! How did Lidya take that?'

'As if she couldn't take in what he'd said.'

'What a man!'

'Ralph was furious.'

'And how did Eaton say it affected the probabilities?'

'Pooh-poohed it. Said there was no evidence special vulnerability occurred. But that if it did occur, it was already included in the measured probabilities, and wouldn't affect his argument.'

'Really?'

'Yes. The judge and the defence lawyer both looked surprised, and Irwin asked him to confirm it was his professional view as a statistician. But nobody challenged the conclusion.'

'How could they? Judges and Counsel don't know about statistics. Nor the police, come to that.'

'But doctors have to, Tom. It sounds wrong to me, absolutely wrong—I must ask Igor, he'll know. If the mother comes from a vulnerable family, it *must* affect the probabilities.'

'I'd have thought so... Look, Jane. *I* can't tell the defence what questions they ought to be asking because I'm police. But there's nothing to stop a member of the public talking to Lidya's solicitor. Unusual, maybe, but not impossible... You were thinking about a support group earlier, weren't you?'

'It never got anywhere.'

'They need more effective medical evidence. And some better legal strategy wouldn't come amiss—what about George?'

Jane looked up. 'Why didn't I think of that?'

Tom nodded.

'But let me talk to Igor about the statistics first.'

'Call him now.'

She wasn't long on the phone. 'Tonight he says, they'll feed me... There's lasagne in the oven. Lock up when you leave.'

*

130

When Tom had closed the door behind her, he didn't turn immediately to the kitchen, but threw himself back onto the sofa. After thinking for a while, he found a number on his mobile, called, and waited impatiently for the response.

'Yes,' said a clipped voice, at last.

'John Smith?'

'Tom?' The voice wasn't encouraging. 'What's the urgency?'

'There's a big risk she'll get convicted.'

'Perhaps she's guilty.'

'She isn't.'

John Smith cleared his throat. 'I told you, Tom,' he said. 'No can do.'

'Think again.'

'Can't, the decision went right up the line.' His voice was still clipped and cool.

'But it may be all over in two or three days.'

'No Tom.' More gruff this time.

'It's her whole future, her life.'

John Smith seemed to be deliberating. '*No* Tom,' he said at last. 'Can't be done.' There was a click.

'*Call ended,*' announced Tom's display.

He raised his eyebrows, dug out his Filofax and after a while turned to the old cases section at the back. He surveyed the page, located another number, punched his mobile's keys deliberately.

This time his call was answered very promptly.

'My dear Tom!' came a light voice. 'Good to hear you. More than a year, I think... What a sad business.'

'It was,' said Tom. 'Upset me a lot.' He explained at some length what he wanted.

There was a long silence. 'Delicate,' said Dr Sampson at last.

'Any chance?'

'They may not be in Cheltenham at all… What did he mean by *right up the line,* d'you think?'

'I don't know,' said Tom.

'He may not have meant cabinet level.' A pause. Then the light voice hummed a lilting tenor line.

Traviata, Tom thought. 'No,' he said aloud.

A sniff, another pause. 'Oh, sweet lady be good,' cooed the voice, contriving a gravelly falsetto this time. Tom smiled, and waited.

'Call you in the morning,' came the voice suddenly. 'Give me a couple of hours. Eleven? Your office?'

*

Jane wasn't surprised to be welcomed by Alice Mikailan to an enormous casserole on her scrubbed kitchen table; the goulash intended for Igor and three hungry teenage sons accommodated a further moderate appetite without difficulty. After the meal Igor suggested a walk in his rose garden. It was getting dark, but he was proud of his scented Bourbons.

'Hospital going well?' he asked. In the gloaming, Jane could just make out he was stroking his beard.

'Yes,' she said.

'Good… You wanted to talk about that dangerous idiot Ambrose Eaton?'

'Awful man. I heard his evidence on Tuesday.'

'What did he say?'

'First, that there was direct evidence of smothering.'

'What evidence?'

Jane explained.

Igor had his nose in a bloom, palely yellow in the dim light. 'Thin,' he said. 'And, from what you say, in

132

flat disagreement with the pathologist. OK... What did he say about the statistics?'

'He started with the probability of cot death for a birth chosen at random in the UK. Said it was one in two thousand.'

'That's correct. I checked after you called.'

'From that he deduced the probability of getting two cot deaths in the same family as one in two thousand *of* one in two thousand, which is one in four million.'

Igor considered. 'Big assumption there,' he said sharply, and paused again. 'For the *first* death, OK, we choose the family at random, as he says. But when he goes on to say "of these", he's changed his sample, hasn't he Jane? It's no longer any old births chosen at random, but a sample of second births to mothers who've already suffered one cot death.'

Jane nodded. 'You mean, if such mothers have a predisposition to cot deaths, you'd expect the probability in the new sample to be bigger? Maybe much bigger?'

'Of course. And not only for genetic reasons. There might be something in the home environment—some toxic chemical in the plastic of the cot mattress, or laying the baby down in a particular way.'

'But Eaton said predisposition didn't happen in Britain.'

'Did he say whether anyone had looked? ... We don't know what causes cot deaths, but some sort of genetic predisposition must be by far the most likely explanation.'

'The defence pointed out that Lidya's aunt lost three babies.'

'That's pretty significant. Genuine cot deaths?'

'I don't know. Eaton pooh-poohed it. Said infanticide was probably more common in Ethiopia.'

'This idiot's got to be challenged, Jane.'

'And he said that even if predisposition did occur, it was already in the statistics, so wouldn't affect his one in four million. He said you mustn't make the mistake of taking it into account twice.'

'*Did* he though? What a remarkably silly statement.'

'What's wrong with it?'

'I just *told* you... Look, Jane. He's right, of course, that predisposition *is* taken into account in the initial one in two thousand, because that includes cot deaths in any specially vulnerable families. But he's completely wrong to say it's taken into account in his *second* factor.'

'You're sure about that?'

'Of course I'm sure.' Igor moved abruptly on to another rose bed and pulled something pink towards his face. He took a long sniff. 'Take an extreme model. Suppose it was the case that all cot deaths were caused by some particular gene in the mother, which had the effect that cot death was *inevitable* for all her babies. If one in two thousand mothers had this gene, then if we chose a mother at random we'd have a one in two thousand chance of a cot death for the *first* baby, just as now. But in this model if the *same* poor mother got pregnant again, she'd be *bound* to have a second cot death, wouldn't she?'

'You mean, in that model, having two cot deaths for two pregnancies would be no more improbable than having one cot death for one pregnancy?'

'Exactly. In that model the probability of getting two cot deaths in two pregnancies is one in two thousand, not one in four million. So he's completely wrong in saying that his probability of one in four million takes predisposition into account—it doesn't.'

'He must be a fool. Why did he say what he did?'

'Convinced himself. A lot of medics have very primitive ideas about statistics. Probably never studied it.'

'But the court treated him as an expert.'

'You and I know something about this guy, Jane. Great on the pathology of lung disease, genuine reputation, sure. *Then* got to be called in as expert witness in smothering cases, acquired a name for it. And *that* involved him in issues of child abuse, where he had no expertise whatever, but got all excited about abusive parents and found himself on a crusade... Chances are he knows no more real statistics than he learned in second MB—never needed it.'

'Like me?'

Igor chuckled. 'Worse—at least you have a good *feel* for when something's wrong. And because he had a handle to his name, people believed him.' Igor was pressing one foot onto the earth around the roots of a standard bush, firming the ground and releasing fragrance as its blooms brushed against his chest. They had now reached the bottom of the garden, the flowers almost invisible. For Jane, the lack of light made the scent even more overpowering by contrast.

'What can we do?' she asked. 'Tom thought we could say something to the defence team.'

'Find a decent statistician for them.'

Team

'So who else will be here?' asked Dr Said, seated on a dining chair at Jane's table and cradling his breakfast cup, his sad eyes moist as usual. It was 8.30 on Thursday morning.

'Tom?' asked Igor, slumped on the sofa.

'Can't be seen to be involved.'

Igor leant forward to take his cup, spreading his knees. 'But he reckons she's innocent?'

'Yes, he does.'

Dr Said worked marmalade dextrously into his warm croissant. 'I have to leave at ten,' he said.

'I know, Raja,' said Jane. 'Igor can't stop for long either.'

'Who else?' said Igor.

'George. George Devenish.'

'The barrister?'

'Yes.'

'Your defence silk last year?' said Igor

'Yes… I'm not sure whether you knew, Raja: eighteen months ago, I thought I might have to face a rather serious charge.'

Dr Said smiled. 'We all knew, Jane.'

'George is good,' said Igor.

'The Western Morning News had three scorching paragraphs on Sir Ambrose's history yesterday,' said Dr Said. 'From their court reporter.'

'This isn't a publicity campaign,' said Jane.

'But he sounds like a useful ally,' said Igor. 'Anyone know who he is?'

Raja dipped into his briefcase and extracted an article snipped from the paper. Igor grabbed it and took his mobile into the kitchen.

The doorbell rang, and a cheerful voice crackled on the doorphone. 'George,' said Jane and ran downstairs.

The new arrival stood grinning on the doorstep, grey curls awry. 'Long time no see,' he said, stepped inside and slid a large avuncular hand round her shoulder. Jane smiled, disentangled herself, and led the way upstairs and went to make more coffee. As she did so she could hear George breezily introducing himself to Raja, and when she reappeared carrying the cafetière he was pottering around the room examining her pastels. Raja was smiling to himself.

Igor reappeared. 'Got him,' he said. 'Seemed keen, so I said join us. Here in a minute, happens to be working just round the corner.'

'Extraordinary thing,' George said, as Jane handed him his cup. He settled onto the sofa and beamed. 'My clerk just called. Another adjournment. The prosecution's withdrawing filed evidence.'

'What evidence?'

'The practice nurse. Marsha Stone.'

'That's odd,' said Jane. 'That must be the stuff about Lidya being an uncaring mother.'

'Correct,' said George. 'I got a peek at the summary of evidence.'

'Clutterbuck promised the judge it was coming later. Eaton said being cold and detached was a leading indicator of guilt, but the judge intervened, and pointed out no evidence of coldness had yet been presented.'

'Ah.'

'What would this withdrawal mean?' asked Raja, his dark eyebrows crinkled.

'Anything. The nurse may have changed her tune, Sandy Clutterbuck may have decided it didn't look strong enough.'

'But not calling the nurse after all that fuss will make him look bad, surely?' said Jane.

'Not necessarily. The judge'll read him a lecture, and he'll say it's all very unfortunate—but he's still contrived to inform the jury that someone reckons she's an uncaring mother. That's what he's after.'

Jane's eyes widened. 'Without producing his witness?'

'Exactly.'

'That's dishonest!'

'My dear!' George's expressive mouth worked and he took a large gulp of coffee.

The bell rang again. 'Arbuckle for Allison,' crackled the door-phone and Jane hurried downstairs. Standing on the doorstep was a fresh-faced young man, his hair an untidy mop, his orange tie loosened, a maroon motor-cycle helmet tucked under one arm. Following Jane's glance he loped up the stairs behind her.

Jane poured him a coffee. He settled at the table next to Dr Said, and produced a reporter's pad and ballpoint. 'Western Morning News,' he remarked, as though it was his habitual opener. 'Arbuckle—call me Andy.' He looked round the room and slurped quickly.

George looked doubtful. 'This is a private working group,' he said.

'And I'm here to work with you.'

'Not for the story?'

'Only later, and only if you'll let me.'

'Think you can *help*?'

'Don't know yet, do I? But I do know what that monster Eaton did to three other women.'

'So you think Mrs Slade is innocent?'

'Don't you?'

'That's why we're here,' said Dr Said, clearing his throat.

'Right,' said George. 'Jane—you and Igor thought we should be putting a few ideas to the defence?'

'If we can. The statistics, specially.'

He asked her to explain, and she did her best.

'You're right to be worried,' said George, at last. 'Quote odds to them and juries feel on home turf—always one or two know their way to the betting shop. Breathe "ten to one she's guilty", and ten to one they'll convict. And one in four million is such terribly long odds... I assume Irwin's calling a statistical expert of his own?'

'That's the point,' said Jane. 'We don't think he is.'

'What's the man playing at? Perhaps he didn't know the statistical argument was coming.'

'He *did*. There was pre-trial argument about whether the jury should be told about the first death, and the judge agreed they should because it was relevant to the statistics.'

'Then he's a fool... But can we find a decent statistician at short notice? A real expert?'

'Last night we couldn't think of anyone,' said Igor.

'Drug companies do statistics,' said Dr Said. 'And isn't here a trial in progress in the Derriford?'

'There is,' said Jane. 'I could find out who's analysing the results.'

'Good as anything, at short notice,' said Igor.

'Hm,' said George. 'He'll need to be an impressive witness, if the jury's to believe him rather than Eaton. We'd need him by Monday. Better find someone today if you possibly can.'

'What witnesses *are* the defence calling?' asked Jane.

George pulled out a pocket book, and fished out a scribbled note. 'A medical specialist of their own. She'll take up this afternoon, and with luck I'll be in court to hear her. Tomorrow morning, character witnesses... Peggy Harford?'

'She's the midwife.'

'Bridget Phillips and Elspeth Cukay?'

'Baby-sitters.'

'Christabel Parker?'

Jane frowned. 'No idea.'

'And dear Father Barnabas Gresley. Anglican high pi.'

Raja smiled.

'Barnabas is all *right*, George,' said Jane, annoyed.

'OK, OK,' allowed George. '... Maybe we ought to go and chat up the defence team this evening, if they'll let us.'

Igor nodded.

'I gotta go,' said Andy. 'Column to file... But keep me in the loop. I'll run a story in the News if you think it'll help. But what you *need* is a national campaign.' He paused and slurped again. 'I can give you some names... If you're interested, that is.'

'Of course we're interested,' said Jane.

'Right. Let myself out, don't you bother.' He picked up his helmet and strode to the door. They heard him thudding down the stairs; the front door slammed. A motor-cycle roared into life.

'Short and sweet,' remarked Dr Said with a satisfied smile.

*

The next few days shot past in a whirl. The prosecution rested their case. The defence opened on the Thursday afternoon with the paediatric pathologist from Sheffield. George reported to Jane and Tom in the evening that her evidence had gone reasonably well. She'd pooh-poohed Sir Ambrose's views on the facial laceration and the degree of hypoxic bleeding in the brain, and agreed with Dr Jones that smothering was no more probable than cot death. But George was gloomy on whether she had enough gravitas to outweigh the solid impression created by Sir Ambrose.

That same afternoon Jane succeeded in running down the drug company statistician. She and Igor contrived half an hour to talk it over with him at the Derriford. Nerdy but enthusiastic, he knew his stuff, agreeing at once with Igor's views and making new points of his own, and he seemed willing to give evidence. Jane and Igor concluded he would do, and it was agreed that George and the statistician should meet Cormack and Irwin during the lunch recess on Friday.

Tom couldn't afford time to sit in court again. On the Thursday morning, as promised, Michael Sampson called him back.

'Stuck,' he said.

'Any real chance?'

'Well, the tapes are definitely in GCHQ.'

'That's a relief.'

'But my best hope isn't. She's in Washington, not back till Sunday. Can't do anything till then.'

Ralph

Jane was determined to hear Ralph's evidence on the Friday afternoon, and at 12.30 she set out for Exeter. While she was eating in the café Andy phoned her to report that the character witnesses had done well. Peggy, Elspeth and Mrs Phillips had all been absolutely clear that Lidya and Ralph couldn't have been more devoted and caring parents; and Christabel Parker (who turned out to be Lidya's school friend now living in Birmingham) had given detail from numerous telephone conversations on Lidya's thoroughness and determination, after Gabriel's death, to make sure that there was no repeat tragedy with Ayana.

This call delayed Jane, and she hurried into the courtroom just in time to hear Ralph take the oath, as smartly dressed as ever. He was clearly nervous, and Lidya was watching him with concern.

'Mr Slade,' began the defence barrister with an encouraging smile. 'The question has been raised by the prosecution of your wife's attitude to her new baby. Would you have described Ayana, who died so tragically, as a wanted child?'

'Of course!'

'Wanted by you *and* your wife?'

'You've no idea… The court has no idea how we felt after Gabriel died.'

'Gabriel being your first child?' Mr Irwin's voice had dropped.

'Yes. It took Lidya so much courage to try again.'

'And, as you say, Ayana was longed for likewise?'

Ralph glanced down towards Lidya and half smiled in his distress. Jane could no longer see Lidya's face.

'Of course she was, even more.'

'Thank you... You said just now it took your wife much courage to try again. Could you describe to the court how she prepared for the new birth, and what special precautions she took to avoid a second trage-dy?'

'Precautions? We read up about cot deaths, of course, discussed it all with our GP, the theories... We went to London to talk to experts, ordered books from America... Lidya threw out all the old nursery bedding and bought new, a new mattress with differ-ent plastic. We studied the post-mortem report on Gabriel.'

'That must have been painful.'

'Very much so... She consulted a nutritionist. We got advice on baby alarms. Innumerable scans and tests... We had the nursery fumigated... '

'Thank you. How would you describe your wife's psychological state before Ayana arrived?'

Ralph closed his eyes briefly. 'Immediately after Gabriel's death, well... she had a breakdown. We both did, really.'

'How serious a breakdown?'

'Unable to act, decide things. She was on anti-depressants for nine months. She got over it in the end, and when we decided to try again, she said we must be strong, steely, get ourselves in good shape to be parents. And that's exactly what she did.'

'Thank you. And her psychological state after the birth?'

'Up to the point when the baby arrived, she had a

143

tight grip on herself. Extremely tight. But once Ayana was there, it all changed. The baby was so special, so *exciting*, for both of us, well, Lidya was just… just *delighted* after that.'

'And how would you describe your wife's mood on the night Ayana died, at the time you left the house?'

'When we left? Happy and pleased, I think. It was our first night out after the birth.'

Mr Irwin paused. 'You don't mean pleased to get away from Ayana?'

Ralph blinked. 'Only in the sense…' He started to cough. 'I'm sorry… Only in the sense that, well, our life was opening out at last. We were leaving Ayana in good hands.' He looked distraught.

'Exactly so.' Irwin paused for a moment. 'Finally, Mr Slade,' he said, 'can you describe to the court what happened when you received the telephone call from the baby sitters?'

Ralph swallowed. 'Well,' he said, 'yes… Mrs Phillips called me on my mobile.'

'You and your wife were at a dinner party?'

'Just supper really.'

'With an old friend?'

'Yes. Raja Said… Mrs Phillips told me Ayana had stopped breathing, but she sounded confused, and she's a bit deaf. I'm afraid I yelled at her.'

'Then what happened?'

'My wife realised what Bridget had said. She grabbed the phone and shut me up.'

'How did she behave then?'

'She swayed on her feet, for a moment. But she… then she recovered and kept her head. We jumped into the Lexus and I drove to the hospital. Very fast.'

'Was she speaking?'

'No… The ambulance arrived after us. The crew

144

rushed the trolley into emergency. Lidya caught sight of Ayana's face, and I think she knew it was all over. She collapsed.'

'How do you mean?'

'She slumped onto the floor. The staff put her on a trolley and injected her.'

'How did she seem when she came round?'

'She didn't come round for eight hours. Then she was groggy. She wanted to know what had happened, of course, and I had to tell her Ayana was gone.'

Lidya's head was in her hands.

Ralph looked down at her and hesitated. 'She wouldn't say anything. For days and days…'

Mr Irwin scanned his notes, and Jane wondered how he would respond.

'Thank you, Mr Slade. No more questions.' The barrister swung his gown around and sat down.

Mr Clutterbuck rose slowly to his feet, his face sombre.

'Mr Slade,' he said, and cleared his throat. 'Where did you first meet your wife?'

Ralph blinked. 'In Addis.'

'Addis Ababa, in Ethiopia? How was that?'

'I was doing some business with her father.'

'Her mother came, I think, from a primitive part of the country?'

Lidya looked up sharply.

'Primitive? Not really.'

'She herded goats? In a tribal area?'

'I believe so.'

'So it would be fair to say that your wife was raised with attitudes to family and children very different from your own?'

Ralph frowned. 'I wouldn't say so.'

'She was used to babies dying?'

'I don't think so.'

'But Mr Slade, the court has heard that her aunt lost many infants.'

'That was in the Sahel, where the infant mortality is higher.'

'Exactly so, Mr Slade. Thank you. And I put it to you that in marrying you and coming to England, your wife was aiming to escape from her restrictive up-bringing and culture. She had become, in fact, a sophisticated woman who didn't want children?'

'That's not true.'

'And this was a persistent source of tension be-tween you, a running sore?'

'I've just said, it's not true.' Ralph's face was red-dening.

Mr Clutterbuck glanced towards the jury. 'So you say. I put it to you that you are shielding Lidya, but the cost to your own peace of mind is almost more than you can bear?'

Ralph took out a handkerchief and mopped his brow. 'No.'

'We shall return to this question later. Now, Mr Slade, let us consider the half hour before you left the house on the night of Ayana's death. While your wife was feeding the baby, you were changing to go out?'

'Yes.'

'Where did you change?'

'In our bedroom.'

'I see. How far is your bedroom from the nursery, where your wife was supposedly feeding the child?'

'Two rooms along the landing. Ten yards, I sup-pose, or a little more.'

'Did you hear any noises from the nursery?'

'Noises?' Ralph pondered. 'No, I don't think so... I probably heard the nursery door open when Lidya came, and her steps on the carpet.'

Mr Clutterbuck looked sharply at him. 'Your wife came from the nursery to the bedroom where you were changing?'

'Yes. Before she started the feed.'

'I see... Do you know why she came?'

'I can't remember... Oh, yes. To fetch a woolly.'

Jane groaned, and Mr Clutterbuck smiled very briefly. 'A woollen garment?'

'Yes.'

'What garment?'

'A jacket.'

'Describe it, please.'

'I'm not sure. Grey-green.'

'Knitted?'

'Yes. Floppy. I think it's mohair.'

'Thank you.' Mr Clutterbuck paused again, gripping the rail in front of him, and for a moment seemed lost in thought. He looked hard at Ralph and smiled grimly. 'No more questions.' He sat down.

Mr Irwin glanced towards the judge, then stood to re-examine.

'Mr Slade.'

'Yes.'

'Where was your wife educated?'

'At a Catholic convent in Addis Ababa, then sixth form at Cheltenham Ladies College. She has a degree in Agricultural Development from the University of Addis Ababa.'

'Thank you. Now, I believe that your wife's mother has been dead for some years. Has your father-in-law been supportive of your marriage?'

'Very.'

'And he wants his daughter to have children?'

Ralph smiled. 'Oh yes.'

'Is your wife close to her father?'

Ralph glanced down at Lidya, and a fleeting smile passed between them. 'Yes, they have a strong bond.'

'It's nonsense to suggest that your wife wanted to avoid having children?'

'Complete nonsense.'

Mr Irwin nodded and paused. 'This mohair jacket. Would I be right in thinking that it was intended for evening wear?'

'I think so, yes.'

'And was your wife in fact wearing it when you both left the house?'

'Yes, she was.'

Useful point, thought Jane, keep it up man.

'Thank you,' said Mr Irwin. 'No more questions.' Ralph looked uncertain for a moment, then left the witness box and walked back to his seat. He sat down and mopped his brow again.

The Higher Court Advocate had risen.

'Yes, Mr Clutterbuck?' said the judge.

'Your honour, the mohair jacket being a new development, I should like to recall Dr Jones.'

'Is he in court?'

'I imagine not. We may need to reserve a little time on Monday morning.'

'Very well.'

*

On the Friday, George and the statistics expert, Jim Matthews, had met Mr Cormack, Frank Irwin and Irwin's junior in the court cafeteria during the lunch recess. As George reported to Jane and Tom that evening, he had argued vigorously the need to rebut Sir Ambrose's statistics, and thought that Jim had made a good impression. The defence team had seemed reasonably welcoming, but said they needed time to consider strategy. They were apparently still debating how to handle Lidya's own evidence, due first thing on Monday.

On Saturday morning Irwin called George back. He still hadn't made up his mind, but seemed afraid that raising statistics again might be a mistake—he felt the better tactic might be to draw the jury's attention away from the issue of probabilities. George countered that the prosecution was sure to make a big play with the odds of four million to one in their final speech, and it was essential to have statistical ammunition available.

Irwin dithered until the Sunday evening, when he rang back again and agreed without much enthusiasm that Jim must be called. He would try to fix this with the court early on Monday.

*

Jane had known for some time that Lidya's evidence would begin on the Monday morning, and she made arrangements in good time to be there, hoping that it wouldn't run on into the afternoon, when she had an unavoidable ward conference.

Proceedings opened with the recall of Dr Jones for the prosecution.

'You remain under oath, Dr Jones,' remarked the judge.

The witness nodded, and Mr Clutterbuck rose to his feet. 'Dr Jones,' he said. 'You told us earlier that the infant Ayana Slade could have been smothered with a soft object. Could you please confirm to the court that it would have been possible to smother her with a woollen cardigan?'

'Smothering of a small child is most often attempted with a pillow or cushion, or some sort of dense pad, or even with the bare hands. But I see no reason why a woollen cardigan would not be effective.'

'And you also told the court that such an attack might be successfully completed within ten minutes. The use of a cardigan would not affect this estimate?'

Dr Jones thought for a moment. 'As I explained before,' he said 'my estimate cannot be regarded as precise. But I don't see why employing a cardigan should affect it.'

Mr Clutterbuck nodded. 'No more questions.'

Mr Irwin rose and then stooped, raised a John Lewis carrier bag and extracted from it something floppy and olive green.

'This is the garment concerned, your honour,' he said.

'Admitted?' asked the judge.

'First time we've seen it,' said Mr Clutterbuck.

Mr Irwin solemnly handed the cardigan over for inspection.

'Do you wish to take evidence of identity, Mr Clutterbuck?' It seemed obvious that the judge wanted to hurry on.

'No, your honour. Admitted.' The green mass was handed back.

'Thank you,' said the judge. 'Mr Irwin.'

'Dr Jones, did you find any fibres of green wool in Ayana Slade's airways?'

'No.'

'Definitely not?'

'Definitely.'

'Would you please examine the garment?' requested Mr Irwin and carried it over to the witness.

Dr Jones looked puzzled, but did as requested.

'You will see that this mohair jacket is knitted using an extremely loose stitch. Does this affect your conclusions in any way?'

Dr Jones hesitated. 'In my experience, as I said, soft pads of various descriptions have been employed, but I cannot recall a case in which a very loosely knitted garment was used. Infant lungs are not very strong… In my opinion, it would still be possible to use such a garment, but it might take longer, and greater pressure.'

'How much longer?'

Dr Jones puckered his brow, and turned towards the judge. 'It's really not possible to quote a time in minutes.'

'Thank you. No more questions.' Mr Irwin returned the cardigan to its carrier bag and placed it on the exhibit table with the baby alarm.

Lidya

'We now continue with the defence evidence,' re-marked the judge. 'Mr Irwin.'

The defence barrister ran one hand over his hair, then selected and opened a new folder. 'I call my client to give evidence on her own behalf,' he said.

Lidya stood up. The Clerk bustled forward and showed her not to the witness box but to the dock. He opened the little gate and stood back. She stepped inside and stood facing the judge, her hands on the brass rail; Jane had a clear view of her face.

The clerk asked whether she was content to swear on the Bible.

'Yes, I am a Christian,' said Lidya, and pronounced the words as instructed, clearly and firmly. A tiny rustle ran around the court.

Mr Irwin looked up. 'Mrs Slade,' he began, 'in his evidence, your husband mentioned that you were schooled partly in England.'

Lidya looked a little puzzled. 'Yes,' she said. 'I was in the sixth form at Cheltenham Ladies' College.'

'How was that financed?'

'My father paid.'

'You didn't feel at any disadvantage compared to the other students?'

'No.'

'Not financially?'

Lidya smiled. 'He gave me an allowance. Not

152

wildly generous, but enough.'

'Nor academically?'

'No. I had good grades, and our School Certificate is a better preparation for sixth form work than GCSE.'

'You made good friends at Cheltenham?'

'Yes.'

'And indeed we heard earlier from one of them.' He glanced at the jury to be sure they'd made the connection. 'Did you find there was a large cultural gap?'

'It was narrower than my friends in England seemed to expect. Addis Ababa is very cosmopolitan, and I'd been at an English-speaking school.'

'Why didn't you take your degree at a British university?'

'I wanted to contribute to the agricultural development of my own country, and the course at home was best for that.'

'That was before you met your husband?'

'Yes.' Lidya glanced down briefly at Ralph, and he smiled back encouragingly.

'Would you say that your attitude to family and children is different from those of English girls you know?'

'Not really. I may have been more certain than some of them that I wanted to marry and have children.'

'Were you confident of being able to cope as a mother in a foreign country?'

'Yes, on the whole.'

'You had a few doubts?'

'I was a long way from family support. But I'd cared for my own brothers and sisters after my mother's death, and I have a very supportive husband. And I thought the medical services would be better here.'

'After Gabriel died, you had a breakdown?'

'Yes. It took me a long time to come to terms with his death.'

'Can you tell the court why?'

Lidya gripped the rail in front of her. 'Why it took me so long?'

'Yes.'

'Because Gabriel had been the culmination of everything we'd hoped for, and he was snatched away from us out of the blue... And because he was such a darling... What else can I say?'

'You loved him?'

'Of course I loved him!' Her knuckles were pale on the rail.

'And later, before Ayana was born, did you feel you were completely recovered?'

'Not from the grief, no. But I'd got my strength back. We were determined. Both of us.'

'Determined not to be beaten?'

'Yes.'

'After Ayana was born, did you enjoy showing her to people?'

Lidya raised her eyebrows. 'Of course!'

'To your own family?'

'They couldn't come.'

'So your father never saw her?'

'No.'

'But I believe that Ayana sent him a letter.' Mr Irwin was smiling.

Lidya nodded. 'With a little help from me.'

'And he very kindly posted it back to us: I have it here. It is written in Amharic, but perhaps you could translate it for the court.' Mr Irwin carried a lavender envelope over to the dock and extracted a sheet of matching notepaper.

Lidya glanced down at it, and the corner of her mouth lifted. 'I'll give a rough translation,' she said. 'Dear *Âyaat*... that's grandparent... I wish to tell you how happy Mummy and Daddy are to be watching over me in my cradle, seeing how healthy I am and how angelically I sleep, with my heart-shaped face. Most of the time though, *Âyaat,* I stay awake to bother them, I'm afraid. I am looking forward to meeting you next month, and sure you will wish to kiss a grand-daughter as beautiful and delicate as I am. With love from your dutiful *Ayana.*' Lidya smiled again, and leant forward to return the paper, with a slight tremor, to Mr Irwin. He carried it back to his seat.

Corny, thought Jane. But effective.

'Mrs Slade,' said Mr Irwin, 'how did you react to the death of your second child?'

Lidya screwed up her eyes and blinked once. 'At the time?'

'Yes, and later.'

'At the time, I collapsed. Later, I felt complete disbelief. How could it happen to me a second time? I was numb... But I wasn't depressed in the same way as after Gabriel. Perhaps my brain knew I knew I was going to need strength.'

'In facing the investigation?'

'Yes.'

'Mrs Slade, I'm going to ask you a very stark question. Did you murder your baby Ayana?'

Lidya took a deep breath. 'No, I did not.'

'Did you harm her in any way?'

'No, no. Of course not.'

Mr Irwin glanced a little anxiously at the jury. 'No further questions,' he said, and sat down.

*

155

Mr Clutterbuck rose very slowly to his feet and settled his gaze firmly on Lidya's face for some seconds. She returned it without flinching. At last he said suddenly:

'In spite of all the talk we've heard of preparation, your pregnancies were *not* planned, were they?'

Lidya hesitated.

'Were they?'

'It depends what you mean.'

'What people usually mean.' Mr Clutterbuck smirked. 'It came as a shock to find, in the common parlance, a bun in the oven?'

Ralph's head jerked back. After a moment's blankness Lidya looked furious.

'They weren't planned, were they?'

'We were preparing for having a baby,' said Lidya slowly. 'It is true I got pregnant earlier than we'd intended.'

'Someone forgot to take precautions?'

'No.'

'Then how come it happened? Disagreement about intentions?'

'Certainly not.'

'You are a remarkably beautiful woman, Mrs Slade.'

Lidya set her jaw but said nothing.

'But you *are*, the jury is aware of it. And pregnancy would spoil that elegant figure, would it not? What a degradation.'

'Pregnancy isn't ugly.'

'Oh but it is. Here you were, a sophisticated young woman, escaped at last from a restrictive society. The last things you wanted were stretch marks and sag, weren't they?'

'Don't be ridiculous.'

'I'm not being ridiculous, Mrs Slade. This is a murder trial. If you wanted the court to believe these were desired children, I wonder why haven't you shown us a little more feeling about them?'

'Feeling?'

'Your evidence has been entirely dry-eyed.'

'I don't produce tears to order.'

'And as well as the lack of tears, I must point out to the jury the clear evidence that you were laying your plans, weren't you, as soon as you realised you were pregnant? *Why did you start the CONI programme so late?*'

'The CONI programme?'

'The Care of Next Infant programme. The special programme, members of the jury, provided by the NHS to all pregnant mothers who have already lost one baby... *Why did you start it so late?*'

Now Lidya was blinking. 'We asked Dr Mayhew as soon as we heard about it.'

'You started it *only two weeks before the baby was due*. You didn't lift a *finger* earlier, did you?'

'We hadn't heard of it.'

'Come, come, you can't expect the court to believe *that* of two such intelligent and well-informed parents. You *deliberately* started the programme late, didn't you?'

'No.'

'So that it would seem natural that the apnoea alarm didn't arrive until *after* Ayana had been suffocated.'

'She wasn't suffocated.'

'How can you say that with so much confidence?'

'Because no one besides me had the opportunity, and I know I didn't.'

'So you accept that no one else could have done it?'

Lidya hesitated. 'That's how it seems to me.'

'You admit that?'

'No one else had opportunity, so far as I can see.'

'Opportunity to suffocate Ayana?'

'That's what I meant.'

'So it must have been you?'

'She *wasn't* suffocated, Mr Clutterbuck.' Lidya's voice had become huskier, and Mr Clutterbuck smiled slowly.

'So you say, Mrs Slade. Now, your counsel suggested earlier it was unbelievable you would have selected the time that you did for the smothering, because there were so many people in the house who might have caught you in the act. And Inspector Tallis seemed to agree with him. But you and I know better, don't we?'

Lidya's mouth tightened and she said nothing.

'Because you needed to create an alibi, didn't you, Mrs Slade? That dinner party was the only way you could organise to be away from your baby, wasn't it? Before the apnoea alarm arrived... Was that luck, I wonder? When did Dr Said invite you?' Mr Clutterbuck had a deceptively benign air.

Lidya swallowed. 'He didn't invite us. Not exactly.'

Mr Clutterbuck smiled. 'Precisely, Mrs Slade. I believe your husband suggested it to him.'

'The two of them got talking, they thought it would be nice for me.'

'*After* you'd suggested it to your husband.'

'I just said it would be nice to get out.'

'To get away from your new-born and vulnerable baby, not yet a fortnight old?'

Lidya flinched. 'Don't you realise?' she said quietly. 'We've been tormenting ourselves with that

158

decision over and over.'

'But you didn't torment yourself much at the time, did you? Why didn't you take this very young infant with you to the dinner party, Mrs Slade? Did you have a carry cot?'

'Yes.'

'But chose not to use it, as any sensible parent would have done?'

'I was trying to establish her sleep pattern.'

'At a fortnight old? No, it was because your plan required it. And the baby alarm—your plan required a baby alarm, too, didn't it?'

'I don't know what you mean.'

'You had to have an alarm set up so you could plausibly instruct the baby sitters not to look at Ayana until some time had passed… *When did you buy it?*'

Lidya looked puzzled and considered. 'Two months before Ayana arrived. When we re-equipped the nursery.'

'And why did you do that? You already had a perfectly good alarm.'

'I wanted to be sure everything was a hundred percent reliable.'

'But more to the point, you needed one with a volume control, didn't you?'

Lidya looked confused.

'Obvious, isn't it? So that the volume could be turned right down when the baby sitters were there—that way the alarm couldn't be used to prove Ayana was dead when you left the house.'

'Is that the knob in the base? We never altered it.'

'You mean to tell the court that you had your alarm set in such a way that you couldn't hear your baby breathing?'

'It was set so we could hear when she cried.'

159

'Why not louder?'

'We never changed the setting. I wasn't even sure what the knob was for.'

'Didn't you ask the nurse visitor how best to use the alarm?'

'I don't think so.'

'Why ever not?

'Why should we? It was working all right.'

Mr Clutterbuck looked towards the jury and raised his eyebrows. 'Now Mrs Slade, your husband has told us you fetched a green mohair jacket from the bedroom. Is that correct?'

'Yes.'

'Exactly *when* did you fetch it?'

'Before the feed.'

'You didn't wear it during the feed?'

'No, it would have been in the way.'

'And you weren't planning to change for dinner in the nursery?'

'No.'

'So I think the court will be curious, Mrs Slade, to know why you took the jacket into the nursery at all... *Why did you?*'

'Why? I'm not sure... I may have been thinking of putting it round my shoulders, and then realised that wasn't a good idea.'

'I put it to you that your real reason was quite different.'

'I don't understand.'

'You had planned to smother Ayana with it.'

'No!' Her voice cracked.

'You needed something soft, didn't you, that could be removed from the nursery without suspicion and would remain under your control, so that if necessary it could be washed later to remove any traces of vomit

160

or blood.'

'That's a wicked suggestion.'

'But it's what you actually did.' Once again Mr Clutterbuck gazed for some seconds at Lidya. She looked down and up again.

'*Say no*, for God's sake!' muttered Jane to herself. But Lidya was waiting for the next question.

Mr Clutterbuck smiled. 'You did, didn't you?' he said.

'*No!*' Lidya looked desperately towards Ralph.

'And what caused the abrasion to Ayana's chin, Mrs Slade? Was that your finger nails?'

'There never was an abrasion!'

'*Really*? I remind you that all three pathologists have described the abrasion to the court in some detail... Did your hands slip? While you were pressing down on your baby's face?'

'I saw Ayana's face for a moment at the hospital. There was no abrasion then.'

'It's your word against those of three professionals, Mrs Slade, I'm afraid... Now, let me turn to your aunt in Ethiopia, who lost three babies, or so you said. How large was her family?'

'How large? She had four others before.'

'So it would be natural to use an abortionist.'

'Not my aunt! Never.'

'Or perhaps, in your society, infanticide would have been more traditional?'

Lidya suddenly folded her arms. 'Mr Clutterbuck,' she said. 'You speak as though you regarded my family as devoid of morals.' Her voice was shaking. 'If there is some deficit of civilisation in this court, it surely, *surely* lies with you and your foul insinuations!'

Mr Irwin was on his feet, violently shaking his head at Lidya. She looked at him and took several deep breaths, grasping the rail. After a few seconds, she turned to face the next question.

'*Would* infanticide have been more traditional?' persisted Mr Clutterbuck.

Lidya threw her head back with a look of absolute contempt, and said nothing.

The prosecutor turned towards the judicial chair.

The judge cleared her throat. 'You must answer the question,' she said, her face impassive.

Lidya turned furiously to Mr Clutterbuck. 'Of course not,' she said. 'I come from a Christian family. We have absolutely no tradition of murdering our children.'

'So how come you murdered at least one of your own?'

'I didn't.'

'How did it feel, pressing down on that innocent little face?'

Lidya stiffened. Her hands flew to her face. She seemed fighting to recover her poise.

'How exactly did it feel? Having to bear down on that tiny face for so very long?'

She was upright again. 'I never did anything of the sort.'

'Oh but you did... How could you steel yourself to be so hard-hearted? Did the little one fight back? Was she wriggling? Banging you with her tiny hands?'

Lidya blinked. 'No!'

'She died quite passively, then?'

'She didn't die at all. Not while I was with her.'

'So you say. But the truth is, you smothered Ayana because you needed her out of the way?'

'No! Never!'

Mr Clutterbuck looked thoughtfully at Lidya for

some seconds. Then he looked up to the jury and smiled gently.

'Thank you, Mrs Slade,' he said. 'No more questions.'

*

The judge nodded to Mr Irwin, who rose again. He was smiling at the jury, but Jane sensed he was less confident than appeared. He turned towards Lidya, who was still standing rigidly with her hands on the brass rail.

'Mrs Slade,' he said, 'let us deal quickly with the molehills that my learned friend has been so industriously magnifying into mountains. This dinner party with Dr Said: it was never part of some dastardly plot on your part, was it?'

'Of course not.'

'You never angled for an invitation?'

'No. All I did was say to Ralph sometime it would be nice to get out.'

'And that was all. You didn't select the date?'

'No.'

'Do you know how the date was chosen?'

'I believe Raja suggested it.'

'And you left your baby behind simply because you were trying to establish her sleep routine?'

'Yes.'

'Thank you. Now, the CONI programme. You started it two weeks before Ayana arrived. When did your GP first tell you about it?'

'She didn't. We heard about it from the midwife.'

'When?'

'The middle of December.'

'And you actually started the programme at the end

of December?'

'Yes.'

'And before the midwife told you, you'd never heard of such a thing?'

'No.'

'You couldn't press for something you'd never heard of?'

'Of course we couldn't.'

Mr Irwin nodded. 'And this baby alarm. You chose to buy a new one. That was because you wanted something more reliable, you said?'

'Yes.'

'You used the old one with Gabriel?'

'That's right.'

'So what was wrong with it?

'It didn't always work properly when the receiver was a long way from the nursery.'

'Making it untrustworthy?'

'Yes.'

'Thank you. Next, my learned friend's suggestion that you feared pregnancy would damage your good looks. Did this ever cross your mind?'

Lidya smiled. 'Not in any serious way. My looks weren't the first consideration.'

Mr Irwin returned the smile. 'And the court can see no damage was done,' he said gallantly. Lidya pursed her lips and did not reply. The young juror in the tank top was grinning appreciatively.

'Now, your background. After your mother died you had to care for your younger brothers and sisters. How old were you then?'

'Thirteen.'

'How many of them?'

'Three sisters and one brother.'

'What did you have to do?'

'Organise things. We had plenty of help in the house.'

'Plan purchases, make arrangements?'

'Yes.'

'Did you have to be motherly, to comfort your siblings sometimes?'

'Oh yes. Especially Zeina, when she was ill. No need to comfort Davit, he kept us laughing through the bad times.'

'Do any of your sisters have children?'

'Desta and Makeda do. I can't get to see them very often, but I send presents. When we can visit, the children are always all over us.'

'So it's nonsense to suggest you hate kids?'

Lidya smiled. 'Of course.'

'How well do you know your aunt, who lost so many babies?'

'Very well. We're close. She was my mother's favourite sister.'

'And it's ridiculous to suggest that she would ever choose an abortion, let alone kill one of her own children?'

'Completely ridiculous. She's tough, a marvellous mother.'

'A practical, sensible country woman?'

'Yes. She still herds goats in the Amhara.'

'Thank you. Now the last of these molehills—the green jacket. Why did you fetch it from the bedroom? Perhaps simply because you felt cold?'

'Yes. It was January. I'd just been out in the garden.'

'Why?'

'To throw dead flowers on the dump.'

'And perhaps you were expecting the car trip to be cold, too?'

165

'Yes, I think so.'

'So there's a natural and completely innocent explanation for fetching it from the bedroom?' Mr Irwin was looking not at Lidya but the jury.

'Yes, of course.'

'Finally, Mrs Slade, may we return to the abrasion on Ayana's chin? Dr Jones in his evidence suggested that it might have been caused by the paramedic team before Ayana reached the hospital—but you said just now it wasn't there when you saw her in A&E?'

'That's what I thought.'

'How well could you see her?'

'Not very. But well enough to see the colour of her face.'

'At that point, weren't you particularly stressed? You collapsed soon afterwards?'

'Yes.'

'Could you have been mistaken?'

'I don't think so. Perhaps, if the abrasion wasn't very obvious at that stage.'

Mr Irwin paused and thought for a second or two. 'No more questions,' he said at last.

Lidya blinked and steadied herself on the rail. The clerk hurried forward and opened the gate. She stepped slowly down out of the dock and walked quietly back to the seat beside her husband. As she sat down, Ralph took her nearest hand in both of his, and after a moment she rested her head against his shoulder.

Jane was suddenly aware she'd been sitting bolt upright for the last hour, her hands so tightly clasped in her lap that they prickled as she released them.

'Mr Irwin?' said the judge.

'It might be easiest to take my next witness after lunch, your honour.'

The judge looked down at Lidya, who raised her head again as though it cost her an effort. Jane could see that Lidya's face, which during her evidence had been tense but animated and at times expressive, was now disturbingly drawn and rigid.

'I think so too,' said the judge. 'Adjourned until two o'clock.'

Reaction

During the afternoon, Jane was back at the hospital desperately catching up on hours missed, but both Andy Arbuckle and George were in court. The support committee was to meet at Igor's at seven to compare notes.

Igor opened the front door when Jane arrived. The kitchen was hot, but rose-scents were wafting in through the open back door and out again by the big side window. Alice was stirring a two-handled iron pot on her Aga, while Dr Said sat head-in-hands at the table. Andy Arbuckle in a lumberjack shirt was perched on a high stool. He grinned at Jane.

'Hi, everyone,' she said, and dumped her medical bag. 'Why so gloomy, Raja?'

The corners of Dr Said's mouth turned down.

'Your statistician,' said Igor.

Mine? she thought, heart sinking. 'What happened?'

'Wait till George comes,' said Igor. 'He'll know better what to think.'

Jane puckered her lips and found a chair, rubbing tired hands over her face.

'Andy thought Lidya did well this morning,' said Igor.

'It was bloody horrible!' said Jane. 'That vicious pompous little man.'

Andy laughed. 'He's just your average one-star prosecuting sheriff,' he said. 'She stood up OK.'

Jane looked at Andy. 'That was the *norm*?'

'Bog standard. Doing his job.'

'Gratuitous licensed torture!'

'Not gratuitous.'

'What did he hope to gain?'

'Come on!' said Andy. 'He thinks she's guilty.'

'I'm sure he doesn't.'

'Well *professionally*, he's got to think she is. If he can break her, force an admission, he's home and dry, isn't he?'

'Well, he didn't succeed.'

'No, he didn't. She stood up well.'

'So all that excruciating strappado went to waste,' said Jane.

'Not altogether.'

'What d'you mean?'

'Think about it. Maybe this jury weren't inclined to take the charge seriously. Then here comes this heavyweight establishment feller, telling 'em in full film-noir detail how this classy black woman smothers her innocent babe. Over and over. Tiny innocent hands pawing the air... So even if he hasn't bullied her into admitting anything, he's still planted all these evil thoughts in the jury's heads, hasn't he?'

Raja looked up. 'Brainwashing,' he said.

'You got it,' said Andy.

Jane said nothing.

Igor said, 'Andy said she shouted at Clutterbuck.'

'She did,' said Jane. 'Only bright spot in a bad day.'

'Dangerous, though,' said Andy.

'Why?'

'Witness needs to stay cool. See Irwin trying to slow her down?'

'But she kept her head!'

'Yes. Luckily.'

There was a pause. 'I gather the pathologist didn't add much,' said Igor at last.

'About the green jacket? No,' said Jane.

The doorbell rang. Alice, slammed the lid onto her pot, and ran into the hall. They could hear George's voice, asking whether he could leave two bags there, telling Alice to be careful with his laptop. She led him into the kitchen. 'Shall I serve the soup?' she asked.

'Please,' said Igor. 'Thank you, darling.'

*

Jane noticed that George was keeping his head down and scowling over his scotch broth. No one spoke, and at last Igor opened a bottle of Chardonnay from the fridge, found and filled some glasses, and passed them around. At last George was mopping his soup plate with a large chunk of granary bread.

'Before you all get going again,' said Alice, 'Anyone object to a few strawberries?' Nobody did and the helpings were generous, but Jane had demolished hers before George had even finished sugaring his and dolloping cream over them.

'*Right*,' said Igor.

George started on his helping, one berry at a time. 'Bit of a disaster,' he said at last.

'What I reckoned,' said Andy.

'What happened?' asked Jane.

'I have to admit,' said George, between mouthfuls, 'young Jim acquitted himself quite well, when you think about it.'

'What went wrong, then?'

'Advocacy.' He looked up and blew out his cheeks comically. 'Irwin contrived to make our new evidence sound bloody technical, and sent the jury to sleep. Jim answered all the questions rather well, but nobody was listening.'

'Damn,' said Igor.

'Damn indeed.'

'Did they manage to bring out how wrong Sir Ambrose had been?' asked Jane.

'*Technically*, yes they did. Plenty of good stuff about *a priori* and *a posteriori* probabilities, modified samples, susceptible families and all that.'

'So did Clutterbuck try to destroy Jim's credibility?'

'No, he didn't. To my surprise… Maybe he realised how young and inexperienced Jim looked compared to Sir Ambrose, and left it to the jury to make the comparison for themselves… Clever really. More effective than trying to trip him up. You have to remember Clutterbuck knows no more statistics than I do, and trying to catch Jim out could easily have taken a wrong turning.'

'So what questions *did* he ask?' said Dr Said, rubbing his chin.

'Stuck to the make-or-break issue,' said George. '"Can I get this clear, Dr Matthews? Sir Ambrose says one in four million. But just now, after a very involved argument that I didn't pretend to follow, you concluded the key probability was more like one in forty thousand. It might even have been as low as one in ten thousand?" And Jim had to agree. So Clutterbuck persists: "Right. So you've come down from Sir Ambrose's figure, but you're *still* telling the court the probability of having two babies dying by natural cot death in the same family chosen at random is as tiny as one in ten thousand—*one in ten thousand*—and could be even tinier?" Jim tries to comment on the figure, but Clutterbuck won't let him: "I'm sorry,

Dr Matthews—*did* you draw that conclusion, yes or no?" Again Jim has to agree. So Mr Clutterbuck says loudly to no-one in particular: "But one in ten thousand is still a *tiny* probability, isn't it? *Minuscule*," and smiles triumphantly at the jury. "No more questions, Dr Matthews," he says, and sits down quickly.'

'But, but, but,' spluttered Igor angrily. 'They *aren't* a family chosen at random! If, as we believe, they're a susceptible family, *then*, on Jim's latest figures, *for them* the probability of one death could be as high as one in three, and the probability of two deaths as high as one in nine. Didn't Irwin bring *that* out when he re-examined?'

'He didn't re-examine,' said George sombrely. Andy nodded vigorous confirmation.

'What?' exploded Jane, leaning forward and banging down her spoon.

'Probably not confident enough of asking the right questions,' said George. 'I got the impression when we talked that Irwin was having trouble following. To be honest, so was I, at times.'

'But Clutterbuck's going to make hay with that one-in-ten-thousand figure in his final speech, isn't he?' said Igor, looking grim.

'Of course,' said George. 'Afraid so,'

'So we made things worse,' said Dr Said.

George frowned. 'Not actually worse,' he said. 'We got the figure for the jury down from one in four million to one in ten thousand. The trouble is they know only too well that ten thousand to one is still a racing certainty.'

'Are the final speeches tomorrow?' asked Igor.

'Tomorrow morning,' said George.

'There's a guy I know on the Observer,' said Andy,

'who might do us a piece… But that's not going to affect the verdict in this trial, is it?'

*

Next morning, having fixed proper leave of absence, Jane was expecting her trip to Exeter on the Tuesday would be decently relaxed. But the summer weather broke, and she had to drive through a thunderstorm, finding the A38 flooded and jammed at Buckfastleigh. She was evidently not the only person delayed: proceedings had still not started when she wriggled her way, damp and anxious, to her usual place in the court gallery.

The courtroom was fuller than it had been the previous week: she could see Andy in the press benches, squashed against a burly neighbour, his pad jammed down on one knee. Irwin was deep in conversation with Ralph and Lidya. He *must* have made up his mind by now what to put into his speech, Jane thought—what *can* they be discussing? Lidya was immaculately dressed, as ever, and seemed animated. She was smiling at Irwin, to Jane's annoyance. On the prosecution bench, Clutterbuck was leafing slowly through some notes, interrupted at one point by his junior. He nodded stony agreement to whatever it was she had to say.

The court usher appeared through a door in the wall facing Jane, like a rabbit from its burrow, and intoned: 'All rise!' The judge made her usual sweeping entry, files in hand, and settled into her grand chair; the courtroom subsided. She looked up and tapped her pencil. Hush descended.

'Members of the jury,' she announced, 'you are now to hear final speeches, for the prosecution first, and then the defence. I hope we can complete them this morning. After that I shall myself sum up the case, and then invite you to withdraw, to consider your verdict.' She looked sharply towards the jury, and one or two of them nodded as if anxious to prove they'd been listening and understood. She turned towards the lawyers' bench. 'Mr Clutterbuck, if you please.'

The prosecutor lumbered to his feet, his hands clutching his jacket lapels. Nervous, Jane thought. Then she realised that Mr Clutterbuck was holding no files, and her heart sank: his speech had clearly been thoroughly prepared and memorised.

'Members of the jury,' he began silkily, 'this is inevitably a highly emotional case, but I must beg you at the outset to clear your minds of feeling, to consider the evidence calmly and carefully... ' His oily voice droned on, moving with the single-minded purpose of a steamroller over the most damning parts of the evidence—Sir Ambrose's analysis of the physical signs that Ayana had been strangled; the baby alarm; the mohair jacket.

Jane had been watching Lidya and Ralph, and found herself quite unable to concentrate on what Mr Clutterbuck was saying. Ralph looked anxious, but Lidya's face had gradually become more rigid, her lips a little tighter, her glistening eyes turned up, as though, Jane felt suddenly, the fly had at last understood the purpose of the spider's web.

Then Mr Clutterbuck referred to Lidya's coldness as a mother. It jerked Jane back to the proceedings: *how* could he bring that in?—there'd been no evidence presented! He *had* brought it in, however: when he did so, Ralph had glanced uneasily at Lidya, whose eyes had narrowed. Though she gave no other sign of distress, Jane felt sure she must by now be feeling something like invading hands clutching at her heart. Irwin, on the other hand, wore an artificial smile as his fingers drummed on the bench. And, remembered Jane, Clutterbuck still hadn't reached his strongest argument—those awful probabilities were still to come. She felt suddenly sick. He'd be sure to use them as his thunderous, clinching point.

She was staring blindly at the door the court usher had entered by, when it slowly opened, and what looked like a very junior receptionist slipped into court, apparently trying to be as inconspicuous as possible. She beckoned the usher, who crept over to speak to her; Jane could see both heads nodding. Mr Clutterbuck droned on. With pantomime discretion, the usher made his way over to the Clerk's desk. The usher was using persuasive gestures, the Clerk's face remained impassive. At last the Clerk nodded, drew a piece of paper towards himself, and started to write what seemed to be a lengthy note. The usher returned to his seat, and the Clerk finished his writing, stood up, walked firmly over to the judicial chair, and handed the note up to the judge.

Mr Clutterbuck stopped in midstream, obviously annoyed. The judge read the note, and re-read it. She looked down at the Clerk, her head slightly on one side, smiling a little grimly. The Clerk waited expectantly.

The judge turned to the prosecutor. 'Mr Clutterbuck,' she said. 'I'm extremely sorry to interrupt you in full flow. An unusual situation has arisen. Most unusual. I fear an adjournment is necessary. Would you be so good as to attend me in my chambers immediately?'

'Of course,' said Mr Clutterbuck, without enthusiasm. His face was reddening, and he abruptly took out a handkerchief and mopped his brow.

The judge looked towards the Clerk again, and said, 'We may perhaps be able to reconvene by two o'clock, but not earlier.' She rose and left the court by her own door.

'All rise!' shouted the usher, a little late. Everyone stood. The lawyers bent to gather up their files. Lidya slumped down onto her seat, as Ralph muttered to her and looked frantically around. Mr Clutterbuck spoke to no one and briskly left court by the door that the secretary and the usher had used. A buzz of talk welled up, and in the confusion Jane saw a dark figure enter the courtroom from below the gallery. The man walked forward deliberately, and followed Mr Clutterbuck through the same door, which closed firmly behind him. It took her a moment to register that it was Tom.

Indiscretion

After a moment's pause there was a buzz of chatter in court. Ralph rose and walked over to the defence bench, but Irwin, looking irritated, seemed to brush him away. Lidya remained seated, her face turned up towards them. As Jane watched, George threaded his way through the throng towards the little group.

She hurried down from the gallery. There were no court ushers controlling movement, and she pressed forward onto the floor of the court. Lidya and Ralph had disappeared but she was in time to catch George.

'Hullo,' he said. 'Did I see Tom rushing through?'

'What's happening?'

'We're not being told, are we? But whatever it is, the judge isn't talking to the defence about it. Did you see Irwin looking daggers at Clutterbuck?'

'Can you guess?'

'Tom must have got something.'

Jane felt a wave of irritation. She'd known for some days there was something he was keeping to himself. George was watching her. 'Cheer up,' he said. 'We'll hear soon enough.'

Not much reassured, and unable to return for the afternoon session, she set off for the car park.

*

The judge's chambers, new territory for Tom, were under the castle eaves. He knocked cautiously.

'Come,' said a voice.

He entered, and realised that the room was high enough for a good view of the Exe, gleaming distantly beneath the haze to the south-east. The judge was standing facing him, without her wig; her white hair made her seem older. Sandy Clutterbuck was sitting in a comfortable wing chair in the window, his legs stretched out over a red Baluchistan rug.

'Chief Inspector!' said the judge.

Tom came forward to shake hands. She gave him a brisk smile, walked over to the panelled wall, and peered into a small cupboard, within which he could see a sherry bottle and glasses. Then she seemed to think better of it, turned back to her desk, and pressed a button on the panel to the right of the knee-hole. Tom settled himself on an upright chair with a needle-point padded seat and nodded to Clutterbuck.

There was a knock on the door. 'Come!' said the judge again, and a woman in severe charcoal entered and closed the door behind her.

'Thank you, Alice,' said the judge, still standing. 'Can you do us coffee and biscuits, please? A cafetière, please, we may be some time.'

'Adjourned?' asked the woman.

'Yes.'

'You'll still be taking lunch here?'

'Yes.'

Alice disappeared, and the judge settled into her desk chair.

Clutterbuck looked up. 'What's this all about, Mrs Stratford?' he asked.

'That, I think, is what we must ask Inspector Tallis,' she said. 'I understand he has something both crucial and confidential to tell us.' She looked at Tom over the top of her glasses. 'What have you to say for yourself

Inspector?'

Tom cleared his throat. 'I don't know whether either of you have any experience of working with the security services?' he asked.

Sandy nodded slowly, as though beginning to understand the nature of the problem. The judge simply waited.

'I don't want to make a fuss,' said Tom. 'But it really is important to keep this conversation confidential. I assume we can't be overheard?'

The judge raised her eyebrows. 'Alice is two rooms away.'

'You don't by any chance tape your conversations?'

'Certainly not!'

Tom thought for a moment. 'Officially,' he said, 'I'm not at liberty to tell you this. But the fact is, MI5 have been interested for some time in Mrs Slade's husband, Ralph. At one point they suspected he might be a terrorist.'

'Indeed!' said Mr Clutterbuck.

'My colleagues and I think he's innocent.'

'But MI5 disagree?'

'They have done, in the past. Currently, their judgement coincides with ours. But they haven't lost interest.'

'Ah,' said the judge.

'At the end of last year, in the course of their investigation, they bugged the Slades' house. I don't know how much of it they covered, but I do know they installed a device in the nursery.'

'Really!' said Clutterbuck. 'Where?'

'On the underside of the basket crib,' said Tom. 'Naturally, we've been trying since Mrs Slade was arrested to find out whether the bug recorded anything on the night of Ayana's death. But MI5 wouldn't

179

say. They wouldn't even let us tell you it was there.'

The judge pursed her lips and nodded. 'Terrorism Act 2000?' she asked.

'Yes. I was told I'd be prosecuted under the Official Secrets Act if I revealed anything.'

'I see,' said the judge. 'Natural justice required you to speak out, but by telling us now, you're putting yourself in jeopardy?'

'I'm afraid that is so.'

The judge looked thoughtfully at Tom. 'How far up the security chain was this decision taken?'

'I was told the very top.'

'Oh dear... So we're stuck?'

'Not entirely,' said Tom. 'I've an old friend recently retired from GCHQ, which is where the recordings are kept.'

'Ah,' said Clutterbuck.

'Fortunately, he agreed with me that justice wasn't being served, and agreed to help. About a week ago he discovered that the recordings from the Slade house were still intact. This morning he rang again, and said he'd been able to audit the relevant archive himself.'

The judge had allowed her eyebrows to rise.

'There are time markings on the tape. He could hear Mrs Slade crooning to the baby as she fed her. The feed started at 7.03 and was over by 7.15. He heard Lidya kiss the baby goodnight, and the click as she turned the light off.'

'And the baby was still breathing then?' said Clutterbuck, frowning.

'Yes. My friend says the individual breaths were easy to hear, absolutely clear and regular. There were occasional snuffles and noises of movement, well after the time when Ralph and Lidya left the house. About 7.45, the breathing stopped for several seconds. Then the baby gave a long sigh, like breathing out, and after that the noises just ended, until the baby-sitters came in and started to panic, about 8.15. He thinks it's absolutely watertight. No smothering—a classic cot death.'

Clutterbuck looked questioningly at the judge.

'Well,' she said. 'Assuming this evidence holds up, Sandy, none of yours stands against it, does it? I think not. So much for those damn statistics... But how do we get hold of this tape?'

There was a knock at the door, and they all paused. 'Come,' said the judge, and her assistant came in with the coffee. 'Thank you, Alice,' said the judge without looking at her; the assistant withdrew.

They all waited as Alice's steps died away,

'We can't get hold of it,' said Tom. 'My contact is retired, and he only got to listen to it by heavy reliance on old boy goodwill. There's no sign whatever the Home Office will release it to the defence. Like me, my friend is for the high jump if it gets out that he's released to us any information about it.'

'And the court can't take cognisance of hearsay evidence,' said the judge. 'As things stand, I think our jury's quite likely to convict... How do you view it Sandy? If we assume that this tape is genuine—and it's hard to see how it could be otherwise—I can, unfortunately, see only one way in which justice can be served.' She opened her eyes very wide. 'Are you and the CPS willing to withdraw, Sandy? What do you say?'

That was what Tom had been praying for: he watched Clutterbuck.

The prosecutor put his head down to think, and ran his hands slowly and repeatedly through his hair. The judge gave a little smile, and waited, leaving the coffee to its own devices.

'Can I hear this tape for myself?' Clutterbuck asked at last.

'I can't see how,' said Tom. 'We can't get you into GCHQ without a high level security clearance—what could we give as the reason? And they won't let the tape out of the establishment... My friend is willing to meet you, though, if it's done discreetly.'

'That's the absolute minimum,' said Clutterbuck. 'You don't suppose he could *copy* the recording?'

'That would be a much more serious breach of security than just telling you about it. I think he just *might* be willing to get it copied if you really didn't believe him, on the basis that you listen to it, and then the copy is immediately destroyed.'

'Damn,' said Clutterbuck. He sighed and looked resentfully at the judge, then down at the floor for a long time. Finally, and very slowly, he looked up again, at Tom, and took a deep breath. ' ... How do I meet this man?'

'He suggests a rendezvous in a quiet café well away from anywhere you usually go... Plymtree, three o'clock this afternoon? The Cheshire Cat. You go up the B3091... '

'I know where Plymtree is.' Clutterbuck looked miserable.

'It needs to be carefully done: the newshounds will be wondering what's up.'

'Andy Arbuckle was in court this morning,' said the judge. 'He's sharp, Sandy.'

'What's your friend's name?' asked Clutterbuck.

'You'll be wanting to check his bona fides, of course. But I'd rather let him decide how much to tell you about himself. Just go to the café. He'll approach you—he knows what you look like.'

'Cheer up, Sandy,' said the judge suddenly. 'You're doing the right thing. This woman's *innocent*, isn't she?'

'I always thought so.' He looked at her dourly. 'It's what the reports showed, pretty much. But how could we fail to prosecute when Sir Ambrose was so damn sure of his ground?'

The judge seemed to take this in swiftly, and Tom guessed she was thinking tactics. 'Well,' she said at last, 'you did an effective job with the evidence you had, Sandy. Sailed a bit close to the wind on the mother's attitude to the baby, Irwin should have challenged you there. Otherwise excellent.'

This brisk flattery seemed to do the trick: Clutterbuck's face broke into a battered smile. Tom smiled too.

'But what will you say to your team?' asked the judge. 'And what do we say to the defence?'

'I've been thinking about that,' said Tom. 'We need a cover plan.'

The judge nodded.

'Best just say *unexpected new police evidence*. Then I and my team are the only ones for the press to quiz, and we know how to keep our mouths shut.'

'Andy Arbuckle will have worked out you're involved anyway.'

'Exactly.'

'But they'll still ask what *sort* of evidence.'

'Safest just to say that can't be explained for legal reasons,' said Tom. 'Let them speculate all they want.'

'Has the merit of being perfectly true,' said Clutterbuck.

'What will your junior think?' asked the judge.

'She'll be deeply suspicious,' said Clutterbuck.

'I reckon,' said Tom, 'if you want to take her somewhat into your confidence, that might be better than saying absolutely nothing. Better to have the top people in your team involved in keeping the secret rather than curious to penetrate it. But no further than that.'

'Will you tell any of your police colleagues on the same basis?' asked the judge.

'I'd best explain to my Sergeant,' said Tom. 'The other person involved already knows.'

'And I propose to tell no one,' announced the judge. 'I'll adjourn again after lunch until tomorrow morning, which will give Sandy time to drive down to the Cheshire Cat.' She smiled. 'And I'll warn the defence new evidence has arisen… Right. That took less time than I expected, but our coffee's been neglected.' She felt the side of the cafetière. 'Black or white, Chief Inspector?'

*

At three thirty Jane finished her ward round and tried to contact Tom, but he was in conference. George didn't answer his mobile either, but at four he rang back.

'Are they still adjourned?' she asked.

'Till nine tomorrow. No explanation. Irwin was furious.'

'How was Lidya?'

'Stood up well yesterday, didn't she? But this afternoon I reckon the adjournment was more than she could take. I thought she was going to pass out. Swaying. Then she put her head between her knees and Ralph was holding her shoulders.'

Withdrawal

The next morning, Jane was back in the gallery. The press benches were packed again. When Ralph and Lidya appeared, Lidya seemed worn, but animated nevertheless; she was soon deep in conversation with Mr Irwin. The jury filed in, and Mr Clutterbuck appeared from the door leading to the judge's chambers. He sat down next to his junior, who asked him a brief question; he nodded, his lower lip protruding. The judge made her usual entry, sat down, and looked around the court. She opened a folder and turned towards the jury box.

'Members of the jury,' she said. 'As I indicated yesterday, a very unusual development has occurred in this case. The prosecution has a statement to make to you. Mr Clutterbuck, please.' She nodded firmly in his direction.

Jane had a strong sense that Mr Clutterbuck's manner had altered: where yesterday he had been heavy and threatening, he seemed now to rise quietly and seriously.

'Thank you, your honour,' he said. 'Members of the jury, I have to inform you that unexpected and very compelling new evidence was presented to the prosecution team yesterday. This evidence has forced us to conclude that Mrs Slade is entirely innocent of the charge with which she is accused. Accordingly, the prosecution wishes to withdraw that charge.' He looked round the court almost apologetically, bowed slightly to the judge, and sat down.

There was a brief moment of silence.

'Thank you,' said the judge. 'The charge being withdrawn, this case is at an end.' She glanced in Irwin's direction. 'Does the defence wish to say anything?'

Mr Irwin rose. 'Your honour,' he said, 'the defence only heard of this amazing new evidence twenty minutes ago, and have still to be told what it consists of. The situation is most unusual. The defence would normally have been informed at once of significant new evidence.'

The judge nodded. 'Yes, Mr Irwin, if the case had been continuing. But since that is not so, it becomes a matter between yourselves and the Crown Prosecution Service, no longer within the purview of the court.'

Mr Irwin hesitated. 'Your honour, my client has been put through a dreadful ordeal, from which, it appears, this remarkably convincing new evidence would have saved her. It is of considerable public interest to understand why it was not produced earlier.'

'I take your point, Mr Irwin, and the court must of course deeply regret the effect on your client. But I reiterate, the matter is now one that you must take up with the CPS. I think I may properly add that, from what I have heard, they acted in fact as rapidly as was feasible.'

Irwin sat down, looking unhappy.

'The defendant is free to go—with absolutely no stain on her character. And the jury is discharged, with the court's thanks for having followed a difficult case so closely, even though, in the end, no verdict was required from them.' The judge gathered her files together. The usher got in his 'All rise' just in time as she swept away, and a great buzz began. Jane saw Mr Irwin looking towards the back of the court and George hurrying forward to meet him; she gathered her things and set off to find the stairs.

*

By the time she reached the floor of the court, Lidya and Ralph were surrounded by flashing cameras. Lidya looked completely dazed, and Ralph had one arm firmly around her shoulders. As Jane approached the group of lawyers, George muttered to Irwin, 'Not here, Frank, not here.' He turned, grabbed her arm and drew her to one side.

'Have you any idea what Tom did?' he whispered urgently. Two pressmen were moving within earshot.

'No,' breathed Jane.

George turned back to Irwin. 'Your chambers?' he muttered.

Irwin nodded twice.

George looked around. 'In my car,' he murmured to Jane. 'Andy too. He deserves his copy.'

A police constable and the court usher were struggling to hold back the crowd and easing Lidya and Ralph slowly towards the entrance; Irwin moved off to join them.

'Let's go,' said George.

*

In Irwin's pleasant panelled chambers a smiling PA was serving champagne. Lidya was slumped exhausted in an easy chair, a full glass on the carpet beside her, and Ralph stood dazedly by the empty fireplace.

Beside him, wigless but bands askew over his shirt front, Irwin was exuding a hastily contrived bonhomie. He motioned George and Jane towards seats. Andy was left standing.

'And who brought *you*?' said Irwin.

'Me,' said George cheerfully. 'I'll vet his copy, Frank. He's been helping.'

Andy grinned and accepted a glass.

Irwin looked around and harumphed; people around him raised their heads. 'Seems,' he said, 'that the defence owes your support group something of a thank you, George,

'Not my group,' said George.

'No? Whose then?'

'It was Jane here got us all buzzing.'

Lidya looked up.

'But it's *Tom* you have to thank,' said Jane, 'not us. None of us has a clue what he did or where he went—but whatever it was, it was nothing to do with us.'

'Hm,' said Irwin. 'I'm *extremely* curious. We're not complaining, however!' He turned to smile down at Lidya.

But Lidya was scrambling to her feet. She walked over to Jane's chair, and Jane stood up.

'The support group was *yours*?' said Lidya. She reached out and took Jane's right hand in both of hers.

Ralph had followed Lidya. 'We thought it was George,' he said.

'We were all in it together,' said Jane. 'Igor did a lot too.'

'And Chief Inspector Tallis, who found this new evidence? You *know* him?'

This wasn't supposed to happen, thought Jane. She nodded uncertainly.

Lidya smiled: it was a very friendly smile. 'You

persuaded him I was innocent?'

Jane shook her head. 'I didn't need to... He was convinced of that anyway.'

PART II

Land's End

Somewhere south-east of Penzance, at two in the morning of a chilly and clear September night, *Ariel* was sailing herself, her mast swaying gently across the stars, a steady chuckling and rippling under her bow, and periodically, as the waves passed, beneath her port quarter. James, the self-steering gear, was creaking to himself, his tall vane silhouetted astern against the moon. The house-glow of Penzance had mostly flickered out, but Miranda, alone on deck, could still pick out in her binoculars a far-away necklace of orange street lamps just above sea level.

She was mulling over their plans. Back in June no one had anticipated quite how intrusively the press would continue to pursue Lidya, or the ghastliness of much of the public reaction. That was when Jane had suddenly suggested that a day's trip to Fowey and back might take her mind off things. How right she'd been: sailing had come like a glowing revelation to Lidya. She'd wanted more, and whenever they met she had some new energetic query about points of sailing or slab-reefing or chart symbols or sea-sickness tablets.

Hamish, Miranda remembered with a glow, would be meeting them in Oban, full of life and of himself. Jack would be joining them there too. Tom, though, was missing. A week before the start some unforeseen police duty had ruled him out. He'd been exceedingly annoyed—a shame, he deserved his break. For the moment, then, it was the three of them.

*

Ariel ploughed on. By three, when the alarm clock went off in the cabin below, Miranda was finding it hard to keep her eyes open. She heard the buzz switched off, and the gas lit on the galley stove. A few minutes later Jane clambered up into the well, the heavy night glasses bumping on her chest.

'All quiet?'

'Yes. Lovely night.'

Jane nodded, and looked around, ducking to peer under the moonlit sails. 'Wolf Rock just where it should be.' She raised her binoculars and watched the bright flashes from the south-west.

'There's a yacht over there.' Miranda pointed to the right. 'Parallel course.' She gave a little shudder.

'Swig of cocoa?'

'Thanks.'

Jane went below again. A few minutes later she reappeared with two steaming mugs and a bag of fudge. Miranda slurped thankfully, and felt her chilled gut warmed from within. There was a slug of rum in the cocoa.

'James behaving himself?' asked Jane.

'I had to reset him once.'

They were quiet for a while. But when Miranda had downed her drink and two more pieces of fudge, Jane said:

'Round Land's End, it might be a good idea to have both of you on deck for a bit.'

'How soon?'

Jane calculated. 'Hour and a quarter.'

'Then I'd better get some sleep.' Miranda pulled herself upright.

'How do you feel the day's been?' said Jane quickly.

'Still talking nineteen to the dozen.'

'Not quite at ease, though.'

'*Nonsense*, Jane. She's been smiling at you all day.'

Jane pushed the question away, and grinned.

'OK if I go down now?' said Miranda.

'Sure...   Don't set your alarm. I'll fetch you if you're needed.'

Miranda wriggled down the steps and slid the hatch to over her head. She yawned, kicked off her sea boots, and worked her way into her sleeping bag in the portside quarter-berth. The water tumbling on the other side of the fibreglass sounded oddly comforting; putting one hand to the hull as she dropped smoothly into oblivion, she could feel its gentle vibration.

*

Off Gwennap Head Jane sailed to pass half a mile south of the Runnel Stone. The wind gradually strengthened a little, but remained northerly: once round Land's End they would have a lively beat against it.

For a moment she decided against calling the others. But then she remembered that her novice crew-member had been wanting to see how night navigation was done. She went below and tapped on the door of the fore-cabin. There was no response.

She fetched a torch, lit it, and opened the door cautiously. Lidya was lying curled up in her sleeping bag, deeply asleep, one dark wispy curl on the white pillow catching the beam. Jane hesitated, then took one shoulder and shook it gently.

Lidya muttered something lilting and unintelligible, and turned right over, away from the light.

Jane grinned, and shook the other shoulder.

Lidya sat up suddenly, bumped her head on the deckhead, and fell back. She laughed and rubbed the place. 'Jane!' she said. 'Is everything all right?'

'Yes, quite all right. Are you OK?'

'Oh yes.' She finished rubbing and smiled.

'It's four-fifteen. We're just coming up to Land's End, and if you want to see some night navigation, now's your chance.'

Lidya was suddenly serious. 'Give me five minutes.'

Jane grinned. She went back on deck to check for traffic, then down again to work with chart and tidal atlas, and after a few minutes, Lidya joined her.

'Better get your harness on,' said Jane.

Lidya buckled in and came to look over Jane's shoulder at the chain of pencilled GPS plots extending westwards on the chart.

'We're here. Well south of the Runnel Stone for safety.'

The pupil studied the chart.

'GPS has made everything terribly easy, of course. We *could* navigate if we wanted without looking outside at all. But let's do it the old-fashioned way. After all, GPS sets can fail.'

Lidya nodded.

'We'll try getting a fix.' Jane collected a hand compass from the shelf over the chart table. 'You bring that notebook and torch.' She climbed the ladder; Lidya was close behind. 'OK? Now we need to select some lights…' Jane pointed forward and to the left. 'See that white flash?'

Lidya ducked down to see under the sails.

'That's the Wolf Rock. D'you know how to count

196

seconds?'

'No.'

'Like this: *nought* two three four, *one* two three four, *two* two three four, *three* two three four... It should be one flash every fifteen seconds.'

Lidya tried, watching the light. 'I made it thirteen.'

'Near enough... Now I take a bearing on it.' Jane raised her compass and squinted through the sight at the flashes. 'Two-four-one magnetic.'

Lidya scribbled by the light of her torch.

'Now the Longships.' Jane pointed again. 'That's the rocks off Land's End.'

'The red one?'

'Red at the moment—we'll soon be into its white sector. It's five seconds on, five seconds off.'

'Hardly worth counting.'

'No, it's obvious... Three twenty-nine magnetic.'

'Three twenty-nine?'

'Yes... And over there we can still see Tater Du.'

'Three white flashes,' said Lidya, peering at the tumbled Cornish cliffs.

'Every fifteen seconds. And there's a fixed red light lower down.'

'Why do they have that?'

'You can only see it on certain bearings. It's a warning that we lie in the direction of the Runnel Stone.'

'But we're actually further away?'

'Yes... Sixty-eight.'

'Can I try a bearing?'

'Better practise by daylight first...' Jane held her watch to the binnacle light. '0432 BST... Let's go and plot them.'

But Lidya was still looking ahead. 'What's that one? Fainter.'

'The Seven Stones. Other side of the shipping lanes,

treble flash... And there to our left can you see an even fainter double flash?'

'Ghostly.'

'It's reflected by clouds, below the horizon from here. That's the Bishop Rock, over by the Scillies.' Jane led the way down and settled at the chart table. In the notebook she carefully subtracted off the westerly magnetic deviation from her bearings. Then, using parallel rulers from the compass rose on the chart, she plotted the bearings backwards from the light positions. Her three pencil lines crossed making a small triangle, very close to the last pencilled GPS mark.

Lidya watched. 'The three compass bearings fix our position?'

'That's it.'

'But the GPS does it anyway. '

Jane smiled. 'Yes,' she said. 'Life's got very much easier since I bought it. And GPS fixes where we are within a few yards.'

'So do you still bother with bearings?'

'Yes I do, from time to time. Just in case the electronics fail or start giving wrong readings... Now, back up top.' Jane climbed the ladder again. 'You take the wheel. I'm going to disengage James.'

'What course?'

'Due west will do.'

Lidya struggled to see the swinging compass card in the dim binnacle light, and Jane closed the companionway hatch to shut out the cabin light. 'Better?'

'Thank you.'

'Right,' said Jane. 'Now, I'm going to haul in the sheets. As I do, turn *Ariel* towards the wind, and see how close to it you can go.'

'Turning right?'

'Yes.' Jane hauled in a few yards of mainsheet,

jammed its cleat, found a winch handle and wound in the jib steadily. 'Just as close to the wind as you can.'

'I can't see the flag,' said Lidya, peering up the mast.

'Try to judge where the wind is by feeling it on your cheek.' The sails above them flogged suddenly, and *Ariel* came upright and slowed. '*Too* close! Steer left!'

Ariel heeled sharply and staggered. 'I can't!' said Lidya, her feet slipping on the sloping floor of the well.

'Yes, you can!' Jane eased the main sheet a little. 'That's too far—let the wheel run a bit.' *Ariel* leaped forward, the wind humming in her shrouds, and Jane hauled the sheet back in. Lidya struggled, turning the wheel alternately a little left and right. Gradually things became steadier. Gripping a spoke with one hand, she pushed hair out of her eyes with the other.

'You're doing very well,' said Jane. 'Keep going as you are, I'll just plot the new course.' She disappeared below. Lidya anxiously adjusted the wheel to keep the sails just drawing, and *Ariel* buckled down to the beat, crunching steadily out to sea, well to the left of the Longships flashes, which after a while changed from red to white. Some time later Jane returned.

'Most unusual,' she said, looking around, 'no traffic. The northbound shipping lane is only two miles to our west now, and usually you'd see quite a procession. We'll keep out of it, all the same.'

'Is it out of bounds?'

'Small craft are allowed to cross, but it can be dodgy, especially at night... Is this OK, Lidya? Would you rather be getting your sleep?'

Lidya shook her head. 'No, no, I want to see it all... You make it feel so ordered, so routine!'

Jane laughed. 'I thought it might feel a bit adventurous.'

'Well, that too. Could it be dangerous where we are now?'

'Yes it could, specially if we had no GPS and the weather were different. Suppose we had a Force 8 south-westerly ripping into the sails, big swell, heavy rain with visibility down to a hundred yards, and half a dozen big ships around us funnelling towards the shipping lane. We'd be going by dead-reckoning from our last compass fix, maybe two hours earlier, not quite sure where we were, with *Ariel* bouncing around to make chart-work all but impossible, forced to beat out against the gale to keep off the Land's End rocks, but terrified of being run down when we got near the shipping lane.'

Lidya laughed. 'What would you do?'

'Pray! Claw off to the south-east. But the thing is, think ahead, never get into bad situations, pay attention to the forecasts.'

'But even if you do, sometimes you get taken unawares?'

'Yes.'

'Like life,' said Lidya and glanced quickly at Jane.

Jane hesitated.

Lidya made a face. As *Ariel* threatened to come upright, she hauled the top of the wheel to the left. Once the course was steady again, she said again, 'Like life… You want this wind to blow my troubles away.'

Jane said nothing.

Lidya looked across at her and smiled. 'And,' she added, her mouth a little twisted, 'maybe it is doing… You're being very good to me.' She pushed hair out of her eyes again, checked the compass, and announced, 'We're pointing well to the left of that lightship.'

'And so we should be,' said Jane.

Ariel ploughed on, and after another five minutes

Jane went below. 'OK,' she said on returning. 'I've checked the position. Time to start zig-zagging. I'll manage the jib.'

Lidya nodded.

'Go ahead.'

Lidya let the wheel spin to the right. *Ariel* turned and swung upright, sails banging. As they came head to wind, Jane let fly the port jib sheet and hardened in the starboard one, and the boom swung over their heads from left to right. With the wind now blowing on her left cheek, Lidya steadied the new course, and Jane went below to record it, dropping the winch handle into its companionway pocket as she did so.

Ariel plugged on towards the jagged tip of Cornwall, only just visible against the inky eastern sky.

Irish Sea

By breakfast time the wind had backed to the west, allowing them to ease the sails and leave *Ariel* creaming northwards over a quiet sea in bright sunshine. Their course to the North Channel would take them close to the tip of Pembrokeshire, but first the rocky north coast of Cornwall fell away to their right, and the wide expanse of the Bristol Channel opened up, freckled with the shadows of a few small clouds. Lidya had settled for her bunk as soon as it got light, but reappeared at eight when Miranda started rattling pans in the galley.

'Bacon and egg OK?' asked Miranda.

'Is there cereal?'

'Corn flakes,' said Miranda. 'Take some of the warm milk.'

Jane set James to work, and they ate their breakfast together in the well, Lidya perched on the coaming and the other two settled on the seats. Once Miranda had served Jane her bacon and fried bread, she paused reflectively with the frying pan in one hand.

'So,' she said.

Lidya smiled down at her.

'So what?' said Jane.

'No men.'

Lidya looked puzzled. Then she glanced down and caught the half-grin on Jane's face. 'No men,' she echoed, and continued spooning corn flakes. The

202

whistling kettle boiled, and Miranda disappeared to make coffee. When she'd returned and filled mugs, she went on very dreamily:

'Hamish *says* he's a new man.'

'Ah!' said Jane.

Lidya seemed to be thinking. 'And is he?' she asked at last.

But Miranda was lost in private reflection and didn't reply.

'And what about Tom?' Jane prompted her after a while.

'Tom?'

'Was *Tom* a new man?'

Miranda returned to the here-and-now and considered. 'When we were growing up?'

'Yes.'

'I don't think he changed nappies, if that's what you mean... Not from what I heard. But he was a good dad.'

'How?' asked Jane.

'You know... silly games, fantastic stories, making toy theatres, camping. He and Mum used to take us out on the Moor... I think he was really fond of Jack and me when we were kids.'

'You *think!*' said Jane.

Miranda grinned cheerfully. 'Know.' She nodded and poured herself more coffee.

'*Ralph* changed nappies,' said Lidya after a while.

Jane looked at her and there was quite a long pause.

'And what about your father?' said Jane at last. 'I don't imagine *he* was a new man.'

Lidya laughed. 'I never even saw my father when I was a baby.'

'Really never?' asked Miranda.

'Not till I was six. But they must have told him how

I was doing, because he knew all about me when I first sat on his knee.'

'Did he talk to you after that?'

'Yes. I was the oldest, and we talked a lot when I was growing up, never stopped. When I was older, he would ask what I thought about *everything*, politics, even. The girls at school were amazed.'

'I saw him once,' said Jane. 'In Noss Mayo. Tall and rather handsome.'

Lidya nodded. 'It does a girl good to have an attractive father,' she said.

'Does it?' said Miranda. 'Why?'

Jane laughed. 'Come on,' she said, 'Tom's not that bad.'

'I know,' said Miranda, 'I've painted him... But I don't *think* of him that way.'

'You might sub-consciously,' said Lidya.

Jane hesitated. '*My* father didn't talk very much,' she said at last.

'That's sounds sad,' said Lidya.

'Not really... He was forty-five when I was born and my mother was quite old too... I'm sure they were both very fond of me. We were a good family, with a lovely house and things... But I did so want to have a sister.'

*

The wind remained steady, and they made rapid progress northwards. Jane set a course to pass inside Grassholm, and by lunchtime, having dodged a large oil-tanker that was forging across their bow towards the Milford Haven terminal, they could see clearly the snowstorms of sea birds circling around Skokholm and Skomer, as St Bride's Bay opened up to the north. As they were munching ham rolls, Miranda struck again.

'D'you think Hamish *really* wants babies?' she asked.

Jane frowned. 'Surely you know that by now!' she said sharply.

'Oh yes,' said Miranda, 'he seems very keen... But, seriously, do men *really* want them?'

'*Yes*,' said Lidya.

'Not all,' said Jane.

'All men want *descendants*,' said Lidya. 'My father does.

'That's not what I meant. Do they want babies the way women do?'

'Of course not,' said Lidya. 'It's not the same... *You* want them, Miranda?'

'Yes.'

'Then you know how strong it is.'

Jane hesitated. 'You could test Hamish out,' she said to Miranda at last. 'See where *he* stands on changing nappies.'

*

Jane's first impression was that the talk about babies, far from disturbing Lidya, seemed to have released something for her. During the afternoon she was again bubbling over with questions about sailing, and enjoying exercising her new helming skill, talking delightedly to *Ariel* as though she were steering a companionable but sometimes obstreperous child along a crowded street. To Jane's continued amazement, she even chatted a little to Miranda about the management of newborns and her recollections of Gabriel and Ayana seemed surprisingly happy. If she was feeling her loss as she spoke, she contrived to conceal it.

But this observation proved to be misleading. Once again, Miranda took the first night watch alone. At the changeover the wind remained westerly, but a shifting bank of cloud had obscured the moon and stars, making the sea very dark. There was at first almost no traffic about, and Jane left Lidya alone on deck, but at five she returned to help with the complexities of the Anglesey separation zones and the Holyhead ferries. As she climbed the companion ladder the cabin light caught Lidya's face, and her cheek was wet with tears. But she simply dried them, smiled, and said nothing.

*

'How difficult was it working out the childcare thing?' Miranda asked Lidya at breakfast. Wales behind them was almost out of sight.

'With Ralph, you mean?'

'Yes.'

'Why should it be difficult?'

'Coming from such different backgrounds.'

'But they *aren't* so very different... It wasn't a problem'

'It's funny,' went on Miranda, back in her dreamy mood, 'thinking about being actually married... A wife is so stuck...'

Jane laughed out loud. Lidya looked quizzical.

'Well, she is! ... You have to live with your man's limitations.'

'You're leaving these alarming reflections a little late,' said Jane tartly.

'Not really. Hamish is gorgeous and I love him... But he's not very organised.'

'There are worse things,' said Lidya, and finished up her cereal. The wind strengthened a little, and as *Ariel* heeled she adjusted her position on the coaming and tucked a strand of hair into her jacket hood.

'Coffee?' asked Miranda. 'And shall I make some toast?'

'Yes please,' said Lidya. Brown bread please.' She watched the sea for a while. 'Ralph has a drink problem,' she added.

Again there was a pause. Miranda poured the coffee and went below. After a while she returned with a stack of toast, butter and a jar of marmalade. Lidya helped herself and started spreading.

Jane took a deep breath. 'Ralph doesn't *seem* like an alcoholic,' she said.

Lidya thought for a moment. 'No,' she said.

There was another pause. '... There have been times when he's cut drink out altogether,' said Lidya at last. 'But at the moment it's wine at dinner and pub binges with business partners.'

'Not too serious, you mean?'

'That depends. Every so often, something turns up that he can't face. And *then* it's gin, secretly and he won't stop.'

'What do you do?'

Lidya made a face. 'Make sure he's not left alone. Bully him, sometimes... So far he's always been able to pull back. After three or four awful days... I don't understand how he does it.'

'But he's a support to you, in spite of it?'

'Oh yes...' Her eyes lit up. 'You know he's a swimmer?'

Jane nodded.

'Serious?' asked Miranda.

'That's how I first really noticed him.'

Jane grinned. 'Where?' she asked.

'In Ethiopia. Lake Abeye.'

'He was visiting your Dad?'

'On a business trip. We all drove out from Addis for a break.'

'Do you swim too?'

'Not like Ralph… I did that day, though. It's a very beautiful place.'

Ariel swayed to a puff of wind, and drove on.

*

By lunchtime they had passed to the west of the Calf of Man and the island shores were slipping steadily past. The bank of cloud had moved on, leaving an almost cloudless sky and sparkling sea, and treating them to a splendid view of the sharp crags of Snaefell, with the distant Lake District fells tucked hazily behind. To their left the green Mountains of Mourne glowed fifteen miles away, and the entrance to Strangford Lough had opened up.

Suddenly Jane said: 'Ralph's drink problem must have been made much worse by what happened.'

Miranda looked up.

Lidya's lips tightened, and she looked towards the western horizon.

'I'm right out of order, I know,' said Jane. 'I've been trying for so long just to imagine what it can have been like for you. But what *did* all that stuff do to you both?'

Lidya looked down at her. '*Do* to us?'

'Not losing your two babies—I can't even *begin* to imagine that. I meant the court case and all that, the threatening legal stuff.'

After a moment's thought Lidya slid down from the coaming and settled herself into the corner of the cockpit seat, arranging her plate and mug beside her.

At last, she said, 'I don't mind your asking, Jane.'

Jane waited.

'But it's hard to explain. When Gabriel died, and the police wanted to investigate, it was a shock, of course—but actually, it was a *relief* to be in a country with a decent legal system. I thought to myself, it just shows how thorough they are. It never occurred to me they'd think I *really* killed him—and they didn't think that, so I felt safe. Of course, we were totally devastated about losing Gabriel, but we weren't worrying about the law. Why should we?'

Miranda nodded, and Lidya looked thoughtfully at her.

'Then, when I was pregnant again, I felt peaceful at first. It felt like hope, sweeping away the bitterness... Until that day when Tom came.'

'That was bad?' said Jane.

'Well, he made us afraid that Ralph might be whisked away and held on evidence we couldn't be told, let alone challenge... *That* felt like Ethiopia again.'

'How did *he* take it?' asked Miranda.

'Badly.'

'Drinking?'

'As usual. But after a few days he threw it off, decided he trusted the system, confident MI5 would clear him.'

'What about you?' asked Jane.

'I was afraid much longer. Now, though, about this terrorism stuff, I don't know. They haven't questioned Ralph for a long time. Perhaps the security services *have* got him right at last... And that mysterious new evidence Tom found, the evidence that saved me...'

'He still won't explain it.'

'No. But Ralph and I think it must be linked somehow with MI5… Perhaps I've reason to be *grateful* to them. Who knows?'

'You sound so calm.'

Lidya looked at the horizon and shook her head. 'Not really. I get nightmares… I had one the night before we left. Reliving the night Ayana died… That one keeps coming back, it's a millstone that won't stop grinding… Night after night…'

Jane nodded.

'*Why* did Ralph have to persuade me to go out?'

'Oh Lidya—he was trying to make something nice for you.'

'I know. I mustn't accuse him.' Lidya forced the heel of one hand briefly into her eye, rubbed, and looked up again at Jane. 'But that one's not the worst.'

'What is?'

'Sir Ambrose.'

Jane nodded. 'He made my flesh creep.'

'He scared me from the moment we knew Dr Jones wanted his opinion.'

'Cormack knew about him?'

'Yes, and I read him up. That nightmare started even before I knew what he looked like.' Lidya laughed. 'He *comes* for me like a red turkey-cock: gobble, gobble, gobble.'

'D'you have horrors about Clutterbuck too?'

Lidya considered. 'I do about my cross-examination. He was so unfair.'

'*Unfair*? Appalling, more like. Tricky, devious. Unprincipled.'

'Yes. But he was doing his job.'

'How can you *possibly* say that?' said Miranda.

Lidya turned to her. 'I'm not saying he wasn't scary. Of course he was. It was touch and go whether I could keep my nerve with him, I nearly broke down.

Ask Ralph what I was like in the evenings. But that man's not a *nightmare* for me, not any more. In the end, you know, he realised he'd been wrong.'

'Unlike Sir Ambrose?'

'Yes… And because Sir A's treated as such an expert, he can subvert the whole legal system'

'How do you mean?'

Lidya shook her head impatiently. 'It's true! They would never have prosecuted me if he hadn't told them to. He said totally false things in court, but the lawyers and the judge didn't have the nerve or the expertise to question them. He had the presence and reputation to sway the jury even when the other experts showed he was wrong. He's done it to scores of innocent women before and he'll do it again. And he's so sure he's right. Who can stop him? … And he isn't going to leave me alone.'

'Why d'you say that?' asked Miranda.

'What I just said. He still thinks I'm guilty.'

'Why are you so sure?' asked Jane.

'He said something.'

'He talked to *you*? When?'

'After he gave his evidence. We were packing up to go home, and he came over to the defence bench.'

'What on earth did he say?'

'He looked me full in the face, smiled, and said quietly: "That was terrible for me, it must have been awful for you!"'

'Impossible man!'

'We just stood there. Ralph nearly hit him. Then Mr Irwin told him to go away, and he went.'

'What an extraordinary thing! But why did that convince you he'd never accept your innocence?'

'Think about it. What he *meant* was, he was sorry he'd had to expose my *guilt*, my awful guilt. He was trying to let me know, for God's sake, that he *cares* about crazy women who murder their own children. In his warped mind it was the moment to give me a little care and attention, to give proper consideration to my peculiar motives. He'd moved on *far* beyond any possibility of innocence.'

'He persuades himself.'

'Exactly.'

'And it doesn't seem to cross his mind he might be wrong,' said Jane. 'So far as we could find out, he's always used this simple-minded first MB statistics, and never consulted a real expert.'

'That one–two–three mantra of his is so powerful,' said Miranda, and Lidya nodded vigorously. The wind had eased a little, and *Ariel* was sliding forward almost silently, her wake very straight astern. A puffy cloud had for the moment obscured the sun, but distant waves still sparkled.

'Thank God it didn't depend on the jury, in the end,' said Lidya. She looked down and picked up her cold toast. 'I was lucky.'

*

By the following night, the coastline to their right was Scottish. Jane had kept well to the east of the separation zone, close under the Mull of Kintyre, arriving at slack water so as to avoid the race, and now the tide was helping them up the sound towards Oban; the westerly wind had been very kind, and she was hoping to be in port a day early. She and Lidya were together again for the second watch. They were already past Gigha, the sky was clear, and the moon was making it easy to see the faint outlines of the Paps of Jura to their left.

Lidya had been silent for a long time. 'Being religious has made it harder,' she said at last.

Jane hesitated. 'God uncaring?'

Lidya nodded.

Again Jane hesitated. 'You might also wonder,' she said at last, 'why did he have to create someone as evilly stupid as Sir Ambrose?'

'That too...' said Lidya. She looked up again, gave Jane a quick smile, and there was another long pause.

At last she said: 'There's something I need to ask you, Jane.'

'Me?'

'Because of my religious belief.'

'Ask away,' said Jane easily. She was busy adjusting the self-steering gear.

Lidya said evenly, 'You shot a man, didn't you?'

Ariel butted nonchalantly onwards, shouldering waves aside.

Jane's throat tightened. At last she nodded.

'I need to understand how someone like you could bring yourself to do something like that.'

Jane closed her eyes.

'Dr Said told us. You discovered someone on your boat with a rifle. In the middle of the ocean... I'm not saying what you did was wrong.'

Jane still said nothing.

'And I know what false accusation feels like.'

'You seem to be supposing I'm really a good person at heart,' said Jane, distressed. 'But I'm *not*. That wasn't how it seemed to me. That's what's made it so hard.'

'Made what hard?'

'Believing I can be a proper partner to Tom.'

'That's all wrong,' said Lidya. '*Tom* doesn't think you're evil, does he?'

'No, thank God.'

Lidya waited.

'But you can't understand?' said Jane at last. 'How I could bring myself to shoot a man?'

'No, I can't.'

Jane shivered. 'I'm not sure I can, either. I keep asking myself how I did it... Survival instinct, I suppose.' Jane was looking forward, where the sound ahead of them was gradually narrowing in the moonlight. The wind sighed in the rigging as *Ariel* swayed to it.

'Him or you?'

'Yup.'

'But how could you be *sure*?'

Jane laughed shortly. 'I knew.' She pushed hair out of her eyes.

Lidya looked at her.

'I knew Carl. I *knew* he was there to get me. If I hadn't shot him, I'd have been dead.'

'How quickly did you have to decide?'

'You want the grisly details? I was able to grab his rifle... I knew instinctively.'

'That you had to pull the trigger?'

'Yes.'

'I don't think I *could* have.'

'Then you wouldn't have survived.'

'I know...' Lidya narrowed her eyes. 'How was it for you afterwards? Living with yourself?'

'Well,' said Jane. 'It's been fucking awful... Tom supports me. But I think in my position he might have shot to incapacitate, not to kill.'

'He's not a woman.'

'Is it so different for a man? But the thing is, unlike you I drew it all on myself.'

'What d'you mean?'

214

'By my crazy behaviour.'

'Crazy?'

'When I was a student.'

'Getting involved with this Carl, you mean?'

'Yes,' said Jane, with some sense of relief. 'If I'd had any sense, I'd have realised what a monster he was.'

'Students do lots of crazy things.'

'I can't see *you* doing what I did as a student. Not in a month of Sundays.'

Lidya looked at her. 'In Ethiopia, there was this coup. The communists strangled the Emperor, and my father criticised them. He was young then, but he wouldn't kill. They ostracised him, threatened him, he felt humiliated. But he wouldn't do it....'

Jane nodded. 'Good for him. But I'm different. My big problem, inside my own head, is: it *wasn't* simply self-defence. I was *glad* Carl was dead, actually *glad*... That's what's awful, that gladness... Killing marks you,' said Jane, and her mouth twitched.

'How so?'

'All last year I felt contaminated, marked off, even after they decided not to prosecute. I even panicked I might finish up like Harold Shipman.'

'The doctor who killed his patients?'

Jane closed her eyes. 'Yes.'

'Jane, that's nonsense.'

'Are you sure?'

'Yes. I can *understand* being glad someone evil is dead.'

'You mean, I need to separate the gladness from the fact that I had to do that awful thing?'

'Exactly.'

'Not so easy...

'You know,' went on Lidya.

'What?'

'I'm *glad* you felt guilty.'

'Why?'

'You *needed* to, didn't you? What sort of monster would you have been if you'd felt fancy-free afterwards?'

Jane had never seen it quite that way for herself; nor had Tom ever said anything quite so helpful. Lidya smiled at her and nodded gently.

A little time passed, and Jane's thoughts drifted for the moment to navigation. She went below to study the chart, and returned to make a small adjustment to James. Lidya had remained sitting quietly on the cockpit seat, studying the moon. She didn't seem sleepy. The wind lifted her dark hair a little. Perhaps there was nothing important left between them that needed saying.

'I'm keeping well up to the west just here,' said Jane.

'Why?' asked Lidya.

'All these little islands off the mouth of Loch Sween. But then at the end of Jura there's the dreaded Gulf of Corryvrecken.'

Lidya smiled. 'What's that?'

'Between Jura and Scarba. A tidal bottleneck with huge currents and a whirlpool.'

'Is it dangerous for us?'

Jane grinned. 'Not if we keep well to the east of the entrance. But to be swept into the tide rip would be a bad idea.'

'Hm,' said Lidya. 'Should I make some cocoa?'

Scottish waters

As expected, *Ariel* arrived in Oban Bay a day early: the wind went round to the south, and as they drove up the channel inside Kerrera, sails spread to catch it, Jane called the Harbour Master on VHF, and he allocated them a temporary berth at the North Pier.

Just after mid-day Lidya swung *Ariel* round into the wind off the Esplanade, and Jane and Miranda tumbled the sails down. As they motored in to their berth, the town spread up the hill was busy with traffic in bright sunlight. The big Mull ferry was easing out of the MacBraynes pier by the station and turning towards them; a line of passengers peered idly down. They made fast and completed a proper harbour furl.

'We could hardly have had a more straightforward first leg.' said Jane, dusting her hands. 'And that looks like a fish restaurant, to save us even more effort.'

A fish restaurant it was, twenty yards from their berth, so they took a lackadaisical lunch there. Miranda called Hamish to announce their safe arrival. But he couldn't leave work early, so she told him she'd take the bus and meet him in Connel.

Through the plate glass Lidya was watching the latest ferry arrival, with the crags of Mull as backdrop.

'They come in from the outer Hebrides with the car decks full of sheep,' said Miranda.

'Everything there depends on the ferries?'

'Completely—

> The Good Lord owns the earth,
>   And all that it contains—
> Excepting just the outer isles,
>   For they are all MacBraynes.'

Lidya smiled. 'And there are hills here,' she added. 'They remind me of home.'

'Not high by your standards,' said Jane.

'And we have lakes beneath ours, not arms of the ocean.'

After lunch, to get some exercise, they climbed up to McCaig's tower, where Lidya could get an even better view: across Lismore and Loch Linnhe and up the Sound of Mull, as Ben More and the lower Mull peaks glowed in the afternoon sunshine.

They wound their way downhill again, and Miranda caught her bus. The other two found a restaurant off the main street that promised well for supper, then found a seat by the water, where they called home on their cellphones. Lidya got through first: she talked for quite a while and Ralph seemed to be in good spirits. But Jane found Tom burdened with work and cross over missing the trip. 'The Guardian had a piece about Sir Ambrose yesterday,' he added. When Jane had finished Lidya said she needed to stock up on sunscreen.

'There's a Boots on the main street,' said Jane. 'Shall we meet back at the boat? I need somewhere selling yachting gear—my oilskin trousers have split,'

They separated. Jane ran her oilskins to earth at a chandlers near the station. Then she pinpointed a supermarket for later stocking up and picked up a copy of yesterday's Guardian. Back in *Ariel*, she found Lidya ahead of her, sitting at the cabin table. She edged around its opposite side to hang her new purchase in the wet locker and set about making tea. When it was ready she poured a mug for Lidya, who looked up and went to dig out some ginger nuts from the galley drawer.

Jane accepted one and poured and sipped her own tea. Nobody said anything for a long time.

At last Lidya remarked: 'Ralph says... that *if* I ever had another baby...'

Jane twisted around.

'I'd have to be chaperoned.' She frowned.

'Meaning what?'

'Never left alone with it.'

'To protect you legally?'

'Exactly... Just in case something went wrong again.'

Jane drew a half breath but changed her mind and said nothing.

Lidya glanced at her. 'Purely hypothetical,' she added, with a half-smile. 'Not what we're planning... Definitely.'

*

Next day Hamish and Miranda arrived by the early bus, in time for the end of breakfast coffee. 'I've been bullying him not to bring too much,' said Miranda.

Hamish grinned, and offered a smallish rucksack for inspection.

'Very good,' said Jane.

Lidya examined it. 'Smaller than Miranda's,' she concluded.

'Oh shush!' said Miranda with a grin. 'Smaller than yours, too.'

Jane found a lifejacket and harness for Hamish, and

allocated him the port settee berth, leaving the other for Jack. 'We need to get on,' she added, 'Only another three hours on this berth. You and Miranda had better be off to the supermarket while Lidya and I sort out the fuel and water.'

By lunchtime they were organised and had motored across the bay to the visitors' moorings at Ardantrive, below the green end of Kerrera.

Jack's train was due at 9.26. 'How do we get there to pick him up?' asked Hamish. They were sitting in the well, Hamish munching a BLT sandwich, his spare arm encircling Miranda's waist.

'I radioed the boatyard,' said Jane. 'The service launch will collect the shore party and bring you back.'

'Hamish and I'll go,' said Miranda.

'Me too, if there's space,' said Lidya. 'New acquaintance.'

'So he is,' said Jane. 'I'd forgotten.'

*

The crossing to the North Pier was a little choppy. By 9.15, in the gloaming, the reception party was in position on the platform, and it wasn't long before Miranda could hear the train squealing gradually louder on the bends as it looped down around the end of the town, at last appearing from under the bridge and groaning to a gentle halt ahead of them.

A solid stream of sensibly clothed and booted passengers appeared under the platform lights; Jack, long and thin, was hurrying along well to the fore and waving. Miranda ran up and hugged him. Hamish shook his hand cheerfully.

He clicked his heels and gave Miranda a naval salute. A passing group of passengers eyed him quizzically.

'*I'm* not your captain.'

Lidya stepped forward. 'Hi!' she said, 'I'm Lidya,' and planted a firm kiss on Jack's cheek. The kiss seemed to take him by surprise, but he returned it, with an interested glance.

Hamish was checking the size of Jack's rucksack. 'How did you manage that?' he said.

'Sisterly insistence.'

'That launch won't wait,' said Miranda.

They hurried off the platform still talking, past a queue of train passengers and a rapidly shrinking line of taxis, then along the waterfront by glowing restaurants and pubs to the North Pier. The launch was waiting on the glittering water, already nearly full, so it was a tight squeeze.

*

Next morning, Jack wanted to be off to Barra at once.

'How many days has everyone got?' said Jane.

'I must catch a train back to London early on Sunday the 5th,' admitted Jack.

'And I've got a week-end duty starting the day before that,' said Hamish. 'Unfortunately.'

'Surely you could get out of that?' said Jack.

'No,' said Miranda. 'He had to promise, or he wouldn't have got leave at all.'

'So we have to be back in Oban by the Friday night?' said Jane.

'Yes.'

'It's the 26th now.' Jane was counting on her fingers. 'Eight sailing days. And we must allow extra time for the return trip in case the weather turns nasty.'

'So we need to start at once?' said Hamish.

'If Jack wants to get to the outer Hebrides.'

'Can we?' asked Jack hopefully.

'We need to get our skates on. But we should be able to make Castlebay.'

'Which way do we go?'

'Up the Sound of Mull, then out past Ardnamurchan and the north end of Coll. That route will give us smooth water early on while we find our sea-legs.'

But it didn't prove quite so easy. From the weather forecast, it was clear that a fast-moving low was bearing down from the north, and they could expect to meet a strong north-westerly and rain in the sound. After that the low was expected to drift away eastwards leaving mist and a very weak westerly in the Sea of the Hebrides. Jane shrugged: the weather was turning unhelpful for a change, but it sounded manageable.

But by the time they'd crossed the Firth of Lorne to Lady Rock and Duart Castle, the wind was driving down the Sound of Mull directly in their teeth, and it was obvious they were in for a long and choppy beat, through heavy rain squalls. As a precaution Jane handed out sea-sickness tablets all round; and by the time they reached Salen, Jack in particular was looking as though they'd been very necessary.

'Are you OK?' she asked him privately.

'I think so,' said Jack stoutly. 'But it would be safer if I stayed on deck.'

By tea-time they were working past the entrance to Tobermory bay. The wind had not abated at all, but was backing to the west, so even after rounding Ardmore point they were still beating. Here they lost the shelter of the land and *Ariel* began plugging into an ocean swell, swoop and crash, swoop and crash. By six it was getting dark and curdled clouds over the Minch were gloomy and threatening. By now Miranda and Lidya both looked pale, and Jack's face was positively green. Hamish was steering, but not looking much more cheerful.

Suddenly, Jack hauled himself to the lee side and threw up over the coaming, his back heaving. 'Jack!' yelled Miranda, and grabbed at his waist, too late to do any good. As *Ariel* heeled, a larger wave than usual slopped over the ship's waist, and conveniently swept the remains away.

'I'm OK,' said Jack, staggering up and wiping his mouth.

Jane looked over her crew one by one.

'Enough!' she said. 'We need to get warm… Helm up Hamish… Supper in Tobermory.'

Hamish turned *Ariel* away from the wind, and as he did so their motion changed to a smoothly modulated rush, and the roaring around their ears dropped to a quiet moan.

'Has it eased?' asked Jack.

'No,' said Jane. 'It just seems less.'

An hour later they were in the smooth water of Tobermory Bay and morale was restored as if by magic. But the sails hung almost limp, and it was another half hour before they crept in towards the lights of the town in the dark. They could find no free visitors' buoys and dropped anchor in a likely spot towards the left, amongst other yachts.

'Hamish and Miranda—supper duty' said Jane.

During the cooking, Jane sat at the chart table to write up the log, and looking up caught sight of Lidya slipping quietly into the loo compartment. It was quite a long time before she reappeared.

But when Lidya emerged she looked cheerfully around at no-one in particular, and Jane thought no more of it.

Northern passage

Jane forgot to set her alarm clock, and next morning, everyone overslept until Hamish roused the crew at eight forty-five. There was a thin layer of cloud overhead, drifting only slowly off the land, and Jane began to worry about sailing times to Barra. At breakfast Jack, who seemed to have recovered his appetite, pitched into Miranda's bacon, mushroom and eggs, and urged everyone else to do the same. Hamish backed him up by rushing out to haul off the sail covers.

'Hold on! We need to think.' said Jane. 'What about shopping, Miranda? Do we need food?'

'Did that yesterday,' said Hamish.

'Only basic shops in Castlebay.'

'I'm sure we're OK for a week or so,' said Miranda.

Jane nodded, but went to check the Clyde Cruising Club pilot book and her tide table. After a while she returned.

'It's fifty miles to Castlebay.' she said. 'The wind's turning northerly, which will make for an easy passage, but it's light. It's going to take us at least ten hours, and I don't want to be arriving in the dark. None of us knows the entrance.'

'So we need to hang about for a bit?' said Jack.

'The Sound of Mull chart shows a quiet little loch a few miles east from here, along Loch Sunart. I think we should pop over there, anchor, explore maybe, and then set off for Barra after supper. That way, we'd be coming into Castlebay at six in the morning.'

'A night crossing?' said Lidya.

'Nothing wrong with that.'

'Where's this loch?' asked Hamish, who had gone to fetch the chart.

Jane pointed. 'Well sheltered. Very narrow entrance, but no hazards.'

Hamish had a close look. 'Loch na Drome Buidhe,' he said, 'I've been in there with the Institute team who check the salmon runs in Loch Sunart. It's a beautiful quiet spot.'

'OK,' said Jane. 'You set the course for us. There are some rocks to be avoided.'

'Big Stirk and Little Stirk.'

'They're the ones.'

*

By lunchtime, they had followed Hamish's directions across the Sound of Mull, and found their way through a steep-sided entrance into the tiny loch, whose shores looked completely wild. There were no other boats, and they ate a picnic lunch on deck at anchor, admiring the view.

'Who's for the shore?' said Jack once they'd tidied away the food and downed shots of cocoa.

'The north side's an island,' said Jane, 'and there must be good views from there over Loch Sunart. There's a little bay where you can land.'

'Sounds good.'

Miranda and Hamish agreed, and went to find their cameras while Jack inflated the outboard dinghy. But in the end only the three of them went: Jane preferred to remain with *Ariel*, and Lidya said she'd stay aboard

226

too, and try her hand at sketching.

'From here?'

'Why not?' Lidya went below, and returned with a big pad of cartridge paper and sticks of charcoal. She settled herself on the cabin roof as the explorers' dinghy puttered gently away from them, sending lines of ripples across almost still water, its noise echoing from the rocks around.

'What will you draw?' asked Jane.

'Water!' said Lidya. 'Always water. I love these sea scenes. And seaweed. Look at all those splendid coarse greens and yellows where they landed.'

Jane fetched her book and settled to read in the well. After a chapter she looked up.

Lidya was frowning. 'Charcoal's not doing this for me.'

'If you love colours, why don't you use pastels?'

'Don't have any.'

'I've got some. Want to try?'

'Why not?'

Lidya had a go with the pastels. She tore off one sheet and started another. 'Hey,' she said after a while, 'this is easier than I thought!'

'Miranda told me to try them.'

'She's an art teacher, isn't she?'

'And very good.'

Lidya smiled doubtfully. 'Then she'll certainly put me to shame. What sort of thing do you do?'

'Still lifes, mostly. Autumn leaves and flowers. *Warm* colours.'

'Do they satisfy you?'

'Sometimes. But more often they depress me... Tom seems to like them, though... I've got to *show* him... '

'Show him what?'

'Warmth.'

Lidya looked at Jane, glanced at the little beach across the loch, and went on sketching. Feeling discomfited, Jane abandoned her book, and fetched the log from the chart table to write up the morning's events. After a while Lidya said,

'What did you *mean* by showing him warmth, Jane?'

'That I can be warm-hearted.'

'To *him*?'

Jane sighed. 'More to kids, I suppose...'

Lidya went on sketching. At last she said:

'*I* don't think you need to show him, Jane... He knows already. At least, that's how I see it. Think how well you get on with Miranda and Jack.'

'That's different. They're adults.'

'So much the trickier. They could easily have resented your appearance on the scene.'

'And I'm a very different person from their mother.'

'Maybe. But whatever you are, they seem to think you're good for Tom, don't they? Both of them.'

'I've been grateful for that.'

'*Grateful*! To hell with gratitude! Think what it says about *you*.'

Jane reflected. 'Have *you* ever found it hard to be affectionate?'

'Not really. It was easier for me.'

'Why?'

'My mother was a loving person, and when she died, it was sort of obvious I had to take up her role... As simple as that.'

'You said she'd been a goatherd?'

'Yes.'

'I suppose that must have been a pretty humble background. And your dad whisked her off into something quite different.'

'Up to a point, yes. But the Amhara tribes have their own class consciousness, you know. She came from an important family with big herds, and he accepted her status, even though she wasn't educated.'

'I suppose she made it feel natural to want more kids? To want to try again?'

Lidya paused and looked hesitantly at Jane. 'Yes,' she said, and went on sketching, re-aligning a few strokes. 'But there are all sorts of good reasons why we shouldn't. Not least that I'm terrified of what might happen. There may be some special reason why my babies die.'

'The experts say no.'

'Yes, you told me. But Ralph and I think the experts may not have got it quite right.'

'Mm... But what about how you *feel*?'

'That's my problem, Jane... My *gut* feeling is, well... The fact is I just really, *really* want to try again. That's it. It's very strong.'

Jane felt uncertain. 'What about Ralph?'

'He's conflicted, too. *He* doesn't want to give up, either. But he's worried about how we'd cope if something went wrong, afraid he'd start drinking and go to pieces... Actually, he's quite terrified.'

'Maybe he's right to be.'

'I know. He *is* right.'

Jane considered. 'Perhaps at some level you don't want to let your mother down.'

Lidya opened her eyes wide. 'That's pretty near the truth,' she said, and deliberately smudged a line or two on her sketch, 'she gave me my *raison d'être*.' After a while she added, 'D'you know, I also have another feeling? Very odd.'

'What?'

Lidya laughed. 'I want *everyone* to have babies.'

'Everyone? Why?'

'Shouting to the world! *Everyone* ought to have the right, *nothing* should be allowed to stand in the way… What about you and Tom?   I'd *love* to see you two with a baby. One of your own.'

*

When evening came, but before it got too dark, they motored out through the narrow loch entrance, hoisted sail, and set off west with the craggy lumps of Mull and Ardnamurchan to left and right, the remains of the light dimming ahead of them and the wind now a gentle breeze from the north. The seasickness generated the previous day by the same stretch of sea was forgotten as *Ariel* hissed over smooth water, sucked forward by full mainsail and big genoa.

By midnight *Ariel* was well abreast of the point of Ardnamurchan, and the light on its tip had come into view, flashing twice every half-minute. Lidya and Jack were paired as night watch for the first time, and with Jane's help they set a course for Barra, making sure they would pass well outside the Cairns of Coll. The mainland of the island was now ahead on their left, marked by the faint lights of a few crofts, and occasionally the flickering headlights of a car, but the outline of the land itself was too low and dim to be made out against the darkening sky beneath the red glare of their navigation light.

An hour later the daylight had disappeared completely, they were out onto the deep water of the Sea of the Hebrides, and Jane had gone down to find her bunk, leaving the self-steering gear disengaged so that the watch could practise compass steering in the dark. The wind had strengthened a little to help them on their way, and a noticeable swell was rolling down from the north. The sky ahead was prickly with stars.

To Jack's annoyance, Lidya could hold the course more precisely than he could. 'It's the waves, swinging us about,' he said, peering to windward, his lanky frame silhouetted against the binnacle light.

'I don't watch the compass all the time,' said Lidya. 'I use a star.'

'Like a temporary course marker?'

'Yes…' As Jack was trying out this suggestion, she looked a little uncertainly at him. 'You work in a merchant bank?'

'Yes… Lazards.'

'It sounds very high-powered, big bucks and all that.'

Jack looked down at her. 'Well, I get a lot by Dad's standards.'

Lidya thought about this for a while. At last she said, 'Your Dad and Jane need to get on with things.'

Jack peered down the companion way and gently slid the hatch shut.

Lidya smiled. 'Not if you don't want to.'

He paused, then nodded, his head on one side. 'It's hard for her'

'I wish I understood better. This man she shot, Carl. Do you know about that? Is he the origin of her uncertainties?'

There was a pause. After some time, Jack said,

'I'm not sure that I ought to talk about that… And we don't know, not really, Miranda and I.'

Lidya nodded. 'OK,' she said.

*

At two an alarm clock buzzed below, and was swiftly switched off. A few minutes later the hatch cover slid back, and Miranda climbed up to sniff the night air.

'Hamish is just coming.' she said. 'Gosh it's dark… And the wind's dropped.'

'Thick cloud drifting down from the north,' said Jack. 'Is Jane awake?'

'Yes. But she said just to carry on, and only call her if there are problems… Course?'

'Two ninety-eight,' said Lidya.

'Two-nine-eight. Thanks.'

Lidya handed over the wheel, rubbed her eyes, smiled, and climbed slowly down the companionway to find her bunk.

'How did that go?' Miranda asked Jack when she had gone.

'No problems… She wanted to talk about Jane.'

'Oh,' said Miranda doubtfully. With a huge yawn, Hamish, still buckling on his harness, was climbing up into the cockpit.

'But I didn't say much,' said Jack, and followed Lidya below decks, pulling the hatch closed above his head.

Half an hour later, however, the wind had dropped even further, the swell had died away, and *Ariel* was making less than two knots. The night was now even darker, and they could see nothing on the water beyond the glimmer of their own navigation lights, and nothing in the sky.

'This is weird,' said Hamish, who was steering. 'Like ghosting through ink.'

'It's quite safe.'

'Yes.'

Ten minutes later the wind failed completely and gradually all water noise came to an end.

'Call her?' said Hamish, spinning the wheel in desperation as he tried and failed to keep on course.

Miranda nodded, and disappeared below. Soon, Jane's head appeared. She peered around, then climbed into the cockpit.

'Oh dear,' she said. 'We'd better start the engine...'

Barra

The engine didn't wake the watch below, and when Lidya and Jack reappeared at six-thirty, they stuck their heads up to find *Ariel* with sails tidily furled, puttering forward over a gently swelling and oily surface, on which was arranged in the middle distance static rolls of pearly pink mist. In some directions they could see lanes of clearer visibility, but no sign of land ahead or other boats. Although they were moving through the water, it felt as though they were stuck at the centre of an unchanging bowl.

'Are we getting anywhere?' asked Jack.

Jane laughed. 'Yes,' she said. 'We should be in by seven thirty. Let's get on with breakfast.'

It was Lidya's turn to cook. By the time the food was cleared away, two or three small fishing boats had appeared out of the mist banks, running ahead of them to the north west. In another half hour the mist started to lift and they could faintly see the land. Jack readied his camera. After a further twenty minutes they were creeping into the bay itself, following the leading marks, identifying strange buoys from the chart, and finally tucking themselves safely into the anchorage behind Kissimul Castle, the roar of their anchor chain startling herring gulls into the air.

*

The mist had gone, and the water sparkled in the morning sun.

'Can we get to see the Atlantic?' asked Jack.

'No,' said Jane, 'It's not safe to take *Ariel* round the west side. It's shallow a long way out, and almost no shelter.'

Hamish, however, had equipped himself with an ordnance map before leaving Oban. 'We can *walk* there,' he said. 'It's not far. Who wants to go?'

Everyone did.

Jane laughed. 'Take a picnic, then,' she said. 'I'll stay with the ship.'

'Pump up the inflatable,' urged Hamish, and in surprisingly little time the shore party had puttered off towards the landing stage.

*

The small town of Castlebay wasn't picturesque: its houses were a small estate of foursquare council properties and its curb stones were concrete. But the shore party turned west along the road and soon found themselves amongst crofts and small hayricks. Then they began to hear surf, and were before long running across a beautiful and deserted expanse of sand onto which Atlantic rollers were pouring out their gigantic hearts. Lidya delightedly pointed north to something large and red by the sand dunes, and Hamish ran after her. But Jack thought he could see seals on the beach ahead, and Miranda stuck with him as he strode seawards, camera at the ready.

They were indeed common seals, lolling with huge liquid eyes on the sand, and surprisingly tame: Jack got within ten yards for his photographs without apparently disturbing them.

The surf was now very loud. 'What was it Lidya wanted to know about Jane?' shouted Miranda.

'Let's get out of this noise.' He put the camera away, and they walked slowly back to the dunes to perch on clumps of marram grass. He looked up, 'She wanted to know about Carl.'

'Did you tell her?'

'No.'

'Quite right—it's up to us not to blab to all and sundry.'

Jack paused. 'Lidya isn't exactly all and sundry,' he said. 'She was concerned… '

'Was she?'

'That was pretty obvious… I thought it was understandable enough.'

'Carl is a pretty sore point.'

Jack thought some more. 'But Lidya's not going to undermine her,' he said at last. 'Come on, let's catch them up.' He pulled Miranda to her feet and ran northward ahead of her along the sand.

In the distance they could see Hamish and Lidya, now standing by the red structure. Lidya was inspecting it closely and Hamish seemed to be laughing; as she got nearer, Miranda realised it was an old style GPO telephone box.

'Just look at it!' called Hamish as they came up. 'Crazy!'

The box was standing lopsidedly on the seaward side of the sand dune, not a building in sight, the nearest track half a mile inland. No telephone wires on poles led to it, and its door was hanging open, held from swinging too far in the Atlantic westerlies by a pair of leather straps. Its floor was smothered in blown sand. But its scarlet paint was fresh.

Lidya emerged. 'It has a *dial*,' she said.

236

Hamish laughed again.

'Is it working?' asked Jack.

'I didn't try.'

Lidya went back inside and lifted the receiver. 'There's a tone!' she called.

'A Gaelic *Tardis*!' said Hamish delightedly.

'Telephone books, too,' said Miranda, pointing to the shelf to the right of the receiver, and Lidya pulled them out. There was a Barra local directory and a Western Isles Yellow Pages, dog-eared and damp, but usable.

Jack dug out his camera again.

'Oh!' demanded Lidya suddenly. 'Take one of me in it... Please...With the sea behind.' She smoothed and fluffed her hair and propped herself inside the box with the receiver to her ear and smiled beguilingly, one elegant elbow resting on the little shelf. 'For my cousins.'

Jack took several. Then he propped the camera on some driftwood and managed to get a picture on delayed exposure showing all four of them, arms around each other, crammed into the box together.

*

From the mysterious phone box they wandered cheerfully north, and came eventually to a rocky headland, where they stopped for lunch with the sighing of the breeze in the grass and the squabbling of black-backed gulls as background. Afterwards they climbed the ridge, but found themselves forced inland by a wire fence running along its crest. Beyond the fence there were a number of shaggy-looking Hebridean sheep grazing, and when they had walked a few hundred yards away from the sea, they saw ahead of them a group of three ewes standing around a fourth, which was lying on the turf near the wire.

Lidya looked at them. 'What time of year do the lambs come in Scotland?' she asked suddenly.

'Springtime,' said Miranda, confidently.

Lidya frowned and ran up to the fence to take a closer look. The ewe on the turf let out a piteous bleat, and the others surrounding her turned towards Lidya and bleated too.

'She's in *trouble*,' said Lidya.

'Where is the farmer?' said Miranda.

'Miles away,' said Hamish doubtfully.

Lidya pursed her lips and looked all around, but there was no help in sight. She nodded firmly to Hamish and ducked to wriggle under the wire.

Hamish looked doubtfully at Miranda, then stepped forward and held up the strand. Lidya slid beneath and ran over to the sheep.

'Should we?' said Jack doubtfully.

'Come on,' said Miranda, and she and Hamish squirmed through after Lidya. Jack followed more slowly.

Lidya was kneeling beside the ewe. '*Not* always in springtime!' she said. 'Look!'

'God!' said Hamish. Jack, his eyes wide, said nothing.

The small greasy head of a lamb was protruding from the rear of the sheep; as they watched the lamb feebly shook its long ears.

Miranda squatted down beside Lidya. 'Jane would have known what to do,' she muttered.

Lidya threw a look of exasperation over her shoulder. '*How* would she know?' she said. '*Not* the same as babies. Not at *all* the same.' She stood up and took off her waterproof jacket.

'But *you* know?' asked Miranda, taken aback.

'What d'you think?' said Lidya, and laughed. She rolled up both sleeves, squatted down and patted the ewe's side firmly. '*Rega bel!*' she crooned in a gentle singsong. '*Rega bel, Kes bel! Ati denaget!*'

'Shouldn't we fetch the farmer?' said Jack.

'No *time*,' said Lidya. 'They could both die.'

'But you think you can save them?'

'Of course... Anyone got any string?'

'String?' said Hamish.

Jack hesitated. 'I have,' he said, and produced a hank of reefing cord from his trouser pocket.

Lidya took it. She tied a loop of cord around the tiny head. The ewe bleated again, but didn't try to move, and Lidya again patted her firmly on the flank. 'Good lady!' she said.

'You aren't going to yank it out by the neck?' said Jack, horrified.

'No, no, push it back in.'

'*Back in*?' chorused the three watchers.

'The forelegs have to come first,' said Lidya firmly. She cupped both hands around the tiny head and pushed. At first nothing happened, and she grimaced, the others watching doubtfully. 'Help me!'

Miranda shrugged, and placed her hands behind Lidya's; and after much easing and wriggling the slippery object at last slid back inside the ewe. One of Lidya's hands followed, halfway to her elbow. The others could tell she was feeling around.

'Got one!' she said, and wriggled her arm out. Her hand followed, grasping a slender fetlock and hoof. 'More string!'

Jack with his knife cut off a new piece of cord, and Lidya tied it around the tiny limb. Her arm went inside the ewe again, which let out another piteous bleat, and tried to gather her legs together.

'Hold her down,' shouted Lidya, and Jack and Hamish leapt forward to do so. The ewe accepted the constraint silently.

After much further exploration, Lidya at last found and pulled out the second foreleg, and tied a cord to that too. 'Good!' she said, with a nod of satisfaction. '*Amat'ac!*' she shouted to the ewe, and slapped her side. '*Amat'ac*! Push!' she shouted, even louder. To Jack's amazement the ewe seemed to understand. Her body convulsed and after a few moments, following the slender forelegs, the small head reappeared, and then, quite suddenly, the whole lamb slithered out onto the grass, followed by a thin trail of umbilical cord.

Lidya wiped her hands on the grass and stood up. 'Now rub it,' she ordered. Miranda massaged the floppy lamb doubtfully at first and then more vigorously. The lamb wriggled. 'Good, now show it to the mother. Leave the cord. Don't touch it.' Miranda lifted the lamb and placed it at the ewe's head, the cord trailing behind. The ewe raised the front part of her body and started to lick her lamb's face, as though this was all in the day's work.

Miranda felt her legs shaking, and tried to wipe her arms on the grass. Lidya found in her jacket a small box of tissues and offered Miranda a handful.

Jack untied the strings from around the lamb's head and legs. 'You didn't use them,' he said doubtingly.

'They're just in case something goes badly wrong,' said Lidya. 'But it didn't… We're safe now, no more rush. Perhaps we should try and find the farmer.'

'I'll go,' said Hamish.

*

Not until five did Jane see Lidya and Jack returning slowly to the quay. They settled themselves on the shingle beside the inflatable. 'Waiting for the others,' she said to herself, refilled the kettle, and put it on to boil again.

It reached whistling point without anyone further appearing. Leaving the kettle to stand, she dug out wholemeal rolls, butter, tomatoes, and Bute cheddar. She washed the tomatoes and a somewhat sagging lettuce, and arranged everything on plastic plates in the cockpit. Then she decided something warm was called for, and emptied three tins of cock-a-leekie soup into a saucepan, before noticing that the inflatable was at last on its way.

There was only Jack in it, however, crouching low over the outboard, leaving the bow cocked up. He brought it in to *Ariel*'s stern and handed up the painter.

'Hi,' said Jane, making fast. 'Where is everyone?'

He clambered aboard, and looked back. 'Bit of an adventure... Not sure where the two lovebirds have got to. Lidya said she'd wait for them.' He noticed the food and grinned appreciatively.

'What adventure?'

He settled onto a cockpit seat. 'We found a sheep giving birth.'

'Wrong time of year, surely?'

'Yes... We were miles from anywhere. But Lidya knew what to do and she saved the day.'

'Didn't you call the farmer?'

'There wasn't time. The lamb was the wrong way round.'

'She *delivered* it?' A distant memory from medical school slid into the back of Jane's mind.

241

'Miranda helped her a bit.'

'The farmer was all over Lidya, once he got there. We all went down to his croft, Lidya rode with the ewe and lamb in the back of his pick-up. His wife gave us all whiskey... Don't think they'd seen anyone Lidya's colour before, but it didn't put them off. The missus kissed her and asked if she wanted a job.' Jack looked longingly at the supper but restrained himself, popped down into the cabin and returned munching an apple.

Jane laughed. 'Start properly if you want,' she said. 'I'll join you.'

'They talk Gaelic to each other... He hadn't realised the ewe was pregnant.'

'Did he explain how that could have happened?'

'Yes, he did. Very weird... They always leave the ewes to run with the ram in mid-September, and the lambs arrive in mid-February.'

'I thought it might be later.'

'That's what he said, five months gestation. Of course, they don't let the ewes have any more contact with the ram, but the new lambs run with the ewes for quite a while. He said the ram lambs are sometimes mature at two months, and, very very occasionally, they impregnate their own mothers.' Jack looked disturbed by this male irregularity.

'Bizarre!'

He nodded. 'It's extremely rare, he said, because the weather and the grass aren't good enough to mature the ram lambs that quickly. But he seemed to think it must be what happened... Extraordinary, isn't it? The whole thing was pretty amazing for me,' Jack admitted.

'Seen a birth before?'

'Never kept guinea pigs.'

Jane was watching the quay. 'Lidya's waving,' she

said.

'There they are,' said Jack, looking up. He slipped a slice of Bute cheddar into one cheek and climbed down into the inflatable. Jane tossed the painter into the bow, and watched as the little craft took a zigzag course to the quay, and then, after a few minutes, returned more slowly, much deeper in the water.

'I hear you've a heroine on board,' she said rather seriously when they arrived.

Lidya made a face. One by one everyone climbed aboard.

Hamish stayed for a moment in the cockpit as the other three went below. He looked to be sure they were out of hearing, and said quietly to Jane, 'Jack told you what happened?'

'Yes.'

'The farmer wanted to be sure I understood something—it seems there's a health hazard in lambing for pregnant women. '

'He's quite right, there is.'

'He was too embarrassed to say anything to Lidya directly, but he wanted to be sure someone told her.'

'I'll do that,' said Jane.

*

Before supper Miranda and Hamish went down below to fetch extra woollies and stayed there rather a long time. Jack looked down the ladder, and turned back to Lidya. 'They've shut themselves in your cabin,' he said apologetically.

'I expect they need somewhere to talk privately,' she said, and raised her eyebrows.

'What about?' asked Jane.

Lidya smiled.

'A *wedding* venue,' said Jack quietly.

'Hamish,' explained Lidya, 'wants it in Edinburgh. But *she* wants Plymouth.'

'She says that's what Mum would have wanted,' said Jack.

But Miranda and Hamish were returning. They climbed the steps, took their soup mugs and settled on opposite sides of the cockpit. Hamish looked around, his face determinedly cheerful. 'What's the forecast?' he ventured

'Westerlies tomorrow and Tuesday,' said Jane, and lowered her mug to her knee. 'But for Wednesday they're talking now about a south-easterly gale… We need to make plans.'

'Why?' asked Jack.

'To be sure of getting Hamish back to Oban by Friday night, I think we must use the westerly while we have it and sail back across tomorrow.'

'But we only just arrived,' urged Jack.

Hamish was just about to comment when Lidya said suddenly, 'Where is Fingal's Cave?'

'Staffa,' said Hamish.

'What about it?' said Jane.

'I was remembering Mendelssohn. The *Hebridean Overture.*'

'Ah!'

'And you'd like to see it?'

'Not if it would slow us up.'

'Well, said Jane. 'If we get across in good time tomorrow we would have time in hand to give it a flying visit. And if you're interested in places with connections we could visit Iona too.' She went below to fetch the chart, and on reappearing sat next to Lidya to study it. 'Iona's easy,' she said at last. 'But we'd need calm weather to land on Staffa.' Her finger pointed, and Lidya bent down to look.

'I'd like to see Iona,' said Lidya. 'Because of Saint Columba. He always makes me think of the Nine Saints.'

'Who were they?'

'They brought Christianity to Ethiopia at the same time as Columba was bringing it to Scotland.'

'I thought Ethiopia was Christian from New Testament times,' said Jane. 'You said it was.'

'That's just a legend,' said Lidya. 'Historically, we were Christian after the Nine Saints... They built monasteries everywhere.'

'You know the Abbey on Iona isn't mediaeval?' said Jane. 'It was rebuilt quite recently.'

'But there is an ancient chapel,' said Jack. 'With the graves of Scottish and Norwegian Kings.'

'You know a lot about it,' said Lidya. She seemed pleased at the thought.

'I've never actually been there,' said Jack.

'Nor me,' said Jane.

Iona

Next morning Jane's plan was to reach Arinagour on the south-east side of Coll by sunset. After that the expected south-easterly gale would make returning to Oban via the Sound of Mull a pain, but a passage around the south of the island, taking in Staffa and Iona as Lidya wanted, seemed workable.

The wind was westerly as expected, but disappointingly weak. Anxious to be safely across the Minch before dark, Jane roused the ship at six, and by eight-thirty they were on their way. She set full main and their largest jib, which Jack and Lidya poled out to catch what wind there was. For the first hour they took it in turns to steer, but eventually got bored, so as the wind strengthened slightly, Jane set James to work, and the three of them relaxed on deck as the low crags of Barra dwindled behind.

By lunchtime, they were within ten miles of the lonely white tower of Oigh Sgeir and beginning to get a clear view ahead and to their left of the jagged peak of Askival on Rhum. There had been the excitement of seeing a group of minke whales blowing only a hundred yards away, which even brought Miranda and Hamish on deck.

Towards evening, the wind died away as expected. Jane started the Volvo, and they motored sedately into Arinagour, picking up a visitor's buoy without difficulty. Lidya made supper, Jack tidied up, and they all turned in early.

*

Next morning the wind was a little stronger. It had swung round to the south, making it a beat down to Iona, but the distance wasn't great and the tacking took them through the line of the Treshnish Islands and allowed them a close look at Ulva and Gometra. Everyone cheered up a little, and in surprisingly little time they were near Staffa.

Jane sailed *Ariel* across the south side of the isolated island and they got a magnificent view from three hundred yards of its black basalt columns topped and tailed with volcanic tuff, making the whole lonely island a lopsided Greek temple, pierced by incongruous dark eye-sockets on either side.

'Which is Fingal's cave?' asked Lidya, who had the binoculars.

'On the right. The other's the Boat Cave.'

'Boat Cave looks bigger.'

'The water's deeper there,' said Hamish, 'and the tourist boats sometimes go right in. But Fingal's is longer. It stretches right under the island.'

However, the wind was blowing towards the shore. Big waves were curling into the cave and breaking on the landing spit to its right. 'I don't think so' said Jane at last. 'Not today. The anchorage is too exposed. And you'd have big trouble getting ashore.'

'Oh!' complained Lidya and Jack together. Hamish too seemed ready to question the decision. But then two particularly large waves washed completely over the landing spot, and he kept his mouth shut.

'Cheer up,' said Jane. 'The forecast gives us a better

chance tomorrow.' They sailed on, and by three had found their way into the Sound of Iona, the gentle green island gleaming in the autumn sunshine and calming tensions. Lidya was glued to the binoculars as they came in, inspecting the squat buildings of the Abbey.

'There's a village,' she said.

'And there's an ancient paved road all the way from the landing place to the Abbey,' said Hamish. 'It's the way they brought the old kings for burial.'

They downed the sails, and Jane motored cautiously into the Bull Hole, between rocky islets on the Mull side of the Sound, just north of the ferry slipway. 'There'll be a bit of swell with the wind this way,' she said, 'but it's a good anchorage.'

*

The small ferry in MacBrayne red and white was embarking sensibly wrapped Iona pilgrims from the slipway.

'Is there time to visit the abbey this afternoon?' said Miranda.

'I don't see why not,' said Jane. 'There'll be another chance in the morning.'

'Hamish?' said Miranda firmly.

'OK.'

'Me too,' said Jack.

'I'll wait,' said Lidya.

Jane looked at her with some surprise. 'Are you sure?' she asked.

'Yes. I'll do some more sketching.'

The inflatable was sorted out in double quick time, and had to dodge the ferry on its next crossing: the tide being low, the little vessel was making a wide detour to avoid shoal patches.

Jane watched as Lidya made a start on the Abbey, and after a while felt encouraged to try something herself. To keep it simple, she went for charcoal, and chose the ferry slipway: there were various small craft on buoys in the foreground, and as time passed, she was pleased with how it went.

After about an hour Lidya stretched and started to gather up her pastels. 'Coffee?' she said.

'Thanks,' said Jane. '... Oh, and before you go down...'

Lidya looked up.

'There's something I need to tell you... A message to pass on... That lamb you delivered. You do know there's some slight medical risk involved in what you did?'

'*Risk*?'

'The farmer wanted to be sure you knew. It's only if you're pregnant.'

Lidya stopped returning the pastels to their box.

'You didn't know?'

'No.' Lidya placed one pastel carefully in its slot and picked up another. 'What sort of risk?'

'Some sheep infections can be transmitted to women.'

'Affecting the baby?'

'Yes. Sometimes abortion.'

Lidya thought some more. 'But the lamb *wasn't* aborted,' she said. 'And the ewe was healthy.'

Jane nodded.

Lidya was still pondering. 'I don't think my mother can have known that,' she said, and laughed. 'But the danger's very small, you say?'

'Yes.'

She collected up the pastel box and paper and disappeared below.

*

The shore party divided. Jack chose to turn left, following the track that crossed the island, while Miranda and Hamish set off to explore the abbey.

Jack was back at the rendezvous on time, and soon saw Hamish and Miranda hurrying down the hill towards the pier.

'We took a detour,' said Hamish, with a little laugh.

'How was the Abbey?'

'Very good,' said Hamish.

'And we bought this map at the visitor centre,' said Miranda. She opened it. 'Show us where you got to.'

Jack examined it and pointed.

'The "Bay at the Back of the Ocean",' she read. 'What a gorgeous name!'

'We need get a move on,' said Hamish, and they set about manoeuvring the inflatable down to the water, watched by a queue of visitors waiting for the final ferry of the day.

*

The morning next day was still but chilly, and Jack made porridge.

Miranda arrived last for breakfast. Settling at the cabin table, she put one arm firmly round Hamish's waist, and he looked down at her with a big smile. She waited for a lull in the conversation, then said very loudly, 'You'll all be glad to know…'

Jack banged an encouraging spoon on the porridge saucepan for silence.

Miranda grinned. 'You'll be glad to know that

Hamish and I have made a *decision*...'

Hamish slid his arm around her shoulder.

'... we're going to get married!'

'Oh!' said Lidya. 'Lovely!'

'And we *think*... but we're not sure yet... that we're going to get hitched here, on Iona.'

'In the Abbey?' asked Jack. '*Can* you?'

'They told us at the visitor centre.'

'But what about the reception?' asked Jane.

'There are two hotels,' said Hamish.

'And there's a village hall. We can have a ceilidh! They told us you can ship in a band from Oban.'

'Great idea,' said Jane. 'It sounds absolutely splendid.' There was a moment of silent porridge handling as everyone took the news in, followed by a great deal of debate about details.

At last Lidya asked rather diffidently, 'Are some of us still going back to the island this morning?'

'Of course,' said Jane. 'I want to see it... But if I go with Lidya, are Hamish and Miranda happy to stay behind as anchor watch?'

'Sure,' said Hamish.

'Is it OK if I go again?' asked Jack. 'I want to photograph the graves of the kings.'

Once again, therefore, the inflatable crossed the sound.

*

Jane had brought binoculars and an ordnance map: she wanted to climb Dun I, the highest point on the island, for the views. Lidya said she'd accompany her and Jack left them at the Abbey gate.

The little peak was only two hundred feet high, so Jane and Lidya were soon at the top, surrounded by quietly grazing sheep. To the north-west on the horizon stretched the low strip of Coll, and to its south Tiree, peakier, but more distant and dimmer in the haze. To the right, nearer and sharper, lay the scattering of Treshnish Islands, the Dutchman's Cap particularly clear in outline, and then the dark smudge of Staffa. Behind that stood the purple lumps of Ulva and Gometra.

'Not bad,' said Jane, taking a deep breath. She raised her glasses for a closer inspection of Staffa, then studied her map. 'Those are the Cliffs of Gribun,' she said, pointing to the right of the tiny island. 'And the big peak behind them is Ben More.' She swung to her right. 'Over there's the Paps of Jura, sticking up over the Ross of Mull, down-sun… Got them?'

Lidya had found a rock and seated herself on it.

'And there,' said Jane, swinging round further to the south and looking out over the sea, 'I should be able to spot two lighthouses… A bit west of south— that must be Dubh Artach… Skerryvore seems to be lost in the haze…'

'Jane,' said Lidya sharply.

'What?'

Lidya sniffed and looked up, the curls at the ends of her hair framing her dark face.

Jane looked down at her.

'I've got a problem,' Lidya said quietly.

Jane waited.

Lidya drew a deep breath. She raised her eyebrows, swallowed, and looked down again. 'I'm pregnant,' she said.

'Oh! … Oh. How sure are you?'

'I've done a test. What you said about that sheep made me think I ought to.'

'Unmistakable result?'

'Yes.'

'What brand?'

'*Clear Blue.*'

'But when did you get the kit?'

'In Oban... I did a test then too, but it was negative.'

Jane counted on her fingers. 'Six days ago... What made you try then?'

'I got a taste I remembered.'

'Ah yes... Were you late?'

'Not then.'

'But you are now?'

'Yes.' Lidya looked down and up again. 'And I wasn't altogether surprised, you see.'

Jane raised her eyebrows.

Lidya nodded. 'I didn't want to disappoint him, it was the night before I left... But I'd run out of gel.' She looked up. 'I did use the diaphragm, though.'

Jane paused. 'You were unlucky,' she said at last. She looked uneasily at Lidya. 'How d'you feel, now you know?'

Lidya didn't reply, but dropped her head to her knees and wrapped her arms tightly around them.

Unsure whether she was doing the right thing, Jane moved to sit next to her, put an arm around her shoulders, and sought and squeezed one of her damp hands.

Lidya seemed to be weighing things up. After some time, she dropped Jane's hand and said in a matter-of-fact voice, 'Ralph will probably say we should get rid of it.'

'But you don't want to?'

Lidya turned her head sharply. '*No,*' she said. 'I don't. But *on the other hand* if something goes wrong this time that man will be back. He will...' Her fists

253

tightened, and she grated her knuckles fiercely together.

'Sir Ambrose fucking Eaton,' mouthed Jane privately to herself.

But Lidya had heard, and her face became rigid.

*

As they scrambled down to the road, Lidya made Jane promise to say nothing to the others. She needed time, she said, to get her bearings. She wouldn't even call Ralph, not straight away.

'What d'you feel now about Fingal's Cave?' asked Jane cautiously. 'Should we give that a miss?'

Lidya thought for a moment. '*No!*' she said at last. 'Of course not. I *still* want to see it. And why the hell should Sir Ambrose fucking Eaton stop me?'

Staffa

Back on *Ariel* Lidya everyone wanted to set off as soon as possible. 'The landing place is called '*Am Buchaillie*,' Lidya announced, having consulted her Blue Guide.

'That's where the tourist boats come in,' said Hamish.

Jane studied the chart. 'If it's the cave you want,' she said, 'you can get the inflatable ashore nearer, just to the east of the entrance.'

However, as soon as they'd motored out from the Bull Hole, Jane began to have doubts. The southerly wind, so slight at the top of Dun I, had risen. She hoisted just the big jib to carry them the short distance to Staffa with help from the engine, and as they approached it was clear that the swell, though weaker than Tuesday's, was still substantial.

'It's a beautiful morning,' said Jack encouragingly.

'That won't make landing any easier,' said Jane; and as they approached she turned *Ariel* and coasted back and forth along the south face of the island three times, inspecting the shore line through binoculars.

'All right,' she said at last, 'if you all really want to, we'll give it a try. I'll anchor as near as I dare, and give *Ariel* plenty of cable. Anyone want to stay here with me?'

No-one did.

Jane laughed. 'Right then! Hamish and Jack fore-deck, please. Eighteen fathoms…' Watching the echo sounder she judged her position and turned into the wind.

'Lower away the jib!'

Jack obliged, and put a tier around it.

Ariel slowed and stopped. 'Let go!' shouted Jane. The chain roared out, and jerked to rest at last. She checked the echo sounder. 'Another three fathoms, please!' Hamish measured the chain and eased it out, and Ariel settled herself, facing upwind away from the landing point. Jane recorded their exact GPS position.

'Right,' she said, when at last she was certain the anchor was holding, 'Now then… Hamish has most experience.'

Hamish looked around. 'OK,' he said.

'Be *damn* careful as you approach. And if you have any doubts about getting ashore, don't risk it. Remember the outboard motor is your return ticket, so be sure you don't whang the screw on the rocks. *Don't* try to take the inflatable into the cave, get ashore on the spit to the right. All right?'

'Yes.'

'If the anchor shows the slightest sign of dragging, I'll give you a single hoot on the foghorn, and you *must* set off back at once.'

'OK.'

'And if the wind rises and I want you to return anyway, I'll give two hoots.'

The inflatable was pumped up and launched, and Hamish climbed in. Jack handed him the outboard, which he clamped in position. He checked the fuel. Miranda and Lidya climbed in, followed by Jack with his camera in a plastic bag. Hamish started the engine.

'Off with you!' shouted Jane against the din, and threw the painter to Miranda in the bows. Hamish opened the throttle, and away they roared.

*

As they approached the spit to the right of the cave, the swell rose higher. Hamish throttled back, and steered first left and then right to inspect the landing area.

'What an extraordinary place!' said Miranda.

To their left, basalt columns rose tall on both sides of the cave entrance, like the pillars of a cathedral nave. Deep waves were sweeping headlong into the opening every twenty seconds or so: they could already hear the sucking echo as each passed into the hollow chamber beyond. The low spit ahead of them consisted entirely of the ends of yet more columns, two or three feet across, like the hexagonal ends of a bunch of huge unsharpened pencils, sticking up irregularly, alternately exposed and submerged as the sea rose and fell. There was no shingle.

Hamish stared anxiously. At last he found a place where a gap between slightly taller columns made a shallow valley.

'Right,' he said. 'Miranda, ready with the painter?'

Rope in hand, Miranda got one knee up onto the rubber bow.

'Jack and Lidya, ready with the paddles.' Hamish stopped the engine, unclamped the outboard and lifted it right into the boat, away from the rocks. 'Now drive like stink!'

The inflatable staggered forward, and there was a long squeak as its rubber floor grounded on one of the columns. Miranda leaped onto the head of another and managed to hold the bow steady. Jack scrambled out sideways, and Hamish passed him the outboard. A wave suddenly lifted the lightened boat and flung it three feet higher, Miranda scrambling up the rocks ahead of it, holding the painter tight.

Jack placed the outboard safely on rocks well above the water, and Hamish waited while Lidya high-stepped out, then left the inflatable himself, one deck shoe plunging under water. He and Jack grasped the grab handles, and with Miranda and Lidya hauling they lifted the boat safely ten feet above the sea, stepping precariously from the top of one column to another.

'Right,' said Hamish, his legs unsteady. He sat down, and the others followed suit, laughing a little. Looking seaward, *Ariel* seemed small and far away, her stern pointed towards them. Hamish thought he could see Jane in the well, watching their progress through binoculars.

'I'm going to climb up to get a few pictures,' announced Jack at once, and the others watched doubtfully as he clambered slowly up the headland to the right of the cave entrance, and spent some time on its crest, snapping in all directions.

'Shall we get up there too?' asked Miranda. But Jack was already returning, so they waited.

'Marvellous light,' he said as he rejoined them. 'Now, I want some from inside, looking out.'

The other three followed. At the cave entrance, they discovered a crude path entering on the right hand side, running over the irregular tops of further exposed columns. It was very narrow, and to its right someone had fixed an iron handrail to the cave wall—very necessary, for there was a sharp drop on the left into deep gurgling water.

Jack was moving forward quickly. 'Dodgy place, this,' he called back. 'Just stop there a moment!' He took several shots of their figures against the light, then turned and hurried on deeper into the cave. Lidya pressed forward and followed closely behind him.

Miranda and Hamish followed more slowly. As they worked onwards, stepping from one column top to another in deepening gloom, the sounds of the cave became more sharply defined. As each luminous wave passed, moving relentlessly into the cavern, it made a deep rushing noise, which, as it moved onward, changed gradually into an ever-deepening boom. Much later, after what seemed like thirty or forty seconds, they heard the wave break on some distant strand hidden under the bulk of the island. But instead of the usual clatter and sucking of a breaking wave the sound returning to them was transmuted by the echo-chamber of the cave into a musical note, or rather a series of interwoven musical notes, a fantastic hooting, as though of strange prehistoric beasts or the whistling of a breeze through gargantuan pan-pipes.

'You can hear why it had such a big effect on Mendelssohn,' said Miranda.

Hamish put one arm firmly round her shoulder. 'In Gaelic they call it *Uamh-Binn*,' he pronounced, '*Cave of Melody*.' They stopped and listened to the cave-cadences for some time.

But then, unexpectedly, from some distance ahead, they heard a muffled double thump, its second part louder than the first.

'What was *that*?' asked Miranda uneasily.

Hamish was listening.

Then came something like a distant shout, half lost in the resounding echoes of the cave, and very quickly after, another, more extended. Its pitch was quite high.

'Lidya?' whispered Hamish. He listened, but they heard nothing more.

'How far ahead were they?' asked Miranda.

'Thirty yards? More?' Hamish moved forward as

fast as he could, one hand guided by the rail, and Miranda followed. After fifteen yards or so he stopped and bellowed, 'Jack! Lidya!'

There was no reply.

'We're totally on our own here,' murmured Miranda.

'Too right,' said Hamish, 'got to be damn careful.' He pressed on slowly. But the column-tops of the path were getting harder to see.

Five more times Hamish stopped and shouted, to no effect.

'Why ever didn't we bring a torch?' said Miranda. It was getting too dark to see anything clearly.

'Where the heck *are* they?' said Hamish. 'There's a bit more light if you look back,' he added. Behind them they could see at the mouth of the cave a cameo image of Iona etched on the distant horizon.

'This place is dangerous,' said Miranda. 'Look how sheer the columns drop down into the water behind us.'

Hamish followed her pointing finger. 'What's that?' he said suddenly.

'Where?'

'In the water.'

'How far back?'

'Only twenty feet!' He started to scramble back. Dimly against the light, he could see two orange lifejackets rolling in the water below the path, lifted three feet or so with each wave that passed. 'We passed them!'

Miranda had seen too. 'Dear God!' she muttered.

Hamish reached the spot and realised that the handrail there was swinging loose. The path was a good fifteen feet above a sheer drop; looking down he could just make out in the gloom that Jack was floating inertly. Lidya was waving, her dark arm, face and hair almost invisible in the swirling water, but he could see her eyes shining.

'Are you all right?' he shouted.

She replied, but the sound didn't reach him: it was reflected back from the basalt face and lost in the unending hooting of the cave. He let go of the springing rail and bent down to get his face as near above hers as he could.

'Hamish!' yelled Miranda, and clung to his knees. Disconcertingly her hand discovered beside her in the dark a woven camera-strap, and she clung to that, too, without conscious thought.

'Louder, Lidya! Louder!' shouted Hamish. 'We can't hear you!'

Faintly came back: '… banged his head.'

'Is he knocked out?'

'… Yes… Bleeding… '

'Can you keep his face out of the water?'

'… trying… '

But looking down he realised how hard it was for her. 'I don't think we can climb down to pull you out,' he shouted

'… not safe … ' came Lidya's echo.

'We'll pass you a rope!'

'The painter,' said Miranda, 'That's all we've got… I'll go.'

It was a long wait. Hamish could see that Lidya was finding the waves difficult to handle, but she seemed unpanicked. He could see no sign of life in Jack. His heart beat faster.

Miranda returned at last.

Hamish explored the length of the painter in the dark. 'Too short!' he said at once. 'Even if we don't make a loop.' He lowered it down. The rope just reached Lidya, but there was no way of getting a purchase on it to haul Jack up.

'Damn,' said Hamish.

'… give it me…' called Lidya, Hamish passed the rope down, and watched as she eventually managed to lash Jack to herself.

'Can you pull him along at all?' called Hamish.

Lidya tried, and managed to drag Jack a foot or two through the water.

'That's no good,' shouted Hamish. 'And there's nowhere further along we can get down to you… We'll have to bring the inflatable.'

'Is it safe, bringing it into the cave?' asked Miranda softly.

'We don't have any other option.'

'Shall I stay here?'

'No,' said Hamish, after thinking. 'The inflatable is our lifeline, and two are better than one for managing it safely.'

Lidya must have heard this: their voices from above were evidently reaching her relatively easily. '… you go… ' she shouted. '… anchor us… '

'Is she going to tie herself on?' asked Miranda.

'I think so.'

Lidya managed to loop the free end of the painter round the top of a column. Having seen this safely accomplished, Miranda and Hamish hastened back to the daylight, adrenaline pumping. As they at last blinked in the sunlight, they heard two hoots on *Ariel*'s foghorn.

'Can't be helped,' said Hamish. 'Can't risk the outboard in the cave entrance. Have to paddle.'

They eased the inflatable towards the water, and Miranda held it while Hamish fetched the outboard and laid it on the bottom boards. With a struggle they paddled the little boat out across the area of swelling waves and round towards the cave entrance. As they entered the cave they heard Jane hoot again.

'Now paddle *hard*!' shouted Hamish.

On a switchback of green luminous water they forced their way forward into gloom and deeper water, but it seemed an intolerable age before they had penetrated far enough to be searching again for the two life jackets; as before their eyes failed to pick them out, but Lidya's shouts drew them in the right direction. Her glistening eyes when they reached her seemed to Hamish dreadfully exhausted.

'He's breathing,' Lidya shouted, untying the loop that held Jack. 'But it's not going to be easy getting him into the boat.'

She was right.

'We need that under his armpits,' said Miranda.

Lidya nodded, untied herself, and passed up the rope, hanging on to a grab handle with one hand. Leaning over the side, Miranda managed to get the painter into position and nodded. Hamish hauled, the inflatable wobbled perilously, Miranda grabbed Jack's thighs and heaved, and at last he slithered in over the side.

'Same for you?' called Hamish.

Lidya nodded, and before long she too was wriggling over the edge. Arms shaking, Hamish and Miranda paddled as strongly as they could towards the light, while Lidya massaged Jack's hands with fingers scarcely less cold. At last they were past the cave threshold, and Hamish could fit the outboard and start it.

The sputtering roar and sparkling sunlight seemed to affect them all, including Jack, who twitched, sneezed, then put one hand jerkily to his head, where blood was oozing thickly from his matted hair. Concerned, Lidya slapped his hand, and when this had little effect, his cheek.

Jack spat out gobs of sea-water, crinkled his brow opened his eyes, and muttered something incomprehensible.

Lidya bent down shivering, and kneaded his hand again.

*

'Where the hell have you been?' shouted Jane as they came alongside. Then she saw the blood on Jack's scalp and forehead.

'He banged his head,' said Miranda.

'Badly?'

'Yes,' said Lidya.

But Jack was trying to speak. '... camera?' he slurred.

'Got it,' said Miranda sharply, and showed him.

Jack half-grinned. He tried to stand, wobbled and sat down again. Hamish climbed aboard over *Ariel*'s stern, leant over the inflatable and grabbed Jack's right arm. Jane grabbed his left, Jack stood up and they hauled him into the cockpit, water draining off him. He sat down quickly.

Jane glanced at Lidya, sodden as she was, and caught her eye, but she simply nodded towards Jack. Jane leant over him and parted the hair on his scalp. There was another gush of blood. She pressed gently on the area, frowned and swallowed. 'Not good,' she said, and looked around. 'Now then, ship safety first... Hamish and Miranda, foredeck please.' She started the Volvo. 'Don't fuss with the inflatable, Lidya... Leave it towing on a short painter.'

'Up anchor?' called Hamish.

'Of course!' Jane got the engine into gear and eased *Ariel* forward.

The foredeck crew wound in furiously. 'Up-and-down,' shouted Hamish at last.

Jane opened the throttle. A safe quarter mile from the island, she eased it back, and after Hamish and Miranda had stowed the anchor, she got them to help Lidya haul the inflatable aboard.

'Don't deflate it,' she said. 'We need somewhere quiet to sort ourselves out, and there's a decent anchorage over there.' She opened up the throttle again. 'Now, warm clothes for Lidya, you help her Miranda... Wheel, Hamish, please. A bit to the left of Iona for the moment, I'll give you a proper course in a minute... Let's get Jack down in the cabin, too.' She went ahead, and turned to help him down the steps, then threw an oilskin onto Jack's berth, settled him on it, and examined his scalp again.

Jack winced.

'That needs hospital... How are you feeling?'

'Jus' woozy,' said Jack. He slurred the 'z' badly.

Jane looked at him sharply. 'How the hell did you do it?' she asked.

Jack looked puzzled.

'Don't remember?'

He pursed his lips and at last shook his head.

'What's the last you *do* remember?'

Jack took his time. 'Graves of the Kings,' he said at last, uncertainly.

'Yesterday.'

'Was it?' asked Jack.

Jane raised her eyebrows. 'It was... Miranda!' she called.

'Coming!' Miranda wriggled out of the fore cabin.

Behind her Jane could see Lidya, comfortable now in pyjamas, hauling an Arran sweater over her head.

'What was it happened?' she asked.

'I didn't see. Lidya knows.'

'What's that?' said Lidya, settling at the cabin table. 'What happened, exactly?'

'The handrail gave way, inside the cave. He fell.'

'And banged his head?'

'Yes, dropped about eight or nine feet, fell sideways and banged his head, then rolled into the water.'

Jack looked amazed, and cautiously put one hand to his scalp.

'Was he unconscious?'

'Yes. I was afraid he was going to drown.'

'So what did you do?'

Lidya made a face. 'I jumped in after him.'

'Just like that!'

'At first he wasn't breathing. I managed to blow one or two good breaths into his mouth. How they told me at school.'

'While the two of you were bobbing around in the water?'

'Then he did start to breathe. But his head kept flopping.'

'How long before he came to?'

'That was much later. After we got him into the inflatable.'

'How long?'

'Fifteen or twenty minutes.'

'More,' said Miranda.

'Oh dear,' said Jane. 'Got to take this seriously, I'm afraid… I'll put a dressing on your head in a minute, Jack. Can you start getting him dry, Miranda?'

'Of course.'

Jane went on deck, looked around, came back down

to study the chart, and returned to talk to Hamish. 'Pretty sure it's a depressed fracture,' she said. 'Is there a decent hospital in Oban?'

'On the main road south... A skull fracture, you said?'

'That's what it feels like. If we go in now to Bunessan, how soon can we get him there?'

'Bus or taxi across Mull, ferry to Oban, taxi to hospital... Three and a half hours if lucky. Probably the best we can do—the nearest rescue helicopter's in Prestwick.'

'Could you go with him? I'd better stay with *Ariel*.'

'Of course!'

'OK... Now, well to your left—you can see the entrance already...'

PART III

Communications

From: lidya.slade@hotmail.com
Date: 23 Oct 2003 13:07:32
To: jacktallis3@btinternet.com
Subject: A very very big thank you

Dear Jack,

Ralph and I are both so glad to know you're home and back to
normal. And thanks very much for the kind things you said. We
had a marvellous cruise, didn't we?

Lidya

SAFEGUARDING CHILDREN BOARD
SOCIAL SERVICES

30th Oct

Dear Mrs Slade,
Just to confirm with you tomorrow at 11.30
Doreen Kent

Hi Lidya,

So here I am, settled in at last! Miranda and I have agreed to share the cooking whenever she's here, so for the big day I did the turkey and she did the pudding and mince pies and a really splendid cheesecake as well.

I'm already halfway through your ikon book— beautiful, and, to my eyes at least, quite extraordinary. Thank you.

Tom's lying on the rug snoozing by a crackling log fire, and it would be just too *unkind to wake him to solicit his thanks for the elegant cashmere enclosing his torso, so let me express them on his behalf!*

Hamish is with us too, of course. The love-birds are up in Miranda's bedroom, totally taken up yet again with wedding plans, and Jack, his scull magically restored, is floating around the house being discreetly helpful to everyone.

I know Tom may not have said very much, but I just wanted to be sure you understand how very deeply in your debt he feels—which goes for all of us as well, of course. Thank goodness *over and over again that the great rescue left you (and yours) unscathed.*

Much love and see you soon,

Jane

2nd Jan 2004

Case 135(b)/2003:
Baby Slade

Dear Mr and Mrs Slade,

As you already know, having been informed in November of Mrs Slade's pregnancy, and in the light of the two
earlier cases of unexplained infant
death in your family and the subsequent
court proceedings, the Safeguarding
Children Board decided in late November
that it should institute a Section 47
Investigation to determine whether your
child to be born might be in need of
protection.

I am now writing to inform you that
the Board has as a result of this investigation concluded that protection is
necessary.

Their decisions are:

1) that Mrs Slade ought to have no un-
supervised access to her infant;

2) that the infant should be delivered
in hospital, where it will be cared for
initially in the Special Care Baby Unit;
and

3) that the baby should then be trans-
ferred to appropriate foster parents.

Accordingly, the Board has made appli-
cation to the Family Division of the
High Court for a Protection Order, and
we expect the case to be heard in March.

I should like to assure you that the
members of the Board are acutely aware
that their decisions are likely to prove

distressing to you, and were only taken after the most careful consideration. I must remind you, however, that the well-being of your unborn child must be paramount.

If you have any questions about the procedure, please do not hesitate to contact me. You may also find it helpful to contact the Children and Family Court Advisory and Support Service (CAFCASS), which can provide you with independent advice.

Please acknowledge receipt of this letter on the enclosed form.

Yours sincerely,

Jean Hoskins

Senior Social Worker
Secretary to the Board

10th January

Dear Mr and Mrs Slade,

I hope you are bearing up under these very distressing circumstances.

As we agreed, I have now consulted James Pierce QC of Salisbury who is familiar with Family Court work, and will, I am sure, be able to represent you there effectively.

Yours sincerely,

Cyril Cormack

22nd March

Dear Lidya and Ralph,

Jane has told us something of how deeply the Family Court's decision has affected you both, and on behalf of the support group, I am writing to let you know how distraught we all feel. We were shocked, really shocked, to hear that Sir Ambrose had given evidence, blatantly biased against you as he is.

Jane also passed on your lawyer's warning that we mustn't campaign publicly, but it is surely a scandal that such a flagrant injustice cannot be discussed or even reported in the newspapers.

We all wish you the very best of fortune in your appeal, which we understand will be heard in mid-April.

Raja

'Tom here, Ralph...   Just to wish you luck for Tuesday.'

'We certainly need it ... Half a second, I'll turn that down...'

'How are you both?'

'Doing our best to conserve strength, Tom.'

'I bet.'

'And, to be honest, rattled.'

'But you said James Pierce was optimistic?'

'Cautiously, yes...'

'Bloody hard...   We just wish we could be more help...   Now, you probably don't have any spare energy for chit-chat just now. But the fact is, Ralph... we've got a bit of news.   If this isn't the moment, just say so. Jane thought we shouldn't be troubling you with it...'

A noticeable pause. 'It's OK, go ahead'

'Well... The fact is... Jane's pregnant!'

'Say that again.'

'Jane's expecting.'

'Expecting a *baby*?'

'Yes.'

'Tom! ... I can't believe it. Hold on!'

A rapid-fire explanation, Lidya's startled '*No!*' Then a confused noise and rattle.

'Tom! Where is she? Let me speak to her!'

'She went out...   She knows you've got so many awful things on your mind.'

'She's an idiot!' Lidya seemed to be sniffing back tears, but with some determination nevertheless. 'Congratulations, oh, congratulations!'

'Are you OK? ... We weren't sure this was quite the moment.'

'Don't be silly, Tom, please. It's *good*... Of course it

is. How's she feeling about it?'

'Jane? Over the moon! *Really*. Me too… And a bit overawed, I suppose. She's still worrying about motherhood, you know—but only about once a week now.'

There was another extended sniff, but then Lidya was laughing too, in her husky voice, and Tom found himself laughing back. 'Tell her to call me,' she demanded, 'the *moment* she gets in… And tell her from me she's an idiot… Twice over. A *double* idiot… As if we could *possibly* not have wanted to know!'

From: t.tallis@dandc.pnn.police.uk
Date: 30.03 2004 10:02:57
To: super.plym@dandc.pnn.police.uk
Subject: Slade Family Court decision

The Board **did** contact us. We told them in the strongest terms we were confident the acquittal was correct, no foul play in either death.

Can we talk?
Tom

April 23rd 2004

Dear Mr and Mrs Slade,

Allow me to congratulate you on your success in the Court of Appeal. I felt there must be light at the end of the tunnel once I'd heard Mr Pierce's demolition job on Sir Ambrose's line of argument. I believe we got as much as we could reasonably hope. We owe Mr Pierce quite a debt of gratitude.

Yours sincerely,

Cyril Cormack

SAFEGUARDING CHILDREN BOARD
SOCIAL SERVICES

21st May 2005

Case 135(b)/ 2003:
Baby Slade

Dear Mr and Mrs Slade,

This letter is confirmation of the final revised arrangements for the birth of your baby.

Your infant must be delivered in the Derriford Hospital. Provided it is healthy, you will be permitted to take it home with you one week after the birth.

Once home, however, neither of you must

278

be left alone with it. You have indicated
that you are willing to pay for suitably
qualified attendants to be present, by day
and by night, and I must now request you
to pass their names to Mrs Kent, who will
arrange for them to be vetted by the police.

Kindly acknowledge receipt of this letter on the enclosed form.

Yours sincerely,

Jean Hoskins

Senior Social Worker
Secretary to the Board

Zeina

There was no hesitation this time about the name: Lidya's third child was to be Zeina, after Lidya's youngest and favourite sister. As required, she was born in the Special Care Baby Unit of the Derriford on 7th June, and the following day, Jane was able to visit.

She found Lidya propped up in bed in a solo ward, breast-feeding. Seated watching her were two nurses, one wearing a staff nurse's belt. An empty crib on trolley wheels stood by the door. The ward was lit by fluorescent lights, the venetian blinds covering its windows closed against the June sunlight. Ralph was there too, pacing the limited space.

Lidya glanced up from her charge.

Jane hastened forward to press her hand, and in-spect. The tiny scrap's eyes were brown-green and intent: she was sucking strongly. She had her mother's high cheek bones, but her skin was milky-coffee, paler than Ayana's. 'Gorgeous!'

Ralph caught Jane's eye and raised his eyebrows.

There was a pause. Lidya switched the baby to her other breast. The junior nurse stood up to make sure she had latched on properly, but Lidya stared her down with an angry face.

Jane looked around for a chair, but there was none spare. 'Ralph told me you had a rough time,' she said quietly.

Lidya nodded.

'A breech.'

A weary smile, without looking up. 'Yes.' The smile vanished as quickly as it had come.

'But they sorted it?'

'After quite a flap.' said Ralph. 'They had to fetch the consultant.'

'Stitches?'

'Thirty-five.'

Jane pursed her lips. 'How are you feeling now?'

Lidya looked around, and at last faced Jane. 'Sore... And frightened,' she added.

Jane nodded. 'But you *mustn't* be,' she said. 'You really mustn't. There'll be good people watching over her absolutely 24/7. You *know* there will. It's going to be all right.'

The corners of Lidya's mouth twitched and she looked quickly at the senior nurse. She seemed to be thinking. 'That's not the only thing I'm frightened of,' she said.

'What, then?'

'Losing control,' she said quietly, to no one in particular, and shivered.

Jane, aware of the nurses, said nothing.

'You *won't*,' said Ralph quickly.

Lidya gave a tiny shake of her head.

But Zeina had lost interest, one tiny fist was waving in the air. Lidya hoisted her up and began to knead her back. The staff nurse rose but Lidya paid her no attention and she sat down again..

'You'll feel better when you're home,' said Jane.

'Will I?'

'Of course!' said Ralph.

But a tear was running down Lidya's cheek. After a few moments she wiped her eyes on her sleeve, gripped her daughter, held her up high, and stared into her tiny face.

The junior nurse rose, and put out a steadying hand.

Lidya snatched the child to her shoulder.

The staff nurse coughed. 'Better put her down now,' she said, and pulled forward the crib on wheels. The junior nurse held out her hands in expectation. Lidya kissed Zeina tenderly, stared at her for a moment, then handed her over. The nurses tucked Zeina in, working together, one on each side of the crib, and wheeled her away.

Lidya's eyes followed them until they were out of sight, then closed tight, as if the compliance had cost her a good deal. Ralph sat down and put an arm round her shoulders. Jane took the other vacated chair and sought Lidya's free hand. It was clammy. Looking up she saw beads of sweat springing on Lidya's smooth dark forehead, just below the hairline.

*

After the specified seven days Lidya and Zeina were dispatched home in an ambulance, and Ralph's organisation swung into action. He had a team of seven chaperones, engaged for eight-hour shifts; Peggy was scheduled for the first, and had arrived at 3 pm, ready to welcome them. The social worker Mrs Kent was also on hand to check the arrangements, but when the ambulance swung into the drive, she withdrew discreetly to her car. Jane was waiting in the hall. The hot June weather had broken, and rain was bucketing down.

Peggy whisked Zeina upstairs and Ralph had an umbrella ready for Lidya. She slipped quietly into the house, collapsed into his arms and burst into tears.

'Good to be home?' he said.

She nodded, but with little enthusiasm. 'Peggy's got her?'

'Yes... Want to go see?'

'Of course.'

She climbed the stairs slowly and walked into the nursery. Peggy made space beside the basket.

Zeina was asleep. Lidya put down one hand and gently stroked the baby's hair and forehead, all that was visible. Then her eye caught the new pink alarm, clipped to the left side of the crib. 'That awful thing,' she said with a shudder.

'Got to have it,' said Peggy.

Lidya made a face. 'Good old Peggy,' she said, and wandered tentatively around, inspecting the arrangements, then seemed to abandon interest. 'I think I'll lie down for a bit.'

'How about a cup of tea?' suggested Ralph.

'Yes, please.'

'You too Peggy?'

'If it's not too much trouble.'

Lidya took one more long look at Zeina, walked slowly to the nursery door and turned left along the landing for the bedroom; Ralph followed her and turned right. Peggy watched them go, listened as Ralph's feet thudded down the stair carpet, shaking her head slowly as she turned back to the crib.

*

Jane had remained downstairs, but heard Ralph's offer to make tea and joined him in the kitchen.

'Could you hang on here for a bit? Please?' he asked, before setting off upstairs with two cups on a tray. When he came down again he poured two more and carried them to the sitting room. 'She's pretty depressed,' he said as they sat down.

'Weepy?' asked Jane. 'Withdrawn?'

'Both of those... You heard her say she was afraid of losing control... And it's bizarre—she seems to think Zeina *hates* her.'

'That's post-natal depression, Ralph,' said Jane.

'Peggy said that too.'

'She's quite right' said Jane, 'It's terribly common after a long period of stress. And just remember what you poor people have had to go through. For *years* now.'

'*And* we had this awful row.'

'A row? Recently?'

'No no, ages ago. It was when we were waiting for the Appeal Court to make up their minds. The tension had been so fucking *relentless*, I rushed out of the house... drove the car like a maniac round the Moor roads. And of course she didn't know where I'd gone. Frantic I'd crashed and killed myself.'

'What had you rowed about?'

'What d'you think? Caught me in the bedroom with an empty bottle... We hadn't been sleeping properly... So she blew up. And it was so obvious she was forcing herself to calm down for the sake of the baby— meaning *I'd* let her down absolutely and completely. Of course I wanted to rush off...'

'Ralph, if it's PND, maybe she needs professional help. I'm trying to remember what's the arrangements are supposed to be now.'

'We carry on this chaperoning for six months... On probation.'

'And after that?'

'They appoint a forensic psychiatrist to assess us.'

'*That's* not going to help her PND any,'

'No,' said Ralph. 'But there's something else. She's

scared… of what she might *do*.'

'*Do*? To herself?'

'I can't tell, can I?'

'To *Zeina*?'

Ralph buried his forehead in both hands.

'She *wouldn't*, Ralph! *Never!*' said Jane.

*

'But it *is* an issue, isn't it?' said Tom. 'With PND?'

Jane raised her eyebrows. 'Technically, yes,' she said. 'A very few patients with PND have a psychosis… But I don't believe Lidya does.'

'The trouble is, Ralph knows what she said. The issue is *there*. So if something happened, and he'd never told the Board… I think we have to advise him to tell them.'

'But if he does that they'll surely want to assess her.'

'Yes.'

'Which would drive her right round the bend.'

'Maybe not.'

'I want to judge her state of mind for myself first, Tom.'

He frowned. 'Better be quick about it.'

*

Lidya sat curled on her white sofa, apparently calmly. 'Dad called me this afternoon,' she said.

'Did that help?'

'Darling *Abayä*—he makes himself out to be so dispassionate and philosophical, stoical, but inside he's smiling to himself and he trusts me—he *is* a comfort… And it's been a distraction of sorts getting the nursery decently organised… But, dear Jane, I can't *stand* the sight of that baby monitor. It makes me retch.'

285

'And Ralph's under pressure, too.'

'Of course,' said Lidya. 'I'm not sure how much more we can take... I can't *stand* this regiment of attendants milling around night and day.'

'Peggy's a support?'

'I'm a lot less happy with that Marsha Stone.'

'Why?'

'I'm sure it was her who persuaded Elizabeth to raise Child Protection with the Board in the first place... And I only just got that snake Mrs Kent out of the house before you came.'

'*Is* she a snake?' Jane had privately made contact with Mrs Kent, and found her sensible, ready to withhold judgement on the danger to Zeina, but dismayed at Lidya's unwillingness to be open with her.

'Well, she doesn't say so to me, but I'm sure she thinks I murdered Gabriel and Ayana.'

'Mm... Ralph did say you had some other anxieties.'

'What?'

'Well... He said you had some fears about what you might do.'

Lidya looked hard at Jane. 'He told you about that?'

Jane nodded.

Lidya's faced hardened and for a while she said nothing. 'It's true,' she said at last, 'that I did get some very weird feelings about Zeina, so it was a worry... But I'm over that. Well over it.'

And with that, Jane felt she had to be content.

*

'OK if I smoke?' said Ralph. Rain was hammering at the windows.

Tom glanced at Jane, who shrugged. 'Of course,' he

said, and went to hunt for an ashtray.

Ralph fished a Sobranie out of his pocket, lit up, and inhaled deeply. He looked uneasily first at Tom and then at Jane, blew out a lungful of smoke, and coughed. Then he ran his right hand over his wet hair and examined his palm, which he wiped on his hand-kerchief. 'Don't know what I should do,' he said at last.

Jane waited. Ralph set down the cigar, and smoke curled up lazily from the ashtray.

Tom considered for some time. 'I reckon you don't have much choice,' he said.

'I ought to tell the sodding Board what she said?'

'Yes.'

Ralph looked distressed.

'This isn't something it's safe to conceal, Ralph,' urged Tom. 'Better tell Mrs Kent what you're afraid of.'

Ralph scowled. 'She probably knows already.'

'How?'

'Marsha.'

'If Marsha knows, everyone will know,' said Jane. 'She'll certainly tell Elizabeth.'

'How did Marsha know?' asked Tom.

'She overheard Lidya telling me me how distressed she was about that mother who drove her car with two kids into a river.'

'Lidya needs counselling, doesn't she?' said Jane.

'But she's scared of what psychiatric assessment might lead to,' said Ralph. 'And our appeal Court Ruling was on the front page of the *Herald* last week. Did you see?'

'Ralph, how horrible!'

'The last thing we want is a news report that Lidya's seeing a shrink.'

'But if she really needs it?' insisted Jane.

'I'm not sure she does. OK, she's depressed. But in spite of what she says, my gut feeling is that her emotions are OK.' Ralph looked questioningly at Jane.

Jane nodded vigorously.

'But you'll inform the Board?' said Tom.

Ralph picked up the dying remains of his Sobranie, leaving a long cylinder of ash in the ashtray. He sucked in one last lungful and ground out the stub. 'I don't know,' he said quietly and puffed out uncertainly.

*

On the Thursday evening Ralph called again and spoke to Tom.

'I told Mrs K,' he said.

'Good.'

'She told the Board. They want a psychiatric assessment.'

'How did Lidya take that?'

'Refused to talk.'

'Oh dear. When will it be?'

'Monday. Mrs K. wanted Friday, but the shrink couldn't make it. It's to be at the Langdon Hospital.'

'But that's the Forensic Mental Health place, Ralph. It's where the secure unit is, near Dawlish.'

'And it's men only... But that's where she has to go.'

Detonation

Early on the Sunday morning, as it was still dark, Jane was dragged awake by the demented trilling of the bedside phone. She felt Tom make a grab at it.

'Yes?' he said sharply, fumbling for the bedside light.

The voice was female.

'My *God*!' he said, and lay propped for a moment on one elbow. 'My God… OK.' He turned and stared at Jane. 'When?' He listened some more, slammed the receiver back onto its cradle, flung back the quilt and stood up.

'What is it?'

'That was Aliza. The Slade baby's been attacked.'

Her throat constricted violently. '*Attacked?*'

'But survived… She's in intensive care.' He began to throw on his clothes. 'Super wants me in quick.'

'He's at *work*?' Jane said stupidly.

'He will be by the time I get there.'

*

'Damn tricky,' the Super said, and pushed his jaw forward. 'I've allocated the case to Andrew.'

'*Andrew?*'

'Yes.'

Tom raised his eyebrows expressively. 'You've decided I'm too close?'

'Exactly,' said the Super. 'And added to that the awkward fact that the organiser of the support group has recently moved in with you, I believe.'

Tom's jaw tightened. 'Why not Iain?'

'*No*, Tom. Last time around he was just as convinced as you that the woman was innocent. It's *got* to be seen publicly as a fresh pair of eyes, and someone of your rank… The evidence is stronger this time.'

'I haven't heard it yet.'

'I know… You still think she's innocent?'

Tom raised his eyebrows and grimaced.

The Super inspected his hands on the desk and looked up again. '*However*,' he said, 'I know what you feel about this woman, and sometimes more angles than one is a wise precaution. So I've asked Andrew to keep you and your team informed through Iain as to what's happening, and he's briefing him now. But understand, it must be seen to be *his* investigation, not yours. If you and Iain conclude that something's going wrong, you can come to me. But *not* to Andrew. And for God's sake keep a low profile. I don't mean just the press. *Nobody* outside this building must know you're involved at all… Is that clear?'

'Yes.'

'You don't feel you *ought* to stay out of it?'

'No,' said Tom. 'I don't.'

*

Iain's office was littered with plastic cups from the coffee machine. Aliza was perched on a tall stool.

'Tell me!' demanded Tom.

'Seen the Super?' asked Iain.

'Yes… Someone attacked the baby?'

Iain nodded. 'Bruising all round the neck.'

290

'Attempted strangling?'

'Yes.'

Tom frowned. 'Who was in the house?'

'The two Slades plus the midwife: she'd taken over as chaperone at eleven.'

'And?'

'Lidya fed the baby and Peggy put it in the crib. Then they all had an Ovaltine together in the nursery. Ralph and Lidya went to bed and Peggy stayed with the baby.'

'Go on.'

'Lidya's story was she got herself to bed,' said Iain, 'and dropped off. About one o'clock, she woke, thinking the baby must be needing a feed, and first went to the loo. Then she heard the radio going in the nursery and thought she'd find why the midwife hadn't called her. She found Peggy deeply asleep. She turned to the crib, and saw the baby was blue and wasn't breathing…

'She screamed, she says, then shook Peggy awake, which wasn't easy. Peggy set about resuscitating the baby while Lidya called 999. The call came in at 1.26 am. The ambulance was there by 1.50, by which time Peggy had got the baby breathing again. It was rushed to the hospital. They both went in the ambulance with it.'

'What about Ralph?'

'They tried to wake him and couldn't.'

'Bloody hell! … It was Lidya herself dialled 999?'

'Yes.'

'I was on duty,' said Aliza, 'and the desk remembered I'd been involved last time. So it was me who got her story.'

'You went to the hospital?'

'No. Lidya came here.'

Tom's eyebrows shot up. 'She left her baby in order to talk to us?'

'Yes.'

'Mm… Did they secure the house?'

'Of course. The squad car got there at four thirty, and they managed to wake Ralph. He's here too, but too groggy to talk.'

'Looks like they'd all been drugged?'

'Yes. But Ralph was taking sleeping pills anyway.'

'Where were the Ovaltine mugs?'

'In the kitchen, unwashed.'

Tom nodded. 'Was the house properly locked up overnight, before the attack?'

'Ralph did that,' said Iain, 'after the previous chaperone left. There's a mortise lock on the front door. No-one else had keys. The ground floor windows were locked.'

'So opportunity-wise it was just these three? Peggy, Ralph and Lidya?'

'That's what it looks like.'

'Who was the previous chaperone?'

'The practice nurse.' said Aliza. 'But she'd left by 11.20 and the next one wasn't due until the morning.'

'This looks rotten bad for Lidya,' said Tom. 'What state was she in?'

'Really exhausted,' said Aliza. 'But not crazy when I saw her. She said she'd screamed when she first saw the baby, and broken down for a bit at the hospital. But then, she told me, she knew she had to do something, because Ralph wasn't there to help her. So she came here.'

'Did she say why?'

'To make sure we understood it was an attack and not an accident.'

'Not depressed? Not hysterical?'

'No. She seemed absolutely convinced that someone *else* must have done it, somehow, and that we needed to find out who and how, as quickly as possible… She wanted me to call you… She slumped down after the interview, and I called in the police doctor. She wanted to talk to Ralph too, but I said she couldn't.'

'Forensics?' asked Tom.

'Blood samples taken on all three,' said Iain. 'The team'll be in the house today.'

'Mm,' said Tom. '… And who prepared the Ovaltines?'

'She did,' said Iain, looking hopelessly at him.

*

'Can I see her?' said Jane.

'No.'

'And it's looking bad?'

'Very.'

'I don't believe she did it.'

'Nor do I,' said Tom. 'The psychology makes no sense at all.'

*

When interviewed by Andrew, Ralph became extremely angry at the suggestion that Lidya might have attacked Zeina.

He said he'd drunk the whole of his Ovaltine on the night of the attack. His regular sleeping tablets were Temazepam, and he reported that soon after Lidya and Zeina had come home he'd mislaid a blister pack of twenty, of which he'd used one.

When re-interviewed, Lidya confirmed independently that Ralph had lost a pack of twenty

293

Temazepam. On the night of the attack she'd only taken a mouthful of her Ovaltine, felt she didn't want the rest, and tipped it down the bathroom sink, eating a peach instead. Peggy and Ralph subsequently confirmed this, and everyone agreed that Lidya had used her usual distinctive mug.

Like Ralph, Peggy couldn't believe it was Lidya who had attacked Zeina. She confirmed that she had drunk the whole of her own Ovaltine.

*

The preliminary toxicology report was emailed in at mid-day on the Monday, and Andrew photocopied it for Iain. Ralph and Peggy both had Temazepam in their blood, Ralph the equivalent of three normal doses, and Peggy two. The Ovaltine dregs left in their mugs also contained Temazepam at a concentration corresponding to two doses per mug, as did the milk saucepan. Lidya's mug also contained dregs of Ovaltine but the lab had not so far detected Temazepam, though they had found a trace in her blood.

The forensics team found an empty Temazepam blister pack inside one of the rubbish bags in the family dustbin, which had been emptied two days before the attack. If someone had stolen Ralph's pack and put six doses from it into the milk saucepan, that left thirteen tablets unaccounted for. But no trace of them could be found, in the drains or elsewhere. Nor was there any evidence in the kitchen or elsewhere of anyone having crushed tablets to disperse the drug in the milk.

*

On 4th July the Child Protection Committee made an interim order that neither Lidya nor Ralph should have any further contact with Zeina.

Andrew soon decided that the attacker couldn't have been anyone from outside the house.

'I can understand his conclusion,' said Tom. 'But I don't *like* it.

'Nor do I,' said Iain. 'But that's very much how it looks... Whatever can her state of mind have been?'

Tom set his mouth in a thin line but said nothing.

Iain looked at him. 'The house was properly locked and there was no sign of any break in,' he said at last. 'And more to the point, we've no outsider to point a finger at. None of their acquaintances had any apparent motive, and casual burglars don't strangle babies.'

'A nutter?' said Tom.

Iain shrugged expressively and the corners of his mouth sagged. '*Inside*, if it was Ralph or Peggy they'd have had to deceive the other two into *thinking* they'd drunk drugged Ovaltine when really their mug wasn't drugged. To make that work, they'd have had to subsequently doctor the dregs in their own mug, and *also* take the appropriate doses after the attack in order to explain the blood tests. Too elaborate. Not believable.'

'Yes,' agreed Tom. 'Moreover, we think it's likely the attack took place not long before Lidya woke Peggy, or it wouldn't have been possible to revive the baby. Lidya might even have interrupted the attack when she went to the loo.'

'And if that argument is right,' said Iain, scratching his head vigorously, 'it makes both Peggy and Ralph very unlikely candidates, Peggy because she would have had very little time to take the appropriate dose and pretend to be asleep, and Ralph because you'd think Lidya would have heard him leave the bedroom.'

Tom said nothing.

Iain looked at him. 'She had very little Temazepam in her blood, and the others had lots.'

'But Iain,' said Tom. 'The alternative makes no sense either. Whatever sort of post-natal depression would it have to be? She would have to have planned the attack a week in advance, and in such a way that all the evidence pointed to herself. *Why*? And then gone for her baby, but leaving the job unfinished and waking Peggy almost at once. *Why*?'

Iain looked at him. 'If you're bringing private opinions into this, I agree,' he said. 'But it's what the physical evidence points to. And the CPS will tell Andrew that it isn't up to him the assess the psychology.'

'They don't always prosecute when it's PND,' said Tom, 'if there's no long-term damage to the baby.'

'We don't know that yet.'

'But does it *sound* like PND?'

'No,' said Iain, and shrugged. 'This is a carefully thought out crime, not a distraught woman in a moment of madness.'

'But for something so carefully planned, what motive would make sense?'

'Something us simple-minded chaps can't grasp.'

'Jane doesn't think she's a psychopath,' said Tom.

Iain shrugged. 'Nor do I,' he said. 'But Andrew can't conceal from the CPS what he's got.'

'I know that,' said Tom.

*

Next day Andrew proposed, and the Super agreed, that the Slades should be warned there was evidence apparently incriminating Lidya which would have to be forwarded to the CPS. Given the evidence, Tom and Iain could see no reasonable objection.

As Andrew reported it later to Iain, Ralph was again furious, but managed to keep his cool. Lidya, on the other hand, after a moment's total incredulity shrank into herself like a woman hollowed out inside. There was no shouting, nor tears, nor even words. They couldn't return to Victory House, which remained a crime scene. Ralph had arranged for the two of them to move in with his aunt in Salcombe.

Acceleration

Jane was infuriated by the police decision to forward evidence to the CPS, raged at Tom for failing to prevent it, and for two days was near to walking out on him.

The Protection Board insisted that if Lidya and Ralph were to have any further access to their baby, Lidya must first be psychiatrically assessed. The forensic psychiatrist at the Langdon concluded she had serious post-natal depression and needed further assessment as an in-patient for three weeks. To keep her away from Zeina the assessment was to take place in an Exeter hospital rather than the Derriford.

Ralph drove her to Exeter, and Tom and Jane, barely reconciled to each other, offered him a bed. He accepted, and asked them to clear their house of alcohol before he arrived. When the Super heard, he threatened to order Tom off the case entirely. But Tom shrugged and chose to ignore him; and the Super said no more about it.

On 11th July the News of the World splashed the case over their front page, complete with family photos, demanding to know why Lidya's earlier prosecution for infanticide had been withdrawn.

*

Jane visited Lidya three times in the Exeter hospital. On the first two occasions they met in a patients' lounge, and Jane was able to describe her visits to Zeina in the Derriford. Lidya hardly responded. 'They *may* not keep you from her,' Jane urged, but Lidya's lips merely tightened.

On the final visit she found her in bed in an open ward. It became apparent, though little was said, that she felt deeply betrayed by Tom for allowing her case to go forward to the CPS.

Jane's heart sank. When she left, Lidya, lying back on the pillow, accepted her kiss, but shivered and made no other response. Jane's own morale was low. She was now three months pregnant, and her alarms about herself as mother were beginning to feel out of control.

*

On 14th July Iain came once again to sit on Tom's desk, cracking his knuckles. 'The damn CPS are ploughing ahead,' he said gloomily. 'No queries at all.' Tom's fan was buzzing lazily in the summer heat. 'But Andrew's case implies that this woman's a psychopath. Neither of us *likes* that conclusion. But does it stand up logically?'

Tom screwed up his mouth.

'I can imagine a woman killing her baby if at some deep and hidden level she hated the prospect of kids… But you'd think she'd make some minimal effort to avoid being prosecuted for it.'

'I can't believe that of her anyway,' said Tom. 'A more comprehensible possibility is that she was afraid of Zeina being taken away, and chose to kill her to make that impossible. An extremely passionate and irrational woman might have done that.'

'She *did* say she was scared of what she might do.'

299

'But Iain, a crime like that would be a desperate scream to the world—never something coolly planned and concealed.'

Iain looked thoughtful. 'And in fact there *wasn't* any immediate threat of her being taken away,' he said, 'nothing to provoke a crisis… In that scenario it would be essential she should *succeed*: if the baby didn't die, it would *certainly* have been removed, and she'd know that. Yet if we assume Lidya did it, she also woke Peggy, and the timing would suggest she *intended* the baby to survive.'

'And from the very first she was determined we should investigate. Her own reaction was that it could only have been an outsider.'

Tom's fan buzzed on.

'Amateur psychology won't help us anyway,' said Iain at last, cracking his knuckles again. 'The CPS will be recruiting their own psychiatric assessment.'

*

On 22nd July, Ralph brought Lidya home to Victory House. Two days later the Protection Board, having considered Lidya's in-patient reports, decided that Zeina should be fostered as soon as she was well enough to leave hospital. Lidya and Ralph would be permitted fortnightly access in the presence of the foster mother and Mrs Kent.

On the same day, Tom heard that the CPS had taken a provisional decision that a charge of attempted murder would probably not succeed and were considering instead grievous bodily harm.

Somehow, however, this decision was leaked to the Daily Mail, who in response hit on the idea of inviting Sir Ambrose to write a feature article on mothers who harmed their babies, which he did. He also, it later appeared, wrote in strong terms to the Exeter CPS office.

Nine days later the CPS changed their minds and charged Lidya with attempted murder. The preliminary hearing was taken very quickly, and she was bailed by the magistrates. The News of the World celebrated, again on the front page. The Mail boasted that Sir Ambrose had very properly been allowed to influence the decision.

*

Jane wanted to discuss the situation with the Slades, but feared that direct contact would do more harm than good. In the end she called Ralph anyway, and to her relief he begged her and Tom to drive over.

'She's upstairs,' he said when he opened the door to them. 'Wants to stay there, I'm afraid.'

'Perhaps this isn't a good idea, Ralph,' said Jane.

'No, no,' he insisted, 'please stay.' He led them into the sitting room, and went to the kitchen to make tea, his broad shoulders slumped. Jane looked doubtfully round the room. After a few minutes Ralph returned, and stood ready to pour out. 'She's furious with you, I'm afraid,' he said to Tom. 'But I guess some charge or other was just inevitable? The evidence was too bloody incriminating?' He poured and passed round the cups.

'They didn't have to make it attempted murder,' said Tom.

Ralph nodded. 'But bloody hard to take,' he said. 'She keeps telling me she never did anything to Zeina. And at first I believed her—of course I did. Still do, really... And I do try to keep her morale up... But I suppose I've got to reckon with it.'

'Reckon with *what*?' said Jane quickly.

Ralph turned to her. 'With her being unhinged,' he said miserably. 'By all this bloody pressure.' He drew in an unsteady breath.

'*No*, Ralph,' she shot back fiercely, with a glance at Tom. 'Whatever Tom's horrible evidence seems to say, she's *not* unhinged… And I don't believe Tom thinks she could ever have done it, either.'

'Hell, Jane!' said Ralph. 'I'm *not* forgetting what she's like… But it wasn't me, and it can't have been Peggy.'

'No,' said Tom.

'And no way it could have been anyone from outside.'

Jane looked at him. She closed her eyes, and wiped away with one hand a few tears of frustration.

Ralph clenched his hands. 'Thank God we got bail,' he said at last. 'At least she isn't rotting in Exeter jail.'

'That would have done for her completely,' said Jane.

'And Cormack's booked George Devenish for us. We're ditching Frank Irwin.'

'Thank goodness for that,' said Jane. 'George will do you proud.'

'Not sure whether he can.' Ralph handed round biscuits, his hand shaking a little. 'They're going to bring back Sir Ambrose with that crucifying 1–2–3 argument, and my gut feeling is Lidya's done for, whoever we get. We're going to have the respected and distinguished Sir Ambrose chasing us from pillar to post all over again.'

'How's Lidya taken it?' said Tom. ''

'Knocked her right back, of course… And her Dad's letter just finished her off.'

'Her *Dad*? … Whatever did he have to say?'

'She's not being rational,' said Ralph. 'It was a very *supportive* letter. All he got wrong was to ask why she hadn't been in touch… I'll show you.' He got up and hunted in Lidya's bureau.

'Please don't bother.'

'I *want* you to see it… Not here, she's got it with her.' He went to the door and stumped slowly up the stairs.

After a while they heard Lidya crying in the bedroom, and Ralph trying to calm her. At last he came slowly down again, his face red.

'Doesn't want you to see it,' he said.

'D'you mean she'd broken off with him, or something?' asked Jane.

'No, no, nothing like that. She'd just been so miserable she couldn't bring herself to phone him.' Ralph looked distraught.

'There's a heck of a lot of pressure on you, too, Ralph,' said Tom. 'How are you coping?'

'I've thrown out the cellar, if that's what you meant. Into the dustbin, every last fucking bottle…'

*

She'll *surely* be sensing Ralph's suspicions, thought Jane miserably on the drive back to Plymouth. And, it looks very much as if she can't tolerate contact with either of us, at least for the moment. The wrench of separation felt suddenly so like bereavement that she found herself unable to hold back the tears.

*

That same evening, however, Tom received a phone call, inviting him the following day for lunch in Cheltenham—and a personal lecture.

Seminar

Warm summer rain dripped from the plane trees of Pittville Gardens, stirring up strong smells of freshly cut grass and wet earth. Tom ran up the steps to the pillared front door and selected the best-polished brass button on the panel. There was a buzz. He pushed the door open, and climbed more slowly to the first floor. As he reached the double doors at the head of the stairs, they were swept open dramatically.

'Tom!' Dr Sampson, in blue bow-tie and ochre waistcoat, seemed to have reverted to his whimsical style. He shook hands and waved short arms inwards in welcome.

Tom stepped forward into the enormous sitting-room, still dripping, and removed his issue raincoat. The white grand piano stood in its usual place. He grinned.

Dr Sampson carried the sodden raincoat carefully into the bathroom, and Tom settled himself onto the chaise longue. On the shiny Queen Anne table he could see silver cutlery, soup waiting ready in big porcelain plates, and two starched napkins, each surmounted by a bread roll.

'Eat first,' admonished Dr Sampson when he returned. The soup proved to be chilled watercress and the rolls pleasantly warmed. They consumed it all in silence.

Dr Sampson fetched smoked salmon and salad, and

carefully uncorked a white wine, which he tasted.
'Now,' he said. 'I think we might begin.' He served
and tucked in his napkin.

'I need a lecture, you said?' remarked Tom.

'You do indeed!'

Tom puckered his eyebrows.

Dr Sampson smiled. 'As does that idiot Ambrose
Eaton… I meant to tell you about this after the first
trial, but we got distracted… I read the law report,
you see.'

'The defence team did try to meet Eaton's argu-
ments,' said Tom.

'They didn't do a very good job.'

'But Dr Matthews himself got it right. It was just
bad advocacy that it didn't come over properly to the
jury.'

'*No* Tom!' shouted Dr Sampson. 'Not at all!' He
looked seriously annoyed, and wiped his mouth with
his napkin. 'Matthews *didn't* get it right. He got it all
wrong. *Completely* wrong. …'

Tom looked up.

'*One sudden infant death is a tragedy, two is suspicious
and three is murder, until proved otherwise,*' quoted Dr
Sampson. 'Total fantasy!'

'But Dr Matthews said it was fantasy too,' objected
Tom. 'The chance of two cot deaths in the same family
isn't necessarily one in four million, it could be as low
as one in ten thousand… '

'Tom,' interrupted Dr Sampson. He seemed to be
gearing himself up for a sermon. 'There was something *much worse than that* about Professor Eaton's
statistics.'

Tom waited.

Dr Sampson frowned. 'He fell plumb into the *Prosecutor's Fallacy*. Heard of it?'

'No.'

'Come over here.' Abandoning his smoked salmon Dr Sampson gestured to an untidy desk by the window. The rain had stopped, and leafy trees reared up into blue sky. They sat down, and Dr Sampson found a piece of plain typing paper and a pencil.

'Look,' he said. On the paper he wrote slowly in large letters:

$$1:2000$$

'One in two thousand: the proportion of live births that end in cot death. Eaton argues that the probability of getting two cot deaths in two live births in the same family is one in two thousand for the first cot death, and *of those* another one in two thousand for the second. That's a probability of one in four million.' He wrote:

$$1:4,000,000$$

'That's what he said,' agreed Tom.

'And for three cot deaths?'

'Two thousand times smaller again, I suppose.'

Dr Sampson smiled grimly. 'Yes,' he said. 'For an average family Eaton's calculation gives one in *eight billion*.' He wrote

$$1:8,000,000,000$$

in large black letters on the paper.

'Yes.'

'*And it's all wicked!*' Michael Sampson's voice reached falsetto. 'Counsel waves this figure in front of the jury and shouts. *This chance is so* low, he bellows, *that it can't have been a cot death—it must have been murder.'*

He drew the paper to him again.

'So what do the jury think? *Naturally*, they run away with the idea there's only a one in eight billion chance that she's innocent! *That's* the Prosecutor's Fallacy! Criminally misleading. Yes, *criminally*! … Look, Tom.' Dr Sampson seemed to be beseeching Tom to follow him. 'It's a bit subtle. But only a tiny bit…

Tom grinned, and got a relieved smile in return

'Now first,' said Dr Sampson, 'there's nothing wrong with Eaton's calculation *in itself*, not for an average family… But it's absolutely, terribly wrong to deduce from it that the mother is guilty of murder! Listen! If two children die young in the same family, that's a very rare event—*whatever the cause*. To compute the probability that the mother is a murderer, what you have to do is *not* merely to show how rare it is, but to *compare* the two rare events; you have to *compare* the chance of two cot deaths with the chance of two murders. You absolutely must bear in mind that they're *both* very unlikely.'

'I don't follow.'

Dr Sampson sighed deeply. 'Look!' he said. 'Infanticide is *rarer* than cot death, about one in 26,000… Got that?' He frowned like a stern school teacher, and Tom quailed a little.

'So, you see Tom, in 26,000 births we can expect only one infanticide, on average, but as many as thirteen cot deaths.'

'Does that mean it's thirteen times more likely to be cot death than murder?'

'Exactly so.'

'But if there are *two* unexplained deaths?'

'That's what I'm coming to!' said Dr Sampson testily. 'To understand that, let's consider 26,000 times 26,000 families, in each of which two children have been born.' He fished around in a drawer and found a calculator. 'I make that... 676 million families.'

'Isn't that more families than there are in the United Kingdom?'

'Doesn't matter! This is only a *thought-experiment*, to help us work out the probabilities. Just suppose it were possible to find 676 million families, each with two children to consider...

'The great majority of these children will survive, of course. But in this number of families, we should expect to find one in 2000 cases in which the first child suffered cot death, that's 338,000 cot deaths.'

'And we'd also expect 26,000 murders?' asked Tom.

'Exactly. Now, of those 338,000 cases in which the first child suffered cot death, in how many would you expect the second child to suffer the same fate, Tom?'

'One in 2000, I suppose? That would be... let me see...'

'338,000 divided by 2000,' prompted Dr Sampson.

'Um... 169 double cot deaths?'

'You've got it. And of the 26,000 cases where the first child was murdered, in how many would be expect the second child to be murdered too?'

'One in 26,000... that's only one!'

'We're getting there! So out of this enormous number of families, we expect 169 double cot deaths and only one double infanticide, on average.'

'I see,' said Tom, beginning to get the point. 'So even if there are two deaths, a double murder is *still* much less likely than a double cot death?'

'Precisely!' Dr Sampson beamed. 'Now, have we forgotten anything?'

Tom thought for a while. 'I suppose it's *possible* that the second death was murder even if the first was a cot death?' he said doubtfully.

Dr Sampson nodded approvingly. 'Yes,' he said. 'Of the 338,000 cases where the first baby suffered a cot death, for one in 26,000 cases the second baby will be murdered, that's 13 cases of cot death followed by infanticide. Similarly, you'll find that we expect another thirteen cases in which infanticide is followed by a cot death... Let's set it out tidily.' He pulled up the piece of paper again, and wrote:

From 676 million families, each with two children, we expect on average:
169 double cot deaths
26 with one cot death and one infanticide
1 double infanticide.
Therefore, out of 676 million pairs of births we expect 196 double early deaths, only 27 of which involve infanticide.

'So what's the probability of guilt?'

'I'm not sure,' said Tom.

'Out of 196 double early deaths only 27 involve infanticide, on average.'

'27 in 196?' said Tom.

'Exactly: *totally* different from what Prof Eaton implied. About one in seven. It's a bit higher than the one in thirteen we had for a single death, but still very low—in fact the most likely explanation for a double death is simply two cot deaths, definitely *not* murder. And if you work it out you find that that's still true for *three* cot deaths.'

Tom smiled. 'So it's completely wrong to say that the probability of guilt goes up enormously when there are multiple deaths?'

'Absolutely wrong!' Dr Sampson looked thoughtfully at Tom 'Time for a break!' he said, and took the remains of the smoked salmon off to his kitchen.

Tom sat and thought about juries, and how extraordinarily easy it is for everyday people to be persuaded by an impressive said-to-be-expert witness who is getting something seriously wrong.

There were chinking noises, and Dr Sampson reappeared with cream and thick slices of lemon meringue pie on bone china plates. He served Tom, sat down and armed himself with a slice.

'More to be said, Tom,' he warned.

'I think I can see at least one thing more for myself.'

'Ah!'

'The prosecution will say that a mother who's murdered once is likely to do so again.'

'And how does that invalidate my argument?'

'I'm not too clear. But surely it does?'

'Quite right, Tom! *Our calculation assumed that the probabilities for the second child were the same as for the population at large, even after the first death.* For genuine cot death, that was the point made by your expert at the trial: the probability is *not* the same in all families— if one cot death has already occurred, it makes it more likely that the family concerned is a vulnerable one.'

'That's in Lidya's *favour*?'

'Yes. But equally, if one murder has already occurred, it makes it more likely that the mother will murder again.'

'How can we allow for that?'

'We could try... But I fear Tom that we won't succeed. I don't suppose the Home Office has any reliable statistics on the probability of a woman murdering two or more of her children. I expect you'll find that in general you get two or more deaths in the same family more often than you would expect by pure chance, but sorting out how much of this effect is due to increased probability of cot deaths in some families, and how much due to increased probability of infanticide in some mothers, would be almost impossible.'

'So where does that leave Lidya's case?'

'I don't think statistics has much useful to tell you, Tom. It *certainly* can't be used to prove her guilt. What you need is hard evidence. But in *court* what you have to do is stop that idiot muddying the water again. *Destroy* him as a witness.'

'So we need a more professional expert of our own?'

'I think you might do better than that.'

'How?'

'Last time some of us who understand this stuff wanted to consult the Royal Statistical Society. I think they could be persuaded to take it up. Get them to set out the principles. Make a public statement. Put out a press release.'

'That's quite a thought,' said Tom. He pondered for a while.

'Talk to the defence too. If they want me to stir things up, I can.'

'I shall,' said Tom. For the first time since the attack on Zeina he felt a glimmer of hope.

Interlude

Jane was now twenty weeks pregnant. Her scans were normal, and Tom had brought down from the loft a baby bath and teething rings carrying Jack and Miranda's bite marks.

But she'd not been able to quell her anxieties. In deciding to move in with Tom at Christmas, she'd used Lidya's ordered domesticity as a sort of talisman, a domestic counter-ideal she might somehow scramble into attaining. But by the time she realised she was pregnant, Lidya was becoming trapped in the maelstrom of appalling events, and the camaraderie of the cruise had vanished in the confusion.

She tried to hide her fears from Tom, but he realised soon enough. They talked for a while of psychotherapy, but Jane couldn't face it, and begged him not to tell Miranda.

Miranda and Hamish's wedding was fixed for 25th September, but to Jane's dismay the prospect did nothing to lift her spirits. Because it was to be a Scottish affair the bridegroom's parents took on the major role in planning it. Optimists in all things, they laughed a great deal to Tom and Jane on the phone. Miranda would have liked Lidya to be Matron of Honour, but Ralph said there was no hope whatever of that, and warned Jane not to ask. So Miranda chose as bridesmaids two college friends from Edinburgh, and engaged Jane in endless discussions of dresses exhibiting alternative takes on highland panache.

*

On 10th September the authorities at last des-patched Zeina from the Derriford to join a family of four foster-children not far from Tom's house. Jane was permitted to look in on them with Mrs Kent, who was overseeing the transition. The house was grubby but tidy, the foster mother young and capable.

'This is Dr Allison, Sue.'

Sue shook hands. 'And these are Jason and Mabel and Bryan,' she said, 'and Noelle on the floor.' Noelle looked up and gurgled. 'The little one's asleep. But we can go and see her.' Her accent was Essex, not Devon. '*You be quiet now*, Bryan.'

Everyone trooped upstairs. By the cot Jane's anxie-ties suddenly attacked her. She forced herself to stroke Zeina's forehead; the baby didn't wake.

Sue was watching. 'You know her mum?'

'Yes.'

'Has she told you when her and her boyfriend might be wanting to visit?'

'They're a married couple, Sue,' said Mrs Kent quickly. 'Mr and Mrs Slade.'

'No,' said Jane. 'She hasn't.'

*

'Lidya herself thought so.'

'That it was an outsider?' said Tom.

Iain nodded and frowned 'And if it *wasn't* it certain-ly looks like curtains for Lidya.'

'But Andrew's made up his mind that it couldn't have been,' said Tom. He pushed his jaw forward.

314

'And our problem is, we've no evidence to support that case. Not a thing. All we can argue is that the force has a duty to investigate.'

Tom nodded. 'But you're feeling it's time to go to the boss nevertheless?'

'What I feel, yes…'

'So what do we tell him we want to do?'

'Re-interview extremely carefully the three in the house…'

'And go over the forensics with an ultra-fine tooth comb… Just the usual boring stuff… All right, better give it a go,' said Tom. 'But he isn't going to be pleased.'

*

The trial start date was fixed for 19th October. George Devenish had undertaken discussions with the Royal Statistical Society, and plans were well advanced for countering any attempt by the prosecution to link the new case statistically with the earlier deaths. But George was now unsure whether he could use this line of argument: he wasn't confident of being able to demonstrate in court that anyone other than Lidya had attacked Zeina, and to Jane's dismay his current plan was to accept the evidence against Lidya, but try to reduce or even eliminate the sentence by demonstrating that her mind had been disturbed.

She asked Ralph what he thought about George's plan.

'I don't know,' he said, and swallowed; his jaw muscles twitched. 'He's stuck with having no presentable evidence it could have been an outside job.'

'And he can't argue in court it was you or Peggy.'

'So he may be right it's her only chance, legally…

I hate it. But I'm no psychologist. Maybe my poor Lidya really did have a brainstorm… My job's to be sure she gets the best defence we can afford. And I can't see anyone better than George.'

'But what d'you say to *her* about it?'

'What can I say? She's not stupid. She sees how George's mind is working just as well as I do.'

*

To Tom's surprise the Super agreed quite readily that the three in the house ought to be interviewed again, and that it could be done by Tom's team if it was done discreetly. And Andrew seemed to be content that they should try.

*

Lidya's father announced he wanted to visit. At first Ralph agreed, but then suggested a more attractive plan might be a quick three-day visit to Addis for him and Lidya. He bought the air tickets, and told Jane they produced the first smile he'd seen on Lidya's face for a month.

*

'And when you locked the front door after Marsha left, you used your own keys?' asked Tom.

'Yes,' said Ralph.

'And the back door was locked?'

'Yes.'

'And you checked all the downstairs windows?'

'I always do.'

'And there were just the three sets of keys?'

316

'Mine, Lidya's and the spare set in the kitchen cupboard that used to be Elspeth's.'

'And you didn't see anything out of place that might have suggested an intruder?'

'No.'

'Or notice anything through any of the windows?'

'No.'

'Or hear any strange noises?'

'No.'

'Can you see *any* way in which some outsider could have got into the house?'

Ralph screwed his face up. 'We've thought so much about that,' he said, 'as you might imagine. The answer is no, I can't. Nor can Lidya.'

*

'Yes,' Peggy agreed, 'Ralph let me in when I arrived.'

'And there was never anything to suggest that an outsider might have been in the house?' said Iain.

'No.'

'Nothing out of place in the kitchen or the nursery? '

'No.'

'No strange noises from the garden?'

'Not that I heard.'

'Or from downstairs?'

'No,' said Peggy firmly. Then she stopped. She looked up at him.

Iain waited.

'Mm.' Peggy lowered her eyebrows.

'Yes?'

'There *was* something, you know. Lidya told me... ' Peggy locked her hands together under her chin. 'She told me she'd heard a click.'

'A *click*?'

'She said, when she heard the radio going in the nursery, she heard this little click at the same time.'

'Did she say where it came from?'

'No... She told me in the ambulance, we were swaying along and the attendants were talking and giving Zeina oxygen... She said it was nothing really.'

'But the click was in the house?'

'Yes... It seemed to have stuck in her mind.'

*

Aliza did the interview with Lidya, and reported that although she was taciturn and answered the questions very slowly, she seemed pleased to discover the police were still interested in the facts of the case.

'It's true,' she said. 'I heard a click and I told Peggy about it.'

'What did it sound like?'

'I don't know... Nothing much. It must have been something familiar, or it would have worried me more.'

'Loud or soft?'

'... Soft.'

'Upstairs or downstairs?'

Lidya seemed puzzled. 'I *thought* downstairs; I was coming out of the toilet onto the landing and the cistern was making a noise... I can't be sure.'

'A light switch? A click of crockery? Something falling inside a cupboard?'

'I don't know.'

'Didn't it make you worry there was someone there?'

Lidya thought for a while. 'No,' she said. 'Whatever it was, it seemed familiar but it didn't leave me feeling there was a person there.'

'Why not?'

'I don't know.'

And although Aliza pressed hard for some time, that was all Lidya could remember about it.

*

Ralph mentioned to George the planned trip to Addis.

'*No!*' George yelled. He hammered on his desk. 'You bloody *can't! Bail conditions man! ... Surely* you knew!'

So the visit had to be cancelled. Unfortunately, someone told the *News of the World* reporter nosing around Noss Mayo about the ticket purchase. Soon afterwards a CPS lawyer called at Victory House to impound Lidya's passport.

*

For the wedding, Jane and Tom stayed in the Columba Hotel, just down the road from the Abbey. Iona had lost its magical touch for Jane; in fact, it made her feel sick. But the weather was calm and clear, and the evening before the ceremony she climbed Dun I alone and found a little solace in the distant prospect of the Treshnish Islands, and in remembering Lidya's courage in Fingal's Cave.

She had to admit that the event itself went off very well. Hamish stuttered, but Tom made a great speech and all the highland dress looked splendid. She danced with Tom during the ceilidh and managed not to show too much of what she was feeling.

Miranda and Hamish, happy and handsome, disappeared, and in due course sent home a stream of delighted emails from Jamaica.

*

Zeina lost weight, and was sent back to intensive care for three weeks with a suspected intestinal infection. Then she recovered and was returned to Sue. Ralph reported that Lidya was frantic.

Lidya could still not bring herself to visit Zeina in the foster home, but not long after Ralph went on his own. To his surprise he got on quite well with Sue.

*

'What did you make of the final lab report?' asked Tom.

Iain looked up. 'Dotting i's and crossing t's.'

'Well I noticed two things,' said Tom, 'First, they pointed out it was surprising, if the drinks were doctored using ground-up pills, that they found no solid grains of Temazepam in the milk saucepan. All they found was Temazepam dissolved in the dregs of milk.'

'Dissolved somewhere else and added to the milk in solution,' said Iain.

'But why would the attacker bother to do that?' asked Tom.

Iain shrugged.

'Number two was they confirmed there was no Temazepam in Lidya's mug, none at all. But there definitely was a small quantity in her blood.'

'She could have rinsed the mug when she tipped it out.'

'No,' said Tom. 'The report said her mug had Ovaltine dregs in it.'

'Odd,' said Iain, and thought for a while. 'I don't get that.'

'Neither do I,' said Tom.

Investigation

When Iain arrived for work next morning he found Tom sitting on his desk. 'If Lidya's guilty,' Tom said, as Iain removed his hat, '*why* did her mug contain Ovaltine dregs but no Temazepam?'

Iain too had been thinking. '*Either*,' he said, 'she never put Temazepam in it, *or* she must have rinsed it and *then* put fresh Ovaltine in.'

'Why should she do that?'

Iain considered. 'Either way, it makes her look suspicious: the only one not drugged… That would be crazy.'

'And even supposing she had some pathological reason for wanting to look suspicious, she'd *already* done that by throwing her drink away. There was no point in doing it *again*,' said Tom.

Iain looked doubtful. 'And if she wanted to look innocent?'

'Even odder. She might have provided herself with a Temazepam-free drink without realising we'd be testing the mugs, but why then would she throw it away, which doesn't look innocent at all? Whatever her aim, her actions don't make sense.'

*

Two hours later it was Iain sitting on Tom's desk. 'I've been thinking,' he said. 'Things external. There *was* something.'

Tom looked at him

'It was all so pointless I didn't bother you. Sergeant Ince found a print on the glass of the front door, outside... Hundreds could have made it.'

'But they checked it out?'

'Yes.'

'And?'

Iain laughed wearily. 'They got a match. A petty burglar. But it didn't wash: the guy's home patch is up in the Gorbals... Strathclyde Police faxed his mug shot down.'

Tom looked at his blotter, then up again. '... How good was the match?'

Iain shrugged. 'Fourteen points.'

'Better sus it out.'

*

Ralph didn't recognise the mug shot.

Peggy said at once she'd seen a man rather like that in the lane near the house, but on an earlier evening, not the night of the attack.

Marsha studied the print for a long time and then said she'd seen a man of that appearance on her way home on the night of the attack, but on the lower road, near the lay-by, not near the house. She seemed very definite about it.

The Noss Mayo postmistress thought it looked rather like Jem Stokes in Bridgend, only younger.

'It won't do, Tom,' said Iain at last. 'Burglars don't strangle babies.'

'Could be a nutter,' said Tom, wondering whether the expense of a visit to Glasgow could be justified.

'Jane?' Ralph's voice sounded cracked on the phone, and he was breathing heavily.

'Yes?'

'Can you give me a bed again?'

'Ralph! ... Of course we can... But *why*? Where's Lidya?'

'In prison.'

'*My God!* Why?'

'The CPS revoked her bail.'

'Just like that?'

'Two hours ago. A van, two female warders with a warrant. No notice, damn them.'

'So where is she?'

'Some women's establishment... The other side of Bristol.'

'Can George help?'

'He thinks it gives a better impression not to complain, pointed out it's only three weeks to the trial...'

'But poor, poor Lidya! How did she take it?'

'She was *really* angry. I've never seen her that way before, *screaming* at them... Goodness knows what it will do to her.'

Prison

In the early morning of 14th October a disturbing new idea came to Tom. It made him think he should probably abandon his trip to Glasgow, but he decided to call Cheltenham before making up his mind.

'Yes, Tom?'

He could hear no background noise, and imagined Dr Sampson surrounded by papers in his study, a glass of Chablis in one hand, peering out at the Pittville Gardens trees as an occasional yellowed leaf spiralled towards the lawn below. 'More statistics,' he explained. 'A fingerprint... It's been matched at fourteen points, and the manual says the chance of a wrong match is less than one in eight million.'

A sniff.

'We'd usually say that was pretty good. But I wanted to hear what *you* think... How sure should we be we've got the right man?'

'That depends,' said Dr Sampson. 'There's almost as much nonsense talked about the statistics of fingerprints and DNA as there is about cot deaths... This is Mrs Slade again?'

'Yes.'

'How big a pool of suspects *might* this print have come from?'

'We'd have to consider pretty much anyone, really.'

'Anyone in the whole country?'

'I suppose so.'

'Well, how many people *are* there in the country, Tom?'

Tom wasn't sure.

Dr Sampson chuckled. 'About seventy million. So how many would you expect to give a match purely by accident, if you examined the whole population?'

Tom scratched his head. 'Mm… Seventy million divided by eight million, I suppose.'

'Just so: you'd *expect* to find eight or nine purely accidental matches. Many more if you allowed foreigners as possibilities… So what's your logic for picking out this particular one as the true suspect?'

'It was the only match we found on the national database.'

'So what? Do you know the person you're looking for has a criminal record?'

'No,' admitted Tom. 'In fact the guy we've matched is about as unlikely a suspect as you could imagine.'

Dr Sampson gave a little groan. 'Then he's almost certainly the *wrong* suspect, Tom… If you'd been picking one from a handful of known suspects it would have been a completely different matter. But treating as guilty a match from the database when you've nothing *else* to link the match to the crime is almost always appalling logic.' He coughed deprecatingly. 'I'm afraid, however, it's what you and your colleagues do rather frequently.'

Tom swallowed. 'I see,' he said humbly. 'Maybe I could have seen that for myself… Yes… Thanks.' He rang off and abandoned his notion of visiting Glasgow.

*

Jane was now twenty-four weeks pregnant, and had at last decided she must get some help. She quite liked her therapist in a cool sort of way, and found that the weekly sessions were getting thoughts a little better into perspective, though not doing much to reduce her anxiety. They certainly brought home to her how devastated she'd been by the loss of contact with Lidya. She even began to wonder whether Lidya too might have found the break destructive, and to consider hesitantly how a prison visit might work out. Her therapist, having explained carefully that doling out prescriptive advice on such a issue was contrary to her professional principles, wasn't in any way discouraging.

*

Tom expounded his disturbing new theory to Iain.

Iain listened, then sat up very straight in his office swivel chair and thought for a considerable time with his hands behind his head, swinging the chair slowly to right and left with his heels. At last he brought his arms slowly down and nodded. 'Yes, man,' he said; then frowned.

'Damn hard to pin down,' said Tom. '*If* we can, we ought to get a postponement.'

'But less than two weeks to do it in.' Iain clasped his hands on the desk.

'There's two points we can tackle at once without any risk of alarming the target,' said Tom, and explained.

'I'll take the NHS,' said Iain.

'And I can make a start on Victory House.'

'Right.'

Over the supper table, therefore, as Jane stood

spooning out her risotto, Tom turned to Ralph and said: 'Mind if I ask you something?'

Ralph looked up wearily. 'No,' he said, and Jane looked sympathetically down at him.

'Your garden shed.'

Ralph raised his eyebrows and put down his glass of water.

'Has anything ever suggested to you someone might have been inside it on the night of the attack?'

Ralph looked at him.

'An *outsider*?' said Jane. 'At last! Thank goodness.'

Ralph's brow was furrowed. 'I don't see how,' he said. 'We keep it locked.'

Jane finished serving and sat down to eat.

'D'you have a gardener?' asked Tom.

'He gets the key from the kitchen when he needs it.' Ralph was still cogitating, his lips tight. 'Come to think of it, though, there *was* something.'

Tom waited.

'He asked whether he should put the camp stool away…'

Jane's forkful of risotto stopped half way to her mouth.

'The camp stool?' said Tom.

'Someone had set it up inside the shed.'

'Ah.' Tom smiled in spite of himself. 'Not you or Lidya?'

'No… We hadn't even noticed it.'

'Perhaps because you hadn't been in the shed?'

'I guess. We had no reason to.'

'When did Bill ask this?'

'The same day I drove Lidya to Exeter.'

'How often does he come?'

'Every three weeks.'

Tom thought for a moment, then smiled again. He

nodded.

'Thank God if you're thinking about outsiders again,' said Ralph. 'I've been thinking too. George is good, but he over-persuaded me. The Lidya I've known all these years could *never* have gone for Zeina, never.' He looked rather shamefacedly at Jane and nodded. 'You were right and I was wrong.'

Jane's heart fluttered. She smiled encouragingly back.

Tom too was looking at Ralph with some sympathy. 'By the way,' he added. 'Don't tell anyone I asked about this, either of you. No one at all… It's rather important.'

'Sure,' said Ralph. Jane gave Tom a very sharp look, and continued with her risotto.

*

Still unsure whether Lidya wanted her to come, Jane finally fixed up her prison visit for Saturday 16th October. She drove over and found the establishment close to the M5 in rolling wooded countryside, near a village. Its two-storey modern buildings looked pleasant enough from the outside, but the warders took away her coat, totebag, phone and money, and pat-searched her. After a brief wait she was escorted with a number of other arrivals to the Visits Room, a large space with views out onto grass and trees, and yellow plastic tables and chairs. There were seascapes on the walls in soft pastel blues and pinks.

At 3.45, with a rattling of keychains, the prisoners were led in, those already convicted in slate-blue prison overalls, those on remand in a mixture of clothes. One overweight woman in a grimy low-cut top and short skirt had a baby perched on one hip.

Lidya, in heavy dungarees, was the last to appear. She took a moment to identify Jane amongst the clutch of visitors, then beckoned her over to a free table. Sitting down was a little complicated: the chairs and table were screwed to the floor.

'I thought you were allowed to wear your own clothes?'

'These *are* mine.' The skin of Lidya's face was drawn tight and her dark ringlets screwed back into a tight ponytail. 'Long time no see,' she remarked.

'Yes,' said Jane.

'12th July,' said Lidya. 'In that bloody Exeter hospital.'

'Three awful months.'

Lidya gazed at her and said nothing.

Jane looked around. 'How are you coping?'

Lidya considered. 'With the other inmates, all right,' she said at last. 'My cell mate's in for GBH.'

'Oh... What did she do?'

'Razored a bailiff... Pathetic, all the same. They're *all* abandoned, forgotten.'

'Don't they get counselling?'

Lidya laughed. 'What do you think?'

'Surely there's supposed to be some?'

'There is, I've had some... And guess what?' She gave a little shiver. 'Two suicides last week.'

'Oh Lidya!'

'In their cells. Hanged themselves... The rest start howling when they hear. Like a madhouse.' Her eyes were stony.

Jane swallowed. 'I see there's a baby here,' she said, then wished she hadn't.

Lidya's jaw tightened, and she stared at Jane. 'There's a mother-and-baby unit... Which reminds me. What's my fucking husband up to?'

'Lidya!' Jane swallowed. 'Working fit to bust,' she said.

'Not what he's doing about my case. About *access*, getting access to Zeina.'

'George told him it was safer to hold off on that till after the trial.'

Lidya slapped the table, and nearby visitors looked across. 'How the *hell* can I accept that?' she said loudly.

'Lidya, think! … I know you must be absolutely wretched about Zeina.' Jane felt tears on her cheek and wiped them hastily away. 'Of course you must. But surely, access has to *wait*… We have to save *you* first, for God's sake!'

Lidya's mouth worked. 'And how's *that* for a lost cause, Jane?' she said at last.

'It's *not* lost.'

'It damn well *is* you know.'

'No!'

Lidya shivered again. 'Just bloody *think,* Jane!' For the first time her eyes had come a little alive. '*Think* what your vaunted, world-class British legal system has *done* to me… Skewered me, hasn't it, ground me down, chopped me up?' Her voice had first risen sharply, then shrunk to a whisper.

Jane had no answer.

Lidya stared furiously, then flicked up her eyebrows. 'I'd have been better off back home. In corrupt, despised, underdeveloped Ethiopia.'

'But it *isn't* all hopeless.'

'It *is*… Now, who should I be blaming? … *God?* … He took Gabriel and Ayana. I have to accept that…' Her eyes were shining now. 'But *all* the rest has been your *fucking, useless British institutions*. Just *think* for a moment what they've done to Ralph and me.'

'Which institutions?'

Again Lidya slapped one hand on the table in frustration, so furiously that a watching wardress started towards her, then hesitated. 'First MI5,' she hissed. 'Then the police—and that includes your bloody Tom. OK, maybe he saved me once, but he's given up on me now, hasn't he? On finding out what *really* happened.'

'He *hasn't*!'

'Oh yes he *has*... And what about the CPS, the prosecution, my useless barrister, even the judge? The crude conniving newspapers, what do they care? ... Worst of all that monster Sir Ambrose... He's *coming again*, isn't he? In my dreams... But he's coming again for real, too.'

'Coming?'

'The confident, jolly village butcherman with his razor-sharp knife. To slit the throat of the unresisting ewe... That man wants *my blood*, Jane.'

'But you have allies too.'

'*Who*, Jane? ... Your Tom thinks I may be guilty. My very own new personal barrister, George, thinks my best defence is to plead *insanity*, God help me. Even my poor Ralph, who's working so bloody hard, isn't sure, is he? *Who* is there believes in my innocence now, Jane? ... What about *you*?'

'I believe,' said Jane stoutly.

'*Do* you?'

'Yes. I believe you never attacked Zeina. You're a good mother and always have been.'

Lidya's eyes narrowed. 'I *hope* you do, I hope so...' They opened a little, screwed up as though against the light. 'You've worked hard, I know that. I *am* grateful. You don't always understand, but often you do.'

Tears welled behind Jane's eyelids.

'But I'm *never* going to escape from this bloody awful system, am I?'

'Yes, yes, you are!'

'That's what fucking Father Barnabas tells me.'

'He's been here too?'

'Oh yes he has... I'm *not* going to escape, not ever. But I *can* do something about Zeina. There's all of them, The Court of Protection, Social Services... All *enemies*, all keeping me from her... But Jane, if I'm stuck in here, or if I'm gone altogether, that ought to make it easier for Ralph to get her back, don't you think? *Will you help him, Jane?*'

'Of course! Tom will too... But you musn't give up like this!' Desperately Jane scrabbled for Lidya's hand across the grotty table.

She responded with a violent grip. 'Look,' she said. 'I don't think I'll be able to cope for much longer. And I don't know how poor Ralph is going to manage. But *you* could help him, Jane! With Zeina. You'll be busy, your own little one will be arriving... But will you be able to spare Ralph some time? A little bit of time?'

'Of course, yes!' said Jane. She wiped her eyes with her free hand.

Lidya was still staring at her. At last she released her hand. 'I *think*, Jane,' she said. '... I *think* my father still believes.' Her eyes were glistening again, and for a moment she turned and studied the grass and trees outside.

'You can at least hang on to that?'

'Yes... He believes in my innocence, and in my marriage... I just hope he still does.'

'That's good.'

'Yes... But I haven't heard from him. Not for two weeks.'

Exposure

Iain and Tom worked frantically for two days.

Then, on 18th October, Iain dropped in at Elizabeth's surgery and asked whether he could have a word with her practice nurse. Elizabeth took him to Marsha's room, and she sat upright on a chair beside her desk, knees apart.

'It's like this,' Iain said. 'Mrs Slade's trial is only a week away now, and we're checking various things.'

'Yes,' she said. 'Mr Clutterbuck was doing the same yesterday. He went over my witness statement with me.' She tilted her head slightly to one side and put one elbow on the desk.

'This is mainly about other points,' said Iain. 'But just to check... On the night of the attack, you left Victory House at 11.20, and drove home?'

'Yes.'

'Apart from the man you reported seeing that night on your way home, can you recall any indication that anyone from outside was interested in the house?'

She thought for a moment. 'No.'

'So all the signs suggest the attacker must have been someone inside?'

'Yes.' She nodded.

'And you think it must have been Mrs Slade?'

She looked sternly at him. 'That's not for me to conclude, Inspector.'

'We were just wondering what your opinion was…
After the first two deaths you seemed rather sure that
Mrs Slade was guilty.'

'Yes, I was. I felt she shouldn't have got off so easily.' Her face was impassive.

'Looking back, what made you so certain?'

'What I told you. She was too cool. Quite the uncon-
cerned fashion plate.'

'But in the trial last year, your evidence on that point
was withdrawn?'

She pursed her lips. 'That was Mr Clutterbuck's
choice.'

'Do you know what his reason was?'

'He didn't tell me.'

'That must have been annoying.'

She frowned but made no further response.

'The recent attack,' Iain went on, 'was an attempted
strangling, not a smothering, as I expect you know…
Can you see Mrs Slade as a strangler?'

'No, it surprised me…' Marsha drew a long breath
and let it out. 'Perhaps she wanted to throw the police
off the scent.'

Iain paused, watching her face, which did not
change. He looked down and up again. 'Am I right,' he
said at last, 'in thinking you'd had some previous
experience of a woman who killed babies?'

'Yes, I did.'

'And the culprit was a nurse?'

'Her name was Patience Aken,'

'About ten years ago, wasn't it? … What was she
like? What sort of motive did you think she had?'

Marsha paused for a long time. 'Tidiness,' she said
at last.

'*Tidiness*?'

'Her victims were all babies of unmarried mothers.

She thought they were wickedly conceived and she wanted to tidy them away…'

'Were you closely involved in the case?'

'I was the Ward Sister. I caught her contaminating the drips.'

'Ah!' Iain pushed his lips forward, and considered. 'But did she confide in you? How are you so sure about her motive?'

'I *knew* her… I could tell.'

Iain forced his face to relax, and said: 'So you found you needed to act? Killers like her had to be caught and punished? It had become your task to *avenge* the deaths those babies?'

Marsha looked at him through somewhat narrowed eyes. She raised her eyebrows. 'You could say so,' she said, with a fleeting smile. Then the corners of her mouth turned down. 'She got what she deserved.'

'Can you remind me which hospital it was?'

She looked perturbed, and paused for a moment. 'The Broomsfield.'

Iain looked at her. 'Which is where?' he asked.

She smiled to herself. 'In Chelmsford.'

*

As the ten o'clock news ended, Jane said to Tom: 'You and Iain are up to something.'

He turned off the television. 'Yes,' he admitted, standing by the set.

'But the trial starts on Monday.'

'We're hopeful of a postponement.'

'Really? Are you going to tell Lidya?'

'No.'

'If you've got onto something really hopeful, can't you tell her *now* there's light at the end of the tunnel?

336

She's *terribly* near the edge, Tom, and that prison has an awful reputation...'

'No,' said Tom firmly. 'I can't. She'll hear very soon. Not yet. And they've got her on suicide watch. We've done what we can.'

'That place has a bad track record.'

Tom considered. 'How did you think she was?'

'We went over all that on Saturday,' she said.

'Tough *and* fragile?'

'On the surface, more tough than fragile,' she said. 'But underneath very fragile. I *told* you! And she talked as though a time might come when she wouldn't be there... I'm scared.'

'You're really afraid she might?'

'Tom!' she burst out. 'We've talked through that already. How can I possibly tell?'

He shook his head. After a moment he came to the sofa, sat beside her, and tucked one arm around her shoulder. 'We're being as quick as we possibly can,' he said.

*

Friday 22nd October was windy and wet, and Iain and Aliza took one of the squad cars and found the path to Elizabeth's surgery slimy with soggy chestnut leaves, their stalks awry on the paving. Marsha answered the door. Iain explained that she was needed at police headquarters to go over a few more questions. She seemed a little surprised, but didn't question the request and went to tell Elizabeth what was happening.

Once in the interview room she placed her black handbag on the plastic table under the fluorescent lights, and settled herself on one of the chairs. Aliza sat down with Iain, facing her. Tom came in quietly, closed the door and took a spare chair behind Marsha.

'Miss Stone,' said Iain, having opened a thin file. 'We want first to check one or two things with you.'

She looked steadily at him.

'On the night of the attack on Zeina, you left Victory House at 11.20?'

'Yes.'

Iain placed a tick in his file. 'Can you recall what were you doing in the house after Peggy arrived and before you left?'

'Doing?'

'Were you busy with anything?'

'No. I handed over the nursery and the baby to Peggy, collected my coat and bag from the hall, and left.'

'Mr Slade showed you out of the front door and locked it behind you?'

'Yes.'

'Did you go to the kitchen?'

'No. Mrs Slade was in there preparing the evening Ovaltine.' She smiled.

Iain wrote again. 'And outside, where was your car parked?'

She frowned. 'On the drive. As usual.' Another smile.

'And you drove straight home?'

'Yes.'

Iain nodded. He located a second paper in his file. 'Now, just to check, you told me the other day that Patience Aken killed those babies at the Broomsfield Hospital, in Chelmsford?'

She smiled yet again. 'Yes.'

Iain ticked the new paper and returned to the first one.

'In an interview on 1st October, you told me that on the night of the attack you'd seen a man on the lower road, who looked similar to some photos of a petty thief that I showed you?'

'Yes.'

'What time did you see him?'

'On my way home.'

'How sure are you that he was the man in the photos?'

'Very sure.'

'But you must have seen him only briefly in your headlights?'

'I'm very sure.'

'You don't think the man you saw could have been Jem Stokes?'

Marsha blinked, and looked hastily at Aliza. 'Jem Stokes?'

'Your diabetes patient in Bridgend,' said Aliza.

'No.'

'But Jem Stokes *is* rather like the man in the photos, isn't he?' said Iain.

She considered. 'Not really.'

Iain wrote again, and looked up. 'Could you explain how you came to be on that lower road?' he asked. 'It's not your most direct way home.'

Her face had become a little more rigid. 'My car was facing uphill,' she said. 'I went that way to save turning round.' There was a little pause. Then she smiled happily again.

Iain gave her a long stare. 'Miss Stone,' he said at last. 'We're faced with a very strange situation. In the replies you've just given me, and in what you told me last Monday, you made a number of statements that were, I'm afraid, obviously untrue, and, really, I'd like to know why you told me what you did... Let me go over them. First, you said earlier today that you were parked in the drive at Victory House. If that's true, it means you could just as easily have turned right when you left, as you usually did; it means you *weren't* facing uphill, as you said subsequently, so in fact you had no reason to take the lower road.' He looked up.

Marsha's face was now stony again.

Iain waited. When she didn't reply he went on: 'Secondly, your patient Jem Stokes, who appears to be something of a night bird, told us yesterday he was taking a late walk on the night of the attack and saw you entering your car in the layby on the lower road at about 1.15 am.'

'Not true,' said Marsha. She smiled.

Tom shifted on his chair.

'Thirdly, Mr Slade has told us his wife didn't make the Ovaltine drinks until after you'd left. He also says you came from the kitchen with your coat on when he showed you out.'

'No. He's remembered wrongly, I'm afraid.' This time, she seemed to repress the smile.

'When I interviewed you last Monday, you told me Mr Clutterbuck didn't tell you why he never used your evidence in the last trial. But in fact, according to him, he *did* tell you.'

'He didn't.'

'He told you, in fact, that he couldn't use your evidence because it was worthless. He'd discovered you were in no position to have observed Mrs Slade after either of the first two deaths, because you weren't present on either occasion.'

Marsha looked down at the table, then up again. 'She *was* cold. Too cold.' The smile was back, confiding, almost winning.

Iain took a deep breath. 'Finally, and most extraordinary, we've checked with the NHS and the court records, and discovered that Patience Aken killed those babies, and you were her ward sister, *not* in Chelmsford, as you said, but in Colchester General Hospital.'

'No, it was the Broomsfield.'

Iain raised his eyebrows, and glanced over Marsha's shoulder at Tom, who shrugged expressively. Aliza was staring at Marsha.

'I also have one new question for you,' said Iain. 'Can you explain why your finger prints were found on the metal frame of a camp stool set up in the Victory House garden shed?'

Marsha's eyes widened, and her answer was a little longer in coming than usual: 'That's not possible.'

Iain pursed his lips. He closed his file. 'Miss Stone,' he said. 'I believe that's as far as I can properly proceed without a charge and caution.' He stood up; the little room was very silent. 'I am therefore now arresting you,' he said, 'for the attempted murder of Zeina Slade on 26th June 2004... You don't need to say anything, but anything you do say will be taken down, and may be used in evidence.'

Marsha looked thunderstruck. She leapt to her feet. '*Her!*' she shouted. She banged both fists on the table. '*Her!* The *guilty* one!' Tom stepped forward and grasped her right arm, but she paid no attention. 'You *fool!*' she shouted again at Iain. 'You interfering short-sighted police *fool*... What will happen now to *her?*' Her eyes bored into Iain's. She seemed to recollect herself and sat down, colour draining from her face. Tom let go her arm but remained standing close behind her.

Iain paid no attention. 'We have a warrant to search your flat, Miss Stone,' he said. 'It would save us a little trouble if you would allow me to have your keys.'

Looking completely blank, she stood again, searched her handbag and handed them over.

'This means, of course,' remarked Tom, 'that the case against Mrs Slade must be withdrawn and her trial suspended.'

It took her a moment to take in what he had said. Then she swung round violently to face him, her body twisted, her face once again contorted, reddening in fury.

Tom was prepared for another tirade or some sort of attack, but nothing came. For a moment she stood, rigid. Then she sat slowly down again at the table and folded her hands over her handbag. Her face became again completely stony, apart from a nervous twitch that flickered once in a while across her right cheek.

*

When Marsha had been processed and taken to the cells, Iain said quietly: 'My office?' and the three of them marched there in silence.

'Aliza,' said Tom. 'Iain will be contacting Clutterbuck and the Court. I'll tell Mr Slade himself. But we need to get messages to Mrs Slade and her defence team too. Can you do that? Don't hang about. Contact the prison first. Let her know we expect the case against her to be withdrawn very soon.'

Aliza disappeared.

'If I'm doing the Court, can you give the search team the final briefing?' said Iain.

'Sure,' said Tom. 'But I'd like, if you agree, to go over our new scenario again, check it for flaws. OK? Here again at two?'

Iain nodded.

Tom went off to contact Ralph, and ring Jane at the hospital to explain the development. Suddenly he felt like a wet rag. He told Jane he had more to do, but that he'd try to get home early, and she said she'd do the same.

Departure

'Right,' said Tom. After lunch the three of them had collapsed into chairs in his office.

'What will happen to her?' asked Aliza.

'Secure hospital,' said Iain.

'How sure are you?'

'I'm no forensic psychiatrist. But think how she's behaved.'

Tom looked at him for a while. 'Yes,' he said at last. 'Exactly what the Essex police told you.'

'The avenging angel.'

'And always thinking she can adjust the truth,' went on Tom. 'To suit herself. Every time. Inside her head. Always that big smile.'

'When people get persuaded they can modify truth,' said Iain, hunching up his shoulders, 'it makes them so damn convincing to everyone around.'

'All the same,' said Tom, 'we were terribly slow. I blame myself.'

'She should have been on the opportunity list?' asked Aliza.

'Yes,' said Tom. 'That back-door key. And we should have paid more attention last year to the fact that she was accusing Lidya on the basis of no evidence. Definitely not our finest hour.'

Iain turned sharply to Aliza. 'Get those messages off?' he asked.

'George Devenish was fine. The prison said there was some problem on her wing, but they'd tell her as soon as possible.'

'What trouble?' said Tom.

'They didn't say.'

'Search team under way OK?' asked Iain.

'Working in her flat now.'

'Right,' said Iain. '… Now, this recap, Aliza. Tom and I'll run through it. All look for snags… OK?'

'Yes.'

'First off, the Patience Aken case… Our Essex colleagues never had any doubt Aken was guilty, but it always looked to them as though someone else had tried to hurry some of the deaths along, someone who wanted to make sure Aken got convicted. We only heard that yesterday. Marsha was the obvious candidate, but too slippery for them. Superficially convincing, they said, and they couldn't prove anything. The consequence was, she never got a police record, though she nearly lost her job—there was quite good evidence she'd fiddled the dangerous drugs register.'

'I suppose that was why she pretended to us it had all happened in Chelmsford,' said Aliza. 'She didn't want us stirring the pot in Colchester?'

'That was quite extraordinary,' said Tom. '*Totally* confident we'd be bound to take her word for it.'

'D'you think she believed it herself?' said Iain.

'On the whole, no,' said Tom.

'But she *did* somehow convince herself Lidya was cold, was guilty, and therefore had to be punished?'

Tom nodded. 'Oh, yes,' he said, and Aliza nodded too.

'OK?' said Iain. '… Right. Now her attack. Once the baby was home from the Derriford she makes up her mind to go ahead, lays her plans, and pinches twenty of Ralph's Temazepam.'

Aliza nodded.

'Then on the night concerned she parks on the lower layby, because she knew her car would be there until late, and didn't want it noticed.' asked Aliza

'And Jem Stokes seeing her there later was just her bad luck?' said Aliza.

'Yes. When I showed her our Glasgow mug shots, she realised they looked a bit like Jem, and had to think quickly. Not sure it really helped her to say she'd seen the man concerned. Maybe it did, though. It sent us off on a wild goose chase, at least.'

'Sent *me* off,' said Tom.

'Where was I?' said Iain. 'Oh yes, she brings some bits and bobs with her.'

'What?' asked Aliza.

'A pint of milk ready doctored with the right quantity of Temazepam. Almost certainly the liquid variety, which Elizabeth kept in her surgery. Plus the empty pack of Ralph's tablets to go into the dustbin... She does her stint in the nursery... Then before leaving through the front door she goes to the kitchen, makes sure the doctored bottle is the only milk left in the fridge, and pockets the back door keys.'

'That sounds risky,' said Aliza. 'Mightn't someone have noticed they'd gone?'

'They were on a hook inside a closed cupboard,' said Tom. 'And the back door itself has a Yale spring lock, so it doesn't have to be bolted for the night. There's no reason anyone would have noticed.'

'Then after leaving the house,' said Iain, 'she simply walks around it, goes to the shed, unlocks it, and settles down to watch the kitchen through the window.'

'Why?' asked Aliza.

'She has to be sure Lidya's made the drinks using the milk from the fridge, which she'd have been able to see quite clearly, we checked... Then she waits till about 12.30, when she expects all the adults to be in a drugged stupor, pops the empty Temazepam packet into the dustbin, and gets back into the kitchen using the keys she's taken.'

'She knew the drinks routine, you see,' said Tom. 'Her first job was to rinse thoroughly the empty milk bottle and Lidya's mug, and then put uncontaminated Ovaltine dregs in the mug to throw suspicion onto Lidya.'

'You said she had no fresh milk,' said Aliza.

'You're right,' said Iain. 'Must have brought the uncontaminated Ovaltine with her, in addition to the doctored milk bottle and the empty Temazepam pack.'

'Then she returns the keys to the cupboard,' said Tom, 'and listens to be sure the three adults upstairs are safely drugged. Finally, she creeps up to the nursery and sets about strangling the baby.'

'But then she heard Lidya go to the loo?' asked Aliza.

'Just so. Must have been a shock—the one thing she *couldn't* have known was that Lidya'd chosen that particular night to throw her drink away.'

'So she abandoned her attack, and crept back downstairs?'

'Yes. And Lidya heard the click of her pulling the back door to behind her, without realising what it was.'

'One thing I don't get,' said Aliza. 'If Marsha's plan had worked as she meant it to, Lidya would have finished up with too much Temazepam in her blood, wouldn't she, even though there was none left in her mug?'

'We worried about that,' said Iain. 'We think she relied on us reckoning that Lidya would have deliber-

347

ately dosed herself with Temazepam after strangling the baby, to throw us off the scent.' He put his elbows on his desk, rubbed his hands together, and looked questioningly first at Tom and then at Aliza.

'Is that it?' asked Aliza.

'That's our scenario.'

She thought for a while, then shivered. 'I can't see much wrong with it,' she said.

'Good,' said Tom.

'Why are we searching her flat? Just routine?'

'We may find further physical evidence,' said Iain. 'It's probably where she doctored the milk bottle. She may even have made notes.'

'I suppose her plan needed quite a lot of nerve,' said Aliza, staring at Tom. 'But chillingly simple... And it nearly worked.'

Tom nodded gently, several times.

'Is she very clever, or very stupid?'

'Both,' said Iain. 'Both at once. That's the trouble.'

*

'What a *terrible* thing...' said Jane as Tom walked through the front door, exhausted. She gave him a big hug. 'But thank *goodness* for Lidya's sake'

Tom looked at her.

'When will they release Lidya?'

He shrugged. 'As soon as Clutterbuck can contact the court. Probably tomorrow.' They walked through to the sitting room. 'Where's Ralph?' He sank into a chair. 'How did he react?'

'In his room upstairs. Took a while to take it in. Then he hugged me, cried with relief, kept whispering "Lidya, Lidya" to himself... Maybe I ought to cook something nice to celebrate?'

Tom shook his head.

'Not in the mood?'

'Not yet.'

'Was it very stressful?'

'Less than I expected. Not a *difficult* session. Quite short. Iain put the questions. But as time went on, I got to feel damned uneasy... Once I started thinking about what it all meant.'

'She's a monster?'

'Yes, she is.' He shook his head.

'Criminally insane?'

'Oh yes... The discouraging thing is... '

'What?'

'I keep thinking this. There's not much doubt they'll find *her* guilty and put her away... But our dangerous friend Sir Ambrose will remain at large.'

'Tom! Are you telling me he's mad too?'

'Not clinically... But, just like her, he manages to twist facts, to persuade himself that they're as he wants them to be.'

'And thereby destroys lives?'

'Exactly. And our splendid legal system seems incapable of stopping *him*.'

'Perhaps some of us need to try to change that. You and me... Maybe the support group...'

He shrugged.

Her enthusiasm waned. 'I'd better get *something* to eat,' she said. She wandered to the kitchen, but found herself too distracted to settle easily to the task. She pulled down from the shelf the basic cookery book that had been her mainstay since Christmas, and began to leaf through it, trying to remember what things both Ralph and Tom liked.

The phone rang.

'I'll get it.' she called, and ran into the hall.

From the sitting room Tom watched her lift the receiver. 'Yes,' he heard her say, 'he's staying with us.' She was listening intently for a long time. She sat down suddenly on the stool by the phone. 'Oh!' she said. 'Oh, no!' She lifted her free hand and pressed its fingers against her cheek. 'Of course,' she said, 'nine o'clock... Will you have eaten?' Another pause. 'Thank you for ringing.' She put the receiver down with extreme slowness.

Tom jumped to his feet and ran into the hall.

'Lidya,' she said. There was an odd stillness about her. She walked slowly ahead of him back into the sitting room and dropped abruptly onto one of Tom's armchairs.

He followed. '*What?*' he said sharply.

She sat upright, staring.

'*What?*' he insisted.

She closed her eyes. 'An accident... That's what he said: *Tell Ralph there's been an accident.*' She nodded slowly.

'How *bad* an accident?'

'She's in the prison hospital.'

'He didn't say how bad?'

'No.'

Tom swallowed. 'Who was it? Who called?'

Still she looked distracted, then her eyes swung round to seek his. 'It was Father Barnabas, Tom. Bringing Ralph to the phone wouldn't do... He's coming here. To speak to him personally.'

Tom thought about it. Slowly, he clenched his fists and sank onto a stool. He could see Jane still staring at him from far away, but the sitting room threatened to dissolve; he fought against it, closed his eyes, dropped his head onto his forearms. After what seemed a long time he felt Jane's hands clutching at his shoulders.

350

*

Jane found her hands shaking a little as she took Father Barnabas' damp nylon raincoat; he was wearing a long black cassock beneath it.

'Where is Ralph?' he asked quietly.

'In the sitting room with Tom.'

'Good.' Tall, bespectacled and wiry, he looked sharply at her. 'Does he know who I am, Jane?'

'I'm sure he does.'

Jane opened the sitting room door, and Barnabas marched forward with some determination. 'You must be Ralph,' he said, gently. Ralph rose, his usually ruddy cheeks drained of blood, and they shook hands.

Barnabas motioned for everyone to sit, but remained standing himself, a black pillar in the subdued light. He looked directly at Ralph. 'I'm bringing unwelcome news, I'm afraid,' he said, and paused.

'Yes,' said Ralph, his eyes earnestly searching Barnabas' face.

'Jane told you there had been an accident?'

'Yes.'

'I happened to be in the prison when it happened. In fact I was waiting there to visit your wife.' He glanced down at the carpet, then up squarely into Ralph's face. 'The news is very bad, I'm afraid, and the prison authorities have asked me to tell you... Lidya is dead, Ralph.'

Jane felt her spine freeze momentarily. She watched Ralph: a look of utter despair spread quite slowly over his face.

'*Dead?*' he whispered.

'Yes... I'm so sorry.' Father Barnabas stooped a little awkwardly and took Ralph's right hand in both of his, but didn't immediately add any explanation, and there was a long pause. Tom looked questioningly up at him.

'You said an accident,' said Ralph at last, and pulled back his hand. 'Is what you're telling me that Lidya took her own life?'

Barnabas looked down at him. 'I'm afraid she did…' he said at last. 'For a time the doctor thought he could save her, but she died in the prison hospital about seven o'clock this evening.' He paused.

Ralph looked down at the carpet for a long time. When he raised his head again he blinked, and looked distraught from one of them to another. Gradually his face became more rigid. 'No details, please,' he said. 'No… Not yet…'

'Of course.'

There was another pause. 'I need to be alone,' Ralph said at last, a catch in his voice, looking around distractedly. 'Perhaps you could tell Tom and Jane here anything I need to know?'

'Wouldn't it be better to be with someone?' asked Barnabas levelly.

'No,' said Ralph firmly. He hauled himself awkwardly to his feet, and the others rose too. 'I shan't do anything silly.' He swallowed. 'Please don't pursue me.'

Barnabas nodded, and held up his right hand. 'God bless you,' he said.

Ralph tightened his lips. '*God*?' he muttered, and peered up at Barnabas. 'All is from Allah,' he added uneasily, as though taken aback by what his religion had to tell him, under the circumstances. 'Or so they say.' He turned and walked to the door; they heard him slowly climbing the stairs, with a little stumble at the top; they heard him turn into the spare bedroom.

Jane rose, gazed doubtfully up the stairs, then closed the sitting room door. Tom looked desperately at her, and all three sat down again.

There was another long silence. 'How much do you know?' said Jane at last.

'This isn't easy,' said Barnabas. 'There are, however, two things I need to explain, because Ralph needs to hear them, at some point, from friends.' He looked at Jane. 'From the way she spoke,' he said, 'I think Lidya must have felt close to you. Was that how it seemed to you?'

'I wasn't sure.'

'But you felt close to her?'

'I *wanted* to be.'

Barnabas dipped his head in response, and thought for a moment. 'The way she did it,' he said. 'She cut her own throat, using a cooking knife in the prison kitchen, where she'd been helping to prepare food… It sounds impossible, doesn't it? But that's what she did.'

Jane stared speechless at him.

'I think perhaps,' Barnabas added, 'it was a method she understood, from her background. She knew it could be quick.'

Tom clenched his hands and insisted sharply: '*But she was on suicide watch!* We checked.' He cleared his throat awkwardly.

'I checked too. Only yesterday.' Barnabas blinked several times behind his spectacles.

'So who the hell gave her access to kitchen knives?'

'The prison doctor seems to have assessed her as moderate risk only, and decided she'd be safe so long as she was always with people. That's why she was sharing a cell.'

Tom's head dropped.

'What made you check again yesterday?' asked Jane. 'When I saw her two days ago she was angry and hopeless and I was worried, but there were still things she wanted to get done… Had something changed?'

'She received a letter.'

'A letter?' said Jane, in confusion.

'From her father. It arrived yesterday… She showed it to me. It was in Amharic, but I know a little of the language, and she translated … In fact I have it here.' He searched inside his cassock, and withdrew an air mail envelope. 'I can't leave it with you, the coroner will have to have it. Ralph will need eventually to know what it contains.'

'But whatever did he say?'

'I met him once, and he seemed rational enough, then. But in this letter he concludes that, contrary to his earlier belief, Lidya, for reasons incomprehensible to him, must have killed her first two children and has now tried to kill the third. He offers to bribe her prison guards with a huge sum, begs her at all costs to escape and return to Ethiopia. He urges her to trust no-one, to abandon Ralph and Zeina, and says the only safe course of action is to get back to Ethiopia and build a new life there.'

'My God!'

'The poor man must have been completely unhinged by all that had happened. Lidya seemed utterly broken down by what he had written. But she was still anxious about what would happen to her child, though speaking as though she would no longer be there to care for her.'

'She talked to me about looking after Zeina,' admitted Jane.

Barnabas looked at her as though he might have more to say. But he simply gave a small nod. He drew the letter from its envelope, and passed it to her.

The ink was smudged, and the pages still damp and crinkled in places. An English translation in Lidya's handwriting had been pencilled between the lines. Jane read it through, and passed it to Tom.

Aftermath

Once Father Barnabas had taken his damp coat and driven off through the rain, Jane, still standing on the front step, turned to Tom. His screwed-up eyes were turned in her direction. Then he stepped back into the house, and, as she followed, walked slowly to the sitting room, dropped heavily into one of the easy chairs, and lowered his head again onto his arms.

She went to him: he snatched at her right hand and forced it to his chest, almost, she felt, as if to stop some fierce animal escaping from within. She knelt beside him, put her left arm around his shoulders, and felt them shake a little.

Still kneeling, she wept despairingly for some time, with no hands free to wipe away the tears. But at last the baby within her stirred a little, and she remembered Zeina, and the promise she had made. With that, a measure of calm descended, and a sort of strength. Puzzled and surprised by this change of mood in herself, she made as if to stand, but Tom clung to her hand and raised his head. 'I screwed up,' he said.

'Did you?' she said.

'Of course. Should have paid more attention to what Lidya herself said... Should have checked how seriously the prison was taking the risk... Should have been onto Marsha earlier, *far* earlier...'

'You did your best.'

'No.' He shook his head violently.

She kneaded his shoulder and considered.

'Could you make us some tea?' He released her hand and his head sank again. 'How horribly banal that sounds,' he added after a moment, in a muffled voice.

She stood and went to the kitchen, and the child moved again: she stroked her belly with both hands to reassure it. She decided it was best to leave Ralph for a while. She made the tea, put it on a tray, added some biscuits, and took it to the sitting room.

Tom didn't raise his head.

She poured a cup. 'On the table by your hand,' she said.

After a few moments he roused himself and drank, though the swallowing seemed difficult. 'Sorry,' he said.

'It's OK,' she said.

'She saved Jack... but I failed to save *her*.' He poured himself another cup. When he'd finished that, he stood up and left the room. She heard him go slowly upstairs to the bedroom he used as a study, and quietly close the door.

She sat on alone in the sitting room and thought some more about Lidya and the terrible irreversible choice she had made. The baby remained quiet. At eleven she went to the kitchen again to make Ralph's usual evening Ovaltine. She took it to his room, and knocked.

'Come in, Jane,' he said.

She opened the door. He was sitting on the edge of the bed, his jacket off, his face red-eyed, but alert, as though he had been thinking carefully. She handed over the drink.

'In the morning...' he began at once.

'Yes?' she said doubtfully.

357

'There'll be lots to do… But I want to visit Zeina.'
Jane thought for a moment. 'OK,' she said.

'Will you come with me? We'll have to clear it with Mrs Kent.'

'I'd like that.'

He looked steadily at her.

'Will you be all right tonight?' she asked.

'Yes,' he said. 'Yes, I think so.'

*

Tom came very late to bed, and in the morning slept through his alarm. But while Jane was making breakfast she heard him padding downstairs in bare feet to make a phone call.

'Margaret? … Yes, Tom here.' There was a long pause. 'Iain? You heard then?'

She walked quietly to the kitchen door; she could hear Iain speaking, but not the words.

'I screwed up… No mate, *I* screwed up… Christ man, don't try to bloody *soften* it… You too if you must… ' A pause in which Iain was silent; then he was speaking again. 'Bloody shattered,' said Tom. 'Don't think I can get myself in, to be honest, not straight away… Maybe you're right, mate, thanks… Yes… Not like me at all…'

She stepped further into the hall.

'I'll try to be in mid-afternoon… You'll put me right with the Super, then? … Good man.' He put the receiver down and looked round at her.

'Don't look at me like that!' he said.

'Like what?' she asked, but he didn't elaborate. She explained Ralph's plan for a visit to Zeina.

Tom looked down at the floor and up again. 'Sounds good,' he said.

358

'I'll be back here to be with you by eleven,' she said.

Once breakfast was over she set about swapping ward rounds with a colleague and touching base with Sue and Mrs Kent. News of what had happened had reached them, too. Mrs Kent said little and made no difficulties about the visit, though Jane could tell she was upset.

*

Promptly at ten the Lexus scrunched to a halt outside. Jane saw that Sue was watching for them at her sitting-room window; a moment later she had the front door open. Young Jason was perched on her hip.

'What a terrible thing,' she said, looking anxiously up at Ralph. She took his coat with one hand.

'Yes, Sue, it is,' he said.

She glanced towards her kitchen. 'The rest of them's in there,' she said. 'But young Zeina's still in her cot... Come on up.'

Ralph stumped up the stairs behind her and Jane followed. The baby was squalling. Sue looked down at her, dumped Jason down on the floor, and picked Zeina up. She un-popped the baby-suit, sniffed inside the nappy and raised her eyebrows.

Ralph smiled. 'Shall we do it?' he said. 'You've got plenty to deal with.'

Sue eyed him, then smiled cheerfully in return. 'There's a plastic sheet on the bed,' she said. 'Rest of the stuff's in the bathroom.' She handed Zeina over to Jane, settled Jason on her hip again, and hurried downstairs. Ralph nodded at Jane, and set off to find the kit.

She sat down on a cane chair by the window. Her unborn child reacted to the change of position with a

359

little leap, and Jane found herself smiling. She clutched Zeina to her, and the baby stopped crying, lifting her exploring soft fingers up to Jane's lips. She let them into her mouth.

Ralph returned carrying a clean disposable nappy, a dry wipe, a bin-liner and a pot of barrier cream, all of which he placed on the bed beside the cot.

Jane said, 'I've never changed a nappy.'

Ralph smiled. 'It's not difficult,' he said and disappeared again to the bathroom. Zeina started to cry again, and Jane raised her and patted her back.

Ralph came back with a plastic bowl of soapy water and a wash cloth. He put them on the floor beside the bed, took Zeina from Jane, wriggled her out of her baby suit and laid her back-down on the plastic sheet. 'You have to keep one hand ready to stop them rolling off the bed,' he said. He undid the tabs and pulled down the front of the nappy and used it to wipe off most of the mess, lifted Zeina's ankles with one hand and deftly folded the dirty nappy under her with the other.

'You're supposed to wipe from front to back,' he said as he squeezed out the cloth with one hand and demonstrated. 'Then dry... Can you pass me that cream?'

Jane got the lid off and handed it over.

Ralph applied the cream. 'Nappy, please.' He fitted it around Zeina. 'Not too bunched between the legs,' he said. 'Why don't you get her babygrow on while I clear up?'

Jane took his place by the bed, wriggled Zeina's floppy brown limbs into the right places and did up the poppers on the baby suit. She lifted the baby to herself and felt Zeina's soft cheek touch her own, sensed her tiny fingers wavering on her shoulder.

Ralph disappeared to the bathroom. Zeina was alert, turning her head to stare at Jane's earring. Jane kneaded her back.

Ralph reappeared. 'She seems very easy with you,' he remarked.

Jane nodded silently, held Zeina close for a few more minutes, then sighed and stretched out her arms to pass her back to her father. She folded her hands on her lap and watched.

Ralph took Zeina and jigged her on his knee; the baby's tiny face broke suddenly into a beaming distracted smile. Smiling himself in response, Ralph raised her high, then brought her back to his face for a bristly kiss.

Printed in Great Britain
by Amazon